LIGHTS OF LIVERPOOL

The O'Neils, who have lost brothers and sons into the bowels of London's East End, keep watch over their one remaining young male, a boy named Seamus. Hardworking and good-hearted, they cling together and help each other, and a whole community. Meanwhile, Rosh Allen mourns the loss of Phil, her dearly-beloved husband. Aided and impeded by her mother, Anna, she struggles to raise three fatherless children. Tess and Don Compton are on the verge of separation. An apparently greedy and selfish woman, Tess wants a semi-detached house, and all her own way. Poverty is tearing them all apart but it will be family that reunites them.

LIGHTS OF LIVERPOOL

LIGHTS OF LIVERPOOL

by

Ruth Hamilton

Magna Large Print Books
Long Preston, North Yorkshire,
BD23 4ND, England.

British Library Cataloguing in Publication Data.

Hamilton, Ruth
   Lights of Liverpool.

      A catalogue record of this book is
      available from the British Library

      ISBN   978-0-7505-3690-5

First published in Great Britain in 2012 by Macmillan
An imprint of Pan Macmillan,
a division of Macmillan Publishers Ltd.

A catalogue record for this book is available from the British Library

Published in Large Print 2013 by arrangement with
Pan Macmillan Publishers Limited

Magna Large Print is an imprint of Library Magna Books Ltd.

Printed and bound in Great Britain by
T.J. (International) Ltd., Cornwall, PL28 8RW

I dedicate this work to Daryl Whiting of New Gloucester, Maine, USA.

Daryl, sweetheart, never has the good fight been fought with better equilibrium, more humour, so much patience.

Readers, I beg your support for cancer research. This scourge must be eradicated.

Ruthie

ACKNOWLEDGEMENTS

I thank above all Wayne Brookes who gave me my wings, who appreciates my poetry and makes me laugh.

Camilla Elworthy for bearing with my Franglais.

Louise Buckley who is getting used to me; I'm not easy to digest.

Avril Cain for research into local industries and their placement.

Liverpool just for being here with a rich, fascinating history.

Fudge, one, two, three, four, tail at the back makes five, good boy. It was time to go, sweetheart.

Hello, Blazer – God help me. He's half French mastiff (Hooch) half Lab and completely confused. He understands neither English nor French, so I use German. He doesn't understand that, either.

Readers – you're the main reason for what I do. Thank you. Ruthie.

One

Through a gap in the buildings across the road, a short stretch of the Mersey was visible. On the waterfront, things were back to normal, more or less. Cranes appeared skeletal against a sky lit by an enthusiastic full moon, their metallic limbs stilled for now, because tomorrow was the Sabbath. The repairing of docks had begun almost before end-of-war rejoicing had ended, since the coming and going of ships kept Liverpool alive.

But up the road and further inland, areas of Bootle and the rest of the city waited to be rebuilt by a country impoverished by war. Piles of bricks and bags of sand and cement remained the backdrop of many people's lives. It would happen, though. Eventually, the reconstruction of the community would be complete.

The building behind Paddy still retained the old sign, *Lights of Liverpool,* since it had once housed a factory that had made electric light fittings and lamps, but it had been closed down. Eventually, Paddy had taken it over as a place where hungry dock workers could be fed, and where Irish people could meet at the weekends. It had several nicknames including Scouse Alley and the Blarney, but Paddy still called it Lights when it was used for a function. And today had been a function, all right.

Paddy leaned against a wall and lit a cigarette.

Out of several thousand Bootle houses, only forty had remained safe and steady at the final cease-fire. Roads had been repaired, and houses had been built, but in the year of our Lord 1958, some families remained in prefabs. 'And the Catholics wait the longest time.' Was this paranoia? Of course it was; some Catholics were properly housed, others were not, and Paddy's family happened to fall into the latter group.

Behind Paddy, the wedding ceilidh was in full swing. Irish folk music crashed out of an open front door and into nearby streets, as did the whoops and cries of five dozen guests whose behaviour was deteriorating with every Guinness, every tot of whiskey. The fighting hadn't started yet, but two people had disappeared off the face of the earth, and those two were bride and groom. They couldn't have gone far, since Reen's shoes had four-inch heels, while the groom was no more sensibly shod in his built-up brothel creepers.

Paddy, acting as security, loitered near the front doorway and fingered a whistle. When things got totally out of hand, a football referee's equipment was as good as anything if help was needed. Ah. Here came young Seamus. 'What is it now?' Paddy asked.

The unwilling pageboy, resplendent in a food-streaked white satin suit, shoved an item into the doorkeeper's hand. 'Our Reen's took her knickers off,' the child said gravely, his accent pure Scouse. 'They were under the table with my stupid hat. They made me wear a stupid hat.' He would never, ever forgive the world for that stupid hat. His sister Reen was the chief culprit, of course, but surely some other member of the family could have saved him from such dire humiliation?

'Yes,' Paddy replied with sympathy. 'But you took it off in church, so you did. And that was the most important part of today. It's all over now, but. You need never wear the thing again.'

The little lad almost growled. 'It's on a lot of the photos. I kept taking it off, like, but people were always shoving it back on me head. Why won't people leave people alone, Gran? All me life, I'll be the lad in the hat. Mam will show loads of photos round the prefabs when I'm older. I look dead soft in that white satin thing.'

'You'll live it down. And the prefabs will be gone once our houses are rebuilt, so no bother. Away inside and tell your mammy that your sister is now Nicholas.'

The lad scratched his head. Then the penny dropped. 'Oh. Knickerless.'

'That's the chap.'

He turned to walk away, still muttering under his breath about daft hats and frilly knickers. His own blood relative had forced him to dress up like something out of a pantomime. Liking Reen after this terrible day was going to take a degree of effort. He should have lost the blooming hat, should have put it where it might have been trampled underfoot till it fell apart. In fact, if he'd pinched a box of matches, he could have cremated the bloody thing.

'Seamus?' He was a beautiful child from a beautiful family, and Paddy was prejudiced, of course. But oh, he was gorgeous, and no mistake. Blue eyes, blond hair, good Irish skin.

13

'What?'

'You'll be grand, so. I'll see can I arrange the wedding album with as few photos of your daft hat as I can manage. Just leave it all to me. I'll sort it as best I can, I promise.'

'Thanks, Gran.' He studied her for a few seconds. Patricia Maria Conchita Sebando Riley O'Neil owned Scouse Alley. She also appeared to own the supposedly temporary Stanley Square and all who lived there, though some people railed against her air of authority. The green rectangle, bordered by a tarmac path and twelve prefabricated bungalows, had been organized by the borough to house some of Bootle's many displaced families.

'Did I grow a second head?' she asked. 'You're staring at me like I came down in one of those saucer things.'

Seamus grinned. He was proud of his grandmother. Paddy O'Neil held her drink as well as any man, and she was an excellent doorman. She could spot a gatecrasher from twenty paces, and had been known to lift two at a time towards the exit. 'You make everything right, Gran,' he told her. She was his star, his saint, his everything.

Paddy placed the whistle in a pocket. After patting her grandson on his Brylcreemed head, she walked towards the storage shed. Although this structure was made of thick metal, she could hear them, and they were at it like rabbits. 'Maureen?' she yelled, heavy emphasis on the second syllable. 'Get yourself out here this minute if not sooner.' There were two Maureens, and this one was usually named Reen. Both Maureens were

14

mortallious troublesome, and the younger one would know she was in the doghouse, because she'd been given her full title on this occasion.

The sudden silence was deafening. 'I have your knickers, madam. When the creature you married went under the top table, he was after more than the dropped spoon, so he was. You are a disgrace to your family. No need for you to laugh at my Irish-speak, Jimmy Irons. The day I start losing my accent is the same day I'll start being a bit dead.' She waited. 'Right, now. Will I blow this whistle and get you a bigger audience?'

The door opened. A dishevelled bride did her best to conceal the groom, who was having trouble with his drainpipe trousers. Paddy wondered how he might feel in years to come when children looked at the wedding album. The photographs would be black and white, but the long-line, velvet-collared coat, the DA hair with the heavy quiff at the front, shoes with two-inch crêpe soles, black string tie – these could all become talking points. As for Reen ... well...

'Gran?'

'What?'

The bride swallowed. 'Can you sneak us in the back way so we can have a bit of a wash in the toilets?'

'A bit of a wash?' Paddy looked her up and down. 'Reen, it's fumigating you need. Hair like a bird's nest, cascara all over your face – yes, I know, it's mascara...' The dress, which had started the day like stiffened net curtains from a hundred windows, was now limp and soiled. One bra strap had escaped its mooring rings, so young

Maureen was now one up, one down, a bit like the house in which Paddy had started life in the old country. 'The cake's cut, so away home, the pair of ye.'

Jimmy stepped forward. 'We waited till we were wed, Gran.'

Gran tapped a foot. Who with any sense would get married in a bright blue suit with shocking pink socks and a quiff that tumbled further down his face with every passing hour? Paddy knew for a fact that he used rollers and setting lotion in the front of his hair. Had Reen married a big girl's blouse? 'Then why didn't you start the shenanigans on your way back down the aisle? Or on the church steps? Once you'd signed the heathen English papers, you were married in the eyes of the state.'

She looked them up and down. 'And what a state this is. Just look at the cut of bride and groom, like tinkers at the Appleby horse fair. Away with the both of you. I'll tell your mother you turned an ankle in one of those daft shoes, may God forgive my lying tongue. Go on. At least have the comfort of a bed before you start making babies.' She sighed and shook her head; they were young, full of hope, and had a great deal to learn while navigating the stepping stones of real life.

Jimmy glared at his grandmother-in-law. Built like a brick outhouse without being actually fat, she was unsinkable, unreasonable, unforgiving. And yet ... and yet there was a kindness in her. 'We don't want no babies yet.' His accent was treacle-thick Scouse, but at least he was Catholic. 'We want some time to ourselves first.'

16

'You'll have what God sends to you, so be thankful and keep its arse clean and its stomach filled. Marriage is more than slapping and tickling, so think on. It's a pledge for life, better or worse.'

Think on? Jimmy was thinking on. He and his new wife had to live in a tiny space with Paddy and Kevin O'Neil. The design of Bootle's prefabs meant that the bedrooms shared a wall, and he would be inhibited. Friday, Saturday and Sunday could be all right, because on those nights Scouse Alley became Lights Irish club, nicknamed the Blarney, and Paddy would be out of the house. But would those evenings be free, or would his mother-in-law from next door pay a visit with Seamus, her last resident child?

Paddy cleared her throat. 'Look, I saved this for you as the best present. The O'Garas have a brand new little semi-detached off Southport Road, just finished, it is. I got the rent book for you, so you're to have their prefab in a few days. Your furniture will be a bit of a hotch-potch, but beggars and choosers are miles apart–' She was silenced when the two of them grabbed and hugged her until she could scarcely breathe. 'Let me be,' she gasped. 'I'll be glad to be rid of the pair of you, so.' She glared at Jimmy. 'Nobody wears those daft suits any more. Only the young gangs dress so stupidly, and here's you making a show of my granddaughter.'

He smiled at her. She was all sound and echo, and there wasn't a bad bone in her body. 'Thanks, Gran,' he said. 'Your blood's worth bottling.'

They left hand in hand to continue their marital

17

business in Paddy's temporarily empty house. 'God go with you,' the Irishwoman whispered as the couple disappeared round a corner. They were decent kids. Daft, but decent. And the daftness would be eroded soon enough, because life would move in on them. 'Hang on to your silliness,' she mouthed. 'And hang on to each other, because this is a cold, bold world.'

She lit a second cigarette and sat on a tea chest in the shed. Well over fifty years, she'd been in Liverpool. But if she closed her eyes, she was back in Ireland in that little one up, one down house, white with a black door, stuck in the middle of nowhere, miles of green in every direction. She saw cows and chickens, geese and pigs. It was a wondrous place, pretty, with an orchard full of apple trees, a secret stable where lived two supposedly matchless Arab stallions, and Ganga's rickety sheds where stills bubbled and gurgled, and roofs and walls went missing in puffs of smoke from time to time. The isolation had been total. She just remembered when the house had been packed to the rafters with chattering people at the table, but most had disappeared over to England by the time Paddy was taking real notice.

There'd been no school, and not a solitary book in the house. Ganga slept downstairs near the fire, while the boys had a couple of mattresses at the other end of the same room. Upstairs, a curtain separated Muth and Da from the girl children, so no one had ever been in doubt about the creation of babies. How had they managed when the house had been fuller? Paddy had no idea. Perhaps some had slept in barns and unexploded

18

huts? Ah yes, that row of caravans. Many had slept in those.

Ganga had been a sore trial, mostly because he blew up sheds with monotonous frequency. His life had been devoted to the perfecting of poteen, though he'd never really achieved that. He sold enough of it, sometimes taking off with the horse and cart for weeks at a time, only to return and cause further explosions all over the place. Paddy giggled. She remembered him with no moustache, half a moustache, one eyebrow, smoke rising from his flat cap. It was poteen money that had got everyone out of Ireland. It was poteen that caused all the explosions, but Ganga had blamed the spuds. Spuds, he had declared with every disaster, were not as stable as they used to be. The stud fees had been welcome, too... Paddy shook her head sadly, though a smile visited her lips. She had loved him...

But Ganga had died there, in that little white house miles from anywhere, a jug of home-brewed cider by his chair, a ticket for Liverpool in his pocket. All his adult children and their families were established in England, and he had intended to join them. But when Micky Malone, the nearest neighbour, travelled twenty miles to pick up Ganga's cows and horses, he had found a corpse, three rebuilt sheds full of alcohol, a couple of stills, and some distressed cattle. He tended the cows, led away the aged horses, buried Ganga, took the stills and all they had produced, then sent a message with money to the oldest of the male emigrants.

Paddy drew on her Woodbine. Micky Malone

had been an honest man, but when the money had been divided between all the Rileys, the sum for each of them had been paltry. When everything was sorted out, Paddy had received a pearl rosary from her dead ganga. The pearls hadn't been real, of course. Muth and Daddy, now deceased, had done their best, God love them. They were buried in English soil, but in a Catholic cemetery. Paddy missed them every day of her life. Both had been immensely clever, yet neither had ever learned to read.

But Paddy had mastered the art. In her late teens, Paddy – known then as Patricia – had been handed over to Liverpool nuns. Unable to read or write, she had been placed with five-year-olds and, because of her skill with arithmetic, was nominated as a junior teacher in that area; in return, she was taught to read within months, and was then moved out into society to keep company with her peers. 'I shone,' she whispered now. 'But to what end?' There had been no chance of further education. The Cross and Passionist sisters had taken her, a young adult, out of the goodness of their hearts, but Paddy had wanted to be a qualified teacher.

'No chance,' she mumbled. 'But you won't moan, Paddy O'Neil. You've a good man, a precious daughter and lovely grandchildren.' Even while alone, she made no mention of her sons. She didn't want to think about them. They had followed her brothers into the gaping maw of England's capital of culture, government and crime. More recently, Maureen's lads had made the same journey. Six of them gone, two from each generation. Were they all in gangs? No, she wasn't thinking of them, refused to. Invitations to the wedding had been ignored, and– 'Stop it,' she snapped aloud. Not thinking about them did as much damage as thinking about them.

The lovely grandchild returned covered in even more food and without the dreaded hat. He was worried. She could tell he was worried, because he was shifting his weight from foot to foot. 'Gran?'

'Would you ever consider the possibility of standing on both feet? You'll have me dizzy.'

'I counted, but I think she's gone and hid some near the wall.' The child bit his lip and stilled his lower limbs. He meandered on, throwing into the arena knickers, hat and his cheating mother. There were only seven bottles on the table, but there might be six or more hidden and she'd started singing. 'I was busy with knickers, so I couldn't watch her, could I?'

'God,' Paddy breathed. Maureen was a lovely girl, but she had a singing voice that might have persuaded the *Titanic* to accept its fate. 'What's she murdering this time?'

'Cockles and mussels alive, alive oh.'

'Bugger.'

'That's what Granda said.'

'And she's up?'

Seamus nodded. 'She's up.'

'On the table?'

'On a chair.'

Paddy delivered a sigh of relief. A chair was easy to deal with.

'The chair's on the table, and Mam's on the

21

chair, Gran.'

She gasped, as if retrieving that mistaken sigh. 'Jaysus, she'll be the death of me, Seamus. Your mother's a lovely woman, but...'

There was a rule connected to Maureen, daughter of Paddy, mother to Seamus, to the bride and to a pair of sons who had moved south. She would go weeks and months without drinking, then an occasion would occur, and she needed a counter. Once appointed, the counter was in charge of keeping an eye on the intake. Twelve small bottles of Guinness constituted the limit. Once the twelfth empty hit the table, Maureen was handed over by the counter to Gran, who took her home.

'Could be more than thirteen, Gran.'

She bridled. 'Oh yes? And what's your eejit grandfather doing?'

Seamus swallowed audibly. 'First aid, I think.'

'Holy Mother. So it's kicked off?'

The child nodded.

It was chaos. Or, as Paddy described it, Bedlam with custard. Chairs had taken to the air, curses flew, while small heaps of people on the floor tried to beat the living daylights out of each other. Maureen, apparently oblivious to the situation she had caused, was balanced precariously on a chair, and the chair was far from steady on its table. The ceilidh band had escaped with its drums, Irish pipes and fiddles, while a clutch of emerald-clad young female dancers huddled in the kitchen doorway. The room, long and narrow when disguised as Scouse Alley, had partitions peeled back to make an L shape, and only the kitchen was separate and behind real walls.

Paddy risked her unstable daughter's safety, blew her whistle, and the scene became still life. Maureen, trying hard to balance, stopped inflicting grievous bodily harm on Molly Malone. 'Thomas Walsh?' Paddy yelled. 'Get your stupid wife – my stupid daughter – down from the perch. Any higher and she'll be having a word with St Peter.' She waited until Maureen was back on terra firma. 'Take her home, Tom.'

'But you're the only one she'll–'

'Away with your burden. Time you learned to control the mother of your children. Knock her out if you have to, as we ran out of chloroform.'

A few people giggled, and Paddy's right foot began a solo tap dance. 'Do you know what this place is?' she screamed. She delivered the answer to her own question in a lowered tone, because it fell into total silence. 'Yes, we have a licence for weekends, but our first duty is to the dockers. This is a teetotal establishment to which anyone of any creed or colour may come for his lunch instead of going to the pub. Right?'

The congregation murmured.

'So now, fewer dockers meet their maker or a surgeon in the afternoons. That is our primary function, to keep safe and sober our men. Tomorrow, after Mass, the committee gets its hands dirty and Scouse Alley clean.' Very slowly, she scanned the room with narrowed eyes. 'Do you know what Orange Lodgers say about an Irish Catholic wedding? Oh, yes. They call it a fight with chairs, a blessing and rosary beads. I want this place spotless by noon tomorrow.'

She stood her ground while family and guests

began their attempt to clear the mess. Most of them were drunk enough to need a map to find their own feet, but she let them struggle on for a while. Even the priest was crawling round in trifle, bits of sausage roll and lumps of wedding cake. He was an old soak anyway, and Paddy was glad to see that he'd finally found his true level in life.

With arms folded, Paddy maintained her stance. She knew how they talked about her, what they said when she got 'uppity'. Liver Bird Number Three was one of her titles. Some reckoned she was the one that had taken flight, that she had come down to earth to watch over lesser beings and keep them on their toes. Others had her down as Irish mafia, as an avenging angel from the dark side, as a big-mouthed biddy from Mayo. Till they needed something, that was. Oh, everything changed when they ran out of money, because Paddy O'Neil was no shark, and she treated people well when it came to finance.

When her gaze lit on her husband, she allowed herself a tight smile. He was one of her better decisions. From a family of fifteen children whose mother had died after delivering one final baby, he had made sure that his wife had not been weighed down by a rugby team. All their married life, he had kept a calendar, and Paddy had given birth only three times. Kev was a good man, the best.

Her eyes slid sideways to today's best man, another Teddy-boy idiot in electric socks, crêpe-soled shoes, and trousers that looked as if they'd been painted on. He was spark out on the lino, his carefully cultivated quiff sweeping the floor in its now collapsed state. The world had gone mad.

Girls were as bad, if not worse. Those who couldn't afford stiff, multi-layered net underskirts made their own waist-slips from cheap material with wire threaded through the hem. Occasionally such behaviour led to disaster, because a girl would sit on the wire, and the front of her hoop would shoot upwards to reveal stockings, suspenders and knickers. Boys celebrated such catastrophes, but many a girl stayed indoors for weeks after so humiliating an occurrence. Yes, they were all stark raving bonkers, and parents were mystified.

Maureen was being dragged out by her husband. Her parting shot was aimed at 'When Irish Eyes are Smiling', but she missed by a mile, as usual. Tomorrow, she would be sober; tomorrow, she would make no attempt to sing. The impulse to murder music arrived only with the thirteenth Guinness.

But tonight, Maureen had taken only six drinks, because tonight she needed to be sober. Remembering how to act drunk had been difficult. It was as if the booze altered every atom of her body and mind; she changed into a different person. 'Let me go,' she advised her supportive husband. 'I touched hardly a drop. Michael and Finbar are back.'

Tom Walsh ground to a halt. 'You what?'

'I'm sober.'

'And I'm the pope. What about Michael and Finbar? Why didn't they come to the wedding? Their sister's got married just today–'

'They couldn't,' she snapped. 'God knows who's on their tails.'

Tom swallowed hard and processed his thoughts. 'You let the wedding go ahead when you knew it could have been any or all of us? Who is it this time? The bloody Krays, the Bow Boys, the Spitalfields so-called sodding Soldiers?' Furious now, he grabbed his wife's shoulders and shook her. 'Is it the Greeks?'

'I don't know,' she whimpered.

'But you do know all them London bastards go for family. We could have been blown up. You took our lives into your hands–' His jaw dropped as she took something from her handbag. 'Who the buggering bollocks gave you that? Is it loaded?'

'Course it is. What use would it be without bullets? Fin gave it me. They're hiding with Ernie Avago. Well, they're in his mam's bedroom, God rest her soul.' She returned the gun to its resting place.

Tom groaned. Ernie's mother would be spinning in her grave. 'I'll kill the bloody pair of them,' he said. 'My sons are criminals. I suppose Seamus'll join them in a few years.'

'He won't. My Seamie's a good lad.'

'So were Fin and Michael till they went and found the uncles down the East End of blinking London. Come on, let's sit in the shed for a minute, because my legs don't know whether it's Tuesday or dinner time.'

They had scarcely opened the shed door when it happened. A large, black car slid almost noiselessly to the front of Scouse Alley. Two men emerged with machine guns. It was unreal. The shiny vehicle reflected moonlight, as did the weapons in the criminals' hands. It was real. Tom pushed his wife into the shed, then hid himself behind the partially open door.

He grabbed his wife's bag, pulled out the gun and, with just two bullets, shot the intruders in their heads. He'd been a good sniper, though never with a weapon as small as this one. It was unreal again. But the car door opened once more, and that was very real. Tom felled the third man with professional accuracy; his time in the Lancashire Fusiliers had not been wasted. His knees buckled and he sank to the floor. It was all too bloody real. Never since the war had he killed. Trained for weeks in a firing range, Tom had become an asset to his regiment. He had medals. He had medals for his chest, and British civilian blood on his hands. Yet those machine guns would have killed everyone in the hall. He had saved many lives, but he felt sick to the core.

'Jesus, Mary and Joseph,' his sobbing wife prayed.

The doors of the main building slammed shut, and lights were turned off. That would be Paddy's doing. Tom's mother-in-law was always on the ball, and she was following well-sharpened instincts. 'Stay where you are,' he ordered Maureen. 'There could be a second car. I'll be with you, so don't worry.' He dug in her bag and found spare bullets.

No second car arrived. When half an hour had disappeared into eternity's backlog, Tom left the shed and knocked on the door of Scouse Alley.

'It's only me,' he stage-whispered. He entered a silent room lit only by the small red ends of thirty or more cigarettes.

'What happened?' Paddy demanded. When her son-in-law had supplied the quiet answer, she walked to the door and stepped outside. Three bodies. No visible witnesses. She thanked God for the moon before fetching Maureen from the shed. 'Not a word,' she threatened. Inside, she told the audience that an old car could have backfired, but they must all stay where they were just in case something was about to kick off, since it might have been gunfire. Then she shone her torch and picked out Kev and two relatively sober and trustworthy men. Tom led them out. Three nearly sober men, three dead gangsters, three machine guns. Everything was coming in threes. Guns, ammunition, a car and three bodies had to disappear before daybreak. And Paddy's two eejit grandsons were at the back of it. She would rip the truth out of them even if it took a scalpel to do it.

People were getting restless. 'Look,' she told them.

'We can't look – it's too bloody dark,' replied a disembodied voice.

'Listen, then, Smarty Pants. Very, very quietly, let's sing "Faith of Our Fathers" in thanksgiving for a lovely wedding on a lovely day. The bride and groom are gone, but the rest of us must stay here until we find out what's afoot outside.' She switched on a few of the lights.

So they sang in an almost whisper the battle hymn of all Catholics: *Faith of our fathers living still, in spite of dungeon, fire and sword...*'

Paddy nudged Maureen, who was crippled by near-hysteria. 'When we don't want you singing, you fire on all cylinders. Come on, now. *Fa-aith of our fa-a-ther-ers, holy faith, we will be true to thee till death. We will be true to thee till death.*' Three dead. Three corpses, three semi-automatic guns, one huge car in front of Scouse Alley. Fortunately, all the blinds were closed, so no one could glance out at the horrible scene. She did, though. Tom was swilling blood off the paths. In the moonlight, it looked black, like thick oil. The car and the bodies were gone, and Kev was searching the ground with a flashlight. She thanked God that 'Faith of Our Fathers' was such a long and repetitive hymn.

'Paddy?'

'What?'

'Can we go now?'

'Just stack the chairs, then leave through the kitchens. I want to see none of you at the front in case that was a gun firing. We're not far from bonded warehouses, and some Saturday nighters might have a thirst and no sense. Go on with you. Maureen, pull yourself together and take your son home. Walk with the men. Tom will be back soon, I promise.'

Maureen blinked stupidly, like a woman trying not to wake on a workday morning. 'He killed–'

'Shut up. Shut your mouth before I find a padlock for it. He did what he had to do. He saved my life, yours, Seamus's. Your husband's a good man, and well you know it. This was never murder.'

'But Mam–'

'I've changed me mind. Stay here with me. I don't want you strolling along and letting your brains pour out through that colander you call a skull. I can't trust you not to talk out of the holes in your head, especially the one gaping above the jaw.'

The scraping and stacking of chairs drowned the women's words. Paddy warned her daughter again. 'Not a syllable in front of Seamus. And you'd be best off saying nothing when your daughter manages to separate herself from the Teddy boy she married.'

'I'm scared, Mam.'

'And I'm not?'

They were alone at last when Tom came in. 'Done and dusted,' he mouthed. 'Maureen, your gun's in Davy Jones's locker. Car burned well away from here, petrol tank exploded, everyone of ours safe.'

'And the bodies?' Paddy kept an eye on Seamus, who was picking debris from the floor. 'Well?'

'Cremated in the car.'

Paddy, still strong as a horse, suddenly felt her age. A woman in her early sixties should not be needing to worry about delinquent brothers, sons and grandsons. Michael and Fin had gone south to look for work, and they had probably found it with their uncles and great-uncles. Paddy's brothers, too old now to carry weight in the East End, had passed their unstable crowns to her sons. Those sons, in their forties, were now training their own children and poor Maureen's boys.

'Mam?'

'Leave me alone a minute, so, Maureen.' She

walked into the huge rear kitchen and leaned on the sink. Descended as she was from a determined Irish clan and from shipwrecked Armadaists way back in time, Paddy had a temper fit to strip paint. It was bubbling now in her throat like heartburn after too hefty a meal. 'Ganga,' she whispered. 'Ganga, Daddy, Muth, I've let you down. I'm sorry, so sorry.' She hadn't been the oldest in her section of the huge family, but she'd been the oldest girl – hence her Irish/Spanish name. In the mother country, women kept the men on a path as straight and narrow as possible. But she'd let her brothers go, and they had married southern Protestants. 'And look at the result,' she spat softly.

Her sisters were probably fine. They would have married within the church and were doubtless scattered hither and thither throughout the north of England. A few of the lads were said to be decent and hardworking, so she could be proud of most of the original immigrants. But her brothers Peter and Callum had gone to the bad, and the result had turned life upside down tonight. In her head, she carried a picture of what might have been. She saw Scouse Alley, currently Lights, filled with crumpled bodies, blood and flesh everywhere, no movement, just the odd groan from those who hadn't died immediately.

'Gran?'

She dried angry eyes. 'Seamus, hello.'

'Don't cry, Gran.'

She squatted down and held his shoulders. 'Promise me, lad. Promise me you'll never go to London.'

'I can't,' he said. 'They could send me any-where.'

Paddy swallowed. 'Who could?'

'The army. I want to be a crack shot like my dad.'

A knife pierced her heart. 'Why would you want to be a sniper, son?'

He shrugged. 'I just do.'

It would be all right, she consoled herself. Last week, he'd wanted to be a train driver, and she remembered from months ago his determination to be a fireman or a bobby. He would grow out of the army idea, had to grow out of it. 'Go home with your daddy, sweetheart. I'll see you tomor-row.'

Alone except for Maureen in the hall, Paddy began to focus on Finbar and Michael, Maureen's older boys. Poor old Ernie Avago was lumbered with them. They had brought hell to Liverpool, to their own family, to a lovely old retired dock worker who hadn't a clue about his lodgers' true nature. What was his real name, now? Ernie had been christened Avago by his fellow dockers, because whenever he encountered a man with a difficult task, he always said, ''Ere, lad. Let me 'ave a go.' Avago. He would help anybody, would Ernie. And now, he was nursing in his generous heart two devils from the depths of hell.

Maureen entered the kitchen. 'Mam?'

'Did you calm down at all?'

'A bit.'

'Right, well make sure it's a big bit by morning. I want to go and save Ernie Avago. I can't have him full of bullet holes courtesy of the Kray twins.'

Maureen hung her head.

'Well? What are you hiding from me, madam? All your life you've been unable to lie to me.'

'I'm not sure.'

'And? Lift your head this minute.'

Slowly, the younger woman raised her chin and faced her angry mother. 'Fin and Michael are with the Spits, I think.'

'The Spitalfields Soldiers? Are you sure? Not the Bow Boys?'

Maureen shrugged. 'They've stolen something from somebody, and that somebody sent our visitors to get it back or whatever.'

'Whatever? Whatever's whatever?'

'Blood. They would have shot my sons or members of the wedding party until they got the truth. Fin and Michael must have mentioned the wedding. Each gang has spies in the others. So whatever the Spits know, the Bows, the Krays and the Greeks also know.'

'So who did we kill and cremate?'

Maureen had no idea.

'And you knew this might happen today? How could you let the wedding go on if you knew what could arrive here?'

'Reen would have been heartbroken if I'd stopped her big day.'

'Heartbroken is better than dead.'

Maureen straightened her shoulders and stuck out her chin. 'Always so sodding sure, aren't you, Mother? I stayed sober and did what I could. We can't all be like you, patron saint of the righteous. Just stay out of my way, because you are getting on my bloody nerves. I'll deal with this.' She

33

paused. 'My husband and I will deal with it. Keep out of our business.'

Paddy sat on a stool. It hadn't been easy, any of it. For a start, there was a whole dynasty to think about, and she didn't know half their names. Muth, Daddy, Paddy and her siblings had been the last to be shipped out of Ireland, and all the others seemed to have been gone for years. Muth had been a useful sort of person in the house, and Paddy had pulled her weight on the land, as had her father, brothers and sisters, so they had been kept on until Ganga had saved that final pile of cash. 'Just me, now,' he had declared. 'And I'll be grand, so. In a few months I'll be with you. Micky Malone's missus will do me a bit of baking, and I'll be down to the ferry boat quicker than a bull at a cow, so I will.'

With her head in her hands, Paddy placed her elbows on the huge wooden drainer next to the sink. Ganga had died in the old country. Muth hadn't thrived. Liverpool had crushed her with its crowds, its noise, its busy-ness. At the beginning of the Great War, she had taken to her bed and faded away. After a short period of mourning, Paddy's generation began to disperse, marry and move to various parts of England. 'Including London,' Paddy whispered. 'To hell with London and its gangs.' But she should know where her siblings and their offspring were. Too busy working, too busy establishing Kev's stall on Paddy's Market, the business that had provided the funds for Scouse Alley.

She'd married Kev, and had borne three children. Her brothers, Peter and Callum, were lost for

34

ever. Her sons, Martin and Jack, were similarly doomed. No God would ever forgive the deeds performed by members of those East End gangs. Paddy had learned about her brothers only when two more generations had joined them. The situation had been further clarified by newspaper accounts. Reading about her own son in jail for GBH, seeing his photograph on the front page... Oh, God. That a child of hers could beat halfway to death an old jeweller who refused to pay protection money... 'Stop this,' she told herself.

Maureen was still here, but two of her sons had followed Uncles Peter, Callum, Martin and Jack to hell. Reen had married today, and Seamus had moaned about his white satin cap. 'I'm glad you weren't with us, Daddy.' Paddy's father had followed Muth to heaven within a year, and Paddy felt glad that he hadn't survived to a great age to see the performance here tonight.

What next? Maureen and her husband Tom might well be in danger. Their sons Finbar and Michael were definitely as safe as if standing in quicksand, while poor little Seamus, Maureen's precious afterthought, must be protected at all costs. And what if the London lot knew about other members of the clan? They lived all over the place, and Paddy hoped they were, for the most part, decent and honourable folk doing jobs, raising families, living the ordinary, acceptable life.

She raised her head and looked round the huge room. No matter what, cauldrons of scouse must be ready by Monday lunch time, soda bread must be prepared, with tea or cocoa to finish. For the first time in many a year, Paddy wished she'd stayed in Ireland. She had never been one to look back in anguish, to complain about the English, to mourn the loss of a prettier, greener home. Children got educated here, got jobs, got on in life. She had good company, shops, a business to run.

Maureen. Ah, she would calm down quickly enough, because she'd never manage without her mother. Paddy and Maureen were close, and this was a serious problem, far too tangled and dangerous for Maureen and Tom to handle. But who could manage the unmanageable? Where to start, where to go, what to say?

Oh, God. It was complicated. They had to find out what had been stolen from whom and by whom. Three men, whose provenance remained a mystery because they were dead, would be missed within hours or days. Were they from London? Were they northerners hired by the big boys down south? Would more come to look for the disappeared ones and should a weapon be acquired for Tom? How long did it take for an old woman to go mad in a big kitchen with only her thoughts for company?

No matter what they'd done, Fin and Michael were family. 'I suppose that's how Mrs Kray reasons with herself,' Paddy said out loud. 'She ignores what they do, yet she's reputed to stand up for women everywhere. No, no, I can't go to her for help. Low profile, Paddy,' she told herself.

'Talking to the walls again, love?'

She jumped, a hand pressed to her chest. 'I thought you'd gone home, Kev.'

He shook his head. 'I've been wandering round

in circles outside, kept meeting meself on the way back. No, Paddy. I'll go nowhere without you at a time like this.' He sat on another of the stools and rolled a cigarette. 'What the blood and sand are we going to do about this little lot?' he asked.

'Nothing.' Paddy raised her shoulders. 'I've had the sack from me daughter. She says she'll manage.'

Kev sputtered on trapped hysteria. 'Our grandsons, Pads.'

'I know.'

'And our sons.'

'And my brothers, yes, yes, I know. Three generations of heroes. But we have to sit tight and see what happens. However, no matter what Maureen says, we go to Ernie Avago's tomorrow even if it means missing Mass.' She sighed deeply and rose to her feet. 'Come on, lover boy. Let's go and listen to the eejit grandson-in-law beating the hell out of our spare bed.'

'Paddy, he's a good lad.'

'I know, I know. Just leave me something to laugh at, would you?'

They locked up. Kev stepped away from the door, but Paddy stayed where she was.

'Pads?'

She inhaled deeply. 'You know when you're thinking about something, and something else moves into your head? And the second something has nothing at all to do with the first something? I was thinking about the second something earlier on, but it jumped through a hoop in the middle of my new first something. I wonder do I have dementia?'

37

Kev shook his head. It was a good job he understood Irish. 'No, love. If you've got dementia, God help the rest of us – you're the clearest thinker for miles. What is it?'

'Caravans.'

'Come again?'

'That's how they did it. When there were too many of us in the house, I mean. There was a big stone-built barn with one of the long sides missing. That's where they slept, I suppose. In painted wagons. We used to play in the last one. I think there were four or five of them at one time, then all but one were gone, as were uncles, aunties and so forth. We stayed for years, as I already told you many a time. Ganga minded us well, you know. Strong man. Survived the worst potato blight when he was young, brought his family through some bad times.'

Kev waited for her to reach the end of the path she was currently treading.

'The aunties and uncles will be dead by now, but I've cousins out there somewhere. And second cousins, too.'

'Are you starting a gang of your own, Pads?'

She tutted. 'No, but there's safety in numbers. We must advertise.'

'Under lost and found?'

She clouted him with her handbag. 'Under personal messages, you dope.' She paused. 'Tom did wrong in the eyes of the law, but right in the cause of justice and for the sake of family. We would all have been dead. Now, that's the sort of strength Ganga had. Never a penny to his name, too busy sending everyone over to England.' She

38

leaned on the door. 'And no one could read or write. They were supposed to stay in Liverpool and in an Irish community where they might be found by word of mouth. But they didn't. Their kids grew up, married and sallied forth. I've had tales from hereabouts, so I know roughly where they are, but I need to look for them.'

'Why, Paddy?'

'No idea. Let's get home.'

I saw them, saw what they did. Set fire to a car with three people in it. But I was busy myself, and I've plenty to hide. Cheap tart this time, just a nylon scarf and a pair of poxy earrings, probably Woolworth's best. 'Will you step into my parlour, said the spider to the fly...'

Two

The natives were becoming restless again. Smithdown Road, always a hive of activity at weekends, had slipped with the rest of the country into a chaos made for teenagers, by teenagers, no adults allowed. Grown men could be seen standing in shop doorways scratching their heads and wondering, not always silently, why they'd bothered to fight in the second war. 'Keep your bloody creepy shoes off my door,' yelled many a shopkeeper while washing his paintwork. Teddy boys swaggered along swinging heavy chains. These lads were noisy, greasy, ill-dressed, ill-mannered, up to their quiffs in testosterone and determined to impregnate anything that moved.

There had been a shift, a slight rocking of the planet's axis, because youth had grabbed life by the throat without warning. There was a silent synchronicity at the start. With no obvious discussion on the subject, they had suddenly appeared, males as gaudy imitations of Edwardians, females in wide skirts that hung to mid-calf. These were signals; from now on, older people would be forced to heed the requirements of the young. Curfews imposed by parents didn't always work. There was new music, a new order that was decidedly disordered. Earth had tilted, and nothing would ever be the same again.

On Saturdays, girls promenaded on one side of

the road, boys on the other. Someone with a whimsical turn of phrase had christened the occasion the 'Saturday Prom', and the title had stuck. It was colourful. Females with cash or indulgent parents displayed stiff net underskirts in many shades, and almost everyone was a bottle blonde. Several had hair from which all natural texture had been stripped by frequent applications of peroxide, while their faces looked as if they'd been plastered on with small trowels and finished off with miniature paintbrushes.

Parents might laugh at or rail against such displays, but for young females, this was serious business. They were Dianas, goddesses of the hunt. Although they presented themselves as prey, they were, in truth, the seekers of victims. Their traps were baited, their antennae set on red alert, and their radar was in tiptop condition. Scarcely aware of their goal, these fine, nubile time-bombs were in charge. They needed a boyfriend, a fiancé, then a husband. It was the law. Young women who were not engaged by the age of twenty-one were destined for the shelf. Spinsterhood was dreaded, and the idea of further education never entered their heads; it was marriage or nothing, and nobody wanted nothing.

Dresses in glazed cotton were the order of the day for girls, while boys wore their silly uniforms: long-line jackets in bright colours, thick-soled shoes, tight trousers, dazzling socks and ties like bootlaces. But an uneasiness had descended of late, because fashions were changing, and no one was sure what was supposed to come next. It was time to alter clothes and attitude again, but the new formula was still in its development stage, probably somewhere south of Watford.

Teenagers of the fifties had grabbed their chance by inserting punctuation marks in time, by taking hold of the nowhere years and using them to their own advantage. No longer did they dress as their parents dressed; no longer did they follow family patterns when it came to work. Choice was theirs; they would make up their own minds. Teenagers were a force to be reckoned with; they were challenging the mores of their elders. And their elders were bemused, to say the least of it.

'Why?' Theresa Compton stood in the window of the launderette. Her husband, too disabled for full-time or strenuous work, sat behind her on one of the customers' benches. He had wiped down all the machines while Tess washed the floor. The place stank of Dettol, because Saturday evening was the big clean-up time.

'Mad, isn't it?' he replied. 'What happened, eh?'

She shook her head. The war had been over for thirteen years, and things had started to look up, but the kids had gone strange. It had all seemed to happen overnight. As recently as 1955, young people had left school on a Friday, had started work the next Monday. They followed dads to the docks, mothers to the dry-cleaning company, to the biscuit factory, to shops and offices.

But now, they seemed to have developed a disease that started with a blinding rash that covered their whole bodies. Most were too young for employment, but several of the older ones rushed away from work at the weekend and donned this strange clothing. 'I wonder what me mam would have said about this lot?' Tess's mother, dead for several years, had been an Irish immigrant with no time at all for change. She'd worked hard, worshipped faithfully, died in her sleep. 'I'll bet she'd have clouted our Sean and our Anne-Marie. I reckon these daft swine wear their coats long to hide the splits in their tight trousers. As for Anne-Marie – she has to squash her skirts to get through a doorway.'

She moved closer to the window. Sean wasn't visible, but Anne-Marie was acting all coy and daft in the company of a Protestant in a pea-green coat with the compulsory black velvet collar, and electric blue socks peering cheekily from under the hems of abbreviated trousers. 'Their trousers are too short,' Tess complained. Pea-Green had crossed the road to be with Anne-Marie, who was only fifteen. He'd better keep his hands to himself, or he'd be in serious trouble.

'That's to show off their socks,' Don answered. 'They look like they've all escaped from some bloody circus.'

'Don't swear,' Tess said almost absently. She turned round. 'Did you go and have a look at that carpet I told you about?'

'I did,' he answered. 'And it's horrible.'

Tess bridled. By no means a large woman, she seemed to swell when annoyed. 'But it's all the rage, Don. Are you sure you looked at the right one? Skaters' Trails, it's called. Everybody's buying it.'

'Everybody's buying shocking pink socks and sticky-out underskirts, but we're not. Mind, you're only too right in a way. They're all at it, Tess, not just the kids. Furniture with daft, splayed-out legs, convex mirrors that act like something out of a Blackpool fun house – everybody looks distorted in one of them. What's the point of a mirror like that, eh? There's nothing solid any more. And that carpet you're on about is as ugly as sin. They even had what they called a coffee table. It was curved upwards at each end, looked as if it might take off any minute. Hideous. Made of plastic supposed to look like wood, but it didn't.'

'You've no taste, that's your problem.'

'I have. Utility's good enough for me. And there's nothing wrong with that Axminster square up there.' He waved a hand towards the ceiling. 'It's a nice flat. We don't need carpets.'

Tess held her tongue. The second bedroom had been divided into two smaller rooms for the kids, and they were growing. She wanted a house, planned on letting the flat and continuing to supervise the launderette while Don went into estate agency in the empty shop next door.

She sighed. Menlove Avenue wasn't far, yet it seemed a million miles from this busy road. An ambitious woman, Tess had always pictured herself in a nice semi-detached with gardens, on a tree-lined avenue, among posh neighbours and with a washing machine in the kitchen rather than in a shop beneath their living quarters. The car was paid for, the launderette practically ran itself, and there was money enough for a deposit on a house and for Don's estate agency. Well, she thought there was...

44

But she had just one problem: she hadn't yet advised her husband that he was going to be an estate agent. It was a nice, clean, elegant job. All he needed was a desk, a telephone, adverts in the evening paper and someone to do the running about for him. Oh, and houses. Yes, he would need a few of those.

She looked at him. He was a good dad, a decent enough husband, a man with a total lack of enthusiasm when it came to betterment of self. Injured at Dunkirk, he had been rendered unfit to work in the building trade, but he knew enough about the business to recognize a decent house for sale. He should handle the elegant end of the market. She was thinking the word 'elegant' all the time, wasn't she? But a semi on Menlove Avenue was so important. It was her goal, all she wanted, all she thought about.

'What are you cooking now?' he asked.

'Nothing.' It was probably because of Mam and Dad, God rest them. They'd slept in a gypsy caravan in a barn, children crammed together at the warmer end, the two adults near the door. Yes, there had been a door, but it never fitted properly. Tess shivered. She remembered meals at a huge table inside the white house, an occasional bath in front of a roaring fire, the scent of apples fermenting their way towards cider, sounds like gunfire when a still decided to give up its dead in huts dedicated to the manufacture of illegal spirits. The ganga man had sent everyone to England and, because no one could read or write, everyone had eventually lost touch with everyone else. 'I want us all safe,' she said quietly.

45

'We are safe.'

'I want to own a house,' she said.

'And I want a new knee, but I'm not likely to get one, am I?'

'You can drive. You've got your blessed car. What have I got? What have we as a family got? A rented flat and ten washing machines. I want a house, Don, a house of our own.'

He groaned. 'Menlove Avenue beckoning again? Look, I can't go out to work full-time and pay a mortgage.'

'Yes, you can,' she snapped. 'You can rent next door and help folk sell their houses. Our Sean can be your assistant. It's a clean job, a damned sight better than the one he's got now, all motor oil and filthy nails. Have you seen the state of him when he gets home?'

Don's mouth hung open.

'Shut your gob; there's a tram coming.'

He snapped his teeth together. 'I'd need real money to put next door right. I doubt it's seen a paintbrush this century.'

Tess turned and faced him properly. 'There's two ways to go about it. You can set yourself up, or you can work for Maitland and Corby. They want to open smaller branches in what they call the suburbs. We can make an appointment with them any time. There's a basic wage, gas, electric and phone paid for by them, and you get a percentage of everything you sell.'

Don didn't like the sound of it.

Tess didn't like the sound of whatever was happening outside. She dashed to the door and stared wide-eyed at the scene in the middle of the

46

road. Dozens of teenagers on massive motorbikes had driven up between the Teddy boys and their wide-skirted female counterparts on the opposite pavement. The leader held up a hand, and all the bikes stopped. He cast an eye over the multi-coloured locals. 'Look,' he shouted, mockery decorating the word. 'Still back in the Dark Ages.'

Drainpipe-trousered lads became round-shouldered as if trying to disappear altogether. Even their chains lost sheen and hung limply from hands that didn't know what to do with themselves.

Don stood behind his wife. 'Rockers,' he whispered.

'More like crackers, you mean.'

'Their leathers must have cost more than a month's wages,' Don continued. 'As for the bikes – they'll be on the never-never.'

The Rockers were laughing at the out-of-touch Teds, while pillion passengers, mostly female, dismounted and poked fun at the Smithdown Road girls. Rockers' chicks wore jeans and boots, denim or leather jackets, gloves and roll-necked jumpers. Even on a summer evening, riding was a chilly business.

'So this is what comes next,' Tess muttered.

'Half of it,' Don told her. 'The rest are Mods. They ride scooters and wear army greatcoats, and they want peace. That means ban the bomb, Aldermaston and making love instead of war.'

'I don't like the idea of that,' Tess pronounced.

Don kept his counsel. She wouldn't like the idea of the retort he bit back, would she? When she'd wanted a baby, she'd found a way of making love to a man who could take no weight on one of his knees. She'd been gentle, tender and loving, but it had been just a means to an end. Two children, one of each, and she was finished with all that. Occasionally, very rarely, he managed a pleasant moment when she turned her back on him in bed, but the love had gone out of her. She was allowing him a favour for old times' sake, no more than that. He was a beggar at the queen's table, and the humiliation was killing him. There had to be an end to this unsavoury situation, and he must speak up soon; in fact, he should do it now.

'We have to get away from here,' she said.

Don continued to hold his tongue, because once he started, it would all tumble like Niagara.

'I know it's not far, but it's far enough. I can't see this bike lot roaring up and down a nice residential road with trees and grass verges, can you? Bay windows, too. I've always wanted bay windows.' She looked him full in the face. 'Don?'

He turned and limped back through the door, his hand shaking on the stick that aided his walking. His children were important to him, and he'd planned to drift on until they were on their own roads, no walking stick required to assist them along the way. Why couldn't she stop meddling? She was meant to have been satisfied with her launderette and her flat, but nothing would stay her determination to keep up with the Joneses she hadn't even met.

She came in. 'What's the matter with you?'

His kids were outside but nearby. They were wearing the wrong clothes, articles that had been crossed off the lists of many teenagers twelve months back. He half expected Anne-Marie to fly into the shop at any moment; she had jeans and blouses upstairs. 'Leave me alone, Tess,' he said.

She folded her arms and stood in front of machine number seven. He looked almost as sad as he'd been after Dunkirk, defeated, heartbroken and completely wrecked. Uneasily, she shifted her weight from foot to foot. At the start of the war, she'd already been pregnant with Sean, but she had needed him for Anne-Marie... Yet he'd never complained, and he still managed sometimes to make it happen... He didn't understand her, had never understood what went on inside her head, the memories, the fears, the need not to get pregnant again...

Don looked his wife full in the face. When had she last kissed him? When had she placed a hand on his thigh, an arm across his shoulders, her head on his chest? Why did he have to make love without seeing her face? Love? There was virtually nothing left in him, either, apart from this fierce, protective affection for the children. Yet the cold, hard woman with whom he had lived for twenty-odd years was still the best-looking in Liverpool. Her face, with its almost heart-shaped beauty spot on the right cheekbone, was perfect. He wanted her, but he was no animal.

He took a deep breath. 'I'm here for the kids,' he said quietly. 'I'll go when they go. I don't want to buy a house with you, live with you, eat with you. If we had another room here, I'd be sleeping in it.' There. He had said most of it. Yet he derived little relief from opening his mouth and speaking his truth. He felt terrible, as if he had trodden on a small creature with no means of defending itself. Because she couldn't help being what she was. Why she was what she was – that was another matter altogether, and not quite a mystery.

Tess closed her mouth so quickly and inaccurately that she bit her tongue.

'I'm still a man,' he reminded her as gently as possible. 'I might walk like a ruptured duck, but I'm all there apart from that. We've lived a lie since our Anne-Marie was born. Everybody managed without all sorts while you worked and saved for this business – and all power to you – well done. But you never asked what I wanted. When you go to the chippy, you always fetch me a steak pudding. I might fancy cod once in a while, but you don't ask. In your mind, I'm just a steak pudding, a body at the table, a man whose stiff knee holds you back. It's no way to live, Tess.' This wasn't living; it was an existence, no more.

She felt as if the world had shifted sideways on its axis. 'Where will you go?' she asked, her voice cracking.

'I've somewhere to go. It's a bit late for you to start worrying about my welfare, isn't it? I got married where you told me, when you told me, let my kiddies go to RC schools. When I came back from war early and less than perfect, I realized I'd got more affection out of the ancient mariner who brought me back in his leaky boat than I've ever had from you.' He was being cruel, yet he couldn't stop the words pouring like hot magma from a tear in the earth's crust.

Tess stared at the floor, wished it would open up and swallow her. The expression on his face, or rather the lack of expression, made her sick, ashamed and ... and alone. She was suddenly terrified. Anne-Marie would leave school in a few weeks, and she wanted to go in for hairdressing. Apprentices and improvers worked long hours. Sean was doing mechanics in a garage, and he was already talking about getting a flat with a couple of mates. 'Don't leave me,' she begged, hating herself before the words were out. She couldn't be left, mustn't be left.

He stared hard at her before answering. 'You left me years ago, Tess. I've read that many books, I'm an almost-walking encyclopedia. Invasion by Danes, Romans, Saxons, I'm your man. I know most poets, the workings of the internal combustion engine, how to build a bloody dry-stone wall, how to make a patchwork quilt. Dickens, Mark Twain, even Geoffrey flaming Chaucer; I've digested the lot. And all the time, you've followed your road and dragged this bloody cripple along at the back of you.'

'I'm sorry, I'm sorry.'

Don smiled, though his eyes remained cold. 'Oh, yes, you're sorry. Sorry you won't get a three-bedroom semi with gardens, horrible carpets and a fly-away coffee table. I've no intention of becoming an estate agent. There's very few houses for sale, anyway, because we're still rebuilding what Hitler bombed. No, I'm quite happy manning the phone six mornings a week at Braithwaites, ta. It may not pay much, but a builders' merchants is

51

right for me with my experience.'

That was the point at which Tess suffered her first ever panic attack. It closed in without warning or mercy, removing light from the room, air from her lungs, strength from her limbs. Something hot yet chilling coursed through her veins, while her heart went into overdrive, fluttering and jumping about behind her ribs like a bat in an unfamiliar cave. She was cold to the bone. She was in a caravan on a winter's night, the only warmth available the body heat of her siblings, at least one of which number still wet the bed almost every night.

Don, believing she was having a tantrum of some kind, lowered his chin and drifted back in dream time. 1936. She'd had hair like ripe corn, eyes of the clearest, brightest blue, a neat little figure, and a mind as clear as a bell even then. Her family, with whom Tess had no longer lived, had been dragged into the equation by a local nun who'd learned of the banns. Prejudiced beyond measure, the tribe had fought Tess's determination to enter a mixed marriage, albeit within the Catholic Church. Priests, teachers and even a bishop had been dragged into the ring, but Tess had remained unmoved. She told everyone that she would live in sin, so she finally achieved permission to marry. Don should have known then. From a relatively affluent family, he had been a good catch. But his father's premature death and his mother's second marriage to a wastrel had put paid to Tess's hopes before her marriage to Don was two years old. Then the war, then the knee, then the steak puddings...

Tess loved Tess. She guarded herself against return to the conditions of a childhood that had been impoverished, uncertain and pugnacious. When it came to food and clothing, it had been child against child, and may the best urchin win. A smaller than average girl, she had suffered, so she wanted a warm nest and plenty of space and nourishment. These were her rights, and he had been the one with the duty to furnish her with such requirements. But he had failed by losing his father, his father's money, and the use of one of his hinge joints. She never expressed concern about the pain caused by a shattered patella, by the mangling of connective tissue, by the worsening of everything when arthritis moved in.

'Don?' she managed.

'What?'

She was hyperventilating. 'Get somebody. Heart attack.'

He leapt to his feet, grabbed the stick and made for the door.

With two fingers in his mouth, he delivered a whistle shrill enough to shatter good lead crystal. The leader of the newly arrived Rockers was by his side in an instant. 'What's up? Can we do something?'

'Get the doc, please. Black front door halfway down the block opposite this one, tell him Tess Compton's collapsed. She's on the floor.'

There followed a flurry of activity involving Anne-Marie and Pea-Green, Sean and a couple of friends, the doctor, and the leader of the leather-clad invaders. 'Panic attack,' announced Dr Byrne eventually. 'Get me a paper bag and clear this room.'

The leader of the bike pack ushered everyone but Don and the doctor into the street while Tess blew into the brown bag. Gradually, colour returned to her cheeks and she managed to shift until she rested against a washing machine. Panic attack? She'd been inches from death, and her whole life had run through her head like a fox chasing chickens. 'Pain in my chest,' she breathed before returning the paper bag to its designated place. After a few more breaths, she spoke again. 'Living here's not doing my health any good,' she announced, her tone rapidly approaching normal. 'I think I'm allergic to all these detergents.'

Don shook his head almost imperceptibly. Even now, she was fighting her corner. 'I meant what I said, Tess.' He gave his attention to the medic. 'She wants a house on Menlove Avenue, and I'm putting my good foot down. Just because I'm a cripple, she thinks I'll give her anything she wants. Tess is a bit old for tantrums, but she does her best when she needs to put on a performance.' Molly performed. She sang and played the ukulele, and she didn't moan or mither.

Stephen Byrne placed himself next to Don on the bench. 'What your wife just experienced is very, very real. Something's knocked her sideways. It might be an event in her past, or a recent shock—'

But Don had released a fury he had suffocated for years, and he could scarcely help himself. 'House on Menlove Avenue, doc. Oh, and I have to be an estate agent with our Sean, who gets his hands dirty in his present job, the job he chose

54

because it suits him. I said no to all of it, and you might as well know that this marriage has been over for going on fifteen years. When the kids leave, I leave. I'm not telling them that, but she might. Because, you see, our Tess here is the most selfish creature I've ever met. She thought I would inherit my dad's building firm, but she got disappointed. She thought she'd married a strapping man, but she got disappointed. And to give her her due, she has worked damned hard to get where she is.' He paused. 'Where *she* is, you see. I'm just a steak pudding and mushy peas.' He smiled tightly. 'You can ignore that last bit.'

Dr Byrne was lost for words.

Tess found several. Don had never appreciated her. She couldn't be on her own, would never manage by herself. This panic had happened because she couldn't cope with his threats to leave her all alone after twenty years of marriage. Yes, thought Don, she was doing well considering she'd emerged just moments earlier from a panic attack.

'Well, you're all right now.' Don stood up and made for the door.

'Where are you going?' his wife demanded.

'Out to see a mate. Later on, it'll be a pie, a pint, and a few games of arrows. Even a bloke with one knee can enjoy darts.' He couldn't say any more, because for some reason, he felt perilously close to tears. Even now, after all he'd been through, there was something about her that made him sad, needful, angry, heartbroken.

'See?' screamed Tess. 'He's the selfish one, and it's—'

Don slammed the door, stepped onto the pavement and faced his beloved children. Self-loathing was already diluting his anger; he could not have stayed in the launderette without continuing to rant.

'Is she all right?' Anne-Marie asked anxiously. 'What happened? Is it her heart? She said it was her heart.'

Don shook his head. 'No. She just got upset about something and lost her breath. Go in and look after her when Dr Byrne's finished.' He got into his car and drove away. As soon as he was alone he began to tremble, and he pulled into a side street at the earliest opportunity. Never before had he faced up to her. She was bright, but not bright enough to react to the sarcastic comments with which he sometimes peppered his longer chunks of oratory. 'She probably doesn't listen,' he told the handbrake as he applied it. But he couldn't have drifted along in her wake this time. No. He'd been forced to become a tugboat heaving and hauling HMS Tess into dock, because she would have sold him down the river this time. 'You're thinking in metaphors, Don,' he said aloud. 'And she can't help it. Just remember that.'

But his memories went their own way. Her laughter, clear as a mountain stream running over smoothed stones, her beautiful face, her hands, those wonderful legs. Where had she gone? What had she become, and was he to blame? 'Stop it,' he snapped aloud.

Anne-Marie would have loved to move to Menlove Avenue, because a much-admired rebel named Lennon lived there. A pupil at Quarry

Bank School, he had formed the Quarry Men, and they played at local fetes and fairs, usually with a bevy of girls cheering them on. But Anne-Marie had enough boyfriends. There was Pea-Green, for a start, and the lead rider of the newly arrived Rockers seemed to have taken a shine to Don's pretty daughter. She looked like her mother but, so far, she seemed not to have inherited Tess's selfish streak. Anne-Marie was as engrossed in fashion and music as the next teenager, but she had heart.

'Do you have a heart, Don Compton?' Did he? If he had feelings for anybody other than his children, they were all for Molly Braithwaite, widow of the deceased Matthew. And therein lay the twist in the tale, because he might move on to enjoy all the benefits of Matt Braithwaite's legacy, while Tess, who had married for money, would continue to miss out. He cleared his throat. A part of him understood Tess, because she'd had a bugger of a childhood, and she was a frightened woman. But he couldn't stay outwardly compliant any longer. His wife was frigid in his company, and he needed to get out of the refrigerator, longed to sit near a cosy fire with Molly and her mad dogs.

Molly was a big woman with a smile that sometimes put the sun to shame, and a laugh that was infectious. She would never match Tess for looks, but Don had learned the hard way that beauty was indeed skin deep, and that a pretty face could hide a cruel heart. Oh, Molly. He grinned stupidly and shook his head. Brown eyes, brown hair, a few strands of grey claiming

57

space above her ears. She dyed it. When he'd asked about the colour, she had shrugged. 'Shit brown like the rest of me head. More gravy?' They had looked into the sauce boat, noticed the colour and howled in near-hysteria.

Her house, separated from the business by a couple of acres, was like herself – big and beautiful. She made a man of him in and out of bed, gave him much to be pleased about, including interesting, often inedible meals, and affection. Yes, she adored him. And the increased speed of his heartbeat whenever he approached his place of work reminded him that he, too, was standing perilously close to the brink of love.

He closed his eyes. Was Madam Tess planning to play up? Would she sing to the gallery, to the kids, to the doctor? The man had declared her panic attack to be real... 'I'll get a book from the library,' he whispered. Well, if he could become an expert in car maintenance and dry-stone walling, psychiatry or psychology should be a walk in the park. Panic attacks. Increased adrenalin, the doc had said. Pure fear. What if she went crazy? Could he leave her if she finished up on drugs and all kinds of therapy? What sort of man would behave in such a way?

Well, sitting here would shell no peas, as Molly might have put it. She would be half expecting him, though she seldom demanded a move up the list. He worked alongside her every morning apart from Sunday, and most lunch times were spent in her company, as were several evenings when he was supposed to be playing darts. Sometimes, he felt as if he might be betraying his children, but they were almost grown, and he'd done his best. As a disabled father, he had brought them through their early years while Tess had struggled to save for her own business. He had done his job, and he kept reminding himself of that fact.

Molly had no children. She and Matt had tried for years, but she'd finally settled for a couple of occasionally mad retrievers and some tropical fish. The fish made her sleepy, the dogs kept her awake, nobody criticized her and, taken all round, she thought she was better off with animals. Her one reservation was Sam, who had been expelled from dog school for eating equipment and trying to have sex with a miniature poodle, but she managed to forgive him. She managed to forgive everyone and everything, because she was in love with life.

The dogs greeted Don when he stepped out of the car. They understood his unsteadiness and always made room for him. Molly waved from the doorway. She was losing weight. 'You look good,' he called.

She embraced him and led him inside. 'Well, I've given up the slimming club,' she announced. 'Seven and six a week to be told off in front of everybody like a kid that's never done its home- work? Sod that for a game of hopscotch. So I pinched a diet book and I'm doing it meself. She must have been coining it, that Glenda one. Come in. I've finished the lessons in acupuncture. All the needles are ready, and you've won first prize.'

Don shook his head wearily. In the past couple of years, she'd done massage, which was lovely, cake decorating, which was rather hit and miss, and now she'd been messing about with some Chinese chap and a pile of fine needles. She was ordering him to get his kit off.

'Bloody hell, Molly. Give me a break, will you? I've had a terrible day, and you're kicking off with designs on my body.'

She blew a raspberry. 'Listen, cheerful. I'm only halfway through tattooing, so my designs are a bit limited, just butterflies and birds. No, I'm going to stick pins in you, see if we can get that knee a bit looser.' She studied him for a few seconds. 'What's happened? Does she know about me?'

'No.'

'What, then? Sit down; you look like you've gone eight rounds with a pro boxer. Will I get you a brandy? Cup of tea? Some crayons and a colouring book?'

'Shut up, Moll. No. First, promise me you're not studying to be a tattoo artist.'

'Joke,' she said before shutting up while he told her the lot. Rockers, bikes, Menlove Avenue and estate agency were all delivered wrapped in Skaters' Trails carpet while she sat quietly and listened. 'So,' Don concluded, 'she went and had a panic attack. I didn't notice at first, then, when I did notice, I thought she was putting it on, but Dr Byrne said it was genuine. She's scared. I told her I'll be leaving her when Sean and Anne-Marie have gone – if not before. Terrified of being on her own, she is. And to be honest, I've never been sure about her nerves. At least my bad knee's visible because of the way I walk. What's wrong with her could well be in her head, and we've no bandages or calipers for that.'

Moll watched his face and shared his pain. 'And you drove off before the doctor left?'

'I did. I was in such a bloody mood, I had to park away from the road until I stopped shaking.'

'Not nice, Don.'

'I know that.'

She touched his hand. 'I've seen her, you know. I got dressed up in all me muck and took a load of washing there. She's pretty.'

'Yes, she is.'

'So you want me for me money, eh?'

'Of course.'

Molly threw her head back and guffawed. She had a laugh only slightly lighter in weight than that of a dock worker, and her whole body shook. Well, the bits that weren't encased in an over-enthusiastic all-in-one girdle shook. She was his oxygen, his entertainment, his comfort. 'I love you, Moll.' There. He had finally said it.

That put a stop to her merriment. She wanted this man, but not at any price. 'Don, I don't care if we live tally, cos we don't need certificates except for proof of insanity. But I do care what happens to her. If Tess's price is a house on Menlove Avenue, a bit of carpet and a bent mirror, she can have all that. I've two hundred thousand doing nothing, and a business I'll flog as soon as I feel like it. She can keep her launderette, live on her tree-lined avenue and have new furniture if she wants it. We're off to Harley Street, you and I. There's a chap who does knees with metal and plastic or something. He can use putty for all I care, as long as we can get that leg a bit better.'

61

He blinked back a reservoir of emotion. Chalk and cheese? No. Molly was solid gold, while Tess was steel, shiny, cold and heartless. She was also frightened halfway to death, because she needed scaffolding all round to preserve her air of normality. 'She wouldn't take it off you, love.'

'No, but she'd grab it from you and bite your hand off at the wrist.'

'I haven't got it, have I?'

Molly sucked in some air and delivered a shrill whistle. 'Then get it, you mad bugger. What happens to men's imaginations, eh? A policy. You took out a policy years ago and never told her about it. Or you've won the pools – whatever it takes. You want to live with me, she wants to move to Menlove Avenue, so that's what has to happen. With my money, but sod it.'

'And when she finds out I'm living with my dead boss's wife?'

'Leave her to me. I've buried bigger dragons than your Tess, mate. Look how many builders I deal with on a daily basis. Cheeky bastards, most of them, but if they don't toe the line, they can beggar off to Mike Merryfield's dump. Cut price? He couldn't trim his toenails, never mind his prices. The government will deal with him, because we're still technically in a period of austerity as far as building's concerned.'

That was another thing about Molly: she knew her onions, her cement and her bricks. Judging from some of the offerings delivered to table during her Italian period, she confused the three occasionally. But she was an experimental cook, and life was never dull. 'I'll think about it,' he promised. 'The kids are still there, so I should have time.' Whichever way he looked at it, he was going to be a bought man. Still, if he had to be someone's property, he would choose Molly any day. 'And thanks, Molly. It's really generous of you.'

She beamed at him. 'I'll be getting the better deal. I'd swap a house on any avenue for you. Now. How do you feel about rainbow trout?'

'Are they found at the end of a rainbow with leprechaun's gold?'

'No, they're found at the wet fish shop, and they cost quids.'

He shrugged. 'I'll give them a go, but don't forget the brown sauce.'

'Heathen,' she hissed before making for the kitchen.

Don sat with her children, Sam and Uke. Uke had won his name by breaking Molly's ukulele as soon as he entered the house for the first time. Molly had a George Formby party piece that she sometimes performed in local hostelries, and the ukulele was a vital prop. So she'd bought another one, forgiven Uke and carried on as before.

They were grand dogs, lively, gentle and caring. Don would have loved to get the kids a dog, but they'd never lived anywhere suitable. Perhaps Menlove Avenue would be suitable, though he couldn't see himself depending on Tess to look after a puppy. There was too little love in her.

'What am I going to do?' he asked Uke, who always pushed his way to the front in a queue of canines, even if the queue consisted of just one pair.

No answer came, of course. 'Molly?' Don called.

A flustered face pushed its way through a serving hatch. 'What?' she snapped with mock anger. 'I'm still tickling me trout here.'

'Are they alive?'

'Well, they're very fresh.' She paused. 'How do I know when they're cooked?' she asked.

'When they stop flapping about.'

She thought about that one for a few seconds. 'Do I cut their heads off? Because they're staring at me. I feel like I'm stood in the dock on a murder charge. What did you want, anyway?'

'Only to say I meant it.'

'Meant what?'

He put a hand to his mouth. 'Bugger. Can't remember.'

'You love me.'

'That's the one,' he said.

She disappeared, and a few swear words accompanied by the smell of burnt fish and a clattering of implements travelled through from the kitchen. The head reappeared. 'Don?'

'What?'

'Will you go down the chippy?'

He managed to suppress his laughter. 'What about the trout, love?'

She shook her head gravely. 'Cremated. I've sent flowers. They said family only, but I thought a little bunch of freesias would do no harm.'

And it was all compressed into those few minutes and seconds. He loved Molly because she didn't mind being laughed at, because she courted attention with her ukulele and her Formby songs, because she liked to learn and have a go, even with acupuncture and rainbow trout. She was alive,

64

funny, generous, as mad as a frog in a bin, and beautiful. Lovely eyes, soft skin, open mind.

They ate cod and chips from vinegar-soaked paper, watched an old film on Molly's television, played tiddlywinks and fought over which was a tiddle and which was a wink. Dogs joined in the fun, made off with the tools of the game and left two adults spread out on the carpet.

'You'll have to help me up, Molly.'

'I know. You're a bloody liability. Tell you what, you stay where you are and I'll build a cage round you so you can't go home. I'll put Sam and Uke in with you so you won't be lonely. Hey.'

'What?'

She pushed the next words out of a corner of her mouth. 'They're staring at me funny.'

'You what? Who?'

'Me fish. Don't look now, they're watching. It's the trout. They'll never forgive me for the trout.'

'They never saw the bloody trout.'

'But they have ways, Don. Look at that angel fish–'

'You told me not to.'

'Why do they call them angel fish? Delinquents, they are. That one there's a bastard. They know I murdered trout.'

'But we sat here and ate cod–'

'Anonymous cod. Cod with no heads.' She stood up and helped him to his feet. 'I've committed fishslaughter,' she said.

'Moll?'

'What?'

'Shut up and get a bloody head doctor. I'd better go before she smells a rat. If she smells a rat,

I'll decapitate it and get done for ratslaughter. That way, you won't be on your own in court.'

She clung to him. 'Don't let her drive you any madder than you already are. No matter what she does or says, stay cool, not angry.'

'I'll try.'

He drove from the edge of Woolton to Smithdown Road, his foot easing off the accelerator as he neared his destination. The kids would be in bed. Tess might be in bed, or she might be waiting with one of her prepared diatribes. He wasn't in the mood. He'd never been in the mood for lectures, but what could he do? Tess would have her pound of flesh, wouldn't she?

He climbed the stairs to the flat, his leg throbbing fiercely. She would have put his name down for gardening in her new house, he supposed. Gardening? A potted plant was his limit. Cutting lawns and trimming hedges lay well outside his restricted range of abilities.

Ah, she was trying a different tack. For a woman approaching forty, Tess Compton was in excellent shape. She was wearing an almost transparent nightdress, her face was made up, and she had spread herself out like Marilyn Monroe on the sofa. His immediate reaction was born in hope, hope that his children were asleep. But he couldn't look at her, since she was so annoyingly beautiful. God, he wanted her. What sort of animal was he?

'Well?' she asked.

'Well what? Wishing well, artesian well, well done? It's too late, Tess. You're beautiful, but there's no point. You go to bed, and I'll have the sofa. Sean and Anne-Marie will think it's because of my knee. We can't fill in the missing pieces of our jigsaw. It's not about sex; it's about respect, fun, talking. You look stunning, and you always did, but lovemaking was always the payment you made for something you wanted, like Anne-Marie. So thanks, but no, thanks.' To get her own way, Tess was prepared to act the whore.

She shot up like a rocket on bonfire night. 'So you won't try?'

'I've tried long enough. Now, listen to me for a change.' He swallowed nervously. 'A while back, I took out a policy, and it will mature soon. That will get you your house. Anne-Marie will probably go with you, because she's Quarry Men mad, and one of them lives along that avenue. Sean will do whatever he wants.' He held up a hand when she opened her mouth to speak. 'I've not finished. You say nothing to the kids until we've found the right house. When they learn about everything, it will be from both of us. Together. For once, think about them, not about you.'

She stood up, turned away, and walked into the bedroom.

Don lingered for a while at the living room window. Last order stragglers meandered homeward, some whistling, some singing out of tune. One maniac had fallen in love with a lamp post and was whispering sweet nothings into its corporation-green paintwork. A late bus trundled by, a tangle of multicoloured youths fighting on its upper deck. Rainbow. Rainbow trout. 'That angel fish hates the bloody sight of me.' Burnt supper, down to the village for fish and chips twice, plenty of vinegar. An ordinary woman who still worked

67

in spite of her wealth, who still spoke like a native, who sounded just like George Formby when doing her bit at the pub. 'Turned out nice again.' Yes, she was a mimic. She was a giver. It was time to make things happen; it was time to move on.

Leather's hard to sew, but I managed to cobble together a close-fitting mask with eye holes, a space for my nose, a gap for my mouth. Buggeration, this one was a fighter. I didn't give her enough chloroform before sticking her in the sidecar. She's in some woods up a side road off the A580. Scratch marks on my arms. Must wear closer-fitting clothes.

I'll be all right for a while now...

Three

There is a nowhere place, a morning twilight that hangs between night and day, between sleep and wakefulness, and its nature is cruel, because it shelters us for so brief a time from recent miseries. When sense returns, memories pierce consciousness like shards of glass cutting through bone and tissue, embedding themselves in a heart that felt repaired just moments earlier. It refuses to be managed, eliminated or curtailed, as its nature is elemental and buried in the id of every human creature.

Life was getting no easier. Today, Roisin Allen sat bolt upright in the bed, reality crashing into her chest, heart racing like a lorry down a cul-de-sac, impact inevitable, petrified, waiting for the grinding of gears, the scream of brakes, the stench of burning rubber. She was both victim and perpetrator, since she was the one who must mend herself, and she could not stop her own machinery.

What would Phil have said? 'Pull yourself together, you've kids to mind.' Or, 'You can't stand still; you have to move on with life.' *Oh, Phil, how shall I carry on without you, and why didn't I treat you better? No, I didn't want more children, but we could have—Well, I could have held you and loved you when you needed that.*

Guilt was the worst part. Within moments of

69

waking, every cross word she had uttered, every dirty look she had delivered, came back to her on a vivid Technicolor screen, sound included, in her weary head. He had called her his Rose, his Rosie. Roisin, pronounced Rosheen, was a beautiful but unusual label, so most people named her Rosh. In the mornings, he had nominated her Dozy Rosie, because she'd been a reluctant riser.

Phil had been dead for three weeks, and Rosh Allen continued to suffer these early morning symptoms. She slept next to a bolster that was not him, but fooled her when she shifted during slumber, giving her false security, false hope. Drugs sent her into unconsciousness, but they hung over her like black rain clouds, and she seldom woke properly until after lunch time. Mother had moved in, of course. She had taken over the children, the cleaning, cooking, washing and ironing. Mother, usually Mam, in her late fifties, could not carry on like this for ever. An amazing little woman, Anna Riley coped with whatever life threw in her direction. *I continue selfish, Phil. My poor mother is weighed down by it all, and I know I should be–*

The bedroom door crashed into an item of furniture. 'Why ever do you keep the chest of drawers just there? Every morning the same, and I nearly lose your breakfast. We've eggs scrambled all the way to glory and back just now.' The tray was dumped unceremoniously on a bedside table. 'Get yourself on the outside of that lot, then out from under the blankets.' Anna paused. 'I've given up me house, so. The keys go back this afternoon.' She sighed. 'Some of us have to make the decision to get on with life, you see. We can't all go

Shakespearean and lie round like Desdemona in a fit with her leg up.'

'I haven't got my leg up.' The woman in the bed glared hard at her mother.

'Neither did Desdemona, but she'd every right to, poor soul. Anyway, like I said, I've given up me house.'

'Right.'

'And it's grateful they were, because a family can take it now. I was rattling about like the last pill in the bottle. When you're better, I shall find myself a sitting bedroom not too far away from you.'

'A bed-sitting room, you mean.'

'Perhaps I do. But we have to get Winston and Lucy-Furr. You must come and help me. I have a vehicle for their transportation, but cats can be troublesome, as you are quite possibly already aware.'

Rosh groaned. Troublesome? Her mother's cats were from the dark side. Their behaviour was criminal; had they been human, they would have been in Walton Jail. There had been four of them, but two had gone off to ruin wallpaper and furniture in cat afterlife; however, the two worst had managed to survive the busy stretch that was College Road. And now Anna intended to bring them to the relative peace of Lawton Road in Waterloo, Liverpool North. 'I don't want them.' Rosh would rather have mumps or scarlet fever.

Anna made no reply. Her daughter had spoken, had referred to something other than her grief. This was progress indeed. An inch at a time, Anna's precious Roisin was going to be dragged back to life.

'Mam?'

'What?'

'Does Winnie still talk all the time?'

'He does. He comes home and delivers a lecture, especially if there's rain about. Blames me for the weather, so he does. And every time, I have to show him it's raining at the front of the house as well as the back. Or vice versa. Always, he demands tangible proof. The boy's a fool, but handsome enough for a ginger tom. You'll grow used to them, I promise.'

'I shall get a very large dog,' Rosh threatened. She cast an eye over her scattered breakfast. Winston was not the naughtier of the two felines. Lucy-Furr, pronounced Lucifer, had definitely been booted like the first fallen angel out of heaven by God the Father, who would have needed the assistance of God the Son, with God the Holy Ghost riding shotgun. Lucy destroyed things. She did it secretly, frequently and thoroughly. 'I noticed extra holes in your funeral mantilla. She even ruined a sacred item.'

Anna sniffed. Back to the funeral. Again. 'I've sold all me furniture as well,' she said. 'So we've money to live on until you get back to work. We need just a small new bed for me in the box room. Stuff in there will go into your roof. But you see, Roisin, when you work, you won't be here for the kiddies when they get out of school. You could be gone already when they leave in a morning. I've taken a couple of evening jobs to help out–'

'Mam, you're doing enough.'

Anna sat on the edge of her daughter's bed. 'Now, you just listen to me, young lady. Phil Allen was one of the best, but he's gone, God bless him and have mercy on his good, brave soul. I'm still here and not in bad health. We muck in. We're Irish, so we do what needs doing for the greater good within the family. I know you don't want me here for ever, but I know also that you love me. Now, don't start crying again, or we'll need a boat. Eat. We're going for me cats.'

Alone, Rosh did her best with the scrambled eggs and toast. Mother was right about the chest of drawers too near the door; perhaps the room was due for a change. And she must take Phil's clothes down to church for the poor. Yes, Mother was right yet again; it was time to make an effort. Mother was almost always right; that was the most annoying thing about her.

Phil had given Mam the name 'Mother'. She deserved the full title, he had said. Anna Riley was small in stature, huge in soul. Had Rosh needed any proof at all, these past weeks would have provided it. Until the funeral and after that sad occasion, Mam had kept house all day, had sat all night with her daughter, seldom sleeping in her chair, always ready to respond to the moans of a child in another room. And she was right, because a young widow needed to work, while children wanted minding. Energy would have to be found, as would the urge to re-enter the workplace. None of it was going to be easy.

'Roisin?'

Here came Mam again, door crashing inward once more.

73

'Open it.' She held out an envelope and waited while her daughter released its contents.

Tears surfaced quickly. It was a postal order for twelve pounds from Phil's workmates at Wilkinson Engineering. 'Aren't people good?' she said. 'We'll get your bed with this.'

Anna produced a second envelope, manila, with a little window on the front. 'And this arrived along with that one.' She held it out. 'There.'

'Oh, heck.' Rosh dried her eyes on the bed sheet. 'I don't like brown letters. You know I hate them. You do it.' Phil had always dealt with such items. The idea of being responsible for all the workings of a household held no appeal for Rosh. Going back to a full-time job would be enough without all the bills and the budgeting.

Seating herself in a small rocking chair by the window, Anna opened the envelope. She had learned to read in her thirties, and she was proud of how quickly her eye could cover a page. 'May the saints preserve us,' she exclaimed. 'What a man that was. He was a pearl.'

'Mam?'

'Thought of everyone but himself, didn't he? I mind the time when he came to me and said–'

'Mam!'

'No, he called me Mother, so he said that, then went on to–'

'Mam!'

'Oh, sorry. It's from an insurance firm in Manchester. Your man kept his payments up, God bless him. They're waiting just now on the coroner's confirmation of the report. But when they have that for their files, and when death by accident is

74

official, you will get ten thousand pounds. Had he died naturally, it would have been just three. But because it was a road accident, well – there you go.'

Rosh's jaw dropped. Just three? That was enough to buy two houses and a car. But ten? Philomena could carry on with piano lessons, the old instrument downstairs could be tuned properly or replaced, while Kieran might realize his dream of becoming a doctor. As for Alice – well – she could just be happy. Little was expected of poor Alice, who had been late to crawl and walk, who still seemed to have difficulty reading and writing... 'Thank you, Phil,' she said aloud.

'Amen to that.' Anna waved the letter. 'And this is a sign, Roisin. You don't need to rush out to work, don't need to–'

'Oh, but I do. That nest egg is for my babies, Mother. I can get a tutor for Alice, someone who can get her learning. Kieran needs books, and Philly could use a new piano.'

'And you?'

'I'm coming with you. For the cats.'

Inwardly, Anna thanked the saints with all her heart. Money had never held a high position on her daughter's agenda, but the policy had made her think about a future, about the children, even about the cats from Satan. It would all take time, but life was about to be reclaimed by the beautiful Roisin Allen, God help her. Because men noticed her, and there was no Phil to guard her now.

Half an hour later, two women could be seen walking the short distance from College Road to

75

Lawton Road. The smaller pushed a coach-built pram, while the taller held down a tied-on sheet of glass under which two cats spat and scratched with great ferocity. 'What would they have been like if you'd never had them neutered?' she asked.

'There would have been more of them,' was Anna Riley's smart response. 'They've no rules about incest. Heathens, they are. Hell will be full of them, so it will.'

'They keep managing to scratch me at the edges of the glass,' Rosh complained. 'They've claws like needles.'

'Well, don't let go of that glass, whatever. I know it's tied on with the rope, but it shifts and slides, so hang on to it. These cats are all I have of your father now. I mind the day when he brought all four into the kitchen. They were half drowned, and we had to feed them through a little glass dropper with a squeezy bit of rubber on the end. Ah, his neck was scratched to bits when he fetched them into the house, bless him. Two dead now, and just the angels from Hades to remind me of a very fine man.' She sighed. 'We were both fortunate in the husband department, Rosh.'

'There are no angels in hell, Mam.'

Anna winked. 'Just wait. Just you wait and see.'

They buttered the cats' paws and sat watching while the pair of miscreants licked avidly at their gilded pads. Lucy-Furr, after studying her new surroundings for a while, jumped on Rosh's lap and curled into a ball.

'Good heavens,' Rosh said.

'She's comforting you. She knows you're in pain.'

'Rubbish.'

'You'll learn, missy. Oh yes, you will learn. Cats have more than one personality, you see. Like the facets of a diamond, they throw out all kinds of light.'

'You mean they're insane?'

Anna chuckled. 'They very well might be. But it's our kind of craziness, so they could be Irish.' She glanced at the clock. 'See, I'll go now and get the older two from the library and Alice from her friend's house. You peel spuds and carrots, and I'll pick up some cutlets on the way home.'

So Rosh was left with two schizophrenics of the feline persuasion. She topped a carrot, and the green-fringed end shot across the table and landed near the cooker. Winston was on it within a split second. He batted it at Lucy-Furr, and she tried to eat it. Her male counterpart, taking offence at this offside behaviour, became referee and dashed across the room. In a blurred ball of fur, half ginger tom, half black queen, they rolled round the kitchen at a fair rate of knots. Their language was coarse; Rosh knew immediately that they were swearing in Cat-ese.

To confuse the issue further, she threw a few more carrot tops into the field of play. Madness of the very finest quality ensued. Lucy grabbed two tops and sat on them. Winston picked up a third, held on to its green bits and waved it about under his nose. The female, infuriated by this uppity boy-cat type of behaviour, displayed confusion that put Rosh in mind of Alice, her younger daughter. It was clear that Lucy-Furr had no idea what to do next. If she stood up and went for him, she would reveal her hidden carrot tops. If she allowed him to carry on tormenting her, he would continue to feel superior. So she meowed at Rosh, who picked her up, removed the treasures and placed them in a pocket.

The wrestling match continued. Lucy leapt from Rosh's arms, and pandemonium resumed. They were funny. But potatoes and carrots needed peeling, and the cats would have to get on with life. 'Just leave my walls and chairs alone,' warned the head of the household. 'No plucking, no picking, or you'll end up Manx, because I'll cut your tails off. In fact, I'll have your whiskers, too.'

Her heart lurched slightly. She had gone five or more minutes without thinking about Phil. Guilt and hunger combined to make her stomach ache. How shallow she was, how uncaring. She didn't want cats, yet she had allowed them to distract her to the point where she had forgotten the love of her life. *You liked carrots, didn't you? And lamb cutlets, though you always said a man-sized belly needed about twelve of the buggers to feel even half-full. And mint sauce. We often had lamb at Christmas because you loved it with mint sauce and roasties and parsnips ... oh, Phil. Come home, sweetheart.*

'Mum's crying again.' Thirteen-year-old Kieran had entered the kitchen before his two sisters. They stood behind him, Philly with a protective arm across Alice's shoulder. Alice was five, and she couldn't stand change. She needed the same routine every day: socks, underclothes, blouse and skirt laid out in that order on the landing ottoman. Shoes, highly polished, had to be placed on the floor near the landing window. Her cardigan or jumper must be folded and left downstairs on the hall stand, with her coat hanging to the right of it, little satchel under the coat. Philly, at twelve, often opined that Alice said little because she couldn't be bothered with niceties.

'I'm not crying,' Rosh lied. 'I've laughed till the tears came.' She dried her face on a cuff. 'Mother, your cats have had me helpless. They ran off with bits of carrot, and we nearly had World War Three.'

The two older children smiled, but Alice displayed no emotion.

Rosh continued with her peeling, hoping against hope that Alice would react. Since Phil's death, the little one's patterns of behaviour hadn't altered; they had stopped completely. A huge part of Alice's backdrop had disappeared. Her father, knowing that his baby was special, had treated her like a little princess. She had almost listened to him. In his presence, she had carried on in her own little world, a place from which she had occasionally paid a visit to the here and now. It was almost as if the child had stopped existing since the loss of Daddy.

But, as the saying went, where there was life, there was hope. And here came Alice with one of her precious habits. She picked up carrots and put them in the cream colander, potatoes in the silver-coloured pan. This had been one of her chosen jobs since she'd been able to reach the table top. She was a strange child. Ten steps to the garden gate. Her legs were growing, but she continued to need that decade of paces from door to pavement. Rosh had explained about longer legs, but that idea involved development, which was change, and Alice did change at her own speed, and usually not at all.

'Twenty-seven in there,' the child said, a finger pointing at carrots cut lengthwise. 'And twenty-three in here. Spuds.' She stalked out of the room. The occupants of the kitchen stood open-mouthed, listening while Alice hung up her jacket. 'Alice hook,' she said. Then she started to laugh. It was a rusty noise, as if it needed a squirt of oil. 'Stoppy, stoppy,' the child yelled.

Rosh crept to the doorway, her right arm held out to order the rest to stay where they were. Alice could count beyond the ten paces, and she could do it quickly. Rosh had noticed on several occasions the child's lips moving while vegetables were transferred – for how long had she been counting? Since babyhood, this youngest one had 'talked' to her inner self, but was she absorbing knowledge, was she learning? If she was learning, then someone, somewhere, was getting through to her.

The newly widowed mother stopped in the doorway and watched the scene in the hall.

It was Winston. Sunlight, split by a crystal figurine in a window, deposited spots of colour all over the walls. Rosh held her breath. Phil had bought her the crystal angel after the birth of Alice. He was here. She could almost feel him breathing next to her. Winston, too, was here; so was every colour of the spectrum.

Mother's male cat was determined, arrogant, but far from elegant. To describe him as overweight would have been a kindness, since he was roughly the size of a three-month-old St Bernard. He leapt up the walls, tried to capture and eat a bit of green, a drop of orange, a slice of blue. His tail wagged more furiously with each failed attempt, and Alice was helpless on the floor. Here was a child who noticed just three or four objects in her own room, who failed to hear the honk of a vehicle's horn, who seldom responded when her name was called. This was a miracle, and Phil had made it happen. He had returned to look after Alice. She would be all right.

The cat gave up his fruitless fight. He landed badly, rose to his feet, shook himself and twitched his tail twice, as if sending a vulgar signal to the audience. They could bugger off out of it, because he didn't care.

Alice stood up, walked past the cat and up the stairs. She would doubtless position herself on her bed with Teddo. Teddo, a one-eyed bear passed down by Rosh to Philomena, by Philly to Alice, was the little girl's constant indoor friend. Rosh remembered sewing on a new eye, an item Alice had removed immediately. Teddo had one eye, and that was law.

Rosh returned to the kitchen and related what she had seen. 'It has to be Hans Asperger's illness,' she told her captive audience. 'Leo Kanner's paper was about the truly autistic. We can find a window into Alice. A real autistic would not have laughed like that. Well, from what I've read, I mean.'

Anna placed her shopping basket on the table. 'Mrs Green said Alice and Beth were playing swap dollies, but there was no talking.'

'She'll improve,' Rosh insisted. 'She spoke just now, didn't she?' There was no point in mentioning her own certainty about Phil's presence in the hall. Such declarations would serve only to upset Philly and Kieran. The latter had assumed the role of man of the house, and it was he who had gone to the doctor to ask about the papers on autism.

'Both Austrians,' he said now. 'As was Hitler, I believe.'

Anna blessed herself hurriedly. 'Wipe the name from your lips, Kieran. Think of what he did to the Jews, and to Liverpool.'

'They're very advanced medically,' the boy replied. 'Kanner discovered autism in 1943, and Asperger wrote his paper in '44. They leave us standing when it comes to medical research.'

Anna began to prepare the meat and boil water for the vegetables. The two older children abandoned the kitchen and went up to their rooms. Rosh left the meal in the capable hands of her mother; she was going to spy on Alice. But someone knocked at the front door and distracted her. She knew who it would be; she also knew that he would have seen her through the frosted glass in the door. 'I wonder if I can get heavier frosting?' she asked of no one, since she was alone in the hall. Yes. It was Roy Baxter. He had deposited a basket at one side of the step, and was on his way back to the gate.

'Oi,' she shouted.

He stopped and turned. 'Sorry. I just left a few things from my allotment – onions, spuds and stuff. Oh, and a bunch of flowers. From the allotment. I didn't buy them...'

He hadn't changed. A tongue-tied lad had become an awkward man. Did he really think he had a chance because Phil was dead? No. He was just being kind, she supposed. 'Thank you, Roy. Please don't worry about us. We'll be all right, I'm sure.'

He opened his mouth, delivered no more words, raised his cap and turned away. Stumbling over something or other, he crossed the road at a pace that was uneven, to say the least. Why was he such a damned fool? She'd turned him down fifteen years back, had chosen Phil Allen, and that should have been an end to it. It wasn't his fault that the Allens had moved into Lawton Road during the war. Phil's job had been listed as essential, because he'd been in charge of a unit at Wilkinson Engineering that made stuff too special to mention. The Official Secrets Act had been involved, and rumour had it that Phil and his friends had been involved in the manufacture of electronic equipment that had played a part in code-breaking, though no one was sure.

Roy's reason for non-participation in the battlefield was less glamorous, of course. He'd broken a leg during a football lesson at school, and had lost an inch of bone after surgery performed months later because the limb had refused to mend. So he'd sat the war out with Mum and Dad, had tried to ignore the people across the road, had never married. He needed a lift in his left shoe, would always be a cripple, and she would never look at him. No one would look at him.

Dad was waiting, of course. The usual sneer was in place as he addressed his son. 'She'll not glance at your side of the road in a million years, so I don't know why you bother. Knocked you back the first time, married a man with a good trade, so what would she want with you now?'

Occasionally – no, frequently – Roy felt like killing his dad. Every time the bully had beaten Mum, Roy had wanted to kill him. She'd died relatively young, of course.

'Look at the state of you.' Joseph Baxter threw back his head and laughed. 'No guts, no sense, one leg.'

Roy stood his ground on both legs. Normally, he would have been upstairs or in the kitchen by now, but this time he seemed to be glued to the floor. And he'd been so excited yesterday, as his boss had promoted him, and he'd felt proud of himself. The war had been good to him, because a shortage of manpower had allowed him to progress and, after years of dogged determination and exams, he was now an articled clerk. He knew the law; he knew if he hit his dad, he would end up on the wrong side of a locked gate.

'Well?'

'The moustache looks daft with your lip curled. Oh, I knew I had something to tell you. I'm fully articled now, with an improved salary, so I'll be looking for a place in town, somewhere nearer to my work. Just a room, of course. I may come home at weekends.' Because this was his home. He'd made sure of that, hadn't he?

'You what?'

'Unless you're going deaf, you heard me. While Mum was here, you belittled her and beat her up. Now you throw all your nastiness in my direction. I'm not violent by nature, and I may be disadvantaged because of my leg, but I'm thirty years younger than you. Watch your mouth, or I might just split it open and lose you even more of those rotting teeth.' Roy blinked. Had he really said all that, or had his imagination gone into a higher gear?

Joseph, who had always refused to be reduced to Joe, had a ready answer; he usually had a ready answer. 'You'll not manage on your own,' he said, the tone not quite steady.

'I think the boot's on another foot, Joseph.'

'Joseph? Who are you to be calling me Joseph? I'm your father, for God's–'

'No. You're no father to me. Mum told me. She married you and pretended I was yours. She wanted to comfort me from her deathbed, so she told me the truth.' Roy was making it up as he went along and yes, he knew he was being vengeful. 'You are no one's father. How many times have you said there's no lead in *my* pencil, eh? Well, listen to me for once. Your pencil's never been sharp; neither has your brain.'

'You bastard.'

'Exactly. I'd rather be a bastard, as it happens.' It was happening. After all these quiet years, Roy was shaving off his pound of flesh. Today, he had made the longest speech ever. And he still couldn't walk away, because his father was looking unwell. Or could he bugger off and let the mad beggar take his chances?

85

The older man's face was grey. He seemed to be experiencing difficulty with his breathing and, after a few seconds of increasing discomfort, he sank to the floor.

Roy stared blankly at him; was he dying? Was there justice in the world after all? But Roy's nature forbade him to stand and watch anyone struggle for breath. He pushed himself to move, returning as quickly as possible to the house outside which he had so recently left a basket.

Rosh answered the door. 'Ah, Roy,' she breathed wearily. What the hell did he want now?

'Sorry,' he said. 'But will you ask Mrs Riley to sit with my dad? He's collapsed, and I need to go up to the phone box.' Without another word, he walked through the gate and turned towards College Road.

Rosh gathered her thoughts. Alice was sitting at the kitchen table with Mother. Alice had to grow used to living with her grandmother. So, after advising Anna of the situation, Rosh crossed the road herself and entered the Baxter house through its open front door. He was unconscious near the fireplace. He had a thready pulse and colourless skin, and his breathing was shallow. The place wasn't untidy, but neither was it clean. There was something about a house without a woman; it acquired a film, as if the very air it contained was opaque.

A collection of law books sat on a shelf. Beneath them on a small table, a photograph of Roy's dead mother kept company with a radio. The fireplace was Victorian, the sideboard and gateleg table Utility, the hearthrug maroon. It was a dingy, lifeless room; there was no love in it, nor one pretty item. Two battered armchairs in worn leather flanked the rug. The walls were mottled brown and cream with patches of damp here and there. She didn't want to look at him.

When she did look, she saw no improvement in the health of the creature on the floor. Rosh knew what he was, what he had been to his wife. He'd been her jailor, her abuser, her enemy. Roy had struggled to get home from work at lunch time, because Joseph seldom fed his cancer-stricken wife, and none of the neighbours dared go near in case he was in. In the end, Roy had put her in hospital, as he could not keep his promise to let her die at home.

'You killed her as sure as if you'd taken an axe to her. Is it your turn now? My Phil died just weeks back. Roy came to the funeral, but you couldn't be bothered, thank God. Because my Phil hated you, and that wasn't in his nature. He was a good man. Your son's a good man, but you–'

'Hello again, Rosh.'

She hadn't heard Roy re-entering his house. 'Sorry,' she said quietly.

'Not your fault. I turned on him for the first time ever. Just words. I didn't hit him, but I wanted to. I just told him what I thought of him.'

'About time, too.'

Roy gazed at the man on the rug. 'I said I wasn't his son, that I was a bastard. Told him my mum said that to me on her deathbed. That did it, I think. He took a funny turn and collapsed. This damned article hurt my mother over and over

87

again. There was ... there was rape, too. I know the law wouldn't have accepted it, because she was his wife, but...' He raised his shoulders for a moment. 'But I heard it, lived with it, was too terrified to do or say anything. I thought he might kill me, her, or both of us.'

'I saw her bruises, Roy. Many people saw them.'

An ambulance arrived. Joseph Baxter was given oxygen and placed on a stretcher. 'You can come with him,' one of the men said.

'No, thanks. I want nothing to do with him.'

The older of the pair frowned. 'But ... er ... aren't you his son?'

Roy shook his head. 'He brought me up, beat me up, beat my mother. Shove him in a bin somewhere, because he's one evil bugger. Just get bloody rid.'

When the vehicle left the street with its bells clanging, Roy allowed a sigh of relief to escape. 'Sorry you had to witness all that. But while I can, while I'm angry enough, I want to show you something else, another symptom of his evil. It's important that someone sees what he used to do. I know you're in mourning, but you're just about the only person I trust enough to... It's embarrassing and shaming, yet I have to do it.'

She followed him upstairs to his father's room. The stair carpet was threadbare and filthy, though an open door framed a sparkling bathroom. Roy probably cleaned that, she guessed. Everything needed a lick of paint. The banister felt greasy under her palm.

Roy stopped on the landing. 'His room's a disgrace, but I can assure you that mine isn't. Take my word for it.'

He led her into the squalid front bedroom. It stank of long-stored dirty washing, of mould, damp and dust. From the wardrobe, he dragged a small chest and threw open its lid. 'There you go, Rosh. That's what he is and was.'

It was filled with implements and weapons. She saw handcuffs, leather whips and belts, rope, a wooden article shaped like... 'Good God.' She slapped a hand to her mouth. 'That thing there – is the stain blood?'

'It is. My mother's blood. She died of cancer of the cervix. It was discovered too late, and it spread. But yes, he used that thing on her. Made it himself, I think, and he used too little sandpaper. She must have been full of splinters.'

Rosh took several deep breaths. 'Why did you stay after she died?'

Roy smiled sadly. 'To watch him. To make sure he hurt no more women. I suppose it's a kind of penance, my way of apologizing to my poor mother. Then all of a sudden, I'd had enough today. It just boiled over. In fact, I wish I'd said more. I suppose the hospital will want me to take a case in – pyjamas, dressing gown, soap and so forth. When they unpack it, they'll find a selection of the things he used to torture Mum. I'll put a little note in– *These are the toys he used on his poor wife.* Perhaps that will make them let him die.' He closed the lid of the chest. 'I need him to be dead.'

'Roy–'

'No, I've had enough, Rosh. I'm angry with me, because I should have stuck a knife in him ages ago. She used to cry in my arms, and I did nothing, nothing, nothing.'

'You'd have hanged or got a life term.'

'She was my mother!'

'Yes, she was. And if you'd committed murder, she would have blamed herself just as you blame yourself now. She could have left here when you were little, taken you with her.'

'He would have found us. You'll never understand his power, Rosh. You didn't live here. The man's not right.' He tapped his forehead with a finger.

They returned to the front living room. After a few minutes of silence, Rosh went to make tea. Like the rest of the house, the Baxter kitchen was in reasonable condition, though rather less than clean. Light was diminished by a cloudy window, and the room's contents were in a far from sensible order. She dug round and found the necessary items, discovered that her hands were shaking after the shock she'd received upstairs. 'Roy?'

'Yes?'

'He is your father, isn't he?'

A few seconds elapsed before the answer arrived from the next room. 'Unfortunately, yes.'

She stilled her trembling fingers and brewed the tea. Love thy neighbour as thyself? Joseph Baxter wanted roasting alive on a spit with a rod of steel right through his body. Poor Roy. She carried the tray into the living room. 'Isn't your real name Roylston?' she asked.

'It was my mother's maiden name, but we shortened it to Roy. He sometimes uses the full Roylston, because he thinks it annoys me. But what angers me more is his breathing. I'd rather it stopped.'

Rosh scarcely knew what to say. She had just suffered a massive loss, and here sat a man who prayed for the permanent removal of his father. It was difficult for her to understand, because she had adored her dad and had never stopped missing him. It was sad that Roy hadn't really had parents. His mother had been beaten into the ground by his father, and the result was this hatred. 'Don't let it consume you,' she said.

'Too late, Rosh. The love I had for my mother was massive, but this is bigger. I feel like I've exploded.'

She had to get back to her mother and the children, but she didn't want to leave him. With the way Alice was, Rosh was reluctant to introduce another new face, so inviting him to the evening meal was not a possibility. Yet he scarcely seemed fit to be abandoned. 'I'll get home now,' she said, 'but I'll come back later just to make sure you're all right.'

'You're very kind. No need for you to put yourself out, though, because I'm sure I'll be better shortly.'

She stood for a few moments and watched him. In her opinion, he was becoming calm – too calm. It was as if he had removed himself in the direction of an alternative universe, because this one had been unkind to him. The fury of recent minutes had left him; it seemed that everything had left him, because he scarcely moved, while his cup of tea had been ignored apart from the odd sip. 'Roy?'

'What?'

'You won't do anything daft, will you?'

He blinked. 'Such as?'

'I don't know.'

Roy managed a slight smile. 'Make a list and submit it to management. I'm management. And I'll tick off the daft things one by one. No, I'm not going to kill myself. Neither am I going to let him back in here. Ever since he signed papers that put me in charge of paying the rent, this is my house. It's mine because I don't pay rent any longer; I pay a mortgage.'

Rosh swallowed. 'Where will he go?'

'It's a pity they closed the workhouses,' was his reply. 'Let the state look after him. I can't do it any longer, Rosh. Apart from school and work, I've been in the company of this mad man all my life. Most of Waterloo knows what he is. And half of Crosby. Go home to your kiddies and your mother, Rosh. Alice might start thinking you've disappeared for ever like– Sorry.'

'It's not a problem. Phil's dead, and I have to face facts.'

'He was a good lad. One of the best.'

'Thanks. I'll ... er ... I'll see you soon.' She left him to his thoughts.

Outside, a posse of women bearing gifts had gathered. Rosh was assaulted by a barrage of questions, some of which she answered. No, Roy hadn't gone in the ambulance. Yes, he was in, though he seemed to want to be left to himself. No, she hadn't seen him eating anything. Yes, she was sure he'd appreciate dishes of food left in the porch. When asked about 'that evil old bastard',

Rosh offered no reply save her opinion that he had suffered a heart attack.

Mother was waiting, of course. She jumped up as soon as her daughter entered the best room. This was an area for adults only, as there was a middle room that served for Sunday dining, piano, children and homework. 'How is he?' Anna demanded.

'Which one?'

'Either or both – I don't mind.'

Rosh sank into an easy chair. 'Well, Roy was angry, then quiet. He refused to accompany his dad in the ambulance, ranted a bit, got mad with himself for not saving his mother some grief. He showed me stuff I could never describe to you in a million years, instruments of torture that had been used by the old man on his wife. And Roy swears that Joseph Baxter will never set foot in that house again. I think it was some sort of heart attack, by the way.'

Anna tutted and shook her head slowly. 'Glory be. All this terrible stuff going on under your nose, and you never get a whiff of it.'

Rosh was used to her mother's odd statements. She was also used to the grim determination with which Anna Riley hung on to her Irish accent. 'There was never a smell, Mother. Mrs Baxter was a clean woman. We saw some bruises on her, though, if you think back. And now the house does want a damned good clean. Roy tries his best, but there was more than a whiff in the old man's room.'

Anna nodded sadly. 'Aye, we did see bruises, bless her. But tell me, how will he keep that festering owld rat out of the house? Hasn't Mr Baxter lived there since Adam got chucked out of Eden?'

Rosh explained that the rent book had been transferred into Roy's name. 'And then he bought the house, Mother. He's got a mortgage. Oh, my God!'

'What?'

Rosh stood up and gazed across the street. 'He's in his dad's room – look. And he's throwing everything out of the window into the front garden.'

'Looks like he means it, then, Rosh.'

The younger woman dashed outside. 'Roy?' she called. 'You're ruining your geraniums.'

He stopped for a few moments. 'Is this on the daft list?' he asked.

It wasn't. She knew it, he knew it, and each was aware that the other knew it. She shook her head. 'What's the plan?' she called.

'Decorating.' Roy returned to his task.

'He's wiping him out,' Rosh told her mother a few minutes later. 'Painting and wallpapering over him, I shouldn't wonder.'

'Roy will not manage that,' Anna replied. 'The man needs to be dead.' She paused. 'I know we shouldn't question God, but I sometimes wonder why the good die young, and old sinners like Joseph Baxter survive.'

'I know, Mother.'

Anna grinned. 'And Alice can write her name.'

'What?'

'You heard me. Something's clicked. She's in bed with Teddo, two cats and some crayons. Does

94

it matter if she draws on the wall?'

Rosh shot from the room and crept upstairs. In damped-down illumination provided by a night light, she saw her beautiful baby, Winston and Lucy as good as gold at the foot of the bed and, on the wall, a perfect drawing of Frank Smith's butcher shop. Even the rainwater goods were there, as was the drop-down awning blind that served to keep sunlight away from the window display.

Alice was finally claiming her place among the living. And, while her mother wept tears of joy, Alice smiled in her sleep.

See, I'm fine with most of them. They come in the shop with their kids, a quarter of dolly mixtures and a Woman's Weekly, *pay the papers, ask am I all right. It's not all women; it's the ones with a certain look in their eyes, as if they think they're too good for the rest of us. It's the beautiful ones. My mother was beautiful...*

Four

A funeral took place at about five thirty in the morning on the day after the wedding. The sun was urging a weary eye over a misty horizon, and starlings were tuning up in the orchestra pit, while a lone blackbird, who seemed to have elected himself maestro, shouted orders from the roof of Jackson's bakery. If he wanted crumbs, he was in for a long wait, because Sunday was the bakery's single day off. Emily Jackson did her wedding and birthday cake icing on Sundays and, unless a major accident occurred, Sunday was a crumb-free zone.

Paddy was sole witness when her adorable, precious grandson emerged at snail's pace from the side entrance of the prefab next door. He looked left, then right, before stepping out onto the path with a huge knife and a bundle that was wrapped poorly in a crumpled mass of newspaper. A man on a mission, he frowned determinedly, and the end of his tongue expressed a high level of concentration as it poked from a corner of his mouth.

Paddy failed to control a wide grin. Seamus closed the door with untypically meticulous care, turned, and dropped the hat. It slid out of its newspaper coffin and fell at his feet, though the despised satin suit remained where it was. She started to laugh aloud when he forgot himself and

96

jumped on the hat with both feet. Why on God's good earth was she laughing? She had to face up to Seamus's older brothers in a few hours, had to save the life of poor old Ernie Avago, make sure that Lights of Liverpool was returned to a condition fit for its other incarnation, Scouse Alley, and find room in her head for worry about three dead men and three live machine guns. And here she stood doubled over with glee as she watched the shenanigans of a focused and very angry young man. And he had better not cut himself with that knife, since life promised to be hard enough without visits to hospitals and the like.

Seamus was cutting a square sod of lawn from the tiny rear garden. He lifted it and placed it to one side before getting to work with a spade. There was no ceremony, no prayer, no dignity. Ashes to ashes and dust to dust? He wanted rid; that was all.

The lad stuffed the offending items into the hole, filled it with soil, replaced the turf, and jumped once again on the dearly un-beloved after making sure that the piece of green fitted perfectly. No hymns, no words of wisdom, no goodbye. There. The deed was done. An unsavoury memory had been put to rest, so the world of Seamus Walsh had improved. Of course, there was no marker, no monument, no floral tribute. Instead, a sweaty, pink-faced boy looked down critically at his work. He placed the spade against the wall of a little shed, glanced up and caught sight of his grandmother.

She waved at him and put a finger to her lips, thereby indicating that his secret was safe. They both knew that he wasn't completely out of the woods, of course. Should another wedding be planned, boys of a certain size might be sent along to try on the suit, and they'd need a shovel to get it. But Seamus had done what he'd needed to do, and the fury and hatred were buried in a shallow grave behind Maureen's house. Maureen had trouble enough on her plate today; she and her husband would doubtless be involved in the business with Michael and Finbar, but there was also the problem with Maureen herself, who lost her rag at the drop of a hat. What a temper she had—

'Hello, love.'

Paddy jumped, a hand pressed against her chest. 'You'll be having me with a heart attack, creeping about like a burglar, or a prima ballerina with no shoes on.'

'It's true I've got no shoes on. But me tutu and me tights want a wash, so I've stuck to me pyjamas. And I am stuck, bloody wet through. It's baking in here, love. This place is that hot in summer, we're cooked to medium rare. Stick the kettle on, Pads. Me nerves feel as if they've been back and forth across Wally Ainsworth's bacon slicer ever since last night. Even me eyelashes ache, and I've got pain in teeth I lost years back.'

'I know, I know.' She set the kettle to boil on the hob. 'Kev, I've got a really bad feeling, so.'

'I've got two,' he replied. 'Finbar and Michael.'

She nodded. 'And don't forget the Kray twins and company limited, Dimitri Wotsisname and his Athenian dancers, to mention but a few.'

'Oh, yes.' He leaned against the sink. 'Why were

you laughing a few minutes ago?'

She told him.

And he told her. 'That pageboy suit's on a half-promise to the church. You know they keep wedding stuff for poor folk who can't afford it.'

'Shotgun marriages, you mean. Don't worry. I'll do a Burke and Hare on the suit.' She scalded the pot. 'I'll disinter it, mend it, wash it, and pass it on.' She pondered briefly on the subject of Seamus's older brothers. They wouldn't have buried the suit; they would have sold it. Even at the ages of six and eight, that pair had fixed their eyes on money. They were the same today. Cash was king whatever its provenance. Perhaps they would change? Perhaps they would stay away from London. And, of course, there remained the danger that others would follow the three dead in search of the two lads. Oh, God, it didn't bear thinking about.

The long-married couple sat at the minute kitchen table, each with a pint pot of scalding tea. Maureen and her daughter, the newly wed Reen, had been heard to opine that Paddy and Kevin could win prizes for tea-drinking. They never touched coffee. Coffee was for folk who didn't mind murdering their own taste buds and, since England was a free country, such odd souls were within their rights to fry their tongues with the chicory mixture that currently passed for that drink.

'I wonder what's going on?' Kevin asked. 'Down at Ernie's, I mean.'

Paddy shrugged. 'I know this much for sure, my love. It may be roasting in this house, but my lower vertebrae are frozen solid. Can't get a move out of them. In those very bones, I feel some bad news coming.'

Kev delivered the opinion that his wife's bones were behind the times by several hours, since the bad news had already arrived yesterday. 'I'll bet you any money poor Tom's out of his mind next door. It's one thing sniping during a war, another matter altogether on the streets of Bootle with a little gun pinched from your wife's handbag. What was she thinking of, Paddy? Letting the wedding go on like that when she knew her sons were in trouble?'

She shrugged. 'Well, when I approached that subject, she told me to mind my own business. It is my business. Your stall, Scouse Alley and Lights keep this family going. And we could all have been killed by those London gangsters. She said she and Tom would manage without us, but I must express serious doubt. I bet you she'll be here by nine o'clock, bless her. It isn't every day your husband has to shoot three murderers, so I understand her lack of patience with me. I can be annoying. I even annoy myself sometimes.'

Their second pint was taken into the living room. Paddy lit her first cigarette of the day while Kevin went to make toast. She looked round her home and wondered what these walls would say if they could speak. Martin and Jack, the two sons of whom she seldom made mention, had lived here for a while with their sister, Maureen. Maureen was now next door. The lads had been reasonably well behaved once grown, had done well on National Service with the army, but London had beckoned, and that was that.

Paddy remembered digging Maureen out of her little terraced house, scrabbling in dirt and bricks, fighting to save her daughter and the grandchildren from beneath rubble and dust. Safe now. Hitler had failed to destroy the family, but six members of it had brought grief to the house. Well, to this prefab and the one next door. Her spine remained frozen. The only one left was the lovely afterthought, Maureen's Seamus. 'Dear God, keep him safe,' she begged under her breath. 'Think of something else,' she commanded. Her mind seemed to have a mind of its own, and that was silly.

Ah yes. How proud she had been of this little place. It had a built-in cooker and a refrigerator. She could make her own ice. Shivering, she remembered a rumour about a London madman who hired himself out to the big boys. He specialized in disposal, freezing bodies of murdered folk, jointing them, and feeding the parts into some kind of crushing machine. Freezing made the whole thing less messy. After that, he gave the resulting sludge to pigs. And people ate the pigs. Cannibals by proxy. Why couldn't she think of something halfway decent, for goodness' sake? If her brain didn't kick in soon, her usual quickness of thought would be no more than a pleasant memory.

She had nice furniture, decent carpets, pretty bits and pieces bought by her husband at Christmas time and on her birthdays. The rug was Axminster, and her china cabinet displayed some handsome bits of Royal Doulton and good lead crystal. Kevin dealt in decent second-hand clothing from a stall on Paddy's Market. He'd even invented a fold-away changing room with a cheval mirror so that prospective purchasers could try on clothes. He was a good lad. Every weekday, at lunch time, he left the stall in the hands of another trader, came down to Scouse Alley in his van, and served tea and cocoa. He ate the same stew each time with a side serving of pickled beetroot or red cabbage. She must think of the good, only of the good. Because madness lay–

'Here you are, love.' He handed her a rack of toast. 'Best butter to put hairs on your chest.'

She smiled at him. 'You're still the greatest man I know, Kevin O'Neil. You know, I was thinking. We should start doing meat and potato pies and Lancashire hotpot. Scouse every day gets a bit boring.'

He took a sip of tea. 'I'm the lucky one,' he advised her. 'I was the man who picked you up when you fell over in the street that day.'

Paddy managed another smile. 'Your hands were all over me.'

Kev shrugged. 'I've always believed in making the most of situations. My ma taught me that before she died, bless her. She made the most by dying. Fifteen kids? The old bastard should have been neutered. But no. He found another daft Irishwoman and remarried within months.' The clock began the slow crawl towards seven. 'Paddy, my darling, we know there's trouble afoot. Neither of us has slept a wink, what with all this, plus Romeo and Juliet darting about at the other side of a very thin wall. We have to stay calm. No

102

matter what happens later on, we take it square and straight, no shouting, no tears, no anger. Your brothers and our sons may be lost to us, but perhaps we can save our grandsons.'

Paddy stared into her cup. 'They've seen the big life, the clever life, Kev. They've also learned that the same life is of little value, because they'll have witnessed killings and might even have performed executions.' She raised her eyes. 'Look at it, my love. If they stay in Liverpool, they may well form a dynasty of their own. I'd rather place them in the hands of the police than let them ruin another city.'

Kev nodded thoughtfully. Ernie Avago was an early riser. Always up with the lark, he had a way with flowers; he also grew his own veg at the back of the house. After his first cuppa, Ernie's primary job in decent weather was the inspection of his garden. 'We'll get washed and dressed, Pads. I'm not sitting here another two hours waiting for my daughter's permission to go hither and yon. We'll be there before madam. And I'm sending Ernie for a couple of weeks in Blackpool while we work out what's what.'

Paddy's eyes widened. 'What's what? What about his whippet and the budgies?'

'Not forgetting the ferrets.'

Her jaw dropped. 'That dog eats furniture. As for ferrets – no. They bite.'

'Paddy!'

'Oh, all right. I know he has to be safe.' She marched off to the bathroom. The dawn chorus had pulled in all the extras, non-professionals and substitutes, and the resulting cacophony had

103

woken love's young dream in the back bedroom. Reen seemed to be enjoying herself, and her grandmother was pleased about that. Too many marriages failed due to mechanical difficulties, and there was no way of correcting problems by fitting a new battery or having an oil change at a garage round the corner. The human body was a mysterious article.

There was an old woman in the mirror again. The face was pleasant enough, but lived in. Kev still loved her, and that was what mattered. He, too, bore the marks of time, yet they still clung together like children lost at sea. What if he died? She'd never cope; if she went first, he'd be completely lost. 'Have a wash, you stupid old crone. Hang about much longer and you'll have the cows home.'

Back in her bedroom, Paddy closed her ears to the noise next door. She lit a night light in a blue glass container and placed it below a statue of the Immaculate Conception. 'Intercede, Blessed Mother.' She then recited from memory, 'Wisdom, understanding, counsel, fortitude, knowledge, piety, fear of the Lord.' These gifts from the Holy Ghost arrived when a Catholic was confirmed, and Paddy needed them reinforced today. She often used the Virgin Mary as messenger; everyone listened to Mary, though Jesus had been a bit snappy with her when she'd told Him off for preaching in the temple at the age of twelve. Mind, twelve was a difficult age, and the lad had been half human after all. 'Oh, pull yourself together, Patricia. This is going to be one very long day.'

Kev had a shave followed by a lick and a promise. There was no point in attending to detail, since Scouse Alley wanted cleaning while half a dozen helpers peeled spuds and carrots for to-morrow. None of them knew the recipe, because Paddy had her secrets, and one of them was her scouse. She had taken the Norwegian dish and injected a bit of the Irish into it; she also used a combination of herbs known only to herself. The women of Bootle and the rest of Liverpool had tried, but no one could get the full list out of her.

Oh, well. He would get a bath later, as a lot of dirty stuff needed shifting first. Finbar and Michael. Old Ernie Avago. Wedding wreckage. Above all, he needed to look after his own wife, because he knew she was terrified.

They travelled in the van and left it in an alley behind Ernie's house. It was better this way; they wanted to attract no attention during this very early morning visit. As expected by Kev, the old man was out in the relative cool of morning. He didn't exist in a tin box that held in yesterday's heat during summer, yesterday's cold in winter, so he lived the more temperate and sensible life when it came to weather. Nevertheless, he always wore a hat, because the sun was not just a friend; it was also a deadly enemy. A slender whippet, older now, lay in a basket under the ferrets' cage.

The visitors entered the garden. The smell of roses was almost overpowering, and Ernie was dead-heading some of his prize-winning bushes.

Paddy was the first to address him. 'Ernie? Still got the ten-gallon hat, I see. You look great, but.'

He half closed aged eyes and peered at her. 'Paddy? Oh, I am pleased to see you.' He gazed over her shoulder. 'Kev. Well, we'd have nearly a full set if the lads had stayed.'

Paddy's stomach lurched. 'They've gone already?'

Ernie nodded. 'It was after two in the morning by the time they scarpered. It looked to me like the boys were waiting for the car, because though they climbed the stairs, they never went to sleep. I was restless meself, what with the heat and me not being used to visitors. At my age, you don't need a lot of sleep. So I saw it coming with its headlights on, though they were switched off when it got here. I saw Fin and Mike jumping into it. And they were gone, just like that.' He tried to click his fingers, remembered the arthritis and gave up.

'Where?' Kev asked. 'Where've they buggered off to, Ernie? They weren't here more than a few hours.'

The old chap shrugged stiffly. 'No idea. They never said nothing about it. But they spent ages writing letters. One left an envelope for his mam and dad, and the other wrote to you two. Oh, and they left me ten quid. Nice lads.' He paused for a few seconds. 'But what's the matter, Kev? They were jumpy as a couple of fleas the whole day and most of the evening – couldn't eat a crumb. Every time there was a noise in the street, they went white and sat down.'

Kevin answered. 'No idea what's going on. But we need to get you somewhere safe for a couple of weeks. Blackpool, I thought. You might enjoy a fortnight on the sands.'

Ernie laughed. 'Look, I can't travel – I'm an old

cripple, as you can see for yourselves. Even a short journey would kill me. Neighbours do the shopping and cleaning, then me granddaughter does the laundry and the ironing, cooks some meals and washes the pots. I can't be buggering off to Blackpool. Here's where I have to stay, but thanks for the offer, it's appreciated. You still living in that sardine tin?'

'We are,' the pair chorused.

'Oh well. Come in for a cuppa, and read your letter. You can take your Maureen's with you, give it to her when you get back home. Nice to have visitors.'

Kev patted his wife's shoulder. 'Do you want to read it first?'

She shook her head. 'Together. We do this together.'

Ernie Avago was asleep within minutes. He drank his tea, then slipped into that happy place so well deserved by those who have spent decades toiling and sweating for a pittance. A child of the Victorian era, the dock worker had to be approaching eighty. There were no budgies. Paddy gazed down at the old man. His dog was on its last legs, his birds were dead, and she had no idea about the state of the ferrets, as they were to be avoided at all costs. 'Life gets taken away a bit at a time,' she said, mostly to herself. 'It's not just the big bang at the end; it's all the bits that drop off beforehand.' She knew he wouldn't replace his dog when it left him. She knew he was preparing for his own departure. 'Cruel world,' she muttered.

'He's Ernie Simpson,' Kev whispered. 'See,

here it is on an envelope. All these years, and we never knew.' The man's bed was under the stairs, and a commode stood close by. Bless him; he was not fit to travel. 'He has to be all right, Pads. One of the best blokes ever. I hope he just slips away when his time comes.'

But Paddy had picked up another letter, one addressed to herself and Granda. Her hand tingled like pins and needles. It was as if the contents tried to reach her via some osmotic process, so she passed the problem to her husband. It was a problem. Bad news had travelled up her arm and into her chest. 'Jesus mercy, Mary help,' she mumbled. She didn't want him to open it, but he must.

'Sit down,' he said gravely after tearing open the envelope and reading the first couple of lines. 'Now, I want you to try to stay calm. Sit down, Paddy,' he said again.

She sat. They were supposed to be doing this together, but she couldn't quite manage to look. There was a dead weight in her stomach; this morning's toast seemed to have turned to lead.

Kevin reached for her hand. 'Your brother Peter died of a heart attack,' he said carefully. 'But Callum was removed.'

Paddy swallowed. 'Removed to where?'

Kev scanned another line. 'Probably Epping Forest.'

Her face blanched. 'They were older than me,' she whispered. 'I was just the oldest girl. So somebody murdered my big brother? He was too old to be a real threat to anyone.'

'I'm so sorry, love.'

She closed her eyes and travelled back once more in time and space, saw Callum running through trees in the orchard back at Ganga's house. Callum liked trees, loved to climb and hide. He was now buried under trees. There was nothing she could do but accept the news square and straight, as Kev had termed it. Then she heard an unfamiliar sound; her husband was weeping. Paddy's eyelids raised themselves quickly. 'Kev? Kevin?' His head was in his hands. 'Martin and Jack?' she asked softly. 'Our sons, Kevin? Are they...?'

He nodded.

'Both of them?'

Again, he inclined his head.

An invisible knife pierced her abdomen. Martin was ripping his way into the world, and what a world it had been. In a cellar dwelling with a filthy, ancient midwife as sole company, Paddy had birthed her son. The almost exclusively Irish slum had teemed with unwashed bodies, wildlife and the stench of effluent. And Kevin had got them out.

John, usually named Jack, had been born into better circumstances. Their home had become a flat in Sefton Park, a place whose non-resident owner refused to give space to Irish immigrants. So Paddy had kept her mouth shut for the most part, while Kev, a first generation Scouser born of Dublin parents, had been forced to do all the talking. And he'd worked so hard, had got them out again...

'Paddy?'

She snapped out of her reverie. 'Removed?'

109

'Yes.'

She inhaled a deep, shuddering breath. 'So Finbar and Michael are next on the list?'

'It would seem so, yes.' He dried his eyes. 'Our sons are in Epping Forest, too. They got above themselves, tried to start their own business. Business? Beating up shopkeepers and pub landlords who won't pay protection? It seems they were all in on the plan. Or perhaps the older ones were removed as a warning to these two boys.'

'They were still our sons and my brothers, Kev.' Peter and Callum, Martin and Jack, three murders and one natural death. Or had Peter died of fear?

'I know who they were, love.'

'If Finbar and Michael had never gone to London with the boxing club–'

'I know that, too.'

'They'd never have been sought out by their elders. Do they say where they are?' Inside, she burned. Was it fury, was it grief? She was unable to separate the two emotions. She wanted to kill; at the same time, she needed to weep a river of tears. Whatever Martin and Jack had become, they had been her babies, hers and Kev's.

He swallowed audibly. 'I don't know what it says further down. Like you, I'm busy mourning two sons. We should go home, love. We'll read the whole thing together, then deal with poor Maureen and Tom. Remember, she has two sons missing and two brothers dead. And you know how she is.'

They left Ernie Avago-Simpson asleep in his chair. Outside, they were assailed yet again by the deep, cloying fragrance owned only by roses. Some of the blooms were so dark in colour that they appeared almost black. Ernie had worked for years on the dark side, but only in his garden. His search for a black or navy rose had occupied his whole retirement. 'Keep him safe,' Paddy ordered the Almighty. She was beyond begging, beyond prayer. It was time the big boss got told what to do, because He had clearly been getting it all wrong. Was anger with God forgivable? Why, why was He allowing all those terrible things to happen to people who tried their very best in this vale of tears?

In the van, she asked Kevin not to start the engine. She wanted to arrive home prepared, because Maureen would probably throw a fit, and full knowledge was the best armour. 'Let's see it now,' she said. 'Because I'd sooner know what's what before facing Maureen.' She took the letter and read it aloud, omitting only the first few lines. That was the bit she and Kev already knew about, and it was, she hoped, the heaviest part.

We feel guilty, because we were approached by others who wanted to work a few patches. It's not as if the new firm was standing on anyone's toes – Ronnie and Reggie don't work that part of London, the Spits weren't interested, the Bow Boys told us to please our-selves, and we got no sense out of the Greeks as per usual. Then Uncle Peter died suddenly, but at least he had a funeral. Representatives of all the firms were there, so imagine our shock when Uncle Callum dis-appeared. It wasn't his fault. He knew nothing about

111

the new firm, so he was killed as a warning to us.

We got an anonymous note to say stop the big ideas, then our uncles Martin and Jack weren't around any more. Evidence was put on our doorstep with the milk. I don't want to upset you even more by telling you what it was, but we knew they were dead. That left just me and Mike. I don't need to tell you that we're in big trouble. We're leaving Ernie's soon. Our women are coming up north for us. No one knows our girls – at least we hope they don't. But we have to disappear, as I'm sure you will understand by now.

Gran and Granda, we're so sad about the uncles, and we don't know who did all that. But we know who didn't do it. The Kray twins' lot are not guilty of the killings. We thought they'd come for us when we saw their car outside the flat, but they hadn't. Reg gave us money and told us to get the hell out of London pronto. This means we're protected by them, but God knows what they might expect in return. We don't know whether we'll ever be safe, and we shouldn't have come anywhere near Bootle, but we just gave the girls Ernie's address in a hurry before we got the train. Even if the old man hadn't been here any more, we could have waited in the alley at the back. Tell him thanks, by the way. He was very good to us not just now, but all our lives.

Mam's already upset, so we didn't tell her the really bad news when we saw her for a few minutes. We gave a kid a few bob and told him to fetch her to the alley. She went mad because of Reen's wedding. With all the trouble down south, we'd forgotten about it. Mike's writing to her now. We may have been followed. The trouble with London gangs is you don't know who to trust. But we trust the Krays. I know they can be *vicious and they won't improve with age, but they're on our side.*

So sorry to bring all this mess to Liverpool. By the time you get this, we'll be long gone. Give our love to Reen and tell her to be happy. Sorry again.

Fin xxx

Both occupants of the car sat in silence for a while. Paddy, who had scarcely acknowledged the existence of her brothers, who had seldom spoken of her sons, felt close to breaking point. She had always expressed the belief that work kept a person going, that the ordinary, everyday routine helped to keep folk sane. The idea of cooking and clattering about in Scouse Alley's kitchen did not appeal. Her usual stand-in was Maureen, her last remaining child. Even Maureen didn't have the complete recipe. On those rare occasions when Paddy became ill, her daughter was given a packet of herbs and told to do her best, but Maureen's best was unlikely to be achievable today.

Kev broke into his wife's thoughts yet again. 'Give me the herbs, and I'll make it. I know it won't be like yours, but I've done it before a couple of times and nobody complained.'

'How do you do that? How do you climb inside my head?'

'Practice.'

She sighed heavily. 'You can help, but I want things to look normal. Our son-in-law killed three men last night, and I refuse to endanger him.' A thought struck. 'And we may have to give up the faith. Because we'd need to tell what we know in Confession. Anything withheld could be

113

sacrilege, and we know about killings. A priest can't intercede for murder or manslaughter until or unless the police are involved. The same with theft. Restitution or a donation to charity is required for theft before a blessing can be given.'

Kev agreed up to a point. Outsiders believed that Roman Catholics could do as they liked and get their souls cleansed every week. This was far from the truth. The bigger sins against society needed to be dealt with by society before absolution could be granted, yet he and Paddy could not hand Tom over to the law. 'But we didn't commit murder, Pads. Neither did Tom, because he saved many lives. If there is a sin, it's his to tell. Ask our priest without actually telling him—'

'Give it up, Kev. If you asked that one his name, he'd need to look for his birth certificate. He's more pickled than a jar of silverskin onions. I'll find a sober priest in another church.'

They drove home slowly, as if they didn't really want to go there. Both blinked back tears; both wondered whether they might have failed Martin and Jack. Had they worked too hard at making a living and climbing the steep rungs of the housing ladder? Had their sons suffered as a result? Maureen had turned out well, but girls were sturdier and more resilient than boys. And even Maureen had her limits. There was the terrible singing when she was in drink; there was also a temper hot enough to boil falling snow before it reached the ground. Paddy voiced her one positive thought. 'Seamus won't go to London, because he'll have no one there.'

Kevin agreed. 'As long as he doesn't grow up

looking for the people who killed his uncles and caused his brothers to disappear. But there's twelve years between him and Reen, and more between him and the lads, so he's like a different generation from Finbar and Michael.' He parked the van. 'Right. Now, we break our hearts again while breaking our daughter's heart.' He mopped his brow with a handkerchief. 'I'm getting a bit past it, you know. Stuff like this gives people heart attacks.'

'Don't you dare,' came the swift reply. 'My boys were scarcely in their twenties when they went south for a look at London life. I knew I'd lost them years ago, God rest their troubled souls. My grandsons are alive and safe, I trust. The other dead ones are my brothers, older than you, older than me. Sixty-five isn't that old. Don't die, or I'll kill you.'

He held her hand. 'A pearl beyond price,' he said. 'Come on. Let's get it over with.'

It was hell. Maureen ranted, raved, tore down curtains, smashed ornaments, clouted her poor husband, broke dishes and threw a frying pan through the kitchen window. Fortunately, Seamus had popped out for the *News of the World* and a Vimto ice lolly, so the worst was over when he returned with a rather soggy newspaper. 'Me lolly melted,' he said. 'See? I was reading this about a burnt-out car in the sand dunes, three bodies in it. It was near Southport. It's in the paper, Dad.' He looked round. 'What happened here?' he asked.

Kev was good at thinking on his feet. 'Now, you're a clever boy reading like that. Give me the paper. Remember we told you your mam's at a funny age?'

The child nodded. 'Is she on a maddy?'

'She is definitely out of sorts.' Out of her mind would have been nearer the mark. 'Come on, we'll go fishing.' He took the boy next door. If Reen and Jimmy were at it again, he would put a stop to it. Seamus's innocence must be preserved at all costs.

So Paddy was left once again with the fruits of her daughter's fury. She'd always been at a funny age, this one. Maureen's temper was swift, hot and soon dispersed. It had occurred to Paddy that Maureen should have been involved in demolition, so quickly did she destroy a room. 'Get her a cup of tea, Tom,' she said. 'If you've any cups left. If not, she can make do with a jam jar, a bucket – whatever.' She eyed her wild daughter. 'Have you finished now? Is the tantrum over – can we call the dogs off and tell the coastguard to stand down? Because you're not the only one in grief. Is the devil out of you?'

'Yes. I want me boys.'

'And I can't ever have mine, Maureen. My brothers and my sons, all gangsters, all dead. Your sons are alive and with their girlfriends. When you've stopped destroying your home, read properly the letter they left for you. I have things to do, a business to clean and run.'

'Don't leave me, Mam.'

Paddy held her unpredictable, feisty child. 'You've got Tom.'

'He killed those men,' Maureen sobbed.

Paddy withdrew her physical support. 'You were

the one with the gun in the bag. Tom did what came naturally to him. Now, you just listen for once instead of feeling sorry for yourself. Had Tom not acted as swiftly as he did, you'd have no son to fetch that silly newspaper. Seamus wouldn't be fishing with your dad; he'd be on a slab in the morgue, and he'd be full of holes. Would that be your preference? Should Tom have allowed that to happen instead of ridding the world of a few more gangsters?'

Maureen shook her head. 'I'm just confused and frightened.'

'You're also missing a kitchen window, and half a tea set. It's time to put your temper to bed once and for all. You indulge yourself, kicking off like that. There's a seven-year-old boy living in the house, and he's better behaved than you are. Your carryings-on could force him to leave home early, just as his brothers did. You can't possibly expect him to be content living here with you and your moods.'

A very silent Tom entered the room and pushed a mug of tea into his wife's hand. The younger woman rallied. 'Are you saying it's my fault that Finbar and Michael went away?'

'No more than I'm asking whether Martin and Jack were driven away by me. But think about it. Seamus was angry enough already because of the satin suit and hat. Then he comes home with the newspaper and finds his house wrecked by his own mother. And has it not occurred to you that the police might be on their way? I know none of the wedding party will betray us, but are we completely sure that no stranger saw what went on? Well?'

Maureen dropped into a chair. 'I didn't think–'

'And there's the answer. You react like an animal when it senses danger. Now, I'm off to my work, because we have to carry on as normal. I believe that kitchen window of yours has been broken more times than a bowl of new-laid eggs. Tom still keeps the right size of glass in the shed, so get him to replace it before the bobbies turn up. As for the rest, shift the breakages and put your furniture in the middle of this room. You're decorating. I mean it, Maureen.'

'All right.'

'And stop these eejit tantrums. What you're short of is a good hiding, madam. Oh, and remember, when you get time, read that letter again. Have Tom with you when you do. No kicking off.'

There was no van, because Kev had taken Seamus out of the war zone for a few hours. It was quite a walk from inner Bootle to the edge of the Mersey, but Paddy had done it before. On this occasion, however, she was not exactly full of energy. Her brothers were dead. That alone was enough to knock her sideways, but her sons? Those two little lads had learned to read at her knee. How proud she had been of her ability to teach them that vital art. Reading was the key to all else. It opened doors to history, geography, science...

As soon as they were at school, they'd started bullying. Nothing major at first, but they learned in time how to terrify, subdue, dominate. Any teacher who tried to control them suffered, and

118

they excelled at boxing. Michael and Finbar had travelled a similar path with the noble art, though they hadn't been quite as naughty as their uncles.

Martin and Jack, one at each end of the pram, barely twelve months between them. That had been Kev's idea. He'd wanted her to get it all over with while she was young enough to cope. Maureen had been born in a proper house, and Kev had been right, because his wife had managed. Their love life had, of necessity, become inventive, and he had stuck to that calendar like glue, as three children were enough for any marriage. Like all good Catholics, he had refused to employ real contraception. He was one in a million.

The sons of that man in a million now lay in Epping Forest. The only decoration for their graves would arrive in the form of autumn leaves. She mustn't cry. She needed to arrive in Scouse Alley's kitchen full of life, advice and complaints about people not tidying as they went along, about carrots being cut too thick or too thin, about the wedding, Seamus's suit, the drunken celebrant, Maureen's singing, the fights...

But. No mention could be made of blood lying black in moonlight, of bodies, guns, a car. It occurred to her for a brief second that Tom had meted out the family's revenge; three dead for three dead, since Peter had died naturally. Or had he? Had terror stopped his heart? Whatever, she must stop thinking like a gangster.

She rounded a corner and saw her newest baby, Scouse Alley. There was no sign of police, no sign of trouble. Walking up the path, she checked for bloodstains, found nothing. Turning, she gazed

119

down at the river and the street that led to it. Nothing. She hoped the car had burned thoroughly, because there might have been a scrap of paper bearing names and addresses. 'Worrying like this will have you crackers,' she whispered. And had the invaders from London known about Ernie, they would have bypassed the wedding and gone for their real targets.

Ernie Avago-Simpson seemed to have no idea of what yesterday's visitors were involved with. She hoped that no surviving piece of evidence in that car would leave even the smallest clue, but beyond that there lay deeper disquiet. Who in London knew where the three dead men had been going? Had Finbar and Michael been careful? Had anyone else been given Ernie's whereabouts? With the incident spread all over Maureen's rag of a newspaper, the whole country would doubtless be aware of the cremated corpses. So who was safe? Those three had known where the wedding reception was to be held...

She entered the kitchen by a rear door and met with a barrage of questions. Had she heard the news? Wasn't it terrible? Three teacups and one dead man. The number three again. 'Minnie?' she asked wearily. 'Can I have it from you?'

Minnie Walker did the talking. Ernie Avago's granddaughter had found him dead in his chair not half an hour back. He had a smile on his face, but the aged whippet wasn't happy. The old man had a couple of male visitors yesterday afternoon, but his Christine had found a warm pot and three unwashed teacups today. So someone had been there early this morning.

Paddy placed herself on a stool. 'It was me and Kev,' she said, her voice shaky. 'Ernie was fine, so he was. We went a few times before Mass on a Sunday, and I usually remembered to wash up, but I was in a hurry today.' They hadn't visited him in months. Lie upon lie. Venal sins, but piling up like layers of paint over a huge blemish that would break through again and again. 'He was asleep when we left him, God bless and save his good soul. Messing about with his roses when we got there.' Another death. *How many more?*

Another walk ensued. After pushing her package of herbs into Minnie's hands, Paddy cut through back streets in order to catch Ernie's Christine. If Christine knew the identities of yesterday's visitors... Lying was bloody hard work. A good liar needed a good memory, and Paddy's powers of recall were not what they had been. Then there were the teacups – what if Christine wanted the police to check her dad's cup for poison? There wasn't a phone box on Ernie's street... 'Please, God, please.'

But she needn't have worried. Christine stepped out of her husband's embrace and into Paddy's. 'Mrs Moss said you'd been. She saw you with him in the garden. Bless you and Kevin.'

Ernie was still warm. He'd always been warm, generous, open-hearted. Christine and Alan, her husband, had laid him on his bed. Paddy stroked the wiry, grey hair. She was saying goodbye to several people, and Ernie was the only one she would ever reach, so this poor, innocent man represented them all. 'Is the priest coming?' she asked. 'Ernie should still have the Unction, because I'm sure his spirit is standing at the back door looking at roses.'

The answer from Alan was affirmative.

Christine mopped her face with a tea towel. 'Who visited him yesterday?' she asked. 'Two young men, we were told.'

Paddy, who felt sick with relief, light-headed through exhaustion, managed a slight shrug of her shoulders. 'You know how your grandfather was, Chrissie. His door was always open, and he had friends of all ages. They might have been ferret-fanciers, rose-growers – whatever. Will I have a quick look round for clues? Because if we can find them, they might want to be at the funeral.'

So while Extreme Unction was delivered by a priest, Paddy got the freedom of the house. After making sure that nothing of her grandsons remained, she re-entered the kitchen. The priest had gone. 'No idea who his visitors were,' she told Christine's husband. 'But they'll perhaps read the announcement in the newspaper.'

'Thanks,' Christine said absently. She was sitting on the edge of the bed. 'He has oil on his head.'

'Leave it be.' Paddy stood by the grieving woman. 'It's holy oil.'

'It'll be a big funeral.' Alan sniffed back all emotion. Grown men didn't cry.

But Paddy did. She finally opened her mouth and released a sound that was almost primeval. Like a sad, wounded wolf baying at an unresponsive moon, she mourned her brothers, her sons, and this man who had represented all that was good, all that was disappearing with Ernie's generation. She, a child of the later Victoria years, had done a poor job of keeping in touch with her wider family, of rearing her boys to be decent. As for today's youngsters – she disapproved whole-heartedly. Some people, somewhere, had got it all wrong. And she was one of those people.

'Paddy?'

She pulled herself together, though it took some effort. 'I'd better get home.' Her breathing wasn't right, so the words were born fractured.

She was forced into a chair and given a glass of brandy. Alan went off to borrow a car. He would be back to take Paddy home once he'd dealt with the doctor and the undertaker.

Chrissie patted her companion's hand. 'I never expected you to be as upset as that,' she re-marked.

Paddy sipped her brandy. 'I'm tired,' she ad-mitted finally. 'The wedding and so forth. I'll be better shortly, but.'

She didn't remember much after that. The brandy seeped into her blood, and she began to nod off. Alan helped her to the car, and she re-turned to an empty house. In the overheated liv-ing room, she slept on a sofa. Reen and Jimmy had probably gone to look at the O'Garas' prefab, and Kev was ... somewhere. He was with Seamus.

Paddy slept for six whole hours.

People don't bother with me, yet I could have been something of a wit. I went home one day to the Dingle hovel, and Edie next door told me that Dad had gone out. 'Pour some more petrol on him,' I told her smartly.

123

I was only about nine at the time. Another evening when he was following me home, a man asked me, 'Is that your dad?' So I told him no, I was just looking after him till the appropriate authorities found him a place. But I didn't become a comedian, did I? Instead, I'm a street cleaner. I clear away the human rubbish. Oh, and I work in a shop.

Five

Tess was about to put her foot down and, when she did place it on the floor, it would be cushioned by Skaters' Trails. The carpet had become a symbol, a physical expression of her depression and frustration. Don didn't want to live, eat or sleep with her; he had the money to buy her a house on Menlove Avenue, and he was prepared to spend it to be rid of her. Hating him should have been easy, but she couldn't quite manage it. How easy life would be if she could detest him. But she could annoy him, oh yes. What she failed to work out was her reason for needing to upset him. He held all the trump cards, and he might well withdraw his offer of a house if she stepped too far away from the oche.

She was still pretty. Her reflection in every shop window she passed proved that point. Men looked at her. They saw beauty, yet knew nothing of her mindset, her secrets. For behind the handsome facade, a disconcerting thought niggled. She was not a loving wife, had never been a satisfactory one. And she'd been stupid enough to believe that he would stay in the marriage because of his leg.

Don was a good-looking man. Lately, she had begun to view him differently, and the limp gave him character. Everyone liked him. Leader of a local pub's championship darts team, he was greeted with smiles and waves every time he walked out of the launderette and into the street. His popularity had been earned because he was a decent man and a good player of darts. Don deserved to be treated well.

Tess, on the other hand, was seldom spoken to. She could sometimes be a bit cool when customers asked for change to dispense a cup of detergent or to work a machine. They should have sorted all that before dragging their dirty washing through the streets. *I am already a bitter old woman,* she told her inner self while walking to the carpet shop. *And the kids love him more than they love me, because he raised them while I was busy filling daily needs and saving towards freedom. Freedom? Customers can't even remember to bring the right change or a packet of soap powder... And now, he's going to abandon us, and the children will hit the roof, since it's all my fault. But even though I might well be leaving the flat, I'm still going to have this carpet.* The carpet had become a matter of principle.

But a husband was a prerequisite. Widowhood carried with it a degree of dignity, but widowhood was impossible to arrange without committing a mortal sin, and she didn't want him dead anyway. Divorce, for a Catholic, was supposedly impossible. It was also an admission to the world that a woman had failed, that she had been placed in the reject bucket. *Do not touch, do not feed this animal.* Tess dreaded the shame of it. Those who had suffered her terse replies in the launderette would gossip. They'd say she deserved it, had pretended to be a cut above and no wonder poor Don had

126

left the scene, bless him with his bad knee.

'I'll have the grey,' she told the shopkeeper. Red was such a common colour, and grey was the only available alternative. She gave him the address of the flat and asked him to measure and fit before lunch time tomorrow. When Don came home from work, he would see her statement; whether or not she stayed in the flat, the carpet would be a fait accompli. Axminster square, indeed. Everyone had fully fitted these days, because polished floorboards or lino edging were very pre-war. Even if the flat was to be let, a new carpet was required.

The kids knew there was something wrong. Their father was sleeping on the sofa, which was doing his knee no good at all, while Sean had been heard to deliver the quiet opinion that his mother's face looked like a squeezed lemon. But neither Don nor Tess had spoken to them yet about the planned separation. Would they suffer? Well, they weren't babies any more, and this world was full of hard knocks...

She sat with a cup of stewed tea in a small café that could not be listed as having seen better days, since it had always been scruffy. But Tess needed space to think, and there was plenty of that in this oily hole. The flat no longer felt welcoming, the launderette was noisy, the streets were too busy. She was the only customer here. Even the cup stank of rancid fat, while the table was chipped and marked by the scratched initials of today's young. The decadent establishment was soon to change hands and become a milk bar with a juke box and non-alcoholic drinks for a generation of nomads.

They wandered. They came home from work, ate in a hurry, then beggared off to places they would never discuss. Sean was a quick wash man, but Anne-Marie took hours to get ready. She was now apprenticed to Dolly Pearson, a hairdresser from ... from Menlove Avenue. The hairdressing shop was a Smithdown Road lock-up. Dolly was divorced, and was looked upon as damaged goods, though she seemed not to care. Was that the answer, then? A hard shell, a layer of nonchalance, a permanent smile and a permanent wave always well set with a fringe on the forehead?

Sean was old enough for pubs, but Anne-Marie wasn't. She was, however, old enough to spend her leisure time riding pillion behind a man who had renamed himself Marx. His real name, Mark Wells, was clearly not good enough. Mark, as Tess insisted on calling him, was something of an oddity, since he was a quiet Christian of sorts with a loud motorbike. He'd brought the doctor, had ushered everyone out of the launderette while Tess had sat stupidly with a paper bag. Mark voted Labour... Still, he'd got rid of Pea-Green, which was surely a good thing?

Oh, she couldn't drink this tea. Was it tea? It smelled like something that should go straight down the toilet without the need for processing by a digestive tract. But it was her ticket to silence, so Tess remained where she was. Mark. He was doing accountancy, seemed decent enough apart from motorbike and leathers, and he knew John Lennon. Anne-Marie had been a devotee of the Quarry Men for at least three months, so perhaps

Mark was merely the key to a golden gate? Children were so secretive these days.

Anne-Marie would favour a move to Menlove Avenue. To be near her hero, the girl would probably move to the moon. Sean was different. For a start, he was male and not particularly communicative. Anne-Marie, now under the influence of a male, was slightly less talkative these days. Men were the deciders, the breadwinners, the leaders. But not in Tess's household. Her husband had returned damaged by his very brief war. Because of his disability and periods spent in hospitals, Tess had taken the reins, and she had held on to them tightly.

Look what you've done today, she chided herself silently. Should she cancel the carpet? Should she take the policy money and move to Menlove? *Answers on a postcard, Tess. No matter what, you've lost him. So. Do you want to be abandoned on Smithdown Road or on Menlove Avenue? Answers, as already stated, on a postcard to... I am definitely going strange. If I don't buck up, I might well find myself in a padded room strapped down in a straitjacket, and that's not my style.*

A degree of intelligence prevailed. While the greasy tea cooled, Tess Compton found some of her senses. On Smithdown Road, Don's abandonment of his family would be noticed immediately, and she would be stuck in that flat with boisterous women and noisy washing machines below. On Menlove Avenue, fewer people would comment at the start, and she would own a house. It was time to talk to the children. It was time to take the money and to plan a graceful exit.

Tess Compton left the café. She returned to the carpet shop and cancelled the order, offering as reasons the fact that her husband hated Skaters' Trails, and the almost-lie that they had decided to move from the flat. 'I'll be back,' she promised. 'I'd no idea about his plan to buy a house. It was meant to be a surprise.'

She walked homeward, though she passed the launderette and carried on all the way up to Menlove Avenue. There were two for sale at this end, both stating *Apply within.* So she applied within. Each house had separate living and dining rooms, a decent hall, three bedrooms and a bathroom. The kitchen was small in one, extended in the other. There were gardens front and back. The extended house had a slightly smaller rear garden because of the improved kitchen, but the owner was leaving carpets and curtains at no extra cost, and the front sitting room had Skaters' Trails, the grey version, of course. Surely this had to be an omen?

Tess sat down there and then in 'her' new kitchen and wrote a contract of sorts. She left a small cheque as deposit, returnable should a survey find fault. Meanwhile, the For Sale sign must be removed. And that was that. She stood in the front garden and admired the house. It was beautiful, newly painted in black and white, while Anne-Marie's hero lived diagonally opposite. Also, this was a good address, since Woolton was, for many people, a statement of arrival. Don worked just outside Woolton, so the children would be able to see him...

She looked up and down the avenue, her

heartbeat suddenly louder and erratic. Lots of trees, houses well cared for, several cars and... And he had another woman. This sudden realisation arrived like a punch in the solar plexus. *Why did I never turn to face him when he was ready in the bed? Why was I stupid enough to make him use me in that way? Even a prostitute would serve him better. I am a cold country, and he has gone somewhere with a warmer climate. How stupid am I? Men need relief and release – my mother warned me about that. Who is she?*

Joy about her semi-detached paradise evaporated. How much did she have left after that deposit? Was there enough to pay Injun Joe, the private detective? But there was really no point, because she couldn't apply for a divorce. Still riveted to the spot, she worked on her breathing. A panic attack threatened. Sometimes, she had one because of worrying about having one. And she couldn't have one here, not on Menlove Avenue. People here owned new cars and Skaters' Trails, bay windows, even an oriel in the smallest bedroom, and decent net curtains. Some had gone as far as Venetian blinds and pretend shutters on outside walls...

No, she couldn't have a panic in this place. It was a coffee morning area, a cheese and wine evening location, a keep-your-garden-nice avenue. She managed her breathing before walking back towards home. *You did well, Tess. A person looking for a house is expected to stand and stare at neighbouring buildings. But keep taking the pills, woman.*

No. She couldn't apply for divorce, but he might. Wasn't there a get-out-of-jail card after

131

seven years of separation? If there was, she wouldn't contest it, because she was being bought out, wasn't she? It was a house, a house, my wifedom for a house. That was Shakespeare's King Richard, she seemed to remember from school, but his had been a kingdom and a horse.

The only other way to get a quick divorce was via Injun Joe and his photos. Joey Dodds had earned his nickname in childhood, because he'd always chosen to be an Indian rather than a cowboy. Now, he'd decided to be a private detective, and he earned most of his money by catching people in flagrante and in seedy hotels. Well, Don would find no evidence of that behaviour from her, though she could get it from him and his partner in adultery. Because there had to be another woman. But was proof required? The truth was that no matter what, a Catholic remained married. Even if Don had the marriage terminated after seven years, she would not be free to marry again. She would never do that, anyway. Once was enough for any woman with a degree of common sense.

Yet if she looked at it another way, knowledge was power. She wanted the extended-kitchen house, so she needed to move fast. If she knew the identity of his mistress, she might be able to apply pressure and negotiate for some new furniture and a washing machine. It was September, and she didn't want to spend another winter in that flat if she could help it.

Even so, there was a huge void where her stomach had been, because she was losing a massive thing – her status. She was going back on

132

the shelf, would be considered soiled goods, a reject, even a danger. A pretty divorcee was to be avoided in case she made a move towards someone else's husband. It worked the other way round, too, as many men didn't want their wives to associate with a female who might lead them astray. Did they think separation was a communicable disease?

She'd never been inside Injun Joe's wigwam. It was above a tobacconist shop, and was reputed to have totem poles, feathered head-dresses and, on the walls, pictures of native Americans. That was where Joe's flamboyance began and ended. Access to his office was through a rear yard, and he was the soul of discretion. Dolly Pearson was reputed to have used him, though no one was completely sure.

Tess lingered outside the wool shop. At this time of year, she had used to start on her children's winter knits, but they were beyond the winter knit stage. Should she make one for Don? No, he'd think she was trying to get round him. Was she thinking of arranging another attempt to get round him? Seduction had failed, so she couldn't imagine a cable knit making any difference. But she went inside, picked up a pattern and some blue double-knit wool. It would emphasise her startling, bright blue eyes. Tess would begin to knit for herself and live for herself, since the kids would leave sooner or later.

She entered the launderette where four women were doing their weekly wash. 'I'll be upstairs, ladies. If you need change for something or other, just ring the bell. Oh, and you'll have a tea and coffee machine soon. I ordered it about a week ago. I think it even serves cocoa or drinking chocolate of some sort.' She then delivered a beaming smile before climbing the stairs. The expressions on those four faces had been priceless.

Becoming nice was not going to be easy. 'We'll have to work at it, won't we?' she asked her shepherd's pie before leaving it next to the oven. It would be heated through for tonight's meal, and the children would remain at the table this time, because they needed to be told properly and by both parents. Menlove Avenue. She kept saying the name in her head. She needed to continue excited.

Sitting near the window, she began to cast on the bluebell-coloured wool for her new sweater. No one could have everything. There was even space for a small breakfast table in that kitchen. A house was nearly everything, and a husband was not absolutely essential. And the gardens were neat and simple. It was her pride that was giving her pain, and pride was expensive. She might assume the air of the grievously wounded, one whose man had been whisked away by a younger woman. That would work with other single females, she supposed as she began the first row of ribbing.

He was on the stairs. Her insides trembled slightly, and her knitting picked up speed when the door opened.

Don glanced at her. It was clear that she had a plan, because her back was ramrod straight, and she was occupied by something that didn't require too much concentration. Tess was a poser,

134

though she seemed happily oblivious to that fact. 'What's happened?' he asked.

Tess bit her lip; he thought he knew her so well. Perhaps this was a demonstration of familiarity breeding contempt. 'I found a house,' she replied. 'On Menlove. This end, of course.'

'Of course.'

'And I put down a deposit out of my own money. She's leaving carpets and curtains, so that'll save a few bob. Do you want to look at it? We could go together.'

'That won't be necessary. How much is it with its carpets and curtains?'

'And light fittings,' she added. 'I forgot about them.'

'How much?' Don repeated.

'Nineteen hundred. It's got a nice new kitchen. There's another house for eighteen, but that has a tiny kitchen and no soft furnishings included.'

'Or light fittings?'

He was making fun of her. 'Or light fittings,' she answered obediently.

'OK. Write the address down, and I'll get it looked at. Is your deposit returnable if there's anything wrong?'

'Naturally.' She changed needles. Did he think she'd arrived in the last shower of rain? He knew only too well that she was a damned good businesswoman, that she'd fought every inch of the way to make a decent home. Everything here was hers, right down to table mats and cruet. For a minute or so, she stopped knitting and wrote down the details of the house. 'There you are. She'll have taken down the For Sale sign.'

Don picked up the sheet of paper. 'What are you making?' he asked.

God! Surely he wasn't attempting to start a conversation? 'A jumper for me,' she replied. 'Isn't the wool a lovely colour? It matches my eyes.' *Pick that gauntlet up,* she said in her head. *You'll find no one with eyes prettier than mine.*

Don's thoughts ran on similar lines. Tess was the best-looking woman for miles. Her eyes were stunning, as was her body, while her legs stopped many a man at work. Builders, glaziers, window cleaners and coalmen showered her with attention, but she'd ceased to notice. Had she ever noticed?

Tess turned her temper down to simmer level. The other woman needed to be left out of the recipe until the deeds of that house were parked in the vault of her bank. He was staring at her. She couldn't be sure of his expression without looking directly at him, but he wanted her. All men wanted her. Even Anne-Marie's Rocker gave her the eye from time to time.

'Tess?'

'What?'

He paused for a while. 'The sofa's killing me.'

She didn't hesitate. 'Then come back to bed. I'll have the sofa.'

'Oh, I see.'

Did he see? Did he really? 'I have to use the sofa if you use the bed, or we'll be giving mixed messages to Sean and Anne-Marie.' The welt of her knitting needed at least another inch. 'It's time to talk to them, Don. We should do it tonight after the meal.'

He had no idea why he was suddenly pre-varicating. He didn't love her, did he? And even if he looked at it from a pragmatic viewpoint, Molly was paying for the house. Without Molly, there would be no move, no change... He was being bought, as was Tess. For under two thousand pounds, Molly would become his owner; for the same sum, Tess would get the house. What was the matter with him? Molly was a joy to be with, while this one was ... she was a challenge. A part of him of which he was less than proud still wanted to tame his legal wife. Just once, he needed to make her scream with joy. But she wouldn't. She couldn't relax, was incapable of physical excitement– Good God, he still desired this cold, calculating woman.

'Shepherd's pie,' she said apropos of nothing at all. 'A bit of salad on the side, I thought. Weather's still just about warm enough for salad.'

Don almost grinned. He was thinking about sex while she concerned herself with lettuce and tomatoes. That was probably the case in most households. Men pondered the wonder of orgasm while women knitted and made sure the family was adequately fed. Molly wasn't brilliant with food, but she was great in bed. And on the floor. And in the car. 'Tess?'

'Yes?'

'Did you ever have a climax?'

She was studying her pattern. 'No,' she said eventually. She would not be ruffled; no matter what Don said or did, she would be ruffle-free. But the flame under her temper was suddenly burning at a slightly higher temperature. She must

137

not allow the mixture to bubble; it needed ice.

'You pretended.'

'Yes.'

'Why?'

She shrugged and swapped her needles again. 'It seemed the polite thing to do.'

'Then you turned your back on me and allowed me to help myself.'

At last, she put down the work and looked him squarely in the face. 'I'm sorry. Anyway, it's too late now, isn't it? You've made your decision. I was frightened before getting used to the idea.' In that moment, she realized that she did want the house more than she wanted this place and him. 'I suppose you could move with us if you wanted to.'

He couldn't. He couldn't take Molly's money and abandon her. There was no real endowment policy, and there was no turning back, because Molly was the pretend policy. No. He was having doubts about radical change, about losing his children, this road, familiar faces and places. 'I don't want to talk to them tonight,' he said carefully. 'I'd rather wait until we know your house is steady. I know you need to get a house at this end of the avenue, because you'll have to be near the launderette. But there's no point getting Anne-Marie all excited about living on John Lennon's street if it all falls through.'

It wasn't a street, it was an avenue, but she must not correct him. 'Fine,' she said. 'Whatever you like. Now that you mention it, that would be better. The house is near his, by the way. I wonder if it's wise to take her there, because those boys attract some wild ones. She's daft enough without getting involved with a rampageous fan club.' *Hold on,* she advised herself. *Don't erupt, or you'll destroy this lovely new wool. Do what you always do; sit on your temper. In all these years, he's never seen you in full flood.*

A sliver of sunlight pierced the window and illuminated her hair. Like molten gold, it glowed, providing a halo above a perfect face. Even now, she fed something in him. Yes, she was selfish, careless and unforgiving, but the Irish in her kept her young. Tess was like poetry. She sat there on her own page of life, but if you looked closely, she was a piece of art. There was elegance in her movements, in her stillness, in everything she did or didn't do. 'Tess, I did love you.'

She raised her chin, and the halo moved so that it was behind her whole head. And suddenly, the fuel that fed her temper leaked and engulfed her. 'You don't even know me; you never did know me.' In a trice, she was gas mark nine, and she was shouting. 'I am a determined protector of myself and of my children. You weren't there. You didn't lie cold in a wooden caravan, didn't starve for three days in a row, didn't see your daddy drunk every other night on cider and poteen. You never saw your mammy all bloody with a baby hanging out of her. You weren't there,' she screamed. 'You didn't help bury that little dead thing in the orchard. I was four years old with a baby's corpse in my arms, and I didn't know whether it was a boy or a girl. It wasn't even a person, just a doll in a dirty towel in a cardboard box in a hole in the ground. I swore even then, at the age of four, that

139

my children would thrive.'

Don blinked stupidly. There *was* fire in her, and he could hear it now. But she'd kept it all inside, the fear, the memories, the need to save her own two from anything approaching deprivation. 'I knew your family was poor, but I'd no idea that you'd been through so much.'

'I don't advertise,' she snapped. 'I don't parade my past and serve it up with custard. It's not because of shame; it's because I will not cry. I will never again be broken by life, by you, by that lot out there on the streets, by tramps who offer an apple if I'll take my knickers off.' She stood up. 'Fortunately, we had apples of our own, and we often lived on them, so I hung on to my knickers. Do not *ever* assume that you know me, Don Compton. But I'll allow you this much. Should you or anyone harm my kids, I will kill. And bugger the panic attacks.' She stormed off into the bedroom.

Don shook his head in near-incredulity. He believed what she said, but he had never heard her swear until now. As her anger had grown, the slightly Scouse accent had shifted nearer to southern Irish, and her eyes had blazed like blue flame in a winter fire. This was the source of her panics, then. She would never have peace, would for ever look over her shoulder to see if her monsters were closing in. And every monster had been a man.

Could he leave her? Could he really walk out on a woman whose children were almost ready to fly the nest? She wasn't right, wasn't fit to be alone. Dr Byrne had broached the subject of some kind of electrical therapy, but she wasn't bad enough for that, surely? Don didn't know her? He now had insight enough to understand that nothing would ever be enough to fill the hole created by an almost total lack of childhood. *I'll give you an apple if you take your knickers off.* Small wonder she was frigid if her little body had been judged at the price of a Cox's red.

Her father had dried himself out, though he'd certainly been a drunk when young, and he'd slipped back into the habit after a few dry years. And her mother had been in no condition to protect, care for and feed the ever-expanding family. So the child had become her own parent, and no one would ever break through to the Tess inside.

He left the building in as much of a hurry as his old injury would allow. Tess wasn't the crazy one; he was. It was becoming clear that there were several psychological mechanisms over which he had little or no control. Was everyone the same, or did he need locking up? No one could keep two women. One was enough bother for any man. What the hell was he supposed to do now?

The car made the decision for him. It took him in the direction of a female who was eight years his senior, who was wife, friend, sister and mother all in the one package. Molly was the only person in whom he could confide without worrying about gossip and the trouble it caused. However, the weight of the parcel he needed to deliver might just break her back. He was probably about to lose her. But he didn't want to see Anne-Marie stuck at home with an ailing mother who couldn't

141

be left; wasn't prepared to place a heavy burden on the shoulders of either of his children.

Oh, Molly. She was slimmer these days, quicker off the mark in a chase, especially when running from a disabled man. Her latest decision was that she would remain a poor cook, since the serving up of the inedible would help her reach her goal of nine stone, as long as people ignored her when she begged for fish and chips.

He parked in a lane that led to her house. She would be home by this time, since most business was done in the mornings. Almost absently, he rubbed the knee. Driving affected him and sometimes caused pain, but the bigger discomfort was in his soul today. God, he was tired. He leaned a weary head on the steering wheel. This day promised to continue unhappy, as he would be disappointing both his women. Could he live without Moll? Could he live with a furious Tess who was about to lose a big kitchen, fitted carpets, good curtains and some light-shades? A mortgage? Who would allow him one, and how could he keep up payments? Yet the trimmings Tess had found on Menlove Avenue were what she needed. They were scaffolding, distractions, dressings for a fevered mind. When the novelty wore off, she would probably drift once again in the direction of discontent.

For the first time, Don entered Molly's domain in dread. He wasn't afraid of her, but he didn't want to see her upset. And the shredded remains of his feelings for Tess kept snagging the wheels on his train of thought. Then there were the kids to think about...

Molly sat him down and gave him a cup of hot, sweet tea. 'Now, Don Compton. You've a face on you that might win a knobbly knee competition at Blackpool, but it doesn't match me décor. These days, men get picked to fit in with the furniture, so buck up. What happened? Is somebody ill?'

He leaned back in the chair and closed his eyes for a few seconds. 'Oh, Molly,' he managed finally. 'I don't know whether I'm coming or going. She's found her house and left a deposit, but she's fit for nothing. She boiled over this afternoon, and we both got burnt. In all the years I've known her, she's never lost her temper, not completely. If she gets the house and moves, she'll be happy till the kids disappear, then the electric shock treatment might become a reality. And I don't want my daughter giving up her apprenticeship to look after Tess.' He sighed before taking a few sips of tea.

'What do you mean by boiled over? Are you talking about an accident with the milk pan?'

He shook his head slowly. 'Well, it erupted that way, as if the stuff inside her had found a crack in an outside layer, and she went up like a rocket. At first, I thought she was talking a load of nonsense, but she wasn't. She said I didn't know her, I'd never known her. But when she finally started to come out with it – and I know there's a lot more – it was bloody heartbreaking. She'd nobody as a kid, Moll. They were starving hungry and cold at night. She ... oh, my God.' He was weeping.

'Don? Sweetheart?'

'Buried a dead baby. She was four, Moll.'

'Hell's bloody bells. Who killed it?' Molly asked.

143

'Born dead. That's just the start. I can't leave her. I can't come here and live with you, because she's still full of that stuff, and someone has to be there to listen and make sure she takes her pills. I don't want her in a mental hospital or stuck with nurses drifting in and out of the house night and day. She's the mother of my kids, after all. And I'm not going to let anything spoil their future.' He paused and took Molly's hand. 'So we'll have to stay in the flat, my love. I just can't leave her. I can't be happy here with you while I'm waiting for a phone call to say she's strung herself up or taken an overdose.'

She squeezed his fingers. 'You don't know me, either, do you? There's a cheque on that sideboard made payable to you. It's for three grand, and that'll cover the cost of a semi on her favourite avenue.'

'But Molly—'

'But nothing. I'm a rich woman by most standards, so I've no price, Don. You move with her. I'm quite happy with things as they are, and I've nobody to put in my will, have I? Get her settled and sorted, but don't forsake me. You can't just walk away from Tess, lad. You'd get no respect from me if you did.' She stood up. 'Now, I've a bit of ham salad lingering in the back of me Frigidaire. It's been looking at me funny all day, and I'm sure it's going to ask for its old-age pension if I don't shape. Do you want a bit of pickled beetroot with it?'

She was priceless. Pickled beetroot, a large cheque, ham salad, all the same to her.

In the kitchen, Molly rattled about and heaved

144

a secret sigh of relief. She loved the bones of the man, but she'd found herself a bit unsettled of late. It was nice having a younger chap who came and made her laugh, yet she prized her independence. Everything would have to change if and when he moved in. Could she let him see her ready for bed, night cream pushed into wrinkles, hair in a net to keep it grease-free, Sam and Uke on the bed, a Georgette Heyer propped on that little reading slope? And the reading glasses sliding down her nose?

Molly prided herself on her sense of fair play. She'd been angry with Don when he'd left his wife on the day of the big panic attack, so she would probably be scared to death if he abandoned altogether a woman who might become suicidal. It sounded as if Tess had guarded so fiercely the child inside herself that she had failed to mature emotionally.

Then there was the other point, already considered. Molly wouldn't be able to mooch around in a towelling robe for hours on a Sunday morning. Her experimental cooking, which had been a source of hilarity thus far, would surely cease to be funny once Don became a permanent fixture. She needed to do a course in scrambled eggs on toast before inflicting her culinary disasters on any man. Matt hadn't minded, because he'd loved to cook, and many meals had been eaten in restaurants.

Also, that poor woman deserved her new house. Don didn't sleep with his wife, so he would still be coming here for an hour or two of light relief, doggy company and a bit of a sing-song with accompaniment on the ukulele.

Meanwhile, Don sat with his head in his hands. Had he been completely honest with Molly? Somewhere, deep inside himself, a small flicker of love for Tess tried hard not to be extinguished. And he remembered from moments earlier that brief yet recognizable expression of relief in Molly's eyes. She wasn't ready. And three thousand pounds was so small a sum in her book. He had to accept it. Tess needed the move; Molly needed time to collect her thoughts and wave goodbye to aloneness. She wasn't lonely, since she always found somewhere to go, a pub to sing in, a friend to lunch with, a course to take in the evenings. He was doing no wrong.

In the dining room, he found the cheque resting beside his plate. 'Thank you,' he whispered.

Molly speared a slice of beetroot. 'It'll all work out,' she said. 'You and I do very well as we are.'

He managed a smile. 'I need two thousand, not three.'

'Furniture,' she replied smartly. 'And a better car. That bloody thing sounds like it's got whooping cough or a bad case of diphtheria. And look at me now. Beetroot vinegar all down me new blouse. Twenty-nine and eleven in the sale, that cost.'

Don relaxed slightly. A thirty-bob blouse, a cheque for three thousand – all of similar value according to Molly. He needed to go and face the shepherd's pie, wanted to make sure that Tess said nothing to the children, but he couldn't just pick up the money and run. A degree of discomfort continued to plague him. The part of him over

146

which he seemed to have little control wanted to stay with his family, needed to care for Tess, even win her affection. He shivered. Someone was stepping on his grave, and that someone was Don Compton.

Worse was to come. The dogs were outside, and he and Molly had the freedom of the house. While they played on the floor, the face above his changed for a split second, and he saw Tess with a halo blazing behind her head. Bloody hell. If this state of confusion carried on, he would end up in the hospital with his poor wife.

He drove home with the cheque hidden in his breast pocket. Tomorrow, it would go into the bank, and Tess would have no clue about its point of origin. It was from an insurance company, and he must try to shake off the embarrassment he felt while in the company of this small piece of paper.

She didn't ask where he'd been when he finally entered the flat. He could scarcely remember the last time she'd asked certain questions. But he volunteered a part of the truth. 'I went to see Molly. Her books weren't balancing.'

Still knitting rapidly, Tess advised him that his meal, minus salad, was in the oven and would be dry. 'I didn't say anything to Sean or Anne-Marie.' And she wasn't going to start worrying about Molly Braithwaite, since Molly was a fat frump with no style whatsoever. She was Don's employer, no more than that.

'Your knitting's grown,' Don commented. Life was becoming stranger, as he now felt almost shy in the presence of his wife. 'At that rate, you'll have it finished by the weekend.' He took another mouthful of shepherd's pie. Tess was a good cook, and the meal's time in the oven had made a pleasant crust on top of the mash. 'The money came,' he added casually. 'The house will be in your name, and I'll move in with you if that's all right.'

She remained silent.

'Two single beds,' he added. 'I need a firm mattress.'

'All right.'

And 'all right' was as far as she got for the moment. He waited, but no further comment was made. She was one bloody infuriating, selfish cow. So why did he feel like an unworthy teenager at the feet of a local beauty queen? She'd been hard enough to catch the first time round, and his sex life had been rationed almost as harshly as food during the war. He was mad. He was the one in need of bloody psychiatry. 'I can't leave you.' There. He'd said it.

She stared hard at him. 'I'm not insane if that's what's worrying you.'

Don gritted his teeth. *No, but I very well may be,* was his silent reply. 'I can't leave you,' he repeated. 'Because somewhere, in a well-hidden part of my stupid self, the love is still there.'

Tess raised her head. If there was ever to be a truthful moment, it had to come now. 'That's a debt I can't repay properly. But I'd miss you, Don. I've grown used to you.'

He sighed. People got used to bunions, he supposed. And toothache. Any repeated pain became part and parcel of existence. 'We'll go

148

and look at it together tomorrow,' he promised.

She continued to stare at him. 'You weren't going to bother.'

'I wasn't going to move in.'

'So what's changed?'

'I can't leave you,' he said yet again.

And she smiled. Molly's smile lit up a room; Tess's illuminated eternity. 'You won't like it,' she told him.

'Why?'

'Skaters' Trails.'

The man who loved two women began to laugh uncontrollably. 'How do you manage to get your own way every time?' he gasped.

She didn't even continue to smile. 'Because I'm beautiful.' She stated the fact baldly. 'But, you know, I may be wrong in this instance.'

Don stopped laughing. 'No. You're beautiful.'

'I know *that*. I mean the carpet. It is a bit busy. And common. We don't want to be the same as all the rest, do we?'

He wondered whether she was using the royal 'we', as she seldom spoke about them as a couple. 'How many rooms have Skaters' blinking Trails?'

'Just the one.'

He decided to press her. 'Can I change it?'

'Of course. It's your house.'

Recently, she had begun to forget what he had just said. 'It will be in your name.'

'Both names,' was her reply. 'Because we'll both be leaving it to Sean and Anne-Marie. Your money, your savings, our house.'

She was now being untypically fair. 'All right,'

he said. 'Where are the kids?'

Tess shrugged. 'She'll be with Karl Marx on his bike, and he'll be up to his ears in oil doing a foreigner for a friend. I miss them. Not as they are now, but as they used to be, all shining faces and spelling tests. I felt right. Everything felt right then.'

She was talking to him. He had to answer. 'That's because you were doing what you swore you'd do all those years ago. When that terrible thing happened, and not even a funeral, you buried a bit of yourself, love. Living like that, being hungry and cold, made you determined to give your own a decent chance.'

She nodded thoughtfully. 'But I had to work, Don. And you raised them, taught them to read and spell and count. I missed a lot of that.'

'Blame Hitler.'

'Oh, I do, I do.'

That was the moment when he realized why she was ill. She'd lost her own childhood, and she'd missed a lot of theirs. Her one pledge before God had been broken, and his leg was to blame. 'I'm sorry, love.'

'Why? Did you shoot yourself in the knee?'

'No, I didn't.'

'Then don't be sorry. None of this is your fault.'

Later, when Sean and Anne-Marie were asleep, Don had a quiet bath. Once dry and shaved, he crept into the bedroom and slipped under the covers. 'It's all right,' he whispered. 'I won't be taking advantage. It's just the leg, Tess.' Feeling her tension, he began to stroke her hair until she settled.

She sniffed.

'Are you crying?'

'No.'

'Are you sure?'

'Yes.'

'Once upon a time, the most beautiful princess in the world was born by mistake in a little wooden hut. She knew she was a princess, because she had a birthmark on her cheek, a beauty spot given only to people of true blue blood. She moved with all the pride and grace of royalty, and–'

'And finished up in a launderette on Smithdown Road,' she said.

Don tutted. 'No. On Menlove Avenue with leaded lights in the windows and a horrible carpet on the floor.'

'Shut up.'

'But a prince with a limp tore up the carpet and bought a blue one to match her knitting and her eyes.'

Tess blinked wetness from her eyes; she would not cry.

'And they lived almost happily together.' He lifted her hair and buried his nose in the nape of her neck. So sweet, the scent of this woman's flesh. 'Except for motor bikes, oil on their son's feet and separate beds.'

'Go to sleep, Gordon.'

He hated his full name. 'Call me that again, and I'll tickle you.'

'And I'll have your head cut off by the royal axe man.'

'Fair enough.' He went to sleep.

See, the streets need cleaning. Some women get some men in a pile of trouble, and I'm here to balance the scales. I don't know why it has to be my bloody job, but my mother was lovely. I thought she could do no wrong till she scarpered. I can't be doing with liars. Who said 'to thine own self be true'? Well, I'm being true to mine own self. Cleaning up, clearing out the trash, letting the sun shine through the rain...

Six

Rosh had finally achieved the impossible; she was now in a place where waking, while still painful, was no longer soul-shattering. She had learned to accept a day without Phil, then another, then the next. Some days were sad, others were bearable, while several were satisfying and almost happy. Which was just as well, because Christmas was approaching fast, and the season had always been special. Phil had made it so and, having lost a wonderful father, the three children deserved an extra-special time this year. There was money, though Rosh intended to hang on to most of it. With three children to educate and send forth into the world, she needed that nest egg. But she planned to use some to brighten their lives.

So the wind of change had started to travel through the Allen household, and Rosh intended it to freshen every room. It was more of a breeze than a gale, since the loss of a father as wonderful as Phil had left a massive hole, and speed might have seemed disrespectful. But Rosh would improve the lives of Phil's children, would keep them occupied and as happy as possible. Kieran's bedroom next, she decided, then Mother's.

The girls' bedroom was going to be difficult, because Alice didn't often do change, but she'd seemed happy enough while watching alterations in Rosh's bedroom. Perhaps she might be persuaded? Kieran could work on Alice, get her to choose colours and wallpaper. Fortunately, Philly was easy to please. Immersed in music, she didn't notice the trimmings around her. The only time she complained was if lighting was too poor for her to read her sheets when learning a new piece. Her intention was to become a songwriter, as someone had to lead the world out of its 'silly' rock and roll era.

Rosh sat up in bed and looked round the room. It was pretty and very feminine. Everything had moved. Bed, wardrobe, dressing table and chests of drawers had found new positions in life, while her husband's clothes and shoes had gone to the poor. Newly painted and papered, the room was completely different. This was no longer the nest in which Rosh had lain with her husband. It had all been changed as quietly as possible by Rosh, Anna and an odd-job man called Eric.

Rosh grinned broadly. Eric Holt had since become a bit of a pest, as he had taken a shine to Anna, and the situation was fast moving towards the hilarious edge of the spectrum. Kieran and Philly made many comments about Gran's new boyfriend, his height, his slender stature, his worn-out cap. Kieran had been heard to offer the opinion that Mr Holt needed a ladder to reach the skirting boards. Gran often chased Rosh and Phil's older progeny with a broom, a fish slice, a rolling pin, or anything else that came to hand. If they carried on with the torment, she would kill them.

Mother was still living here, of course. Determined as a Jack Russell down a rabbit hole, Anna

Riley continued *perpetuum mobile*, hyper-alert and full of love. On weekday evenings, she cleaned a couple of offices on Liverpool Road, and she refused to give up her indispendence. This word she had concocted from two others – independence and indispensability, and the Allen household was used to that. Kieran had even put forward the concept of an Anna Riley Dictionary, a DIY volume created for the Irish, the adventurous and the totally daft, but his grandmother was not offended. Years after immigration, she still clung fiercely to her Irish accent. She was grateful to Liverpool, as were many Irish folk, but she had been made in Mayo, and Mayo was printed all the way through her body like Blackpool in a stick of rock.

'You'd be prouder of me now,' Rosh told the wedding photograph. 'I'll probably go back to work after the New Year. They'll have a good Christmas, love – Mother and I will make sure. But we'll miss you so much. It just won't be the same, Phil, but I'll try my hardest.'

Phil had always made a drama out of carving on Christmas Day. When Kieran and Philly had been small, their dad had pretended to choose between them and the meat on the table. So a chase round the house with a fork-wielding father had been normal. 'I only want to see if you're cooked. Just a little prod with the fork,' he would yell as his children fled upstairs screaming happily. He'd never done it with Alice, who had been born after a gap of seven years. Alice, when she did take something on board, treated it literally, and she might have been terrified.

155

The door glided inward and revealed a huge orange cat. Winston had learned how to open doors. Well, some doors. Those that opened towards him remained a mystery thus far, though he was working on the mechanics of the problem. Sometimes, he entered while still hanging from the handle, but this was always done with a complete lack of grace, as the action rendered him wide-eyed, yowling and shaky. This time, he'd remembered to let go. He looked businesslike, tail ramrod straight and stiff, eyes on Rosh, who was the reason for his intrusion. He had come bearing messages, and was doing what Anna always termed a briefcase job.

'Hello, Winnie.'

'Meow.'

'What?'

'Meee-ow.'

'Is she?'

'Mew.'

I am talking to a bloody cat here. Worse than that, I understand what he's saying. This is definitely not normal. I am definitely not normal. I wonder if there's a place for me in a nice, quiet rest home for the terminally bewildered? Are there other people like me, crazy and aware of it?

'MEEE-OW.'

'Is she dressed?'

'Mew.'

Under the dedicated supervision of Winston, Rosh pulled on her dressing gown and walked past the cat onto the landing where she found Alice dressed, but gazing quizzically at her shoes. They were shiny-clean, yet Alice found them unacceptable. As the child studied her footwear, a frown creased her face.

'Alice?'

'Hmm, no.'

Well, that was a promising start. Rosh noticed that the left shoe was where the right should have been, and vice versa. While the little girl could complete a jigsaw in minutes, she remained stumped by ordinary, everyday difficulties like shoes, odd socks, the wrong spoon, a piece of meat in her mashed potato.

'Change over,' Alice said before swapping the shoes' positions. A huge smile decorated her pretty little face.

These were the Christmas gifts Rosh relished. Already, she had detailed drawings of buildings, and sums on paper. All twenty-six letters of the alphabet sat in a pile on Alice's little bedroom table, the same twenty-six on the wall, and Alice could match them. There was a brain, a good brain, but it was behind glass possibly frosted by Aspergers. Rosh was determined to break that glass if it took her a lifetime. 'Hello, Alice.'

No reply, but the shoes were the right way round on the child's feet. And that was Rosh's newest Christmas present, delivered prematurely, but valued all the more for that very reason. Alice knew right from left; she was also displaying symptoms of knowing right from wrong, so the show was making its hesitant way towards the road at last.

The biggest gift had been offered by the school, where Rosh had been shown a sketch of the Victorian building, all false castellation, arched windows and scarred brick. Alice had produced this from memory one wet playtime, but it wasn't the main prize. Although the child appeared not to listen in class, her sum book was full of ticks. 'She's bright enough,' the teacher had said. 'And we're getting help. For two hours a week, her communication skills will be worked on. Oh, and she does better if she brings her teddy bear to school.'

'She talks to him,' Rosh had said. 'And the cats. We have two, and the ginger tom seems to look after her.'

That was when she learned that Alice might need a familiar item with her for some time to come. 'Hopefully, Mrs Allen, the articles will get smaller and less noticeable. But Aspergers children often need to cling to something or other. With luck, hard work and a good following wind, she'll be playing with the others within a year or two. I've had to allow the rest to bring in a toy, because I don't want Alice to stand out for the wrong reasons. But she is special. All your children are. Kieran will go a long way whatever he chooses to do, and Philly will continue with music, I expect.'

'They had a clever dad.'

'And a good mother. Never forget that.'

She had learned something else that day. Alice's condition was thought not to be curable, though the behaviour it produced could be improved in certain cases to a point where it might be virtually unnoticeable. In certain cases. Alice wasn't a case, she was a human child with talent, likes, dislikes, needs, and even some naughtiness. The

158

naughtiness was the item in which Rosh invested most hope. The child reacted. In order to react, she needed to have been involved, however peripherally, in a situation near to her. And she was definitely relating to her big brother and to her older sister.

Winston was having a wash. Alice, all bright and clean in her school clothes, watched him. 'Clean your teeth,' she told him before going downstairs.

A mental picture of Winnie and a toothbrush made Rosh giggle. She didn't want to think about toothpaste. Winston and a tube of extruded white dental cream might prove a lethal combination.

Breakfast had begun. Alice had her egg, her special spoon, the statutory battalion of six soldiers, and a cup of milky tea. The older two were eating Gran's special porridge with thick cream and a soupçon of golden syrup, while Rosh and Anna had toast.

Anna was in full flood with one of her thousands of tales about life in Mayo. 'So Patricia – she was your granddad's sister, and some called her Paddy – had one of her daring and unusual ideas. Sure they were only babies at the time, but they had a problem to solve. She thought if they hid their ganga's clothes and work boots, he would stay in the house and there'd be no more explosions in the sheds. None of them had many clothes to spare, so this seemed sensible enough. Well, Holy Mother on a Friday, he hit the roof in temper. There he was in long underwear with the flap at the back, and an old shirt from before the turn of some long-ago century, and he ranted and raved like a madman.'

'So what did they do?' Philly asked.

Anna laughed. 'Your granddad and his sister ran for the hills, but got tired after a few minutes. When they came back, there was Ganga in a woman's frock and coat, old wellington boots on his feet, going about his brewing as if nothing had happened. Ah, he sounded wonderful, God rest his bones.' She nodded for a few seconds. 'I wonder could we find Patricia? She was with the last lot of Rileys to come over, you know. If she's still in Liverpool, it shouldn't be too hard. I'd like to meet her. She was my husband's favourite sister, backbone of steel, heart of gold.'

'Weren't they all supposed to stay together?' Kieran asked.

Anna shook her head sadly. 'Some went away for work, some married and moved, and I believe a few crossed the ocean for Canada and America. Then the ganga died, so no one was in charge. Lovely big family like that, all split up without thought, without...'

Rosh put a hand on her mother's. Only Rosh could hear the pain. 'All right, Mam.' At times like this, the name Mother seemed a bit formal. Rosh was Anna's sole surviving child. Miscarriages, stillbirths and neo-natal deaths had left the poor little woman devastated. She had one healthy, strapping girl, and all the rest were... 'Eat your egg, Alice, there's a good girl,' Anna said, her voice less than steady.

'You've four,' Rosh told her mother. 'Me and these three of mine.'

Alice chewed on a buttered soldier. 'And Win-

160

ston and Lucy. Six.'

'What about Teddo?' Rosh asked.

She was awarded a withering glance. 'Teddo not walking, not talking,' came the reply from a child who lived on the edge of autism.

'Cats don't talk,' was Kieran's offering.

'Meow,' Alice said. Thus she achieved the last word. Breakfast was over, and she went to clean her teeth.

A disobedient tear wandered down the older woman's cheek. 'Well, that's us told, but. Didn't I always say she'd come right? That child arrived in the world old and in a very bad mood. When she was born, she gave me the dirtiest look I ever got in me whole life. It was as if she knew me already, knew what a nuisance I am.'

'Impossible,' commented Kieran the scientist. 'No one can be born knowing what a nuisance you are. That's something that grows on a person like warts. I was at least four before I worked you out, Gran.'

Rosh squashed a grin. 'Go on now. Teeth, then you take Alice to school, Philly. Make sure you hand her over to someone sensible, preferably a teacher.'

The older children left the room.

Someone knocked at the door. Immediately, the whole of Anna's little body stiffened. 'I'm out. No, I'm dead, and you're waiting for the undertaker to fit me with a nice wooden jacket. Or I've emi-grated to be with our Dan in Philly-delphi-o. London? Christmas shopping? North Pole, South Pole, up the pole?'

'Oh, Mother.'

It was too late, anyway. A mischievous light shone in Kieran's eyes as he delivered Mr Eric Holt to the women in the kitchen. Mr Eric Holt was slightly taller than Anna. The famous cap twisted in his hands as he addressed the two women. 'Sorry. If I'd known you weren't dressed, Mrs Allen, I wouldn't have ... er... Mrs Riley, I didn't–'

'We're going now,' Kieran shouted from the hall.

Rosh went to see her children off. When she closed the front door, she noticed a deafening silence throughout the whole ground floor. He was probably still standing there, torturing the cap in work-worn hands. Well, Mother had to deal with her suitor, so Rosh ran upstairs to dress herself.

She took her time. Underneath all the bluster and harsh words, Anna Riley was as soft as putty. It would take her a while to tell him to bugger off, because she never set out to hurt people. Or perhaps it wouldn't take long, because this time Anna Riley was like a coiled spring; one touch, and she could jump. Such behaviour might be unexpected, but Mother's unpredictability was predictable. She seldom behaved quite as people thought she might.

Meanwhile, Anna was sitting at the table with her jaw almost on the plate. 'Why ever on God's good earth did he ask you, Eric? What in the name of mercy did you do to deserve such a request? I'm shocked right through to the middle of meself. Roy seems to be such a sensible man. Mind, we've not seen him in quite a while.'

The visitor shrugged slim shoulders. 'I was only having a quick look at me Brussels, thinking I could bring some home soon and give them out to people for Christmas. I say looking, but it was still nearly dark. And Roy has the plot next to mine, and he walks over bold as brass and asks me. Well, no. He wasn't as bold as brass. In fact, he was a bit strange, like a puppet talking all on one note, no expression in his voice.' Eric sighed and rubbed his chin. 'He was odd, as if he was in shock. It's good money he's offering, as good as any wage from factory work, but my stomach turned over.'

'I'll make a pot of tea. Stay where you are while I think on things.'

She rattled about and thought on things. The thing she concentrated on mostly lived across the street. It had survived a massive heart attack and was now in need of care. 'Why you, though?' she asked again.

'I was there. Anybody with any sense was still at breakfast, but Roy often goes to the allotment before work, and I've not much else to do unless somebody has an odd job for me. I'm not one for lingering in bed half the day. It's a life wasted, that kind of carry-on.'

Anna mashed the tea and brought it to the table. 'Let that brew,' she advised. 'Joseph Baxter needs a trained nurse.'

Eric swallowed nervously. 'Roy won't let any woman near him. It was a bit ... a bit embarrassing, really, because he told me some terrible stuff about what his dad had done to his mum. Then he asked me to let him know soon, and off he buggered. I stood there for that long, I was near froze to the spot. In fact, when I started to walk home, one of me wellies was stuck in the ice.'

This man was a pest, yet Anna loved his Scouse humour. 'But I still have to ask you again, Eric – why you in particular?'

'Ambulance driver, Liverpool 1942.'

'And what's that to do with the price of fish? I answered phones two nights a week through the war, but that doesn't make me a telephone engineer. Does he think changing gear and steering in a straight line makes you fit for a nursing career?'

'Me and the crew saved a couple of lives, and I don't mind washing folk and popping in to see if they're comfortable, but him? I'd sooner look after a rattlesnake.' Eric accepted a cup of tea. 'I'm ready for that. In fact, I'm probably ready for morphine.' He took a mouthful of the cup that cheers as long as you haven't just been asked to look after a monster. 'I needed that tea, Mrs Riley.'

'Anna.'

'All right. Anna.'

She sat opposite him once more. 'What's your problem? Just tell him no, you can't because you've jobs to do.'

'I can't. Poor lad's had it rough all his life, what with the leg, his mam dying young, and being left in the company of that bloody – excuse me – bastard of a father. It's just twelve noon till six, weekdays only. I can still get to my plot in the mornings and at weekends.'

'And you'll be a rich man, so. But money's not everything. Look. My Roisin's a friend of Roy's.

Let her find out what state the old man's in. Or go and take a look yourself.'

'I'm a coward, aren't I?'

'No. Oh, dear me, no. He's a special kind of bad. Let Rosh get to know exactly what's involved. I know this much – Roy swore he'd never have him back in the house. Roy owns the place, you see. But he's too soft-hearted to see even that bad swine on the streets. The lad will have no peace till Joseph Baxter's six feet under.'

Eric gazed into his cup. 'Well, I'm stopping short of murder, I can tell you that for no money.' He paused for a few seconds. 'What am I going to do all day stuck in a house? What if somebody wants a window fixed or a door shaved? I could be decorating for decent folk. And if I'm not there to do the jobs, people will find somebody else. I like going in different houses and gardens. I like wandering about. Stuck in there with him? I'd be crackers in a week.'

Rosh came in. 'Crackers in a week? My mother could drive you there in ten minutes, and you'd need no petrol.'

So Eric had to go through the tale all over again.

'You're not doing it,' Rosh said. 'Leave it with me. I'll talk to Roy tonight. The money may be good, but if you lose all your customers, you'll be worse off in the long run.' She studied the visitor. It was clear that he felt less than a man, that he didn't want a woman putting things right for him. 'Roy knows me well, Eric. Phil and he were friends at school together, so we go back a long way.'

'And I've grown veg next to him for years. I was just that gobsmacked this morning, I didn't know what to say. Look at the size of me. I'm fit enough for me age, but I don't fancy heaving Joseph Baxter about. And I should have said that; I should have just told him no.'

Anna managed to hold back a nervous giggle. Eric Holt looked as if an autumn breeze might knock him over. 'Look, Rosh won't make a show of you. She'll ask how things are going, then he'll mention you, and she'll tell him you have a lot of work. After all, you might have told us you had a queue of jobs when you were here doing the bedroom.'

Still glum, Eric stirred his second cuppa. 'I just want the ordinary life. Three pints on a Friday, you know what I mean? Then two or three hours a day on me plot or in me little shed on the allotment, read the papers on a Sunday, do a few jobs for people, fish and chips on me way home.'

Anna finally laughed. 'The ordinary life? Whatever's that when it's at home? I lost the best man in the world, and ended up here with this lot and two cats from the dark side. Mind, Winston's helping Alice with her asparagus.'

Rosh refused to react immediately. Anna knew the true name of her granddaughter's possible disability, but she had to make light of it, partly because she tried not to believe in it, mostly because she pretended that Alice was in a bad mood that had lasted years rather than hours.

'She has Aspergers,' Rosh explained for Eric's sake. 'Lives in a world of her own, not keen on talking to people.'

166

'Alice? Your littlest?'

Rosh nodded. 'She doesn't communicate well.'

Eric's eyes were wide. 'She didn't shut up while I was here one afternoon. I thought I'd never get finished. We did colours, the alphabet, Teddo One-Eye, being a tree, hair-brushing and would I teach her to whistle.'

'When was that?' Rosh asked.

'You were hoovering, I think. Being a tree's hard on the arms – I nearly charged you extra.'

'You see?' Anna was triumphant. 'I told you – she's just in a very bad mood with us. She should have been born in Buckingham Palace to a classy family. We are a great disappointment.' She collected crockery and began to-ing and fro-ing between table and sink.

Eric was on his feet and starting to murder his hat all over again.

'She prefers men,' Rosh said quietly. 'She was always with her dad, because she was his princess. And she tries to hang on to Kieran. Can it be as simple as that?'

No one replied.

Rosh led Eric to the front door. 'I'll be tactful,' she said. 'My mother doesn't do tact. She's like a double-decker bus stuck in a narrow alley, all noise and no progress.'

He cleared his throat. 'She's a good woman.'

'She is. Erm ... she likes the cinema. Romantic films with happy endings.'

'Right.' He rammed the abused cap onto his head and walked homeward.

Rosh turned and stopped immediately. Her mother was right behind her.

167

'She likes the cinema,' Anna said quietly, her tone coloured by mimicry. 'What the heck do you think you're up to, Roisin? Are you trying to pair me off with yon fellow?'

'No.'

'Then why ask him to take me out?'

'Because Alice needs him.'

Anna folded her arms and stretched her spine; sometimes, a woman wanted to be taller than she really was. 'Alice needs a man. She seems to like a deeper voice, though Kieran's is still light-weight. You go and find a man. Eric's a confirmed bachelor in his sixties. We're short of a man about your age. You don't have to marry him, for goodness' sake, but...'

'I don't want one.'

'Neither do I. So. What do we do?'

Rosh shrugged. 'Share Eric?'

At this point, both women collapsed against the walls. Rosh used a foot to slam shut the front door and watched as her mother slid down to the floor like a frail maiden in a silent movie. Rosh joined her on the rug. But there was no silence to be had, because they both howled and beat the walls with their hands, the floor with their heels.

'We want locking up,' Anna finally managed. All Rosh's life, mother and daughter had experienced shared lunacy. 'And how would we divide him?'

'Half a pint each,' Rosh suggested.

'And ... oh, my Lord ... and three pints on a Friday. Isn't that ... oh, save me ... isn't that what he said?'

Rosh nodded. 'Fish and chips on the way

168

home.'

'Cheap.'

They pulled themselves together with difficulty and started on the day's chores. Anna boiled ham, skimmed off the salt and set it to roast in the oven. She then tackled beds and upstairs dusting.

Rosh ironed, mended, sewed on loose buttons and thought about her husband. She'd been thirteen when he'd first asked what she was doing tonight, and, until she was fifteen, she'd delivered the same answer. Whatever she was doing would not involve him, was none of his business, and why didn't he move on – Lancaster was nice, or so she'd heard. Sometimes, for the sake of variety, she chose a different location. Madrid, Blackpool, Rome, Venice – the poor lad was urged to relocate in many widespread places.

But Philip Allen had been immovable. Little notes pushed into her hand on the way home, a couple of buttercups and a tired dandelion presented with a flourish as she had neared the house, Valentinc cards and, worst (or best) of all, *Phil loves Rosh* painted on the remaining wall of a bombed house. In purple. Everyone who travelled by bus to Liverpool saw that garish message.

She put down the blouse she was working on. Had he emerged from work thirty seconds earlier or later on that fateful day, the van would have missed him. She would have been ten thousand poorer, but what was money compared to the love of her life, the children's hero?

A little face insinuated itself round the door. 'Stop it.'

'Stop what?'

'Thinking about ... things. Depressing yourself.'

Rosh sighed despairingly. 'How do you know what I'm thinking?'

'I'm your mother.'

Rosh looked up at the ceiling before fixing her gaze on Mother. 'Placing a body in a box in the ground is not about laying to rest. It's about getting rid of matter that will only decay. The putting to rest happens in here.' She tapped her forehead with a finger. 'And I'm getting there. I've reached the stage where it's thinking rather than just feeling. So don't interfere. I have to get through this my way and without those sleeping pills. And with no help whatsoever from you.'

Anna withdrew. There were times when a mother didn't know best, and this was one of those rare occasions. Watching Rosh suffer had been purgatory for Anna. A widow herself, she knew exactly how her daughter had felt, but that hadn't helped. Each person had to learn for him or herself, no short cuts, no assisted passage, just a one-way ticket to despair, the return fare waiting until the mourner was ready to pick it up.

Rosh picked up her older daughter's blouse. Phil had been so proud of Philly. She was an excellent musician, though no one had managed to work out the source of her gift. Gift. Ah, yes, the dining room would need to be locked and the curtains closed, since the new piano would never fit down the chimney, so Santa had made special arrangements. That tale was for Alice only, of course.

170

Kieran was to have a brand new bicycle, while Alice's main present was a dolls' house, fully furnished and with lots of little 'people' to be placed here and there. Those two could be kept in Roy's house, but the piano had to be locked away like a criminal until Christmas Day. In fact, all the gifts could stay here, in the out-of-bounds dining room. She hadn't seen much of Roy recently; perhaps he wanted to keep himself to himself for the time being. Should she stay away? Would he want a visitor?

Anna returned. She was good at returning. 'I'll see to the children while you get ready to go across to Roy's.'

'He doesn't come home till just before six. Anyway, I'm ready enough.' The penny dropped. 'Ah, you want me to look nice for him. Shall I wear my tiara and a full-length evening gown? Do I propose?'

Anna wagged a finger. 'Now you know how it feels when you try to sell me on to Eric Holt. She likes the cinema, indeed. Go easy on Roy, but. He's one of the most unfortunate men I ever knew. If anyone ever deserved help, he does. Anyway, I've been thinking.'

'Don't go straining yourself, Mother.'

'We can do it. We make an extra plate of lunch and take it across. One stays till three o'clock, the other till six. I'll give up me evening job, and I'll be the one staying till six, because you'll want to be here when the kids come home. You won't need to go back to work, and there's neither of us afraid of him. What do you think?'

'No good. Roy doesn't want women in the

171

house.'

'We're not women; sure we're banshees or viragos or whatever. One bad word out of him, and I'll have him chained up like a mad dog. Who's afraid of a man whose ticker's on its last tock?'

'Mother, the job ends when he dies. It has a limited future.'

'Then I'll do it by meself.'

'Oh, will you now? And what if he has a paddy? What if he kicks off and clobbers you with his walking stick? And you're going to give him the bed bath?'

It was clear that Anna had given no thought to ablutions. 'Ah, no.' She shook her head. 'I draw the line at the waist. Just see what Roy says – you've nothing to lose. Now, let's get tidied up so the three urchins can come along and untidy us all over again. Women, you know, are just pack animals. Carry and place, lift and lower, pick up and drop. Who picks us up when we drop? Another woman, that's who.'

Rosh grinned behind a hand. Mother would have made a fabulous suffragette, but even London wasn't bad enough to deserve Anna Riley. However, she had to admit to herself that Anna Riley was magnificent. That so small a body should contain so huge a personality was miraculous.

The children came home. As predicted by their grandmother, Kieran and Philly left a trail of stuff in their wake. Alice didn't. She hung up her coat and satchel before going upstairs with Teddo in search of Winston. According to experts, obsessive behaviour was part of the syndrome. 'Syndrome?' Anna whispered. 'People are stupid.'

She was ready for the Terrible Two. 'Pick up every piece of yourselves, feet included, and return this house to the state it was in before you arrived. Alice has cleared up after herself, but you two are throwing in our faces all the work we did today. Your mother's not a servant, so buck up and pick up.'

They bucked up and picked up. Now she would have another go at Rosh. 'Wear that nice petrol blue skirt. Cheer him up a bit.'

'Torment him, you mean. I'm not the sort that plagues decent folk. If he wants a wife, he can look elsewhere. Now, unless you want me to go across in curlers and headscarf, shut up. In fact, shut up anyway, because you're getting on my nerves in a big way.'

When the meal was finished, Anna put on her coat in preparation for going to work. 'Philly will look after Alice when you go to see Roy.'

'No, Alice can come with me.'

Anna stopped getting ready. 'That innocent child is not going into Joseph Baxter's house, Rosh. I know we've seen nothing of him lately and he's likely confined to his bed, but he still has a mouth like a sewer, I expect. No. I shall stay here and miss my work.'

'And lose your job.'

'So? It's mine to lose.' She paused. 'Stay there, Muhammad, while I fetch the mountain. Send the children upstairs, and take Roy into the kitchen. We want this sorted out for poor Eric's sake. And for Roy, of course.'

Rosh folded her arms. 'Listen, you. For once, shut your mouth and use your ears. This ... conversation has to take place on his territory.'

'With Alice listening? You don't know how much she takes in, do you? So, Miss Clever Clogs, you go alone and I'll go late to my work. The place is locked, and I'm the one with a key, so I'll go into the offices when you return.'

It was turning into another three ring circus. But the younger woman had to admit that her mother was right, as usual. No one knew how much of life Alice took on board, and Rosh shouldn't need to hide behind an infant, shouldn't be afraid of anyone or anything. But she hadn't spoken to Roy for ages, and she felt ... shy. After all that fetching and carrying vegetables from his allotment, Roy had made himself scarce. Perhaps he didn't want to see anyone.

'Go,' Anna urged. 'I don't want to be cleaning ashtrays and desks till midnight.'

'I feel daft. I feel as if I'm pushing myself in where I'm not wanted.'

Anna kept her counsel. The day Roy Baxter stopped wanting Rosh, Anna would eat her best church hat, veil and hatpin included. It was far too soon for Rosh to be thinking of a second husband, but there was a lot to be said for a man friend. Men knew about screwdrivers, electricity and bicycles. They could reach things on high shelves, drive cars, dig gardens and mend most household appliances. For such reasons, a man should be kept on one side until needed. And Roy grew vegetables...

'I'm going,' Rosh said.

'Good. More fuss than an Orange Day parade with King Billy falling off his horse into a sea of good Catholics. Away with you. My grand-children and I have homework to do.'

Rosh pulled on a cardigan and crossed the street. What was she supposed to say? Though it was more a case of what not to say, because Eric Holt's dignity must be preserved at all costs.

Roy opened the door. 'Oh,' he said.

'That's a good start.' She waited. 'Am I to stay on the doorstep? If so, would you pass me a coat or a blanket?'

'Erm. Come in, Rosh. I'm just finishing his bed bath. Go through and sit. I'll make a cuppa in a few minutes.'

She entered the hall, turning right for the living room. It was beautiful. Clean fireplace, new three-piece suite, new carpet square, new paint and wallpaper. Roy's mother's china was on display in a glass-fronted cabinet, and her photograph sat on top of the same piece. A beautiful mirror almost covered the chimney breast, while decent prints hung in groups in the recesses. On the wall opposite the fireplace, a friendly pendulum clock ticked softly.

He'd done the kitchen, too. It sparkled. He'd fitted new cupboards, a nice sink, a central table with place mats and good, solid dining chairs. The room looked so big. The airer, on a pulley in front of the chimney breast, was used now not for drying washing, but for hanging copper-bottomed pans from butchers' hooks. Roy had made a huge statement; this was his house, his décor, his idea of pleasant living. She went back to the living room

175

and sat.

He entered. 'Hello,' he said.

'Roy, this is beautiful. All your own work, I take it?'

'Yes. I may have a crippled leg, but I can still do most things. Eric Holt helped a bit. Tea?' The eleventh commandment in Liverpool was that visitors drank tea. If they weren't offered tea, they were business folk, and that was a different game altogether.

In the kitchen, Roy leaned for support against the sink. He hadn't seen her for a while, but nothing had changed. For over twenty years he had loved the woman, and she still made his heart and his leg ache. The latter gave him pain as if reminding him that he wasn't whole, wasn't perfect, didn't come up to scratch in the presence of the beloved.

'Can I help?' she called.

'No, thanks. Everything's rearranged, so I need to look for stuff.' He found a tray, cups with matching saucers, sugar bowl, milk jug, teapot, spoons.

'Where've you gone?' The less than melodious demand floated down the stairwell.

'Ignore him,' Roy shouted. 'He can dry himself.' He entered eventually bearing tea and biscuits. 'You be mother,' he suggested, 'while I go and see to the one above. He is killing me.'

'How is he?' Rosh asked politely.

'As bad as Satan, but twice as ugly.' Roy left the room.

Upstairs, he finished attending to the man in the bed. 'Who's downstairs?' Baxter Senior asked.

176

'None of your business. My house, my life, my company. You're a lodger till I can find somewhere to dump you. Now, shut up while I have a cup of tea.'

'It's a woman. Little beads of sweat on your forehead, Roylston. If I could walk a bit better without losing my breath, I'd come down and have a look at her.'

'Feel free. Watch the carpet on the fourth stair down, you might break your neck.'

'You'd like that.'

Roy hung the towel on the clothes horse. 'I haven't decorated the hall, stairs and landing yet, so feel free to make a mess. Now. I am going down to drink tea with a friend.'

With a friend. Roy looked at his image in the bathroom mirror. He wasn't ugly. Dark brown hair, plenty of it, dark brown eyes, and he was tall enough, though a bit shorter on the bad leg. With a friend. Phil Allen had been his mate, but Phil's wife was Roy's goddess. She was like a jewel in a shop window; unattainable, but looking cost nothing. Not true. Looking had cost him his whole heart and his whole life. Now he was doing up the house to sell, because he could no longer bear to live near Rosh.

She smiled at him when he returned. 'Still a nasty old nuisance, then?'

'Oh, yes. He's taking full advantage of the order to rest, but I fear he'll be messing up my decorating any day now. Still, I can't keep him out of my hair for ever, can I?'

'I suppose not.' Rosh handed him a cup of tea. For her part, most of the expected awkwardness

177

seemed to have dissipated. The gifts of fruit, vegetables and flowers had ceased to arrive, and she felt settled, almost at home in his company. This was hardly surprising, as they'd known each other since their early years. He was a safe place and a nice man.

'So,' he said. 'Are you here for a particular reason?'

'Er ... no. Just to see how you are, really.' She paused fractionally. 'I was going to ask you to look after the children's Christmas gifts, but there's no need. Philly's having a new piano, so we'll have to lock the dining room until Christmas morning, and I'll keep everything in there.'

'Oh. Right.'

He picked up the plate of biscuits. 'The custard creams are quite good.'

Rosh took one. 'Thanks, Phil.'

Roy's hand froze in mid-air for a split second. Phil? Did she realize she'd called him Phil? And how did he feel about that? On the one hand, she was clearly contented and safe in his presence, yet he wasn't Phil, didn't want to be Phil. But she seemed so relaxed, so at ease.

'How are you managing?' she was asking now.

He explained about giving the patient breakfast, leaving flasks of tea and soup with a sandwich for lunch, making the evening meal after work. 'Weekends are hell,' he said, 'but I've asked Eric Holt to come in at twelve and see to him on weekdays. He can peel veg and start cooking for when I get back at six.'

So here came Rosh's chance. 'Eric's got loads of work on, Roy. When he did my bedroom, he

178

was saying he had too many jobs. So I thought Mother and I could do it.'

Roy closed his mouth with an audible snap. 'No bloody way. I'll advertise.'

'But Roy–'

'No. It's my mess, so let me deal with it. You know how he was with my mam. And you can smile, plead, beg all you like, but no way am I leaving you or your mother with a cruel article like that thing. You don't know him. I hope you never do get to know him.'

Rosh realized that argument would be futile. Even if she came up with something sensible, Roy was dug in deeply enough to form part of the foundations of a new building. Still, she had to try. 'Norma Shuttle,' she pronounced after a ten-second gap. 'Lives at the St Johns Road end, built like a battleship. In fact, Phil said the Navy was using her as a model for an unsinkable carrier.'

He covered a smile with his cup. Sometimes, he forgot the fun side of her. Women as beautiful as this one seldom displayed humour, because they were usually too busy messing with their hair or peering into a handbag mirror. 'So you mean that tall, round woman with a face like a fit?'

Rosh nodded. 'She could hold him down with one hand and clean the house with the other. In fact, when a dray horse was resting, they used her instead. She's pulled more gallons of ale than any barmaid. The other horses made her an honorary member at the brewery stable; she had her own stall and nosebag, plus Guinness in her trough.'

'Sounds very attractive.'

179

'If you like gargoyles, she is.'

'I already have a gargoyle.'

Rosh nodded pensively. 'What about Christmas?' she asked.

He shrugged. 'We've not had Christmas since Mum died.'

'Come to us,' she begged on a sudden whim. 'I'll plate a dinner up for him, and you can carry it across. But whether or not he's well enough, don't bring him anywhere near my house.'

Roy considered the offer. 'Alice doesn't like new people.'

'You're not exactly new. And she's not exactly in charge. I'm the boss.'

'Yes. I can see that.' Roy turned his head slightly. 'He's listening at the top of the stairs. Can't walk to the bathroom, has to have a commode and a bed bath, but he's managed to get to the landing.'

'I can't hear anything,' Rosh said.

'Ah, but I'm wired differently. Like the blokes who find water in a drought, I always know where he is.'

Within seconds, they both knew where he was. The stairs delivered their visitor to a new location just inside the front door. He screamed. It sounded as if he managed to hit every single step during the fall. And two people remained seated through many ticks of the friendly clock; they were riveted by shock to their chairs.

Rumour spreads faster than measles round here. Joseph Baxter's in a bad way, possibly clobbered by his son. Well, I won't blame Roy Baxter. His old man's

180

a right bastard from what I've heard in the shop while pretending to dust the tobacco jars. I hope he bloody dies. I know what it is to have rotten parents...

Seven

The desk sergeant was fed up all the way to his wisdom teeth, one of which was severely impacted. 'Madam,' he said, manufactured patience etched into both syllables, 'you cannot carry on like this.'

'Oh, she can,' said the younger of the two women. 'You should see her when the Orange march is on. You know the row of women who line the route, skirts over their heads, bottoms facing Prince Billy? Well, my mother makes their emerald-green knickers.'

He sighed heavily. Some days were easy. Some days had burglars, thieves and pickpockets. Even drunken fights were simple to deal with when compared to Mrs Anna Riley. The man in the interview room was only being questioned, for God's sake. 'Sit down, please,' he begged.

'Mrs Roisin Allen?' called a disembodied voice. 'Interview room two, please.' The name Roisin came through as dried fruit.

Anna stared at the desk sergeant. 'You said that without moving your lips. And her name is pronounced Rosheen, nothing to do with raisins.' She then turned to her daughter. 'Go in and tell them what happened. I'm away for a few minutes, but I'll be back with reinforcements.' She approached the desk. 'Never underguesstimate the power of the people. Especially when some of

182

us are Irish.' She shot out of the police station while Rosh made her way into the bowels of the building. It was dark, unfriendly, and it smelled of fear and human waste. She experienced a strong urge to run home for a bath.

'Come in, come in,' suggested a friendly female officer from the doorway of Interview Two. 'I'm Constable Lewis, and this is Inspector Clarke.'

Rosh followed the constable into the room. It was cream and green, and the man seated at the table was in plain clothes. 'Is he really a policeman?' she asked. 'He looks like the man from the Prudential, same moustache, same disappointed face.' The table was scarred. Perhaps it had been involved in the Second World War. She was offered a cigarette, and she refused with thanks. 'They kill budgies,' she said seriously. 'Our Bluey never smoked as such, but I think he was a second-hand addict. So we all stopped.' Rosh was nervous. It wasn't every week she was forced to step over a dead neighbour.

'Sit down, please,' the inspector said after casting a meaningful glance in the direction of his partner in crime. 'Full name?'

'Are you sure?'

'Yes.'

'Roisin – that's R-O-I-S-I-N – Carlita Maria Conchita Sebando Riley Allen.'

The inspector stared hard at his victim. 'You taking the wee-wee?' he asked.

She shook her head. 'Not at all. You see, way back to the time of another Queen Elizabeth, the English were no better than pirates. Some of the Armada ships got hunted down and stranded in

183

southern Ireland, and the sailors stayed and married Irish women. The oldest daughter got landed with Irish and Spanish names. Even when my father's family relocated to a different Irish county, then to England, the tradition continued, or so I was led to understand.'

The man passed a sheet of paper across the table. 'Write it there, please.'

She wrote it and handed it back. 'There you go. You have to lisp on the Spanish S. One of the kings lisped, so everybody joined in to keep him company and save him from feeling daft.'

Again, the man's eyes slid sideways. They seemed to have a right one here.

The questioning began. Had she been in the company of Mr Roy Baxter yesterday evening? Yes, she had. What had been the purpose of her visit? To make sure he was all right. Why might he not be all right? Because he worked full-time in town, had a bad leg, and was looking after his father, a heart attack victim. Had Mr Roy Baxter seemed well? Yes, Mr Roy Baxter had seemed well. He'd even been decorating and cleaning up. Had she seen Mr Joseph Baxter? No. Well, yes, but only after his accident.

'You were there when Mr Joseph Baxter fell?'

'I was.'

The man put down his pen. 'You are aware that he supposedly died instantly of a broken neck?'

'I am now, yes. But at the time, I just jumped over him and ran to the phone box.'

'Where you nine-nine-nined?'

Rosh nodded. 'I asked for an ambulance, although when they questioned me on the phone, I didn't know whether he was dead or alive. When I got back to the house, I could tell he was dead. His neck and head looked wrong.'

'Do you think the body had been moved at all? Was it possible that he was only stunned and that his neck was broken deliberately after you had left the house?'

Rosh glared at the representatives of law and order. 'No. I passed a neighbour. You've interviewed Mimi Atkinson. She arrived at Roy's seconds after I left. The door was wide open, because I was in a bit of a hurry. Had anyone been breaking anyone's neck, Mimi would have seen it. The only thing that got broken deliberately was the record for the two-hundred-yard sprint to the phone box. I should be in the Olympics. Anyway, when I jumped over him to get out to the phone, I didn't see his top half. I was so scared, you see.'

A few beats of time passed. 'You were scared, Mrs ... er Allen?'

'Yes.'

'Why?'

'Too much death around me. My dad five years ago, my husband in a traffic accident a few months back.'

'Very sorry, Mrs Allen.'

'Thank you.'

The man undid the top button of his shirt and loosened his tie. 'Some of the questions I need to ask are not pleasant.'

'Fire away. I'm no liar.'

He took a deep breath. 'Did Mr Baxter push his father?'

'No. He did not.'

185

'Are you sure?'

'Unless he can be in two places at once. We were seated opposite each other in the parlour when the old man fell. Also, Roy's the cleanest-living man I know. Roy Baxter couldn't hurt a flea.'

The inspector cleared his throat. 'He hated his father. The neighbours told us that.'

'We all hated his father, God forgive us. He was a nasty piece of work.'

Once again, time passed sluggishly. 'Did you push him?'

'No. I wouldn't dirty my hands. Now, listen to me, please. Roy heard him moving about and thought he might have been listening to us at the top of the stairs. Which went to prove that he could have got himself to the bathroom instead of using a commode and demanding bed baths. Then he fell.'

A glance passed between the inspector and the female constable. 'Mrs Allen,' the policewoman began, 'do you see a great deal of Roy Baxter?'

The situation was ridiculous, and Rosh could not help herself. 'No, he's always fully clothed. And this is stupid. Roy was my husband's best friend. We are not lovers. And if your questions get any dafter, you can fetch me a lawyer from Roy's firm.'

'You haven't been charged with anything,' the woman said.

'You are questioning my character, and I don't like that. Roy didn't kill anyone, and I didn't kill anyone. We have been friends for about twenty years. In case you haven't noticed – which wouldn't surprise me in the least – Roy has a bad limp. He's not steady enough on his leg to break anybody's neck. His hip's been affected by the way he's forced to walk – don't you people notice anything? He's not supple. Phil and I looked after him at school while others mocked him.' She leaned forward. 'Should Roy and I decide to become a couple, we'll be sure to send the two of you invitations to the wedding, but don't start holding your breath in anticipation.'

The two officers rose to their feet. 'Thank you,' said the male half of the inquisition. 'If we need you again, we'll let you know.'

As Rosh emerged from Interview Two, Roy came out of One. She followed him into the desk sergeant's area where Mother was having another go at the poor man. Through the half-open door, the sounds of an uninhibited and unrehearsed choir attacked the ears of everyone in the station.

'Our neighbours,' Anna said when she was close enough to shout in her daughter's ear. 'I fetched them to make a stand for Roy. But they all know different songs, so they're all singing different songs.' She walked to the door and opened it wide. The noise stopped. 'They don't appreciate good music in here, people. Away to your homes, as these policemen are threatening to read the Riot Act.'

Outside, Rosh clung to Roy's arm. 'You all right?'

'They believe me now, though they started asking had I finished him off while you were at the phone box. But you left the front door wide open, and Mimi Atkinson was passing, so she's

187

witness to the fact that I didn't break his neck. You hadn't even reached the first corner when Mimi got there, so I hadn't time for murder. Anyway, there would have been different marks on his body. So, how did you go on?'

She shrugged. 'I think we're in the clear. Our stories probably matched, but not too closely, not as if they were rehearsed. Mother says they're doing a post-mortem at the hospital, because they think he was already dead before his neck broke. Heart attack, probably.'

'Thanks for being there, Rosh.'

'I'll always be there. Phil and I were there for you, and you were there for us. Nothing's changed, except we're missing Phil. You come to us for Christmas and New Year, if you can put up with Mother, that is.'

'She's magnificent, Rosh. I've never met any-one like her.'

'Aren't you the lucky one?'

Anna joined them on the walk home. She was quieter, but she muttered under her breath about the stupidity of the police, the freezing cold, the price of capons, turkeys and bacon, the need to get to work tonight, since she hadn't as good an excuse as she'd had yesterday.

'Mother?'

'What?'

'Shut up.'

Several of the neighbours approached them, some stopping to shake Roy's hand. In spite of all the interruptions, the three eventually reached Lawton Road and entered the Allen house. Roy walked in without hesitation. His own place was the scene of a sudden, violent death, and he would be sleeping on Rosh's sofa until further notice. He picked up a small case containing the few personal belongings he had been allowed to remove from his bedroom across the road.

In Rosh's bathroom, he stared at his reflection in a mirror above the washbasin. He heard his long-dead mother telling him he looked like nobody owned him. It was true. Numbed to the bone, he didn't know how to feel. There was no joy, no relief, no sadness. He was empty. But he could manage a shave, surely? The face in the glass looked like that of a tramp who hadn't bathed in a month.

He was halfway through soaping his face when a small person arrived by his side. She carried with her a wooden duckboard, and she placed this next to him before climbing on to its surface. 'Hello, Alice,' he said.

The child took the brush from him and slathered white froth all over her cheeks, chin and neck. 'Ready, steady, go,' she told him. 'Do it.'

While he used the razor, Alice employed the handle of her toothbrush. Every time he flicked his harvest into the bowl, she followed suit. 'Not on clothes,' she ordered. They shared a towel to wipe their faces before Alice returned the duckboard to its rightful place beside the bath. 'All done,' she said.

'All done,' he repeated.

She disappeared, only to come back immediately with Winston. The animal was so big that he should have carried the child. 'Winston,' she explained breathlessly. 'He is good for me; Gran

189

says that.' She dropped the cat, who seemed displeased. After two flicks of an angry tail, he left the scene, followed by Alice.

Roy crammed all his stuff into his toiletries bag. His eyes stung, and he scarcely knew why. 'Oh, Phil,' he mumbled. For some reason beyond his comprehension, the death of his father prompted the mourning of Phil, his best friend. Alice had played her part, of course.

He managed to reach the front downstairs room without any further encounters. Ready to burst into tears, he sat on the sofa and tried to compose himself. A few seconds passed before he realized that he was not alone. Ah, it was the wild, invisible one, the dark destroyer, the killer of birds. Purring like the engine of a small car, Lucy-Furr joined him, rubbing her side along his left arm. This cat was reputed to deal with grief. On her first day in the Allen house, she had comforted Rosh.

He didn't cry. Instead, he sat with the knowledgeable cat, stroking jet-coloured fur and listening to her expression of contentment.

Rosh entered with a cup of tea. 'Ah, there she is. I've been looking for her. She owes me a pair of stockings in sandalwood, Marks and Spencer. And one of Alice's headbands seems to have gone for a walk.'

'Alice had a shave with me,' he said.

Rosh dropped into an armchair. 'She used to do that with her dad.'

'I guessed as much. And she talked to me.'

'Yes. She even talks to me now. And there's a bit of cheek in her these days. She's been using my make-up, staggering round in heels, pinching the

190

perfume Phil bought me. That's why I think she's nearer normal than she used to be. It's supposed to be incurable, but Alice has a good brain, and she's not completely locked inside herself. She'll surprise us all.'

Roy drank his tea. If he stayed at Rosh's for much longer, Alice might get used to him. There was something about the little girl that tugged hard at his heartstrings. There was something about the little girl's mother, too...

'What's the matter, Roy?'

She could read him like an open book. Phil had often complained about her ability to know what he was thinking, where he'd been, what he'd done. 'My wife is psychic,' he used to say.

'Roy?'

'I think I should stay somewhere else. Alice seems to be getting used to me. Who will she shave with when I've gone?'

'My mother? She does have a healthy moustache. No, I'm joking. While Alice hates change, I've noticed just lately that she's beginning to adjust more quickly. When Phil died, she looked for him all the time. Then she stopped. She'll hang on to Kieran, and she'll survive, Roy. Why don't you start thinking about yourself for a change? Plan a holiday, finish the house, buy a record player and listen to music.'

Was it going to be that simple? A week alone in Paris or Rome, a lifetime alone with Mozart and Beethoven, Jerry Lee Lewis for a bit of light relief? 'I feel numb,' he said.

'You lost your dad. Whatever he was, the man was your father.'

Roy cleared his throat. 'When you came to the house and I went upstairs to him ... well ... I told him to feel free to fall down the stairs. It was as if I summoned demons and wished it on him. Yes, I know what he was and yes, I've long wanted him gone, but–'

'Stop this. Stop it now, Roy Baxter. Remember what he did to your mother. Remember the broken child that poor woman became. He wouldn't even feed her when she was on her deathbed. And if Mother and I come to the funeral, it will be to support you. Until the police let you back in your house, you stay here. That's an order.'

'Yes, ma'am.'

She stood up. 'There's a meal on the table in the kitchen. We put it in the oven on a low light before going to the police station. You'd better eat before our queen bee decides to come through and spoon-feed you. If you think I'm tough, you should see her when she's riled.'

'Yes, ma'am.'

'And stop saying that.'

'Yes, Rosh.'

She glared at him. 'Get in that kitchen now. You've a funeral to plan. My mother's good at funerals. She's in her element when picking hymns.'

In that moment, Roy made a decision. He wouldn't sell the house. He couldn't sell the house. He had to be near Rosh and her family; he had to carry on with the old pain in his heart.

As the months had drifted by, the newspapers

192

had ceased to print reports about three dead men, a burnt-out car and the efforts of police to find the perpetrators. Presses raged on instead about the effects of thalidomide, de Gaulle being elected President of France, Prime Minister Macmillan opening the first of Britain's motorways. Three fewer London racketeers might well be a source of relief for the country's police. London's East End, caught now in the grip of several feuding gangs, was no longer a place in which to begin a new business; the protection game was being run by hard players whose eyes were beginning to fix on the West End, too.

When Christmas loomed on the horizon, Scouse Alley began preparations for an annual event to which many lone pensioners were invited. Each year, women helpers cooked poultry at home, while the rest of the meal was prepared on site, in the large kitchen. Even young Seamus and his friends played a part by setting tables and making paper chains. This was the business's way of repaying the regulars; the dockers who ate here chose the old people who would be fed, while Paddy O'Neil paid not just for the meals, but also for coaches in which the diners would be transported from their homes to Scouse Alley, and returned to their own firesides once the meal was over.

Maureen was late again. So fraught was she these days that little was expected when it came to timekeeping. She dragged her mother to the outer door. 'Can't find him,' she whispered. 'And I don't know how much longer I can carry on, because he's driving me mad. I'll be as bad as him any day now. I think mental illness is catching, because I'm all of a tremble.'

Paddy, Kevin, Maureen and the stalwarts who had helped on that fateful wedding night had begun to relax slightly, but Maureen's Tom had entered a state worse than Russia. He sat for much of the time in his chair, though he no longer rested. Instead, he rocked back and forth, sometimes muttering under his breath, often falling into an exhausted sleep after the constant movement. He ate seldom, refused to communicate, and was fast becoming a problem that could not be contained for much longer, since he had started to wander off from time to time. He had lost his job, his family life and his mind.

Paddy touched her daughter's arm. 'I blame all our lads for getting involved down in London. It's not Tom's fault, and thank God your boys gave you the gun. I thought I'd never have to say such words, but I must, because your man saved us all. And look how he's repaid for his heroism.'

'Well, he's not here at the moment,' Maureen said. 'I've found him a few times near the shed. He ... he killed them from there. I suppose it's what you might call the scene of the crime.'

Paddy tutted. 'Finding Seamus full of bullets would have been a crime. I mean, what was Tom supposed to do? Let them kill every person at the wedding? He's lost his ability to reason with himself, hasn't he?'

'Yes.' Maureen nodded furiously. 'And if I can't find him, I can't help him get his brain back, can I?'

'You're exhausted, but.' Paddy glanced furtively

over her shoulder. 'Do you think he's running round telling folk what he's done?'

'He doesn't talk.'

'He doesn't talk to us, but he may talk when we're not there, and we've no way of knowing, because we aren't there.'

'True, though you're talking Irish again. Have you enough help here? And can you keep an eye on Seamus?'

'Yes, yes. You go.' The diners were beginning to arrive for their small glass of sherry. The pattern was always the same; sherry, soup, main course with wine or beer, followed by Christmas pudding and a tot of brandy before they went home. It was a tradition Paddy had no intention of neglecting. But it was beginning to look as if Tom, her well-loved son-in-law, might get everyone in trouble very soon. 'Did he see the Christmas cards?' she asked.

'I showed them to him, but I don't know whether he actually saw them. I'm worn out, Mam.'

'Find him and get a doctor. This has to be dealt with.'

'And if he tells the doctor what happened on our Reen's wedding day?'

Paddy shrugged. 'Doctors take that hippo-critical vow, don't they? Like priests, they can't say a word.' Internally, Paddy was still struggling with the Christmas cards, two from Michael, two from Finbar. The stamps had been franked in a town not far from Liverpool—

'I think you're wanted, Mam.'

'Yes. Good luck, so.' Paddy pinned a radiant

smile to the lower half of her face. She greeted new people, took care not to ask after those who had failed to arrive. Ernie Avago wasn't here, of course. Ernie, God rest his bones, had been one of the very best.

The Christmas king and queen were chosen and given crowns and white-trimmed scarlet cloaks. These were the two whose birthdays fell closest to Christmas, and they took their place at the centre of one of the large tables. A pianist played soft music, soup arrived, and the party was under way.

When the meal was over, a small choir came to sing for the diners. These children had been plucked from the ranks of a local Catholic school, and they sounded like angels. Paddy stood for a while and gazed at the scene. In this room, the vulnerable smiled, sang and clapped. These were the bookends of life, the overture and the finale. How well they treated each other; how each group rejoiced in the company of the other. She wanted to weep, but she wouldn't. Paddy and Kevin O'Neil were the backbone of the family, a family that had lost four members, while two others were at large and possibly not too far away. Emotion was best hidden. Only at home did Paddy and Kevin weep and support each other.

She offered up a silent prayer for her sons and her brothers, attaching a postscript for Finbar and Michael, her grandsons. Maureen also got a mention, because Maureen was going through hell. Her brothers and uncles were dead, two of her sons were missing, and her husband was showing few signs of returning to the real world. Poor Maureen and Seamus were about to have a very sad Christmas. 'And God help our Tom,' she concluded.

He'd seemed to be all right at first. Never comfortable about what he had been forced to do, Tom Walsh had pushed it all to the back of his mind, where it had festered, grown caustic and burned its way through to his consciousness. No matter what anyone said, he insisted that he was a murderer. Lately, he didn't even listen properly, and he never replied.

But Paddy could do nothing about any of it. As daylight began to fade, she waved off the coaches before joining in the big clean-up. While they scrubbed, Paddy and her helpers found two lower jaw dentures, six pairs of spectacles, three gloves, all odd, a scarf, a wallet and four purses. 'All we're short of is five gold rings and a partridge in a pear tree,' she told the company. The collection was about par for the course, and all items were locked away securely. Next week, dock workers would arrive with descriptions of missing items, and all would be returned.

Meanwhile, Maureen was trudging her way through the streets of Liverpool. By no means the biggest city in England, it seemed sizeable on one of the last shopping days before Christmas, especially when a searcher went into every pub and every alleyway. She fought her way past many bodies, sometimes separating man from wife or mother from child, so high was her level of anxiety.

Exhausted beyond measure, she gave up and went to look for a bus. He would probably be at home when she finally got back, since his inner compass still seemed to be in working order. Oh, God. How was she going to get through to him? It was like trying to communicate with someone who had suddenly lost the ability to see, hear or feel. And her feet were giving her hell.

Then she spotted him. He stood where thousands of Liverpudlians had lingered over the years, arms on the railings, eyes staring out to the steely grey and angry river. He was at the Pier Head. How many had come here for a good think, for a bit of space away from family, for a place in which problems might be thought through without interruption by spouse or by children? Often, there would be up to a dozen or so gazing out at the river and towards the Irish Sea.

Maureen held back. There was something different about him. And it wasn't just that he wasn't rocking in that blinking chair. She couldn't see his face, yet she knew he had changed. Was he worse, was he better? Was he thinking about jumping into that seething mass of water?

A man close by was talking to Tom. What were they discussing? Maureen's heart jumped before picking up speed. Surely Tom wouldn't unburden himself to a stranger? The unknown man displayed a limp when he moved, and one of his feet was in a built-up shoe. *Oh, God, please don't let my Tom place himself in the hands of the law. Why can't he talk to me? I'm his bloody wife, you know. Sometimes, I wonder whose side you're on, God. Just lately, you're not looking after us.*

The two men were shaking hands, and Tom was talking. *So you can talk to him, but not to me, eh? Wait till I get you home, you great big bundle of*

198

washing. Because that's what you've become, just a pile of shirts to be laundered and ironed. As a husband, you're as much use as a guard dog with dentures. Right. Time I sorted you out. Mentally, she pushed up her sleeves and prepared for battle.

The stranger limped away a few seconds before Maureen's arrival at the railings. She stood in silence next to Tom for a while.

'Oh. Hello, love,' he said.

That was an improvement, she decided. Three words. It wasn't much, but she had to be thankful for small mercies. 'Never mind "Hello, love". I should be at Scouse Alley helping me mother. That place'll be like a bloody pigsty by now, and I should be pulling me weight. But no. I have to traipse all over town looking for you. I've had more words out of our Seamus these past weeks. Where've you been?'

'Confession,' he replied. 'And to see Greenhalgh.'

'Who has confessions on a Saturday?'

'A few churches do. But I knocked at the presbytery and spoke face to face, didn't go in the box.' He shook his head thoughtfully. 'I can't even remember the name of the church. Might be St Columba's. It got bombed and rebuilt.'

'Right.' She waited.

'Anyway, I've got absolution. Special circumstances. We both finished up crying, me and the priest. He said I'm a good family man with a conscience and told me to think about David and Goliath.'

'Right.' Maureen's heart slowed to nearly normal.

'You keep saying right.'

'Do I? And you've been saying bugger all for weeks. It's been me, just me talking. The only punctuation I got was from our Seamus, and he doesn't always make full sense. Imagine what he's gone through. Me as well. It's been no bowl of cherries.'

'I'm sorry.'

'I should hope so.' She paused. 'Him with the game leg. What were you saying to him? And who is he?'

Tom moved his head and stared out at the Mersey once more. 'Roy. Found me nearly crying in my beer. Good bloke. He just sat there for a while in the pub before asking what he could do to help. So I told him to take me to a church that was nowhere near Bootle. He waited for me at the presbytery, then we came back here after a cup of coffee in Maggie Moore's caff. I told him I felt better, and he was glad.'

'Good. Are we going home now?'

'In a bit. Roy opened up and talked to me about his dad dying. He'd told his dad to die, and he did die. The dad was a bad man, but Roy felt as if he'd made it happen. The police thought Roy had pushed him down the stairs or broken his neck after an accidental fall, but that was all rubbish. There's this young widow he loves, and he hurts when he sees her, hurts when he doesn't see her.' Tom turned and looked at his long-suffering wife. 'And that was when I felt lucky, because I got my girl.'

Maureen blushed. At her age, she was in no fit state for blushing; it didn't suit her one bit. For a start, it made her look drunk. The singing was not the only result of her infrequent over-indulgence in the Guinness, since she also had a tendency to become flushed and somewhat luminous in the facial department. Tom had been known to declare in the past that they never needed a torch, because they just followed his wife's nose when she'd been on a bender. 'I got my girl,' he repeated. 'And if this was wartime, you'd need a blackout blind for that face. You've lit up like a Christmas tree.'

For answer, she clouted him with her handbag. He was well and safe, and that was all she needed to know. 'Don't go thinking anybody's missed you while you went for your walk on the dark side. And don't go thinking anybody's going to make a fuss of you, because you need a job for a kick-off.'

'No, I don't.'

'You what? Do you think money grows on trees?'

Tom shook his head. 'I told you I went to see Greenhaigh. Roy came there with me, too. Sound as a pound, that lad. Anyway, they're giving me the new Bootle Co-op when they've finished modernizing and fitting it. He said I was due for promotion anyway. I'm going to be the manager. It suits, because I have to build myself up first, and I don't start work for a couple of months. Course, he knew I'd been ill, but he thinks it was a chest infection that refused to shift. I have had that bad cough, so it wasn't much of a lie.'

'And all you needed was confession?'

He shrugged. 'I'm not out of the woods yet,

sweetheart. But yes, confession works. Forgiveness from a man of God is good liquor. One day at a time, eh? And we got Christmas cards from the boys.'

'So did Mam and Dad. Theirs came a couple of days later.' She looked at him quizzically. 'You noticed, then? You heard and saw?'

'Yes.'

Again, she swiped his arm with the bag. 'Why didn't you answer me?'

'Because I didn't want you to see a grown man cry. I couldn't talk about anything. Just give me a chance, Maureen. I feel as if somebody's waved a magic wand, but the miracle might not last.'

It would last, she decided when they climbed on the bus. She would make sure it bloody well lasted. The vehicle was packed with people and Christmas shopping, so she and Tom had to stand. They hung on to leather straps provided for that purpose. His right hand sought her left and clung to her until they reached their stop.

When they alighted, he got the third blow from her handbag. 'What's that about?' he asked.

'Holding me hand on the bus. People must have thought we're having an affair, because husbands and wives don't hold hands.'

He grinned for the first time in weeks. 'Did any of them on the bus know you?'

'Some might have.'

'And if they knew you, they'd know me, and they'd know we're married. If they didn't know us, who cares?'

'I care. It's not natural. Married people don't even talk to one another on a night out.'

'Sad,' he said before dragging her into his arms. Although the daylight was meagre and few people were out and about, she battered him yet again with her bag. He was a good kisser, but she was still going to kill him later. He probably thought he was on a promise, and he could think again. He was a great kisser, though...

It started with the rose bowl. A squat item in mottled pink glass, it was topped by a circle of wire with holes to help arrangements of short-stemmed blooms to remain stable. For several days following the move to Menlove Avenue, the article popped up all over the place. It travelled from landing windowsill to kitchen, to front living room, to dining room, to the main bedroom, to Anne-Marie's domain.

Don told himself it was nothing to worry about. Tess had always been fussy. She could go through half a dozen books of wallpaper samples without finding anything good enough for her. But when it came to the carpet...

He stood in the doorway, his jaw dropping, forehead creased in a frown, hands employed to steady himself by pushing against the jamb. A dart of pure terror pierced his chest. 'Tess?' he managed eventually. On her hands and knees, she looked over a shoulder and smiled at him. 'I thought if I started in the bay and worked backwards, I wouldn't end up painted into a corner.'

'What are you doing, love?'

'Painting them out. You don't like them; I don't like them any more. So they're going. No skaters' trails, just all grey.'

Don swallowed hard. St Faith's Infants' School was still in a state of recovery from deep trauma. Tess, in charge of costumes and props, had accidentally locked everything in the wrong storage cupboard. Alongside the manger, kings' crowns and angels' wings, three terrified children had been entombed. They had suffered nightmares ever since getting out of jail. Tess wasn't right.

Meals were strange. They were also served at some very odd times. Don's mother's rose bowl was currently on display in the centre of the front lawn alongside a frying pan and two tins of marrowfat peas. She wasn't just unhappy; she was absolutely crackers. 'Tess?'

'What?'

'You don't paint carpets. You take them up and buy new ones.'

'Waste of money,' was her reply.

There were times in life when a person didn't know what to do. This was one of those times. 'The paint will come off the carpet, Tess. It might never dry properly, because it's meant for wood, not wool. You can't carry on like this.'

'Like what?'

'Like what?' he repeated. 'Like locking kids in cupboards, cutting up your best curtains for King Herod's cloak, painting carpets, putting tinned veg on the lawn–'

'What?'

'You've two tins of marrowfats, a frying pan and my mam's rose bowl out there.'

'Stop fussing over nothing,' she insisted. 'Anyway, I must get on.'

He watched her getting on. There was no point

in trying to count, but there had to be more than a few thousand trails on a carpet of this size. Although the background was grey, the trails were multicoloured, and she was painting over each one with a fine brush dipped in the contents of a tin marked *Charcoal.*

Three weeks, they had lived here. Sean, who had been on the brink of leaving their previous home for a place of his own, seemed to be settling. Anne-Marie, with a new bedroom fit for a princess, was deliriously enchanted. When she wasn't dressing up, washing her hair or painting her face, she was walking casually up and down the avenue outside John Lennon's house. So determined was her blasé demeanour that she stuck out like a Blackpool tram on Southport beach. But Don's daughter's madness was temporary and hormonal; Tess's was in a class of its own.

He walked into the kitchen. Her dilemma had started here. There were eighteen cupboards and five drawers. This over-abundance of storage space had gone to Tess's head, and she had spent four days and a mint of money filling up every nook and cranny. There was now enough flour to furnish a bakery, the shoe-cleaning equipment kept company with tinned vegetables and fruit, while one large unit at ground level was packed with fresh, ironed linen and a baited mousetrap. She needed a doctor. She needed a lie-down in a darkened room with a cold cloth on her forehead.

Where were the kids? Why were they always there when you didn't want them, and out of sight the minute they were needed? Don returned to the hall and opened the front door. John Lennon was cross-legged in his oriel bay, guitar across his chest, lips moving, quiff tumbling into his eyes. There was no sign of Anne-Marie, no sign of any worshippers just now. The lone Quarry Man, oblivious to anything beyond his music, carried on with admirable dedication. If the lad would just put down the guitar and take up something sensible like plumbing, he would probably go far.

Anne-Marie had a second string to her bow these days. She was wont to visit Allerton, where she had discovered the home of one Paul McCartney. Paul, more conventionally pretty than his friend, had the sort of face that would collapse suddenly. He looked younger than his years, whereas Lennon seemed older, but John's bone structure would serve him better. According to Tess, that was. According to Tess before she went doolally.

And she was very probably continuing to paint the carpet. 'Why am I standing here thinking about a skiffle band? I've a wife gone mental in there.' He picked up frying pan, tins and rose bowl. It had all started so innocently. Failing to find a permanent home for an ornament was normal. But Tess had gone berserk. Dr Byrne had come up with some daft idea about post-partum depression having turned to psychosis, but Anne-Marie was fifteen, Sean was eighteen, and Tess hadn't seemed particularly odd after the births of her children.

Don stood in the doorway with peas, rose bowl and frying pan. The lad in the window across the road saluted him comically, and Don returned the favour with a tin of peas. Yes, Lennon was probably all right, guitar or no guitar. He lived with an aunt who seemed very straitlaced, but at least there were no pans or peas on the front lawn.

Tess was waiting for him in the hall. 'Waste of time,' she told him. 'You were right, but I thought it was worth a go – that carpet's nearly new. The dye didn't take.'

'Dye?'

'Charcoal. But I think it's more for clothes and stuff. Or chair covers and cushions.'

A shard of hope pierced Don's heart. He still loved her. He loved two women. Molly was real, down to earth, a great laugh. This selfish piece of work he continued to adore. 'Will the meal be on time tonight?' he asked.

Tess shook a finger at him. 'Listen, Desperate Don. I've been a bit mithered in case you haven't noticed. A house of this class takes some living up to. I'm still theming the rooms.'

He had no real idea about what theming was, but he didn't bother to ask for enlightenment. One worry went up the chimney with the rest of the smoke: she had used dye, not paint, on the carpet. And, for a few seconds, he hid the other concerns behind more immediate problems. Would Molly want the house back? Could he really give up the generous physical warmth offered by her; was he about to return and worship at the beautiful feet of his beautiful, cold wife? Separate beds–

'Don?'

'What?'

'Will you teach me to drive?'

She had locked three children in a store cupboard for two hours. Her cooking was moving in the direction of Molly's, her timekeeping was hardly Greenwich, and he still wondered about marrowfat peas, a frying pan and a rose bowl. Put her behind a wheel? He'd need to find somebody to walk in front with a red flag. Oh, and a suit of armour. 'Why do you want to learn?' he asked.

'I'm not sure. A job of some kind, I suppose. When I let the flat above the shop, the tenant will look after the business. Littlewoods Pools wants people to pick up coupons from corner shops on Saturday mornings. Johnson the cleaners needs collection points for dry-cleaning. That's to stop launderettes like ours installing dry-cleaning machines. I don't want one. I don't want people keeling over from breathing carbon tetrachloride, not in our shop.'

Don blinked. She'd been reading again. 'Carbon who?'

'Tetrachloride. It stinks. You can go unconscious just like that.' She clicked her fingers. 'Even in frost and snow, you have to drive with the windows open unless you want to wake up on a slab. Newly dry-cleaned items in a confined space can be deadly.'

There was nothing wrong with her, he decided. She was eccentric, no more than that. She wanted a posh house because she'd spent her infancy in a freezing, uncomfortable gypsy caravan. Depression arrived when she became fearful of returning to penury. 'Tess?'

'Yes? I'm going down the chippy. What would you like, Mr Steak Pudding?'

'Steak pudding and peas.'

She stared hard at him. 'Did you mention peas before?'

'Two tins,' he answered.

'Squirrels,' she said as she pulled on a coat. 'See? You still want steak pudding. I didn't need to ask.'

'I like a choice.' Squirrels? Oh, God. What was she on about now? What the hell was the connection between bushy-tailed rodents and two family-sized tins of Batchelor's marrowfats?

'Did you want to ask me something, Don? Only I don't relish the idea of being in a big queue at the chip shop.'

'No.' He'd been about to ask her whether she still had any feelings for him, but it didn't seem right now, not with squirrels as part of the equation. The equation.

She left the house. Don set plates to warm in the oven. Equation? What the hell was he up to? Was he trying to work out her state of mind and heart before deciding which woman to keep, which to let go? If the first onc was broken, would he move on to the other one, who was older but in working order? It was a bit like measuring one car against another: best transmission, best engine, best bodywork. He was the selfish one; he was the bloke behaving like a spoilt child who had to get his own way.

Sean and Anne-Marie arrived together. Don told them their meal would be here shortly, and they ran upstairs. Elvis Presley roared from the Dansette in Anne-Marie's room, doors slammed, water ran. They were home.

He set the table: knives, forks, salt and malt vinegar. Why was there a mousetrap in the clean linen cupboard? Was this enough to make him run away into the ample bosom of a woman with a ukulele, two dogs and some tropical fish? 'I am not a good man,' he whispered. 'I'm not being fair.' He owed Molly. Yet his love for Tess had burgeoned anew over recent weeks. 'I want to have fun with my own wife,' he mumbled. 'I want to communicate with her.' And he should never have taken Molly's money.

Tess came in. She was all smiles, paper bundles and dandelion and burdock. 'What's up with your face?' she asked.

'Why is there a mousetrap in with all the towels and tablecloths?'

'Don't answer a question with a question. You're not an Aquarian.'

Don scratched his head. 'You what?'

'Aquarians answer questions with questions. They're geniuses. It said so in *Woman's Realm.*' She straightened her spine. 'I am Aquarius. I'll have a new carpet for my birthday in three weeks...' Her voice died. 'What's the matter with you?'

He shook his head sadly. 'I think I love my wife.'

A corner of Tess's mouth twitched. 'Warm your feet before getting in my bed,' she ordered. 'And don't expect full service till I feel more settled.' She sniffed. A bitter wind had made her nose wet. 'I've gone ... different.'

'Yes, we noticed.'

'No, you didn't,' she whispered. 'Early menopause. What would you know about that sort of thing?'

A curtain seemed to move at the front of Don's mind. She hadn't wanted more children. She was Catholic. Precautions were sinful... Bloody religion. Not for the first time, he cursed the rod made by humanity for its own back. Holy Moses? He should have left the bloody tablets where they were instead of taking two between meals.

'Sit,' she said. 'Eat,' she ordered.

'Did you mean it?' he asked. 'About warming my feet first?'

'Shut up, the children are coming.'

'Tess?'

'Be quiet.'

They rolled in, the son almost clean, the daughter shining like a new pin.

Tess folded her arms. 'You,' she said to Anne-Marie, 'can get back up the stairs and turn that din off.'

'But it's Elvis,' the girl cried.

Don cleared his throat. 'John Lennon waved at me today.'

'No!' Anne-Marie dropped into a chair, ignored her mother and stared at her dad. 'When?'

Elvis ground to a blessed halt upstairs. 'About half an hour ago,' Don said. 'Bit of a wink with it, too.'

'And what did you do?'

'Waved back. Nearly took my eye out with a tin of peas.'

Anne-Marie blinked. 'Why a tin of peas, Dad?'

'Oh, shut up and eat,' Tess ordered.

They shut up and ate.

That's another one less, then. Working girl, the sort that

211

spreads disease. Trouble is, a courting couple decided to park nearby, and I couldn't bury the corpse. So it's been all over the papers, locals and nationals, and the cops are worrying about the rest who've disappeared. On top of that, my boss is ill. If he dies, what'll happen to me? For ages I've worked in that shop. Oh, and I'm a maniac. Unspeakable things have been done to 'that poor girl's body'. Don't make me laugh, Mr Editor; unspeakable things have been done to and by her for years...

Eight

Seamus had a book. It was a valued possession, not for general consumption by common folk, not available to be borrowed, glanced at or even breathed on. He guarded it fiercely, kept it under boxes and short planks of wood, visited it only when sure that nobody was looking, and he absorbed it like a bear sucking honey from a comb. He always carried a torch, of course, because it was dark in the shelter. For the first time in his life, the son of Maureen and Tom Walsh was learning happily from a book. It was brilliant, informative, and it would change the lives of everyone in the family. The lad had plans that would reshape the world, and he was keeping every card close to his chest, because no one could be trusted.

Wearing the air of a man who had just discovered a whole new continent, Seamus developed a frown and a habit of walking or standing with his hands clasped behind his back. 'Thinks he's Prince Philip,' Paddy had been heard to opine. 'Gone big-headed. We'll be having to get his school caps made specially to fit if he carries on so. He's cogitating, so he is. We must watch him.'

The Thoughtful One kept his book in the reasonably dry Anderson in his sister Reen's back garden, because Reen never went in there. Ander-

213

sons reminded folk of the bad times when Germany flattened Bootle, and few people wanted to think about the war. The shelters were now used for storage of gardening tools and bicycles, though children sometimes played in them when it rained. This metal shed had become Seamus's library, but it held just the one slim volume. He never corrupted the shelter with homework. Oh, no, this was too precious a place for multiplication, division and catechism, because it was an area set aside for real and useful learning.

Reen and her husband had no children yet, and they lived in the O'Gara prefab, since the O'Garas now had a proper house with an upstairs. The boy's relationship with his sister had improved, though he wouldn't look properly at the wedding album. There were three pictures of him and the horrible hat, and that was three too many in his opinion. Even the bride giggled when she looked at the images of her little brother. Perhaps the poor imitation of a sailor's headgear had been a stride too far, but she wouldn't throw the photos away. Perhaps she had a plan for when Seamus was older. She would show them to his friends, and he'd be doomed to a lifetime of *Hello, sailor.* 'And I'll kill her,' he muttered frequently. 'Making a show of me in front of all them people.'

The young hero in Seamus's special book was Harry Burdon Jr, PI, and its author was American. Seamus didn't want Mam, Dad, Gran or Grandpa to see the book, because it was the source of the lad's grand ambitions, and adults should not be allowed to encroach on a boy's ideas. Grown-ups never approved. All they did

214

was moan about difficulties, because they hadn't the imagination to do anything about anything. Why they didn't attempt what he was about to try he could not work out. There might have been a row, he thought. Perhaps Gran had laid into some people with that sharp tongue of hers and they had run away. He wasn't running away. Oh, no. Seamus Walsh was on a mission, and nothing would persuade him to abandon it. Though if Gran found out, he'd possibly end up in the scouse with the rest of the cheaper cuts.

Harry Burdon was a private detective. He was Junior because his dad had the same name, and Junior's dad was a policeman in New York. Seamus did not have the advantages of Junior, as there were no coppers in the family, but the Harry Burdon Junior Private Investigator story had become his textbook. Nothing was impossible. Young Harry had found kidnappers, thieves and shoplifters, so he was definitely role model material.

However, Junior had further help, some of it of questionable quality. His assistant, Beanpole, was a long, thin person who did everything wrong, though he sometimes got it right by accident. Beanpole was probably in the book to make people laugh, but it would be nice to have someone to talk to in real life. The trouble with real life was that school friends and young neighbours were soft. Seamus failed to find one who might just own the staying power. The task he planned to undertake was massive, and he didn't want any babies clinging to his apron strings.

Burdon Junior also got tips from his unsuspecting dad. It did not occur to Seamus that a

215

seasoned New York cop should notice that his son was carrying on like Sherlock Holmes with a tall, thin Watson either by his side or stuck head first in an oil drum somewhere.

Tom Walsh was a good dad, but he was educated to know about spuds, butter, tea, sugar and divi points, because he ran the new Bootle Co-op. Seamus couldn't discuss his complicated secret with his parents. World war would break out, and folk were still waiting for houses after the last lot. And they would stop him, of course. Grown-ups were spectacularly successful when it came to putting a damper on ideas. They got tired, he supposed. Anybody really old, like over the age of thirty, was bound to have started to wear out a bit. They had too much to think about, what with Scouse Alley, weekend events, the market and the Co-op. So it was up to him, because he hadn't yet begun to crumble under the weight of adulthood. He was young, strong, and ready to become a hero; he was clever, resourceful, and quick.

Clues regarding the case in hand were few and far between, so Seamus stuck to the Harry Burdon school of thought. Unlike Beanpole, Seamus would not end up screaming in a bed of nettles, or hanging upside down from a tree in some innocent person's back yard. He would not break the wrong windows, had no intention of being sent to reform school, to Borstal, to prison. No. He was merely going where no adult in his sphere would dare to tread; he intended to find his brothers.

You gotta take what you have and use it, Harry-in-the-book would say to his clumsy, idiotic friend.

And if you ain't got nothing, you look at possibilities and number them in order of merit. All notes in code, remember. Gear up. Army pocket knife, a good length of strong rope, food and water, as much money as you can scrape. Good luck to you, Beanpole.

After a great deal of begging and pleading by Seamus, the knife had arrived at Christmas. It boasted every attachment apart from a kitchen sink, and Seamus was unsure regarding the usefulness of many of its components. There was a thing to take the caps off bottles, the blade, a horse's hoof doodah, and loads of other stuff that looked as though it had been copied in miniature from a medieval torture chamber.

Rope. Stealing thick stuff from the docks might have caused mayhem, and it was too heavy to carry. In view of these problems, Seamus had taken an alternative route, and several prefabs on Stanley Square were now bereft of clothes lines. Clothes line might not be the strongest of rope, but it was better than nothing. He was doing his best, although his only support lay between the covers of a book, so nothing was easy. Discussion was an unaffordable luxury, and that was that.

But the largest part of Seamus's plot was rooted in a lie so huge as to be frightening. It was Easter, 1959. Some of the boys in his class were about to go camping with teachers for five whole days in the mountains of North Wales. Mam had signed the permission paper and had given her youngest son enough money to cover the expedition, and he had stolen it after tearing up the permission paper. This was the most wicked thing he had done in his whole life, and he was avoiding Confession until it was all over. He'd probably get five thousand Our Fathers, a bucketful of Hail Marys, and a few Glory Bes thrown in for good measure.

There was, of course, a distinct danger in the scheme. If Mam met any of the other parents or children, she might learn that her beloved son was not going camping. But, as Harry Junior might have said, *If you don't take a chance from time to time, you ain't getting nowhere.*

Well, Seamus was going somewhere. Nobody else in his family owned the guts, but he had no yellow streak painted down his spine. Eavesdropping, a skill he had perfected during the second reading of chapter one, had taught him that the whole family missed Finbar and Michael. Letters, relieved of envelopes and with no address provided by their senders, had informed him that his brothers were married and that each had a child. 'I'm an uncle,' he whispered proudly before hiding his book. 'They have taken my unclehood away.' One of the kids was only a girl, but that couldn't be helped.

He left his private bunker, dropping to hands and knees to make use of cover provided by the privet hedge. Harry Burdon was virtually invisible. He blended. Because he blended, he could go anywhere in that vast city without being noticed. But Seamus couldn't. Everyone round here knew everyone, and they certainly knew Seamus.

Reen and Jimmy were at work, but Seamus needed to shield himself from the prying eyes of neighbours. Gossip was an almost full-time occupation in these parts. He could hear his grandmother now. *No better than she should be. And did you see the heels on the shoes? She'll be needing an oxygen mask if she goes any higher up. Silver nail polish, too. I tell you she's on the way to Lime Street with a mattress on her back.* Yes, Gran was a gossip of professional standard, but there were many others of her ilk in these parts.

Safer now, he stood up and walked towards home. There were photographs of Fin and Mike somewhere in the prefab. Seamus hadn't seen them and didn't know where they were kept, but he'd listened to his parents talking. Because Tom Walsh had been a substitute manager as, when and where required, he had filled in gaps created by managers' holidays all over the place. 'Rainford, near St Helens,' he had declared to his wife, little realizing that his son was in the hall hanging on every word. 'I recognized the shops in the background. It's a village. East Lancs Road, turn right for St Helens, left for Rainford. A few tenanted farms – Lord Derby owns the land – and the village is pretty. Stone cottages, nice church, a few shops and at least four pubs. They could be in worse places, Maureen.'

And that had been it. But it was something. Seamus had found the village on a map, and had learned the route. 'I could do it with my eyes closed,' he declared quietly as he walked homeward. But he was going to need his eyes open, as he would be on his bike. Mum and Dad wouldn't miss the bike; it was kept in their Anderson shelter. 'My whole life's in Andersons,' Seamus mumbled as he sauntered up the path to his own prefab.

It was half-day closing at the Co-op, and Maureen had taken a couple of hours off between

219

catering at Scouse Alley and helping her dad on the market. Even now, after more than a quarter century of marriage, she and Tom liked to steal time to spend together.

Maureen's lips were pursed as she watched her son dragging his raincoat along the path. 'He's up to something,' she advised her husband. 'He's not one for concentrating unless it's football or cricket. Look at him. Like Loony Lenny from Linacre Lane, doesn't know whether he's coming, going, or on the big wheel at the fair. I get worried when our Seamus is thinking, because nothing good ever comes of it. He shouldn't think. His brain gets overcrowded and his cheeks burn. Looks like a candidate for that spontaneous human combustion.'

Tom joined his wife. Their one resident child was standing in the middle of the path counting. On his fingers. 'Counting,' Tom said. 'What the heck is he counting?'

'Not prayers,' replied Maureen grimly. 'Definitely nothing holy, I can guarantee it. It might be to do with them wedding photos of him in his hat. There's only three in the book, but he hates them.'

Tom laughed. 'He certainly does.'

'But Tom, he wouldn't spoil his sister's wedding album, would he?'

'He would. Remember how he buried the whole suit plus hat? Your mother had to dig everything up for the church. That blinking hat put him in a bad mood for months. And it was a stupid hat. I was surprised when he didn't stick it in the bin before the kick-off. I mean, even some of the grown-ups were calling him Popeye.'

'It was his only sister's wedding day and–' Maureen stopped abruptly. 'Sorry, love. I never meant to make you remember things from that time. Sorry.'

Tom cleared his throat. 'I'll not forget it in a hurry, girl, but I'm all right with it now. That lad of ours out there could have been in his grave if I hadn't ... if I hadn't done what I did. Knowing they were gunning for our other two doesn't help, does it? We can't visit, they can't come and see us, and–' He cut off the rest of his words when the front door opened.

'Seamus?'

'Yes, Mam?'

'Come here, son. Immediately, if not sooner. And I don't want just your head floating round the edge of the door; bring the rest of you as well.'

One hundred per cent of Seamus entered the room. Although he knew it was a dead giveaway, he allowed his weight to swing slightly from foot to foot. His mother's face, when displaying disappointment or anger, made him sway about a bit, but he kept movement to a minimum. She might be on to him. She might have met someone at Scouse Alley or at the market, and that someone could have marked him as a cheat and a liar who mistreated his own parents, and wasn't to be trusted, and wasn't going with school to Wales–

'What's the matter with you?' she asked. 'You look like you're sickening for something. And you can't go camping in the damp and cold if you're not well.'

Seamus allowed a sigh of relief to emerge quietly. If she'd been told he wasn't going camping, she would have come out with it straight away.

'We'll see how you are in the morning. If you're all right, your dad will run you to school in his car.' She was proud of the better car. She wanted everybody at school to know that Seamus's dad was moving up in the world.

'No,' the lad exclaimed quickly – rather too quickly. 'No, not the car.'

'But you'll have your rucksack and first day meals and the little tent. They're borrowing that to keep tinned food in, aren't they?'

'Mam, we've been told to practise walking with the weight on our backs. And I don't want people thinking I'm still a baby. I'd be the only one.' He glanced at the clock. He still needed to get the bike out and hide it somewhere between home and wherever. 'Please don't give me a lift, Dad. Don't make a show of me in front of everybody.'

Maureen sat down and folded her arms. 'You are up to something,' she said.

'Me?'

'Well, I'm not talking to your father, am I? And you're the only other person here now that Reen's married and...' Her voice died.

'And my brothers have gone,' the child concluded for her. 'They don't visit, and we don't visit them. So I take the blame for everything. I bet it's my fault if it rains. Well, I didn't make everybody leave home, did I? It wasn't my fault that we were overcrowded and Reen had to sleep at Gran's and my brothers had to sleep in the living room. They left here to try and get some space to live in.'

Maureen sniffed. They'd gone to make fast, dirty money in London, and she couldn't tell their young brother that. But she could put his mind at rest regarding overcrowding. 'We've had to wait for a house because we want to be near your Gran and your sister. We don't want to be spread out all over the place on Hitler's say-so, do we? Well, our new places will be ready in a few months. I suppose my mam will be pig in the middle, then she can pin her ear to the walls and find out what we're all up to.' She sniffed again. 'And you are up to no good.'

Seamus had trouble when it came to adopting Harry Burdon's innocent look. Harry never blushed, but Seamus had inherited his mother's expertise when it came to changing colour. Harry didn't sway when questioned, but Seamus did. 'Mam, I'm going away for five days tomorrow. I have to learn to put a big tent up with all them poles and pegs, make fire with something called a flint, use a compass, and warm enough beans on the fire for fourteen boys and three teachers. It's a lot to take in.'

Tom grinned. 'Especially when you don't listen to any of those teachers. And if you're living on beans, God help Wales. You'll have all the Welsh running over into England. Well, I hope they don't bring their sheep. I don't fancy waking up to baa-ing every morning. Your mam's bad enough, because she's not a morning person.'

In spite of her husband's attempt to lighten the

atmosphere, Maureen remained on high alert. With her older sons in hiding and her only daughter wed, she had every intention of hanging on to her youngest for as long as possible. There was something wrong. He reminded her of one of those desert lizards. Their feet got burnt in the sand, so they stood on two while the other pair cooled, and those reptiles were ... what was it? *Perpetuum mobile.* That was Latin for not being able to keep still, and the *mobile* was pronounced mobil-ay. Her son was *perpetuum* whatever when lying. 'What are you not telling me?' she asked. 'Come on, out with it. You know I always get to the bottom of things.'

'Nothing.' Seamus felt renewed heat in his cheeks.

Maureen glanced through the window. 'Have you had anything to do with the mysterious disappearance of three washing lines from these prefabs?'

'No,' the child shouted. 'It's always me. It was probably me that bombed Dresden and Hiroshima.' This was what Harry Burdon called fighting fire with fire. 'I'm the one to blame for everything just because I'm the only one of the family here.' At last, he was in his stride. 'Well, I never crossed the border into Poland, didn't blow up ships, and what would I want with clothes lines? That'll be some girls wanting rope for long skipping.' Long skipping had a girl at each end turning, and five or six running in and out of the rope. Sometimes, there were two ropes turning in opposite directions. Oh, yes. Seamus was a born private investigator, because he missed nothing.

'Don't start getting clever with me, lad,' she said.

'Oh. So I'm clever now, am I? You never said that when you were helping me with my geography homework.'

'That's enough.' Tom's tone was ominously quiet. 'Don't ever talk to your mam like that. She's not here for you to wipe your feet on or to sharpen the edge of your temper. Oh, and she's my wife, by the way. I expect people to treat her with respect.'

Seamus hung his head. It was now or never. He knew full well that telling his parents immediately would take more courage than he had. Keeping quiet and going through with the plan was the easier option, so was he a coward after all? What he intended to do was naughty, because he'd told lies and stolen money. But it was also good, since nobody else seemed to have the courage to face Finbar and Michael. Why, though? What had happened for a wedge of such a size to be driven through so close a family? Everyone quarrelled, of course, but Gran always said that it was the Irish in them, the paddy-whack, as she sometimes called it.

'What's he thinking about now?' Maureen asked.

'No idea,' was her husband's reply.

Seamus shook his head slowly. He was in the room, yet they talked about him as if he'd left. He would go now, though he needed to say something first. 'Sorry,' he mumbled. 'It's just this camping business. More to it than I thought.' That wasn't a lie, because he would be camping in his little one-man tent a few miles up the East Lancs. The only

225

camping he'd ever done had taken place here, in the garden, and he'd come inside for his meals. With his head still bowed, the youngest member of the Walsh family left the room. Tomorrow morning, he would become a man.

Maureen sighed. 'Well, me dad's not getting any younger, Tom. I'd best get up the road and help him. I've had enough of me mother for one day. Two stones of spuds she sent back this morning. Not good enough. She was in a right mood, face like a Dock Road crash between two lorries and a train. Blamed me because I put the order in.' She looked at her husband, who seemed preoccupied.

'What?'

'Are you turning weird on me? Because if you think I'm going to drag me legs and the rest of me round Liverpool looking for you, you can think a-bloody-gain.'

'No, nothing like that. I'm going up Waterloo tonight to visit Roy.' He paused. 'Come with me. Your mam'll keep an eye on me-laddo.'

Maureen blinked a few times. 'Is Roy expecting me?'

'He's asked to meet you. He's lonely, love. Never been married, a bad leg, madly in love with a widow across the road who's called R-O-I-S-I-N, pronounced Rosheen, answers to Rosh. And he was good to me that day – remember? Got me to Confession, propped me up all the way to Greenhaigh's office where I got the best job going.'

'I've nothing to wear,' she said.

'Nothing to wear? Nothing to wear? Seven hangers, I've got in that wardrobe. You've more clothes than your dad sells in a year on Paddy's

Market.' He paused for thought. 'Your navy suit, polka dot blouse with the bow at the neck, and new navy shoes from Freeman, Hardy and Willis.'

He always noticed her clothes, complimented her on her hair, told her when he liked her perfume or a new lipstick. It was one of his many good traits, and Maureen knew she was a fortunate woman. 'All right,' she said. 'I'll do an hour for me dad, then I'll come home and get ready. Roy'll forget all about the widow once he's seen me in the fighting gear.'

'You're not available,' Tom said, smacking her playfully on her behind. 'And when our Seamus is away, we can have another honeymoon.'

'Says who?'

'Says me. Now, bugger off.'

She buggered off.

Tom settled down with a newspaper over his face. Within minutes, he was asleep, and his son was on the prowl.

Leaving out the chair on which his father rested, Seamus searched the rest of the upholstered furniture for trapped coins. He found a florin, two half-crowns and some copper. That was the better part of eight shillings, and he wasn't stealing, because he was allowed to keep what he found under cushions. Usually, he was lucky if he acquired a few pennies, so this was a good haul. Was it also an omen, a sign that he was doing the right thing?

He sat and listened to his dad's gentle snoring. Everything about Tom Walsh was gentle. Even when angry, he held himself back, refusing to let rip at the person who'd annoyed him. And that, as Mam repeated frequently, was why Dad had got on at the Co-op. He could work out dividends at amazing speed, was good to his staff and excellent with customers. 'Your dad's a man,' she said regularly. 'And there aren't a lot about these days.'

Seamus had stolen the camping money from Mam and from this wonderful dad who had won special medals for bravery during the war. Dad was a crack shot, a hero, a man who always did the right thing. He'd been ill for a while, a bit strange in his head, but he was back to normal now. Guilt burned through Seamus like summer lightning striking his core. If he got found out, would Dad become ill again?

Harry Burdon Jr didn't have problems like these. No one worried about where he was or what he was doing. Even when he went missing overnight, his behaviour wasn't criticized. But it was a book, just a book. Harry Burdon wasn't real. His mother wasn't real. She didn't have to peel pounds and pounds of spuds every day, didn't stand over hot pans, didn't feed sweaty dock workers bowl after bowl of scouse. Harry Burdon's dad didn't have to tally dividends, add up huge sums of money, take it to the bank, order food for the whole of Bootle on a weekly basis, make sure fresh veg got delivered every other day, because ... because those people in the book weren't real. There was no policeman father, no lawyer mother. All there was... It was a bloke called Richard something or other. He had a typewriter and a desk, and he sat there churning out Harry Burdon books, drinking whiskey and beer, probably, and smoking cigarettes.

Seamus walked across the room and peeled the newspaper off his dad's face. 'Are you awake?'

'Well, I am now.' Tom yawned and moved into a more upright position. 'All right, lad. Out with it. We're not daft, you know, me and your mam.'

It tumbled from the boy's mouth in a rather less than sensible order. 'I just wanted to find them, Dad. So I was never going camping. Well, I was, but on me own. Then well, I looked at you and Mam, and I started thinking. I stole the school camp money and told lies. I read your private letters. But they're me brothers, Dad.'

Tom felt a bit choked, but he dared not weep, not in Seamus's company. He organized his thoughts as quickly as possible, marshalling facts into rank and file, picking up a couple of white-ish lies en route. Some of the truth needed to come out, since Seamus was a long way from stupid. 'There's a very good reason why things are as they are, son. Because of accidents that happened in London, Finbar and Michael have to lie low. They got in with – worked with – some bad people. For safety's sake, they stay away from us, and we stay away from them. It probably won't be for ever, but that's how it is at the moment. Thanks for telling me. If you'd found them, you might have done more harm than good.'

Seamus blinked rapidly. 'You think they're in Rainford.'

'I believe so, yes.' Tom smiled at his youngest child. 'You're eight now, lad. Old enough to know right from wrong, also decent enough to come clean. I'll tell your mother, so make yourself scarce and put the money you took on the mantelpiece. You just leave her to me.'

Seamus went away and sat on his bed. He had three clothes lines to return, and he had been stupid. This expedition was to have been the greatest adventure in his life so far. And his parents wanted something called a honeymoon, so he had better get on the right side of Gran.

Stanley Square wasn't the same any more. People kept moving out, leaving behind the single-storey buildings that had housed them since the war. Empty prefabs looked sad and blind, with no movement, no light shining through windows in the evenings. 'We'll be out of here soon,' he mumbled. 'I'm going to meet Gran,' he called as he walked through the hall.

'Right,' Tom replied. 'But keep away from your mother. I'll not vouch for her behaviour if you tell her what you told me. I can deal with her. Coming to me first was the best way.'

'Good luck, Dad.' Seamus closed the door and began the walk to Scouse Alley. He tried not to think, but failed to suppress the workings of his brain. Gran had to be on his side. Gran was always on his side. He could stay in Gran's house till Mam calmed down, which could be some time between midsummer and next Christmas. She was a good mam, and Seamus loved her to bits, but once she got on her high horse she was, as Dad put it, a bugger to shift.

By the time her grandson arrived, Paddy was locking up. She glanced sideways at him while retrieving the key, then did a quick double-take and gave him all her attention. 'And who are you?' she asked. 'I've a grandson in a mould similar to yours, though he doesn't wear his face in his boots.'

'Don't, Gran.' And he told her. It was much easier talking to her, which was weird, because he and she were like two slices of bread, components of a sandwich with his parents as filling. 'So I told me dad.'

'But not your mam?'

He shook his head. 'Dad said he's dealing with her, because he knows how. Till she drinks too much. You're better with her when she has a load of Guinnesses. And I stole money and clothes lines.'

'You'll be in jail for ever, then?'

'No. But when they thought I was going camping with school, Dad said a few times they could have a honeymoon, so can I stay at yours?'

'Oh, yes.'

'Gran?'

'Yes?'

'What's a honeymoon?'

Paddy hid a smile. 'Well, it's a holiday for grown-ups, but not for children. It doesn't mean they don't love the bones of you, because they do, but would you like your mam and dad there while you're playing with your friends?'

Seamus shook his head.

'Same thing, you see. They want some time to themselves.' Paddy was pleased. Her daughter's marriage was a solid one, but everybody needed a break from children in order to feed a flame often starved by day-to-day drudgery.

'Gran?'

She sighed. The Spanish Inquisition was clearly still in progess. 'What?'

'Well, Dad said about bad people in London. Did they kill my uncles Peter and Callum and Martin and Jack?'

'Possibly.' Sometimes, Paddy ached in the place against which she had held her sons. She missed her brothers, of course, but the loss of a child to whom a woman had given birth was a pain beyond measure. 'We mustn't talk to anyone about any of it. Your brothers, their wives and children, all must be kept safe. We, too, need to be careful.' She shuddered. 'Seamus, should ever a man drive slowly beside you, and open his car window to ask questions, don't answer. I'm not joking now.'

'All right, Gran. And I'll put the ropes on people's doorsteps after dark.' He pondered. 'But two of the prefabs on that side are empty.'

'Then leave all the ropes at the occupied one. And don't be worrying about Confession, because a sin you nearly committed doesn't count.'

They turned into Stanley Square, noticing immediately that all was not well. Paddy wouldn't have been surprised if her daughter's voice could be heard near the Liver Building down at the waterfront.

'Gran?'

'Run to the market and tell your granddad to pack up and come home. Tell him I said. Go on, because your dad can't hold her back for much longer.'

Seamus ran like the wind. With Mam in a mood

232

as bad as this one, he needed to be on a different planet. Maureen didn't hit kids except for a bit of a slap or a flick with a towel, but she was a screamer, and Seamus couldn't be doing with screamers. The only thing worse than Mam's yelling was her singing, and the lad all but flew in the direction of the market.

Paddy strode across the mound of grass that covered the centre of the square and met her furious daughter in the middle. Doors in several of the occupied prefabs opened; people abandoned wirelesses, gramophones and even the odd television set, because fights on the green were often better entertainment than anything available via electricity.

Tom used his arms to encircle his wife's waist. 'Stop showing yourself up,' he stage-whispered. 'And you won't kill him, because you love him, and I'll stop you laying a finger on him anyway–'

'It's her,' Maureen shouted, 'the best gran in the world. Gives him anything he asks for, dotes on him. He was going to go and find my other–' Maureen staggered back and stood on her husband's feet. Shocked, she put a hand to a cheek burning after a flat-handed blow from Paddy.

'Not a word of that while you're out here putting on a show,' Paddy whispered. 'Seamus is a child, but you're not, and here you are, ready to give away your sons just because the lad was anxious about his brothers and ready to seek them out. Now shut up. Some round here would love to gossip about me. They owe me money and want to see me brought down.'

Maureen's mouth made a perfect O. Her

mother had just cracked her across the face with a strong, calloused hand. 'You hit me,' she spat.

'I'll do it again, but, if you don't shut up and get yourself back inside. Watching you having a fit of the hystericals will keep that lot happy till the cows decide to come home. Away with you. Come on, away from the few neighbours we have left.'

'Don't tell me what to do, Mother. My son stole from me. My son. And I know you'll stick up for him, because you–' She was lifted up by her husband and, with limbs scraping the air in the manner of an upside-down beetle, she was heaved across the grass into her home, where she found herself dumped unceremoniously in the hallway.

Mother and husband stared down at the personification of human anger on the floor. 'Ridiculous,' said Tom. 'He's a boy. Boys do stupid things. At his age, I was pinching anything that wasn't tied down, nailed down, glued down or rooted. He misses his brothers, love. And he entered a magic world where he could find them and bring them back.'

Maureen closed her eyes and leaned against a wall. 'I lost two uncles and two brothers to the East End of bloody London. Now, I've two grandsons I can't even visit, because all the boys in this family turn out bad. So when I see Seamus doing wrong and causing bother, I think it'll be him next. What if he had found his brothers? What if his brothers, once dug out of hiding, decided to go back and work with Ronnie and Reggie Kray? What if Seamus joined them in ten years, eh? Just another unmarked grave in Epping Forest.'

Paddy understood her daughter full well, but there was no sense in this destructive way of thinking. 'I'm going to put this right,' she said. 'I'll be visiting London.'

Maureen and Tom stared open-mouthed at the grandmother of their children. 'What?'

'I shall write to the Krays. They helped get our boys back up here, gave them money, wished them good luck.'

'I'm coming with you, then,' Tom said.

But Paddy shook her head. 'No. This will be two women in a room, two women with troublesome boys. Those twins will do anything for their mother, anything at all. Martin told me that, God rest his soul.'

Maureen closed her mouth with an audible snap. 'And what will you ask for, Mam?'

'For my family to be safe.'

Tom sighed and turned away, and the women followed him into the living room. In the age-old stance of a man lecturing his family, he stood with his back to the fire, feet planted apart, one hand pushing hair from his face. 'You could cause deaths,' he said softly.

'I know that.' Paddy paused for several seconds. 'One night last summer, you were forced to protect your family. You became ill, then came to terms with what had happened. Whichever group is after Finbar and Michael, we know it's not the Krays.'

'So?' Maureen sat and folded her arms as if protecting herself from what she was hearing.

'If their mother asks them, they will deal with it. I shall also suggest that my grandsons be chased away if they ever return to London.' Paddy closed her eyes. London, like the moon, was there. It lingered beyond the bounds of imagination, was not as visible as the world's silver companion which came and went on a monthly basis. London was on the Pathé News at the cinema. Nelson balanced on a tall column in some square or other – Trafalgar? There was Hyde Park where daft folk stood on orange boxes and ranted on about politics, religion and what have you, while the queen lived in an un-pretty palace big enough for forty-five married couples with kids, plus guests and lodgers.

The strangest thing about this Bootle family was that Tom knew where to stop with Paddy, whereas her daughter just barged on and on until the tears came. 'You are not going to London on your own, Mam.'

Paddy shrugged. 'I am. I'm going on my own, by myself, with nobody. And I won't even tell you when. No way am I arriving with what they call an enterage.'

'Entourage,' Tom offered, wishing immediately that he could bite back the word. The expression on his mother-in-law's face was sculpted to kill. But he wasn't going to apologize. 'I'll just fetch our Seamus,' he said rather lamely.

'No, you won't,' snapped the angry Irishwoman. 'He's stopping with me and his granddad while you have a honeymoon.' She nodded. 'Yes, he hears everything. We all know there's no privacy in these tin boxes. No matter what, there's always some clever so-and-so can see you, hear you or smell you.' She turned to her daughter. 'Have some time off work and calm yourself down. Honeymoon?' She tutted. 'It'll be more like the Battle of the Bulge.'

When Paddy had left, Tom studied his wife. No way was he going to take her to Waterloo tonight. To say she was in a bad mood would have been similar to stating that the sun was slightly warm. 'There's steam coming out of your nose,' he said.

'There'll be blood pouring out of yours in a minute if you don't bugger off. Go and see your friend. I'll have a bath and listen to the wireless.' She flounced out of the living room.

Tom sat for a while, scarcely realizing that he was engaged in a countdown. Then it happened. He strode down the hall and into the bathroom. Maureen cried like a child, wholeheartedly and with great enthusiasm for the job. Even when her face was screwed up like a sheet of paper in a bin, she remained beautiful. The presence of children and in-laws often stopped the cure, but the couple were alone this time. Roy would be expecting him, but Maureen was, as ever, top of Tom's list of priorities.

He marched away to bolt the outer doors, then lifted his soggy spouse, carried her to the living room and medicated her. She lay in his arms afterwards. 'You're all wet, Tom.'

'I know. So are you.'

She kissed him. 'Why does that always work?'

Tom shrugged. 'Releases tension. I suppose we're lucky. Some women can't abide it. You've always been an easy little tart.'

'I'll bite your ears, Thomas Walsh.'

'Really? Then we'll be forced to deal once again with matters arising therefrom–'

'Braggart.'

'Matters arising,' he repeated, 'and I have to go to Roy's house. You coming?'

'No. I'll go to bed and wait for you.'

'Oh?'

'Matters arising.'

He watched as his wife walked away. There were little white indentations on her belly where unborn children had stretched her out of shape, and the flesh on her thighs was no longer firm, but she was gorgeous. Her beauty lay in the fact that she didn't make herself precious, didn't concentrate on faults resulting from the natural process of ageing. 'A whole week of you all to myself,' he told her.

Maureen stood in the doorway. 'Depends,' she replied.

'On what?'

She shrugged. 'New milkman. Haven't tried him out yet. Oh, and you have to stop Mam going to London. She's not ready for London.'

Tom laughed. 'I wonder if London's ready for her?'

'Oh, I'm going to warm my bath up and start again. Tell Roy hello from me, but I'm out of order due to matters what arose. And on your way back, you can fetch me cod, chips and peas.'

Tom sighed. He would sleep with the smell of malt vinegar, would wake to the same aroma mingling delicately with the odour of cooled fat. There would be newsprint on sheets, escaped chips in the bed, bits of batter adhering lovingly to parts of his person. But it didn't matter, because she was his girl.

As he drove towards Waterloo, he thought about Roy. Roy loved a woman across the road. He busied himself with work and his allotment, enjoyed decorating and improving the house, yet every waking moment he thought of this Rosh woman, the widow of his best friend. He spoke of her with reverence, and repeatedly expressed the opinion that she would never look at him because he was substandard in the walking department.

'What's a bloody game leg at the end of the day?' Tom asked the windscreen. 'He's good-looking, has a smart job, grows his own veg and flowers – what the bloody hell does she want? Gregory flaming Peck?'

He parked the car. Roy was waiting for him at the gate. A neat, proud little garden showed off its residents, early cheerfulness and the gladi-atorial threats of daffodils preparing to show their colours. 'Hello, there,' said Tom.

'I'd given you up.'

Tom shrugged. 'Listen, with my family, you never know whether you're fish, fowl or faggots from the cheap end of the market. We had a situation.'

'Oh. Everything all right now?'

Tom cleared his head of Maureen, the sight of her, the sound of sobs slowing with every move he made. 'It was our youngest threatening to leave home for a while. I had to stay and calm my wife down – she gets upset. Maureen sends her apologies, by the way. She says she'll meet you when she's in a better frame of mind and not in the bath.'

Roy laughed. 'Unusual things, women. I've sometimes wondered whether we're the same species as them. We've one at the bottom of Lawton Road who collects operations. I'm not joking. She looks in medical books, finds an illness she fancies and works on it. Come in.'

Tom hung up his coat in the small hallway. 'You've done a good job in here, Roy. Glad you kept the original mouldings and so forth. So. What's the operation woman working on now?'

'As far as I know, it's ingrowing toenails. She's wearing her sister's shoes – too small for her – and binding her feet at night. If she gets this operation, it'll be number twenty, then she's retiring. The thing is, the hospitals are cottoning on at last. She's had her appendix out twice.'

Tom blinked.

'I know, I know,' Roy sighed. 'But she came over all acute one day, and off she went in a bell-clanger. Turned out to be wind. They rooted round in her belly for a few minutes, but all they found was methane. She stunk out the theatre and three corridors. There was talk of issuing gas masks, and the water board dug up the drains...'

Tom held up a hand. 'Enough. I come from a mad Irish family, so I get plenty of this at home.'

Roy, acting in the mode of estate agent, led his 'client' through the house. In spite of his difficult leg, he had turned the place into a miniature palace. 'I hadn't the heart when he was alive.' There was no need to nominate the 'he', since Tom already knew about Roy's worthless, cruel father. 'But once he'd gone, I noticed what a pretty little house I had. Dirty, untidy, but attractive, it begged to be restored.'

'For her?'

Roy shook his head. 'For me. Though I suppose showing her what I can do did no harm. No, she'll never live here. If – and that's a big word – anything came of our so-called relationship, we'd sell both houses and get a bigger one. She has three children, two cats and a mother.'

Tom tutted. 'I have a mother-in-law. She's a great woman, but she could talk the legs off a grand piano. Good-hearted, she is, only she's always right. When she's totally wrong, she's righter than ever. Now. What's that lovely smell coming from your kitchen? I could eat a bald man on a butty, I'm telling you.'

They dined on a fruity curry served with coconut, sliced banana and home-made pickle. 'By, that was good,' Tom declared when he'd finished off everything apart from the pattern on the plate. 'A lot nicer than a bald man on a sarnie. The last time I had one of them, he was all gristle.'

They ate very English apple tart and drank coffee in the front living room. Tom noticed that Roy placed himself in a chair angled to get the best view of the house opposite. 'Is she in?' Tom asked.

Roy shook his head. 'Isle of Man while the schools are on Easter break. She'll– I mean they'll be back in a couple of days.'

Tom took a sip of coffee. 'You're in pain, aren't you? Like I was when you found me down at the Pier Head. Come on, lad, you can't go breaking

241

your heart over the impossible. She'll either come round, or she won't. Do you want to be sitting here when you're eighty wondering if she'll have you? Wouldn't you be better off looking for a life elsewhere? Selling up and moving on?'

'I can't. In case she needs me. I help with the kids sometimes, and I do stuff round the house for her.'

'You sound like a servant.'

Roy shrugged. 'I'd rather serve her than be master of anybody else. Over twenty years, I've felt like this. When she chose Phil, I grinned and bore it, but he's dead now, and ... and ... well–'

'You'd like to take his place.'

'Not really. Nobody could ever take his place. I just want her. Mad, isn't it?'

Tom was no longer sure. The idea of life without his Maureen was horrible, but he'd been with her for a long time... Yes, he'd been lucky. He took a photograph from his wallet and handed it to his companion. 'There's my trouble and strife,' he said. 'And I wouldn't part with her for all the riches in the world. Roy? Roy?'

'I'll. .. er ... just a minute.'

Roy staggered to the bureau, opened a drawer and pulled out a photograph. 'Here. Have a look at that.'

Tom looked. 'But it's–'

'Yes, I know.'

'Roy, they could be twins, except mine's a good few years older than yours.'

'Yes.'

Each man stared at a picture of the other's beloved.

'We all have a double, or so they say,' Tom said.

Roy cleared his throat. 'And they're not exactly the same. The mouths and eyes are slightly different, but look at the hairlines, the cheekbones.'

'I know. It's uncanny. We could swap photos, and we'd hardly know the difference except for the clothes and the backgrounds. You've good taste, Roy.'

There seemed to be little left to say. Both men sat and stared at the walls for a few minutes, each aware of the other's inexplicable discomfort. Tom picked up the photograph of Maureen. 'She wants fish and chips,' he said quietly. 'If I go now, I'll avoid the rush after the pubs close.'

On his way back to Bootle, he found himself strangely close to tears. Tonight, he had eaten in the house of a grand chap who loved the spitting image of Maureen. As he waited for fish, chips and peas, Tom counted his blessings once again. 'Plenty of vinegar, please. My wife loves her vinegar.' *And I love my wife,* his inner voice said. *Between us, me and Maureen will get Roy and Rosh together.*

He drove the rest of the way to Stanley Square. Maureen and Rosh had to meet.

Well, I'm really done for now. Old Mr Bailey's gone, and his wife wants the shop shutting for a while as a mark of respect? Respect? He loved his tobaccos and his customers, liked chatting to other pipe-smokers about all the different flavours. Respect should mean keeping the place running, but no. She's a woman. Women are daft.

Nine

The house on Menlove Avenue was a huge part of Tess's dream come true. It was pretty, solid, cosy, and it was hers. Housewifery was her main skill and chief employment, but she was spreading her wings, working, making a difference.

Another possession about which she rejoiced was her driving licence, that cute little red book with her name and address printed inside. It didn't record the fact that she had passed first time with scarcely any effort on her part, but that didn't really matter. Well aware of what she'd achieved, she made sure that most people within her sphere were aware of that particular truth. Tess knew of women who had failed five, six or seven times, so she held her head high every time she opened the door of her Morris. The van was not a thing of beauty, but she was in control of it, and that was what counted. Tess now considered herself to be a woman of substance, and that attitude was demonstrated in her demeanour. It was very much a case of *Look out world, here I come*.

She had two jobs, neither of them connected to the Smithdown Road launderette. The tenant in the flat above took care of the business, and she seemed a decent body, grateful for cheap accommodation and a wage. So Tess was free at last and could make her money as she wished. Containment on Smithdown Road had never suited her, and she felt as if she had been released from prison after a long sentence. They were a proper family in a proper house, and Tess had finally reached her main goal.

On Saturday mornings, Tess wove her way round Liverpool, stopping at various small agencies, usually newspaper shops, to pick up football pools coupons and cash, all of which had to be delivered to Littlewoods long before matches kicked off. There was paperwork involved, and Mark rode shotgun, as he put it, so that he could add up and fill in forms while she drove. Tess was beginning to be impressed by her daughter's boyfriend. He wore leathers, had a loud, huge motorbike and a decent shirt-and-tie job during the week. He also hung in patiently while Anne-Marie flaunted herself in front of the Quarry Men, seemed not to mind while the wayward child chased after the Lennon boy, Paul McCartney and anyone else with a guitar or a drumstick.

'Why?' Tess asked him often. 'When she's so … silly?'

And he would smile his slow, beautiful smile, displaying perfect teeth. 'I'm here for the long haul,' he said. 'Anne-Marie may even turn out to be as pretty as her mother, and her mother's the bonus. I like being seen round and about with a beautiful older woman in a clapped-out Morris van.'

'There's nothing at all wrong with my van, I'll have you know.'

'That's not what your Sean says. He thinks if it were a horse you'd have to put it out of its misery, or the RSPCA would haunt you.'

'All mechanics talk like that, Mark. Plumbers are the same, just drama queens with toolboxes. They do that sucking in of breath through their teeth, then tell you to get new taps, not just washers. Our Sean does the same with gearboxes and what have you. Sharp intake of air, head shaking because the job isn't going to be cheap. You don't fool me, any of you. No man can ever fool a woman, and even other women have a hard time fooling me.'

Tess's other work involved clothing. Again, she picked up from assorted agencies, mostly shops, and took the clothes to Johnson's Dye Works, a huge employer in the Bootle area. She would deliver the dirty, pick up the dry-cleaned, then return items to the same shops from which she had collected earlier. Always aware of the dangers of chemicals, she drove windblown and rain-damped, because carbon tetrachloride was a killer. But she loved driving, enjoyed being out and about with just herself or Mark for company.

Life was good and safe. The fear of a return to childhood poverty had lessened in its intensity. She had a beautiful home, two attractive and hardworking children, a car of sorts and, on Saturday mornings, the company of an interesting and very handsome young man. All was well. No. All was almost well. There was a niggle in her head, and it was making its relentless way to the forefront of her consciousness.

She pulled into the driveway. She had dropped Mark in town, where he had muttered darkly about an expected invasion by Mods wearing army greatcoats and riding girlie scooters. It was Saturday lunch time, and the children were out.

They would be home shortly, since both the garage and the hair salon worked just a half-day on Saturdays. Don's car wasn't there. He worked some weekends for just a few hours, but he had spent more time at home of late. They were closer. She liked being closer, being valued, even loved. He was delighted with her, and she enjoyed his delight.

'I gave him a hard time,' she told her nutkin tree. She had no idea of the tree's real genre, but she called it nutkin because of the squirrels. A slight smile decorated her features. 'What the hell were you doing with a frying pan, a rose bowl and two tins of peas?' she remembered Don asking.

'Merely temporary measures,' she had replied loftily. He had thought she was crazy. She was a long way from that.

The tins of peas had been replaced by bricks, then by a bit of carpentry performed by Don. The tins of peas, then the bricks, now the proper fixings kept steady a plank along which the squirrels scampered to their little house, another item built by Tess's husband to her design. They travelled along rope, frail branches and tree bark, tails positioned for balance, one eye on the birds, the other on fellow squirrels. They were cunning and fun, and they had become Tess's hobby.

The frying pan had held the creatures' water containing a tiny pinch of salt to hold off the ravages of frost, while the rose bowl was filled with nut-and-fat lollipops pushed through the metal grille into a mass of Plasticine. Tess's hope that the squirrels would stay in the nutkin tree had been a vain one. They ate anything and everything, while the birds, intended beneficiaries of the lollipops made by Tess, had to be grateful for scraps left by the rodent invaders. She didn't feed any of them during these months of summer. They were wild, they were foragers, and they could get foraging for a change. If they wanted room service fifty-two weeks a year, they were in the wrong hotel.

'Nobody ever said it would be fair,' she mumbled as she stepped out of the van.

'Talking to yourself, Mrs Compton?'

She turned and found herself gazing into the amused eyes of the Lennon boy. He was another good-looking lad. If he'd get rid of the Presley quiff, he'd look nearly normal.

'Well, I'm sure of an audience that way,' she replied.

'True,' he said. 'I see you've got some squizzles. They come down from Strawberry Fields. See you.' He walked off, hands in the pockets of a fashionably scarred leather jacket, jaw moving as he chewed his statutory gum. Squizzles. She would remember that word for the rest of her life.

The house was echoey without the usual number of humans. Tess shoved some braised steak into the oven to heat through before starting on her vegetables. The niggle continued to niggle. There was something wrong with Don. Peas scraped from the pod made music as they tumbled into a metal colander. Where were the carrots? He was awkward, uncommunicative, quiet during lovemaking. No need to worry about gravy; that was in with the steak. He wouldn't talk about how he felt. Don was giving her a taste of her own medicine, and it was not pleasant. No, he wasn't punishing her. There was not a single bad bone in the man, and he enjoyed the new closeness, as did she. 'Surprised yourself, didn't you, Tess?' she said. 'Life in the old girl yet, what?' But yes, he was quiet.

She had been a terrible wife. She should have spoken to him about her faith, her need to abstain because contraception was sinful. These carrots were tough to cut. Sinful? Older and wiser now, she wondered whether Rome wanted millions of Catholics, thereby reducing its women to the status of brood mares, 'I was so bloody selfish,' she told the wall. 'Bitter. I was a bitter, nasty bitch, and he's a good man.' Early menopause had arrived like a gift from above, though she hadn't felt too well of late. A woman's lot had never been, would never be a happy one. There was pain in her belly. She had better go and see the doc again next week.

Carrots, peas, braised steak and a bit of mash; yes, all that would do nicely for Saturday lunch. Weekends were high tea days. The main meal was produced at lunch time, while high tea was a feast of home-made scones, sandwiches with the crusts removed, and Tess's speciality, her cakes or pies. He wasn't completely happy. He pretended to be happy, but he wasn't. She'd made a banana loaf for tea, and a feather-light sponge cake with real cream. Oh, she was a lucky woman, because she had a light touch with pastry and cakes. Edgy. Yes, that was the word for Don. As if he could never get really comfortable.

She remembered the conclusion she had

reached months ago: there had to have been another woman. Don adored his children, had stayed for their sake. 'And all I did was moan about the flat, the business, my own precious self, a house on Menlove Avenue, and Skaters' Trails blooming carpet. Idiot.' He couldn't be blamed for seeking comfort elsewhere. How did she feel about it? She hadn't the slightest idea. Well, no, that wasn't quite the case. She was empty, yet there was no jealousy. 'I understand,' she admitted aloud after a few seconds. 'Don was lonely. Marriage can be the loneliest place.'

While slicing carrots, she failed to concentrate, cutting quite deeply into the middle finger of her left hand. There was very little pain, just a twinge when she moved her hand. Orange circles of carrot and red droplets of blood did not look well together. Who was the other woman? Where was she? Did he love her? As she made to stand, all strength drained suddenly from her body. She felt it leaving her head, her chest, her abdomen and, finally, her legs. There was blood everywhere. It was all over the floor. How could so much come from a nick in a finger?

With Saturday's lunch unfinished, she began to lose consciousness, fell off the chair and lay on a black-and-white chequered floor across which a pool of bright blood began to spread. Her last thought was that the braising steak might burn. There would be no dinner and ... and...

Fortunately, Don was the one who found her. As he dialled 999, he thanked God that his children were absent, because the scene was truly terrifying. And she couldn't die, mustn't die. He loved

250

her. And there was Molly, then all this blood; it was coming from Tess's womb, he thought. And there was Molly and this house and Anne-Marie on her way back from work and– 'Do something,' he snapped. 'Stop Mollying about.'

Cold water on towels pushed up between her legs, blood in her beautiful hair, so lovely, that hair. Face drained of colour, hands so white that touches of pale pink nail varnish managed to look garish. She was a fair-skinned woman anyway, but this was ... different. A finger had been cut; at the same time, the trouble in her insides had shown itself, and she was bleeding towards death. Where the hell was the ambulance?

At last, the tinny sound of distant bells reached him and got louder. Was she breathing? Was her heart beating? As the front door crashed inward, Don found himself hoping that Tess's new panelling hadn't been damaged, because she guarded that with her life. Her life. Did she have one?

Two huge men entered the room. 'Women's Hospital,' said the first. 'Follow in your car, Mr ... er...'

'Compton,' Don managed.

'Yes, well, we'd best be quick, Mr Compton. Leave the room, please, while we get her stretchered. And calm yourself, because blood always looks more than it is.'

Don went into the living room. Through the window, he watched the men pushing his wife into the ambulance. Neighbours stood about in small, chattering clutches. Blood. He couldn't let Anne-Marie find all that blood. But he had to get to the Women's... He couldn't be in two places at

251

once. Even Tess had never managed to be in two places at once. Wife. Blood. Wife or blood? The knee started to throb. Even thinking about cleaning the floor made the whole leg ache.

He cleaned. It was what she would have wanted. Like him, she preferred to shelter the children from unnecessary suffering, so Don worked at shifting blood that had flowed very recently through the veins of his Tess. Two bath towels went straight into the outside dustbin; the remainder of the mess was shifted by a long mop and a bucket of disinfected water. Did the white tiles look a bit pinkish? Was his wife alive or dead? Were the kids almost home? *Oh, God, don't make me have to live without her. She might be a terrible woman in some respects, but she's my terrible woman.*

Here they came, another pair guilty of assaulting Tess's precious panelling by throwing the front door against it. And she rushed into his mind, a tiny girl who slept in a gypsy caravan, an infant too small to fight her siblings for food, and he studied her chosen place of safety for a few seconds. This kitchen was her shelter, her comfort zone. Poverty was Tess's dread, her nemesis–

'Dad?'

He turned off the oven. 'Anne-Marie. Sean.'

'Where's the dinner?' the latter asked.

Don looked at the ceiling and shook his head. 'Haven't you noticed something else missing, lad? Like your mother? That woman you see every day, fair hair, blue eyes, the person who cooks and cleans and–' He closed his mouth tightly. Making his son feel guilty would not improve matters. 'Sorry. I didn't mean to say all that, not to you.

She's on her way to hospital. I stayed to clean up the ... the mess.'

'Why hospital?' Anne-Marie's voice was shrill, childlike.

'I think they call it a haemorrhage, love.'

'Is that bleeding?'

'Yes. Yes, it is. I cleaned it up. She would have wanted that.'

Anne-Marie swallowed audibly. 'Would have wanted? Is she ... dead?'

'No. I don't think so.'

Sean stared hard at his dad. 'Why are we standing here?' he asked.

Don offered no reply. He didn't know why his legs wouldn't move. Yes, he did. His legs wouldn't budge because the rest of him didn't want the answer. Was she dead? He heard himself. *Tess, why is there a mousetrap in the clean linen cupboard?*

She had laughed at him. Her throat, when she raised her head to laugh, was swan-like, slender but firm, white, kissable. *We have a mouse, you nutter. They come out at night. You don't want your foot caught in the trap, do you? So I put it away in the morning, get more cheese, bait the thing and put it out last thing at night.* Yes, there had been an explanation for all of it. Early menopause? Or something else, something that tried to take her life on a beautiful summer Saturday? And he allowed the word through at last. Cancer. Rumour had it that the disease loved oxygen, so after a patient had been opened up... Another old wives' tale.

'Dad?' Anne-Marie was clearly approaching hysteria. 'Come on, please,' she begged. 'She needs us with her. What's the matter with you?'

Sean answered for his father. 'Shock.'

None of them would remember any details of the journey to the Women's Hospital. Don, an automaton, obeyed traffic lights and Give Way signs, but the car seemed to guide itself in the right direction. As soon as he parked, his son and daughter jumped out and leapt in the direction of the main entrance.

He followed on feet of lead. Inside, he discovered that his wife, who had been judged an emergency, was in theatre. He signed something or other without fully realizing that he had given staff carte blanche as far as treatment was concerned, then was led by a nurse to a chair next to his children. 'Your dad's in a bit of a state,' she advised Sean. 'Come with me, and we'll get him some sweet tea.'

As he sipped the hot liquid, Don began his return to the here and now. 'How did we get to the hospital?' he asked Anne-Marie.

'You drove.'

'Did I?'

The girl nodded. It looked as if both her parents were no longer in working order. 'You need that sugar, Dad. Mam's having her... I think it's her womb removed. And blood transfusions. They tried to explain to me, because I'm a girl, and they said a word with fibre in it.'

'Fibroids,' said Don, whose blood sugar level was improving fast. 'They're not cancer, but they're growths.'

'Will she be all right?' Sean asked.

'I have faith in her and in this place. This is a damn good hospital. But the real answer is I don't know. We have to pray, I think.' He drained his cup. That had been the best cuppa ever. Oh, Tess. Surely God wasn't ready for an eccentric who looked after squirrels and birds, who worried lest he caught his foot in a mousetrap, whose fear of poverty had made her outwardly hard and acquisitive? She was so different, so decided, so Irish, so beautiful, so difficult. It could not be her time, not yet. In her late thirties, menopause had not been expected; but it probably wasn't menopause at all. No, it was more likely to have been these bloody fibroids. Bloody was a good adjective in this scenario.

After an afternoon as long as a week, a nurse took Don on one side. 'She's in recovery, Mr Compton. They'll keep an eye on her there for a couple of hours. You won't be able to see her for a while, because she lost a lot of blood, and we need to wait for the anaesthetic to wear off. But she's young, well nourished and in good health apart from this problem with the fibroids and endometriosis – that's a kind of internal bleeding. Her blood pressure's a bit low, but it's an improvement on earlier readings. You were lucky to find her in time.'

'Yes. Thanks.' He returned unsteadily to his offspring and delivered an edited version.

Suddenly hungry, the pair went off to scout the neighbourhood for food.

Don sat. *You were lucky to find her in time.* Where had he been? He'd been paying his dues in Molly's bed, had been recompensing his mistress for providing Tess with the house she had craved. Molly had been his beloved during years of starvation, had spoken to him properly while Tess had screamed or sat silently during meals when the children were present. Molly had given him back his masculinity. He swallowed hard. For some months, he had served two women, and the cost of his duplicity would be high.

Why should Tess pay that price? He knew now that she'd had her reasons for behaving as she had; it had not been her fault. Whatever happened, she would pay. Her life still hung in the balance; the loss of that might be the ultimate price. If she survived, she might lose her place of safety, the house of which she was so naively proud. It was just a semi in an area that sported many pairs of such buildings, but it was her palace, her security, her territory. He remembered fear in her eyes, nightmares during which she kicked and screamed because there were too many siblings in her bed.

I have to talk to Molly. I must go to her as soon as possible and tell her I've been unfaithful with my wife as well as to my wife. When the axe falls, I'll just have to cope. Tess has changed, but her childhood hasn't. She might go back to those awful black dreams if we lose the house, and we have to lose the house. Thank God I never got to Harley Street to have my knee done, because I would have owed Molly for that as well.

'Mr Compton?' A gentle hand touched his shoulder. It was the same nurse who had brought sweet tea. 'Here you are. Two sarnies, one's egg, the other's salmon and cucumber, I think. It's Sister's. She's the only one who can afford red salmon. Oh, and here's a glass of lemonade.'

He broke, tears pouring down his cheeks. The

nurse got help, picked up the food, and followed Don into the sister's office. A porter placed him in a comfortable chair. 'There ya go, lad,' he said in broad Scouse. 'Let our Loosey-Loose look after you, eh? Real name's Lucy, but she won 'er nickname. Loose? Her drawers've been fitted with a lift mechanism – press her nose, and they go all the way down to the cellar.'

The nurse clouted the porter, who left the room wearing a brown overall coat, a sore shoulder and a broad grin.

'Don't cry,' she urged. 'I have a sneaking feeling that your madam will be painting the wards with a two-inch brush come Monday. She woke. And I think she picked up where she left off. Was she cooking?'

Don sniffed back a new flood of emotion. 'She woke?'

'Told me to switch the oven off or her steak would burn. Then she went back to sleep. She might have been tired, but she was bossy.'

Don allowed a long, shuddering sigh to leave his body. The sigh carried with it a story, and Don found himself placing the rather confused weight of his guilt on the shoulders of a very young woman. 'And she'll lose her house, so it'll be back to her childhood when she's asleep, that caravan, too many kids and not enough food. And yes, she's a bossy boots and no, I wouldn't part with her for all the clocks in Switzerland. I've been a fool, haven't I?'

'I'm sorry, Mr Compton, but we all make mistakes, you know.'

'So am I sorry, Lucy. When we moved into the

house, the first thing she did was spend a mint and stash food everywhere. Kitchen cupboards got crammed, and she put tinned food in the bottom of every wardrobe. She can't bear to see birds or squirrels without something to eat, so we're overrun. One cheeky little squirrel takes food from her hands, and we've a robin who comes through the open window to watch while Tess washes up. He likes a bit of arrowroot biscuit.' He paused. 'You won't tell anybody, will you? I'm going to see Molly myself. It has to come from me.'

She squeezed his hand. 'I think you know the answer to that one, Mr Compton.'

'Don. It's Gordon, but I don't like it.' A slight smile touched his lips. 'When I'm in real trouble with the wife, she screams out my full name. Gets my attention every time.'

Lucy nodded. 'Sounds like my kind of woman, Don. Now, listen. Write your phone number on that bit of paper. Give it to me, then go home and sort out her bloody braising steak or whatever it is. The minute there's any change in her condition, I'll phone you. You have got a phone?'

He nodded, wrote down the number, thanked her, left the sandwiches, but drained the lemonade glass.

The kids were outside eating chips from paper. 'They wouldn't let us in with chips,' Sean complained. 'How is she?'

'Asking about her steak when she woke. But she's still in the recovery room. We've to go home. Lucy, her nurse, will phone us as soon as there's any change. Come on. No point hanging

258

round here all day when there's nothing we can do.'

'What can we do at home?' Anne-Marie asked.

Don touched his daughter's arm. 'We can free up three chairs in that waiting room for a start. What would Tess do if I became ill? She'd look after you, and visit me once I was on a ward. You and your brother have been at the top of our list since you were born. She would take you home and wait for the phone to ring.' He thanked God for making Tess mither till she got her phone. She wasn't keeping up with the Joneses; she was setting the pace, determined to overtake the Joneses, the Smiths and any others who thought they were ahead.

They got in the car. She'd be wanting a better vehicle once she left hospital. Oh yes, she would demand a prize after her ordeal. She was a delicious woman, a good housekeeper, keeper of the Book of Knowledge, which she had written herself, good at her part-time jobs. But she remained slightly greedy and selfish due to deprivation at a very young age. Yet she was so damned desirable. Fibroids and endo-something-or-other. Not cancer, not like his poor old mother, and thank God for that.

'Will she be all right, Dad?'

'Yes, Anne-Marie. A woman who wakes from anaesthesia and demands that someone saves her steak is not at death's door. St Peter wouldn't know what to do with her. She'd be polishing harps, haloes and golden staircases, setting mouse-traps and feeding squirrels. I mean, we've had her for years, and can we manage her?'

'No,' chorused the passengers.

At home, Don positioned himself on the third stair so that he would be near the telephone shelf. Anne-Marie busied herself with her version of high tea. She used tray cloths, but drew the line at doilies. Doilies were for if the queen visited or for high days and holidays. The doorbell sounded, and she fled through the hall to answer it, closing the inner door behind her.

Don stared at the phone, willing it to ring. Not with bad news, of course. If it rang within the next half-hour, Tess would be all right. Why was he playing stupid, childish games? If it didn't ring in the next half-hour, would his wife be dead? 'Come on, Lucy. Talk to me. Don't leave me dangling like a fly in a web.'

Anne-Marie returned. She leaned against the inner door, the one that was guilty of attacking Tess's panelling. It needed a rubber stopper. 'He wanted to know how Mam was, said he saw the ambulance.'

'Who did?'

'John Lennon.' She squeezed in next to her dad. 'You know what?'

'What what? Or should it be which what?'

'It's not the right day for stupid jokes. He's just an ordinary lad. Mark's better-looking than him.'

'What did you think he was? The one person in the world who doesn't need toilet paper?'

'Dad, don't be vulgar. He's going places.'

'Yes, the dole for a start.'

Anne-Marie awarded her father a look fit to strip paint. 'You old people don't understand, do you? He's got it.'

'Got what? Measles, scarlet fever, a bad cold?' Why wouldn't the bloody phone ring? His daughter was wagging her finger at him now. She became more like her mother with every day that passed.

'He's gifted. So's Paul. We aren't all stuck with Judy Garland over the flipping rainbow. I am going to make tea.' She jumped to her feet and stalked off.

Don made a note about rubber stoppers. If he saved the panelling from further abuse, Tess would come home fit and well. Underneath the rubber stoppers, he wrote *Bookcase*. She wasn't an avid reader these days, but she'd be pleased if her house looked as if it contained educated folk. *New ironing board* and *Chanel 5* joined the list. He needed a bloody head doctor. How could writing lists help Tess get home safe and well?

Anne-Marie stood in front of him once more, arms folded, foot tapping. 'Our Sean's brewed the tea, and that's a miracle in itself, because he never lifts a finger in the house. Get through there, Dad. We're all worrying, all feeling a bit sick. Would Mam let you eat on the stairs near her new wallpaper? She'd have your guts for garters and your hair for cushion stuffing.'

'I'm waiting to hear.'

'So are we, but we know that staring at a phone won't make it ring.'

His little girl was a woman. In the absence of her mother, she stepped up to the plate and coped. Even if she married young, she would make a good job of it as long as she landed the right man. 'You're special,' he said.

'I know. I'm being moved up from apprentice to improver, because I'm a brilliant stylist. Anybody else has to do a full year, and I've only done eight months. See? All this time, you've had a genius, and you never knew it. So get in there and eat my mother's cake.'

And Don realized in that moment that most of the Irish families he knew laboured under matriarchy. Tiny women brought huge men to heel, and daughters followed in the footsteps of their female predecessors, often learning much of their intricate art from two generations of warm and loving dictators. It was not a bad way to live.

They picked at their slightly lower tea. Tess's high teas were ornate celebrations with matching porcelain cups, saucers, milk jug and lidded sugar pot. In fact, when Don thought about Tess's productions, he wondered why there were no finger-bowls. Anne-Marie had done a good job, but with the ordinary everyday crockery. 'I didn't want to break anything good. There'll be trouble enough, anyway. That nurse told me Mam won't be able to use the hoover, drive or clean up for at least six weeks. She'll go menthol eucalyptus if she can't do stuff. She mustn't make beds, reach up too high, open and close windows, or carry anything heavier than a feather.'

Sean groaned. 'God, she'll be in a mood.'

Don nodded, a wistful smile on his face. 'As long as she's in one piece, I don't care.'

Anne-Marie glanced at her brother. 'We thought ... we thought you were going to split up when we lived on Smithdown Road,' she said. 'We were scared, because she shouldn't be on her own. She needs us, Dad. I reckon she always will, because it's the way she's made.'

'I know. Don't worry about that, because it's more or less sorted out.' There was Molly. It couldn't be put right until he'd seen Molly. 'Your mother had a terrible childhood, hungry, cold and miserable. She never learned to read till she got to England. Quite a few Irish kids in remote areas didn't go to school. The fear of poverty plagues her.'

'I know,' chorused the siblings.

The phone jangled raucously.

Don stood, knocking over his chair so that it lay on its back. He rushed down the hall, cursing Dunkirk for his inability to move at a faster pace. Snatching up the receiver, he breathed a choked 'Hello' into it.

'Don?'

'Yes.'

'It's Lucy. She's fine, on a ward and fast asleep. Don't bother coming, because you might as well talk to the wall, and visiting's seven till eight, so she's not likely to surface by then. Come at three tomorrow. We have longer visiting on a Sunday.' She paused. 'Don?'

'What?'

'Don't cry.'

He hadn't realized that he'd been weeping. After thanking Lucy, he hung up and turned to his children, who stood clinging on to each other. Drying his eyes, he gave them the news. 'She made it. They said to stay away tonight, because she won't even know we're there, and she needs her rest.' The three of them gathered in a huddle, each one clutching the other two.

Sean was the first to break away. 'Synchronized sobbing,' he muttered. 'I'm going for a pint. You coming, Dad?'

'No. I'm off to see Molly. I need to tell her what's happened, because I'll have to have time off when Tess gets home. Anne-Marie?'

'What?'

'Behave yourself while your brother and I are out. No going upstairs with Mark.' Who was he to be telling this young woman how to live? She was nudging sixteen, while he was a man in his forties with a wife, a mistress, and a house he didn't really own. He was the reprobate, the one playing an away game several times a month. Visits had diminished of late, because he was living two lives. And Molly seemed ... different. Was she ill, too? He couldn't hurt her if she was ill, could he?

Anne-Marie, looking for all the world like an infant teacher with a non-cooperative pupil, tut-tutted her displeasure. 'Dad, one of these days you'll have to stop worrying, or you'll get measured for the wooden overcoat. You fret too much. Cool it, Daddy-oh.'

So he cooled it. On this pleasant summer evening, he drove to Otterspool Prom and watched the world go by. Ships, their size diminished by distance, glided silently across the horizon. Perhaps Liverpool sailors stood on deck, their eyes fixed on the Liver Birds. Soon, busy small tugs would start to bob about like little rubber ducks in a big bath. They would fuss and chunter until they got their bigger sister moving in more or less the right direction.

Courting couples walked by, while a pair of pensioners on a bench shared a crossword and a bag of butties. A child kicked a ball, fell about laughing when his dad failed to stop it. 'Goal,' he screamed. Don hadn't played football with Sean, because Dunkirk had put paid to that.

He was stalling, wasn't he? Procrastination, thief of time and all that. He hoped Tess was asleep. If she woke and he wasn't there, would she be afraid and lonely? He remembered how thoroughly he had hated her, but perhaps dislike as strong as that was the reverse side of true love. She used to enjoy concerts, didn't she? And the cinema, even the theatre. He recalled her standing up with Anne-Marie during a pantomime, 'He's behind you.' Oh, he had to start taking her out again. Life was more than work and worry; there had to be some fun as well.

Molly was expecting him. They were meant to be going to a pub, but he didn't feel up to it. If she was intending to perform her George Formby, she would go anyway, because she didn't like letting folk down. Neither did he; the thought of her being upset gave him pain in his stomach. Molly had done so much for him, so much for Tess, that she deserved better treatment, yet he could not love two women. Nor could he go through the motions with Molly just to ensure that Tess kept the house and the stability she drew from its existence.

He climbed back into the car and rubbed his troubled knee. Hanging round here wasn't any comfort, because he knew he was avoiding the issue, and that wasn't in his nature. Hiding away in the physical sense wasn't easy, not with a limp as pronounced as his. Socially, he'd always enjoyed a game of darts, a pie and a pint, and a chinwag, though he didn't have close male friends. Molly had been the centre of his universe for so long that he couldn't imagine life without her. But she was his employer as well as his mistress, and he was likely to lose a job he loved. Job, house, his wife's sanity, all were threatened while she lay in hospital recovering from major surgery.

Molly was waiting for him. 'You all right, love?' The question was coated with concern. 'You look a bit off-colour to me. Get yourself some brewer's yeast. My mother swore by it.'

Don patted the dogs, gave Molly a peck on the cheek and sat down. He had to offload the first part quickly. 'Tess collapsed in a pool of blood today, Moll. I found her when I got back from … from here. She was rushed off in an ambulance and they operated on her this afternoon. Woman's trouble.'

Molly sat next to him. 'Why aren't you with her?' Her tone had become accusatory. 'She shouldn't be on her own at a time like this. Whatever are you thinking of? That poor girl.'

He groaned. 'She's unconscious, so we were told to stay at home. I just went and stood on Otterspool Prom staring at the water. I don't fancy the pub. I don't fancy much, if I'm honest.'

Molly bent and pushed her ukulele case out of view. She was going nowhere, because she was needed here. For some months, she had felt him distancing himself from her. She, in her turn, had been holding back, because she wanted the play-

266

ing field to be level. Although she loved him, he in no way matched her deceased husband, the love of her life. There were other men who liked her, but ... but she would miss Don if he left her.

'Were you meant to be playing tonight?' Don asked.

'It's optional, because I'm not actually booked. It's not a birthday or an anniversary, so I needn't go. Anyway, I'm thinking about your Tess. This is shocking news. Oh, I do hope she'll be all right.'

'Yes, me too.' Suddenly tired, he leaned his head on the back of the sofa. 'I can't go on, Mo. It's as if I'm running at top speed just to stand still. There's no sense to life, no meaning. I keep missing stuff. My little girl's turned herself into a woman while I wasn't looking, my lad can brew tea, now Tess is dragged down by fibroids and some fancy illness that causes internal bleeding. Where've I been while life's kept happening, Moll?'

She closed her eyes. 'Not here. Not all the time, anyway.'

Don sighed. 'It's not so much where I've been physically. It's in my head, as if I went home today and the film ran faster before grinding to a halt. And there she was, blood everywhere, carrots and peas on the table, steak in the oven, her floor all stained. She loves that floor.'

Molly knew that her time had come. Not for one moment did she resent her erstwhile lover's decision, since she knew that nothing lasted. With her husband gone, and her lack of children, she understood full well how disappointing life could be.

Don continued. 'It took a long time to change the first reel, Molly. You changed it. Once she was in that house, she was safe, you see. It ran more smoothly once I found the reasons for her daft behaviour.'

The words crept from her throat to the front of her mouth. 'You still love her, don't you, Don?'

He hesitated briefly. 'Yes. Yes, I'm afraid I do. But that doesn't mean I never loved you. There was a time, as you well know, when I could hardly stand the sight of her. But she's changed. The house changed her, safety changed her. And now...' His voice died of exhaustion.

Molly stood up. 'And now what? What? You think I'll grab it off her? What do you take me for, Don Compton? That house is for your kids and it's legally yours. When you and Tess keel over, it'll be worth enough to buy them each a house, even if they're in a terrace. Your job's safe, and we can still have our lunches. There is no price to pay. You don't really know me, do you?'

An old saying coursed through Don's mind. Friends may become lovers, but lovers never friends. 'It's always felt like taking charity,' he mumbled.

'Pride,' Molly declared, 'is worth nowt a pound, as my old Manchester granny used to say. I've no kids. I've given you a house to leave to yours.' She bit her lip to stop the tears before they flowed. 'Without you, I would have stayed in this mausoleum and let the business down the road go to the devil. When he died and...' She swallowed and began again. 'When Matt died, you ran everything single-handedly and saved me from ruin. So

I saved Tess. No way will I take anything back. I couldn't anyway, because it's not mine. And I'll be all right. We can have our lunch at the pub or here, do our paperwork, go our separate ways and it'll all be OK.'

He knew that the words were choking her. Don was no prize, but he was all Molly had clung to since her husband died. Furthermore, he was sure that she would weep after he had gone tonight, because this was a huge house for one woman and two dogs. 'You need a smaller place with a large garden. Get yourself a plot of land and an architect. Let's face it, you've access to all materials at cost, and you know some bloody good builders. Fresh start, new furniture – it worked for Tess. But no Skaters' Trails.'

She laughed, yet the sound was hollow. 'Look after her, lad. And take time off when you need it. It'll be all right. I'm sure she'll be out of there in no time and driving you mad with her panelling and her wallpaper–'

'And her squirrels. She loves them, you know.'

'Yes, you told me.' He often talked about Tess these days. Molly felt cold, as if an icy hand had fastened its grip round her heart. She remembered the sensation; she'd known it in the weeks after her husband's death. It was loneliness. It was also the realization that she needed a companion, because she was like one pea in an otherwise empty pod. 'I'll build a bungalow,' she announced after a pause. 'Four bedrooms, a couple of bathrooms, orangery, indoor swimming pool and land for the dogs. You're right, it's time I treated myself a bit better. Thanks for everything, Don.'

When he left, he felt as if he had cut the throat of a kitten. Molly had claws and teeth, but underneath the strength sat a weakened woman.

The house on Menlove Avenue was dark and empty. In the bedroom, Don caught a whiff of Tess's *Je Reviens,* a powdery, flowery and sickly kind of smell. But it was posh, so Tess loved it. He would steer her gently towards *Chanel,* a more solid, adult aroma. God, this was funny. Was he turning into some sort of expert in the area of women's cosmetics?

He sat down. Tonight a wonderful, amazing woman had been hurt. He had done the hurting, and she had shown the bravery. Another lay in hospital with some of her insides missing. And here was her bed, a single bed, separated from his by a substantial chest of drawers. Well, that would all change for a start. Both kids had old beds, so these could be their new ones, because he intended to make a nest for himself and Tess. All rules would be broken; to hell with pastels and beige, because this would be a boudoir.

Don laid himself flat on his own divan. A bit of red, a gilt-framed mirror, good sheets with a high-count cotton thread, dressing table, new hairbrush, comb and hand mirror all to match. Manicure set with mother-of-pearl handles, a jewellery box, telephone extension so that she wouldn't have to run downstairs to answer the phone, some pretty nightdresses and peignoirs. What the hell was a peignoir? He didn't know, but the word was in his head, and she was having at least one.

Sleep closed in on him like a sturdy door being

slammed in his face. One minute he was awake, while the next found him in a long corridor. The further he walked, the longer it grew. Through glass doors, he saw women in hospital beds, but none of them looked like Tess. Time after time, he strode past Molly. She was singing about cleaning windows; if he didn't look at her, she *was* George Formby.

'Don?'

Ah, he had found Tess. She was small. Did the removal of a womb plus bits and bobs make a woman shrink? Or was she travelling backwards in time? Would she become a little girl in a wooden caravan, too many siblings and not enough blankets, no toys, no teacher to help her learn to read?

As he entered deeper sleep, the dreams stopped.

Morning found him fully clothed and on top of his eiderdown. Disorientated for a few seconds, he blinked stupidly till his brain kicked in. Downstairs, he came across another pile of occupied clothing, a bundle of denim and leather on the sofa. Someone else had slept where he'd dropped. 'Mark?'

'Go away.' A tousled head raised itself. 'Sorry, Mr Compton. I thought I was at home. I couldn't be bothered going back. We were there till ten, with my mother fussing round Anne-Marie with food, did she fancy a bit of soup, what about scrambled eggs or toast and marmalade. We were both driven daft. So we cleared off and played cards with Sean.'

'I thought he went to the pub,' Don said.

'None of us could settle. Anyway, we kept the noise down in here, because the car was on the driveway and you were in bed.' He sat up. 'Never sleep in leathers; I smell like an overdone turkey complete with burnt plumage and giblets.'

Don and Tess both liked this lad. He was an eccentric mixture of city commuter and mad Rocker. According to Anne-Marie, Mark's chapter of bikers didn't fight. They had become the peacemakers, and their insignia was Churchill's victory sign. 'Victory over what?' Don asked now, indicating the badge.

'Over the atom bomb. They have to stop making them. Did you ever see the Japanese photograph of a man's shadow? He evaporated completely, every bit of him was removed, but his shadow's permanently burnt into the step where he was sitting. It's a reminder for all of us that we shouldn't play with those toys.'

Not for the first time of late, Don reminded himself that there was more to this generation than immediately met the eye. They knew what needed doing, what needed changing, and they were certainly ready to challenge government. It wasn't just riding about on scooters or motorbikes; they had an agenda, they were educated and a power to be recognized. 'Where do you work?' Don asked.

Mark stood up and stretched. 'Family firm. Do you know what I love most about that baby daughter of yours?'

'No.'

'She's not impressed by a sandstone mansion on the Wirral. She likes me for me, for who I am. Did she ever mention my wealthy family? No? That's because she'd rather listen to the Quarry Men, make eyes at Lennon and have a good time. My parents adore her. Anyway, this isn't getting the baby bathed. You have an Ascot, don't you? Constant hot water?'

Don blinked stupidly again. 'Er ... yes.'

Mark announced his intention to make breakfast for everyone before becoming the first baby in the bath. 'I'll drag them out of bed, Mr Compton. They see their mother today, so we want them smart.'

Don stayed where he was and allowed Mark to organize the household. Every day, something new. No, it was more like every hour – Tess in hospital, lonely Molly planning a bungalow, Mark suddenly rich, a new bedroom to be arranged, Anne-Marie's boyfriend making breakfast. 'Get well, Tess,' he whispered. He was going to need her. She might have been rather wobbly of late, but she had a certain way of thinking round a problem before aiming at the core. She was clever; should have been better educated. 'There are no problems,' he muttered. Even so, he needed her, didn't he? Breakfast smelled delicious.

Anne-Marie stumbled down the stairs. Mark dragged her to the table, slapped a full English in front of her, and told her she looked like a panda.

'I fell asleep before taking my make-up off,' she informed him.

Mark shrugged. 'You still look like a panda.'

The panda observed its plate. It didn't like mushrooms, fried bread or black pudding. The offending items were removed, and Panda-Marie played with the remaining egg and bacon.

Sean ate everything apart from the glaze on his

plate, while Don watched these three marvellous people closely. Sean was always hungry, but he worked hard, had an instinct for motors and a liking for beer and company. Anne-Marie was brilliant, another worker with a capacity for fun. She did look like a panda, and she didn't care, because she would see her mother today.

'Eat up, Mr C,' the chef ordered.

Don did as he was told.

By visiting time, they were all clean-ish and almost respectable. Panda was looking human, her boyfriend had lost his overnight beard, and most of the oil had been scraped from Sean's fingernails. Don was wearing his best suit. Tess deserved the best suit.

But as they entered the ward, he noticed an open door. His eyes travelled into the tiny, single bedroom. His Tess was in the bed, white-faced and unconscious. Was she so ill that she needed to be isolated because she required so much attention? This room was very near the sister's office.

A hand rested on Don's arm. 'It's all right, Mr Compton. We've all noticed the similarity. Come and see your wife; she's doing very well.'

He staggered on. The children were already at their mother's bedside, and they stepped aside for him. She looked great. Anaemia had been chased away by transfusions, and she could no longer bleed internally, because the offending aggressors had been removed. 'Hello, love,' he said.

Anne-Marie, busy placing nightdresses, underwear and toiletries in her mother's locker, was dangerously near to tears of happiness. Mark ordered her to calm down, as he was not prepared to be seen in the company of a panda for a second time that day.

Anne-Marie straightened, turned, and faced him. 'Listen, king of the road,' she said. 'Pandas look cute, but they kill. So watch it, or I'll squeeze the living daylights out of you.'

Tess groaned. 'Shut up. It hurts when I laugh.'

Don glanced over his shoulder. The door to the single room was closed. Tess noticed the direction of his gaze.

'She does look like me, then. Everybody's been saying so. Even you think she looks like me. Well, her name's Rosh, and rumour has it that some less than human creature's interfered with her. There's been a little Irishwoman leaping about in the corridor shouting gibberish, and their neighbour's been arrested. So they say, anyway. Poor girl was in theatre during the night.'

Sean wandered off to look through a different window. Mark, in search of a vase for Tess's flowers, was chatting to a pretty nurse. Anne-Marie marched in his direction, pulled him away from the girl and muttered to him, a finger wagging under his nose.

'Just like you,' Don said. Then he bent, placed his head on the pillow and whispered, telling Tess about the planned boudoir and all that would happen within its walls.

When he sat up, she was staring into his eyes. 'Promises,' she said.

He smiled. It was enough.

275

Ten

Rosh had kept her promise about seeking work, though she could afford to be choosy, since she had the windfall from Phil's policy. Not that she intended to depend on it, but she did have the luxury of time in which to make up her mind about the future. She was head of the household now, though her mother thought differently. But Anna Riley had always imagined herself to be in charge no matter what the circumstance, and argument was futile.

Rosh's main aim was to use the money to educate her children to cope in a cruel world, and a plan to make them safe was taking root in her mind. But first, there was something she particularly wanted to do, something that had needed doing for seven years, at least. She was doing it for her annoying, wonderful mother, who would take care of house and children while Rosh made a living. Since Phil's death, Anna Riley had become the core of the family, almost by default, but Rosh needed to be the breadwinner.

Accordingly, Anna's daughter had travelled by bus to Collingford's Dye Works and was interviewed in a small office by a short man with spectacles and a permanent frown. The furrows changed shape when he spoke, and Rosh found her attention glued to the ever-mobile patterns flitting above thick, silver eyebrows. His glasses were a poor fit, as were his teeth. He was flanked by two women, one of whom looked about ninety, while the other, all nail polish and lipstick, seemed very much aware of the competition Rosh might become. While the latter sized up the candidate's clothing and pretty face, the other two fired questions at a pace that few machine guns might match.

Was she a good ironer? What about folding and packing? Did she have experience of invisible darning and garment finishing? Would she be willing to work in the dry-cleaning department? Was she quick to learn, because there was an art to most of the jobs in the dye works. How did she feel about manning the reception desk and telephones? Would she be flexible enough to learn several disciplines and fill in when workers were ill?

Outwardly unfazed, Rosh looked from one to the other. It was clear that they had been impressed by her letter of application and that they wanted her to work here. Well, she had something to say, but it would keep. And she intended to lay it on with a trowel if necessary. A bone to pick? A bone? She had a butcher's yard full of bones, plus a row of skeletons and enough ham shanks for a month's worth of pea and ham soup.

The four of them walked through hats and gloves, through pressing and ironing, finishing, invisible darning and mending, dyeing, dry-cleaning, uncollected items due to be sold, button-matching and packing. The dry-cleaning area stank of chemicals, while the pressing room was scarcely visible through clouds of steam. This

277

place was massive; it looked as if it had been here for ever, like Ayers Rock or the Grand Canyon. People who worked here probably needed a map for their first month or so. Without directions, they might end up lost or mummified in some dry, dark corner.

The older woman sang the praises of social amenities which included keep fit classes, football and netball matches, rounders, cricket, dances, and the occasional trip to Southport or Blackpool. 'You'd be pushed to find a better employer than Collingford,' she concluded, an expression of pride making her younger for a few seconds. 'We look after our employees, and their well-being is our number one concern at all times.'

Rosh coughed politely into her handkerchief. The workers would need days out after working in this place, because the chemicals seemed to close in, as if threatening to choke a person. Not since the war's end had she thought of gas masks as useful items. She shouldn't have come, shouldn't have allowed them to approve of her. They were keen; had they not been keen, this walkabout would not have happened. Perhaps they even had big plans for her, a grand future with a thousand or more a year plus benefits. She felt nauseous, but she had travelled here for a purpose, and she was yet to claim her pound of flesh.

When the tour was over, they returned to the office, where the two females peeled away and walked towards whatever they usually did.

The man poked at his glasses. In dire need of adjustment, they slid down his nose with monotonous frequency. 'You seem very suitable,' he told Rosh. 'Intelligent, probably quick to learn, personable. We have several openings at the present time, and you could go far if you worked hard.' He smiled benignly, and the spectacles' nose piece took off like a careless skier down a very steep slope.

Rosh should not, could not like him, no matter how amusing his mannerisms were. 'Oh, I am a hard worker,' she answered readily. 'I can turn my hand to most things. I got that from my mother, I think. To this day, she's an industrious woman. We're all very proud of her.'

Clearly not listening to her, he shuffled some papers. 'Then we'll start you off in ironing.'

Rosh folded her arms. 'Will you, now?'

'Er ... would you prefer some other area?'

For answer, Rosh shook her head. 'I don't think I would, no. You see, Mr ... what was your name? Oh, it doesn't matter at all. I am Catholic.'

He sputtered. Rosh half expected a set of false teeth to land on his desk, because every S he formed came out as a whistle. 'But that rule was removed years ago,' he managed eventually. 'We no longer adhere to ... to the principles of no, not principles. Er ... things change, usually for the better. I can assure you, Mrs ... er ... Allen, everything is very different now. Race and creed are not considered. We have two black men in packing, and several Chinese in various areas.'

'No Catholics need apply,' said the applicant who was no longer applying. 'So my mother couldn't work here.' She stood up. 'I came here for one reason only. I came to shoot you down on behalf of every family who suffered because of your firm's prejudice. I am very prejudiced against prejudice. Oh, you've custard on your tie. Take it through to that smelly place and get it dry-cleaned.'

He was still fighting with his specs and scrutinizing his tie when the door slammed behind Rosh. The cheek of that woman! He'd better warn the night watch, because she might just find a load of Luddites or Fenians and set fire to the whole caboodle. She was pretty, yes. And there was a look of the Irish about her, the soft, gentle facade that often hid a core of steel.

Rosh stood outside and surveyed an exterior that put her in mind of a cotton mill. About seventy windows stared down at her, and this was just one side of the building. A square tower that reached higher than the main structure was also heavily endowed with glass. A row of vans advertising Collingford the Dyers waited for their loads. She did not belong here. If her mother hadn't been fit for this pile of masonry, the business was unsuitable for Rosh. Well, she'd accomplished what she'd set out to do.

So. What else did Liverpool have to offer? Biscuit factory, sugar works, jam makers, the sausage place. But who was she kidding? This kick-back on behalf of Liverpool's Catholics had been her sole reason for venturing this far away from her base in Waterloo. She had a job offer, and she would accept the position today. It was practically on the doorstep, an interesting shop on College Road, and she had promised to give her answer by five o'clock. And she was meeting

Roy soon, as he was going to help her make a decision.

Someone touched Rosh's arm. She turned and was surprised to see that Lipstick and Nail Polish was standing behind her. 'What happened?' asked the glamour girl. 'Did he not give you a job? I was sure he would.'

'He tried,' was Rosh's answer. 'But I decided not to bother accepting it.'

'Oh.' The young woman bit down on a peach-coloured lower lip. 'Why?' she asked.

'Because it stinks. I don't want to walk round smelling like some chemistry lab. Oh, I don't know. I feel daft now. It's just that my mother needed work some years ago, and they wouldn't even let her apply because she's a Catholic. And I wanted to let them know what they'd done to her.'

Rosh's companion nodded. 'I could see that our Mr Collingford liked you. So did his mother.'

Rosh's hand flew up to her face. 'You mean he was... She was... I thought they were just managers.'

'They're Collingfords, yes. He's a widower, and she's his mother. And the no Catholics thing wasn't their idea. It came from his older brother. They fought it, but they couldn't shift him an inch. He was nasty, and the older he got, the nastier he became. But it was just him.'

Rosh swallowed. Never again would she speak her mind to strangers. Had she listened, she might have heard their names. Roisin Allen could be blacklisted all over Liverpool after this, so she'd better dash back home and grab the job

281

that was on offer. 'I have to go,' she gasped before fleeing round the corner. A voice followed her.

'I'm a Collingford, too. He's my dad.'

Rosh sat on the Waterloo-bound bus. How many times had she told her own mother to keep her thoughts to herself until she was in possession of all the facts? And here sat Anna Riley's adviser, hands shaking as she searched for her fare, cheeks glowing partly because the day was hot, mostly because she had been nasty to people who probably didn't deserve it. She was a sad, hopeless case who could use a sizeable dose of her own medicine. The sins of a deceased older brother should never be blamed on a younger. Oh, she shouldn't have done it, shouldn't have spoken with only half a brain.

She alighted from the vehicle and stood on College Road. Mam was coming out of the green-grocer's. Backwards, of course. A great if somewhat confusing conversationalist, Anna Riley took every opportunity to share her opinions with the world at large and now, addressing a customer or a trapped shopkeeper, she was making sure her words were registering until the very last moment. She had been known to cause a huge human backlog in Woolworth's, because the girl behind the counter had been Irish, engaging, and cousin to a man who had been friend of a friend of a woman who had gone to Dublin and who had come to no good at all.

Rosh crossed the road. 'What are you up to now?'

A startled Anna put a hand on her heart. 'Jaysus, you'll be the death of me, creeping up

282

like that.' She inhaled deeply, as if trying to illustrate the size of the damage done to her by a dreadful daughter. 'He's only gone and got the mumps, hasn't he? I said to Janet in the shop, which grown man goes out and comes back with the mumps? Mumps is something children have, like chicken pox and measles.'

'Mother! What a load of twaddle. You can't blame a man for having a disease. He didn't do it deliberately.'

'Don't be cheeky. If you're going to come over all attitude and righteousness, I'm off home to sort out the dinner.'

'I don't think he went out and chose mumps, Mam. He didn't go into a shop and buy it, did he? I can't imagine anybody looking at the shelves and saying he'd have half a pound of mumps and some mint imperials.'

It finally dawned on Anna that her daughter was looking very well groomed. 'And where've you been in all the posh? Did you forget your tiara and the three rows of pearls?'

'No. I went after a job at the Collingford dye place. They were very impressed with me. I got the distinct impression that they'd want me running the place within a fortnight. Mind, I might have exaggerated slightly in my letter of application.'

Anna placed her burdens on the floor. 'You never went there of all places. Haven't I always told you to keep away after what they did to our fellow countrymen? No Catholics? It was the Irish they objected to, because a man from the Church of Ireland got the knock-back as well.'

Rosh nodded. 'Well, I went. They took me into a little room for an interview. There were three of them. I even got the guided tour–'

'So, they had you marked for possible management?'

'I don't know, Mam. But they wanted to start me off in ironing, so I could see that they were looking for someone to learn the business from the bottom. Anyway, I knocked them back about the no Catholic thing. But I was wrong.'

'You? Wrong? Did the sun turn blue?'

The younger woman smiled briefly. 'They were Collingfords, all three of them. And it wasn't their fault. They'd fought for that stupid rule to be changed, but the older Collingford insisted on it till the day he died. I was hitting the wrong people. I hate myself at the moment, because I didn't even realize who I was talking to.'

'Ah, forget about it. You'll be better off here in newspapers and tobacco. I can walk down any time I like and have a chat with you.'

Rosh thought about that. The concept of Anna at loose in a corner shop was not attractive. Mr Bailey had always kept a couple of chairs in the place so that customers could sit and chat. Perhaps the season of chair-burning was about to occur. Though Rosh had other plans, too...

'It's a shame he died, but. Mr Bailey was a good man, so he was. And you'll be working for his widow, a grand soul with a house near the water. Are you going to tell her you'll accept the job? I saw her walking along not five minutes ago. See? That's her motor car parked outside the butcher's.'

284

Rosh nodded, turned to walk away, then turned again. 'Who's got the mumps?' she asked rather tardily.

Anna picked up her purchases. 'Mary Henderson's chap. They live above the greengrocery. Protestant, of course. He never could stand children, even when he was one himself.'

It occurred to Rosh in that moment that her mother's jokes about non-Catholics were as full of prejudice as the Collingfords' sad history.

Anna rolled on smoothly. 'She's Catholic, and we all know what that means. So he goes and gets the mumps, and the mumps travel downstairs to his underneath regions, and his legs are up in stirrups to relieve the pain in his private bits, and he'll come out of it infertile. So she'll never have a child, will she? The primary purpose of marriage is procreation.'

'You sound like a catechism.' Rosh shook her head. What was the point? 'One of these days, you'll cut your own throat with your tongue. You're talking stupid, and you know it. So why go about making bother? Leave all that to people like Hitler and the IRA.'

'I'm joking,' Anna yelled. 'Did you hear me? This was a joke.'

'Well, I'm not laughing. I hurt an old man today, and his mother. She looked to be in her nineties. And his daughter chased after me and told me the truth about her uncle. One of these days, some sick-to-the-back-teeth non-Catholic will chase after you, but with a cricket bat. Just stop being such a damned nuisance, Mother.'

Mother. Anna knew she was in trouble when-

285

ever she was awarded that title. 'Oh, go and get your job.' She marched off in the direction of home and peace. Some people didn't realize how lucky they were to have a mother who did all the housework, the shopping, most of the cooking, who looked after grandchildren and... Ah. Here came Eric. He'd be happy to carry the bags for her.

Rosh had slipped into a little café and ordered two cups of coffee. Roy was never late. He had booked time off work to help her with a monumental decision, because she had two choices. Mrs Bailey didn't want the shop. It had been her husband's pet project, and he was dead, so its usefulness was minimal. An investor had expressed interest, and Rosh could work for him, but there was an alternative about which she had spoken only to Roy. She had been given first option. The shop was hers for the taking, stock included, for a very reasonable sum. Phil's insurance policy had paid off the mortgage on the house, so Rosh would own two buildings outright if she took this further step, and she needed Roy's advice and support.

He arrived. 'This place gets dingier by the day,' was his greeting. 'Are we safe drinking their coffee?'

'Be an adventurer,' she advised. 'Take a walk on the dark side. If we drop dead, we'll take that as a sign that we needn't look at Mr Bailey's shop after all.'

He sipped, swallowed, shuddered, then pushed cup and saucer to the centre of the table. 'Right,' he said. 'How did Mrs Bailey get on with the powers that be? What did they say about the rest of it?'

'Fine,' Rosh said. 'The plans are not out of date, so I can open a little café round the side of the shop. Let's hope my coffee's a sight better than this muck. So. I'll have to employ women to bake at home, at least one waitress, and somebody to run the shop from two to six. I'm hoping Mr Bailey's assistant will carry on doing the morning shift, sorting out newspaper deliveries and dealing with tobacco. The new café will be my baby.' She paused. 'Is it a good investment, Roy? Am I doing the right thing?'

'I think so, yes. And I'll keep your books tidy. Right. Shall we go? I'm not prepared to drink any more of that muddy stuff.'

They left their table and their coffee, but no tip. Gratuities, like respect, needed to be earned. They lingered outside and looked at Rosh's future domain, which was diagonally opposite the greasy building they had just left. She would scarcely need to shine in order to keep in the shade the café she had just left. 'Roy?'

'What?'

'Thanks for being here for me. You're very good, and I'm grateful.'

'It's OK.' He would have gone to the ends of the earth for her, but he kept quiet.

'Since I lost Phil, you've been a godsend. For my children, for my mother–'

'I love them all,' he said. 'Even the terrible cats.'

'My mother is worse than Winston and Lucy-Furr.'

287

'Yes,' he agreed, 'but I wouldn't like a world without her in it.'

Rosh suddenly felt shy and silly. She'd always known, hadn't she? So why did she feel like a fifteen-year-old on a first date? It wasn't as if she hadn't already noticed him, yet he had been like wallpaper, a backdrop against which life was played out. But since the death of his father, Roy had emerged from his shell, and he was admirable. She mustn't think like this. Her business head should be forced to take over, while her heart needed to be in cold storage – she'd only been widowed for just about a year, for goodness' sake.

Mrs Bailey was in the shop, which had been open infrequently in recent weeks. She was seated in one of her husband's chairs when Rosh and Roy walked in. 'He loved this place.' Her tone was sad. 'Anyway, I must get rid of it. I've decided to sell up completely and go to Australia where our son lives. That house was big with two of us in it. It's like living in some sort of echo chamber now; I can hear my own footsteps bouncing off the walls, as if someone's following me.'

'I know,' Rosh said. Even with Mam and the children, those first weeks without Phil had been as empty as a freshly dug grave.

'I'm sure you do know, dear. So, have you thought about it?'

'Oh, yes. I've thought about little else. And I'd like to work for myself. Roy considers it a good investment, so yes, please. I'm happy with the price, and very happy that the plans for a café are still in date.'

'That's settled, then.' Mrs Bailey rose gracefully from her chair. 'The legal and financial side will take a few weeks.'

'It will be cash,' Rosh told her. 'No mortgage.' How proud of Phil she felt in that moment. He had left her and his children comfortably provided for, and now it was up to her to capitalize on his foresight. This was her business, her own place. She shook the older woman's gloved hand.

'May we look round for half an hour?' she begged. 'We'll bring the keys back later.'

But Mrs Bailey's instincts told her to trust this young woman. 'Keep them. You'll want to be in and out to take measurements. Oh, and get a surveyor. I wish you good fortune, Mrs Allen. You deserve it. I'll talk to Mr Cuttle, make sure he knows what happening.' She left the scene, leaving in her wake a waft of expensive perfume.

Rosh looked at the dozens of jars of tobacco, old newspapers still on display, sweets, chocolate, out-of-date magazines. She was troubled not by any of this, but by the man who was her companion. He'd always been there. Through senior school, he, she and Phil had been the three amigos; as adults, they had been neighbours and now, in widowhood, Rosh couldn't imagine coping without him. But it wasn't enough, was it? The numbness that had punished her after Phil's death had faded away, and the Allens were managing quite well, thank you. But he was here. And he loved her.

She swallowed a sigh. Did she want his love? Would she ever return it?

Roy left her side and went to measure up the

intended café. Rosh was tense, and he decided that the cause of her discomfort was the size of the decision she had just made. Very few women went into business alone. She had bought a going concern, but she also had plans to extend and expand. Rosh had guts; but he had always known that. He ached less these days; he seemed to have settled into the role of escort, but how would he feel if she met someone else? Murderous and heartbroken, he decided.

'I'm not going the traditional gingham route,' she said as she entered the room a minute or two later. 'Floor-length covers in a dark colour, replaceable white cloths on top. The menu will be small at first, but top quality. I'll get a hatch to the kitchen cut in the wall for when we become a bit more adventurous; might as well get all the mucky jobs done before we set off.'

'I can make cakes and pies,' he said.

Roy reminded her time after time not to be surprised. Rendered lame by football and poor surgery, he managed. No. Managed was not the right word, because Roy overcame. His house was a miniature palace, and he'd had very little help from Eric Holt while the transformation was being accomplished. 'Yes, I've eaten your stuff often enough. It's good. A man of many talents, eh? And you're blushing.' She had to treat him as she had always treated him. But... Oh, she should pull herself together. He was Roy, an old friend, and he'd always been attractive. 'You did the house up, you can cook – what else?'

'I grow my own produce, of course. You enjoy it.'

'Oh, yes. Mr All-Rounder, eh?' Once again, she was shy and had trouble meeting his steady gaze. Something was happening, and she didn't know what it was. To find out what it was, she needed to be alone, and the only 'alone' time she got was in her bedroom. 'I have to go and tell my mother what I've done.' 'Alone' time would be postponed until much later, it seemed.

'Yes. I'll stay out of that if you don't mind.'

'Coward.'

'I know,' he sighed. 'And I suppose I'll never live it down. You won't let me live it down, will you? Even at school while you protected me, the pair of you made fun of me.' He tried to sound hurt, but failed.

'You loved it,' was her answer. 'Now, get back to work before you lose your job.'

She watched as he walked down to the bus stop. He was tired. The limp worsened when he did too much, and he often did too much for her. She owed him. Was this pity, gratitude, sisterly affection, friendship, love? Life was about to become complicated. Music exams, psychological assessment for Alice, a business to build. Roy would want to be involved with all those things. And Mam's voice echoed: 'Snap him up before he gets taken off the market by some woman more sensible than you. He thinks the sun shines out of your ears, and you treat him like a servant. And he was reared Catholic, because his mother was Catholic. That heathen father of his didn't count when he was alive, so he's worth nothing dead.'

Rosh continued to stare at him. There had been Phil, only Phil, and Phil had been the for ever person. Nothing was ever going to separate them, yet all it had taken... She wiped her eyes. All it had taken was ten seconds in time, a careless driver, a beloved man who had stepped out too soon or too late. And that man was her man, father of her children and the love of her life.

After revisiting the shop for half an hour and working out the stock cupboard, she had timed the stroll home. It took under ten minutes, and that was reassuring. Thoughts of bus and train rides to and from work had not been happy ones. Rosh didn't realize that she was being followed, that a man with whom she would soon be in uncomfortably close contact was shadowing her every step. With her head full of maroon table drapes and lace-edged tablecloths, she had little time to notice much else, especially when maroon-and-white striped curtains entered the equation. She was a businesswoman, and businesswomen had much to prove in this male-dominated world.

Anna was still feisty and quick on her feet when her daughter walked in. She bounced about slapping things on the kitchen table, all the while muttering under her breath about people who always knew best. Was it not enough that she'd five to feed without being accosted in the street? She wasn't sure that joking about a non-Catholic with mumps was a hanging offence. All this was said to herself; Rosh might as well have been just another brick in the wall. Eric, who had clearly heard the whole tale during the walk from College Road, excused himself and exited via the back door.

Rosh repaired to her room to take off the good suit. It didn't hurt this time. She remembered the day they'd chosen it, remembered her husband's pride shining in his eyes each time she'd tried on an outfit. 'I'm nearly all right now,' she told her reflection. 'Except for her down there and him over the road.' Her down there was still slamming doors; him over the road wasn't over the road, because he was on his way back to work, bless him.

She pulled on a flowered day dress, combed her hair and sat on the bed.

Pity was akin to love, but was this pity? Roy was a rather fine man, handsome, hard-working, personable. As for the limp, it was part of who he was, who he had been since childhood. She was sorry about the limp, as it gave him pain, but she didn't mind it. 'We're probably meant to take care of each other. The kids like him, Mam thinks the sun rises out of him, and I... I don't know, do I? Send me a sign, Phil.'

When Rosh reached the ground floor, Mam was on a slightly lower light. Still simmering, but not ready to boil over like a neglected milk pan. 'Sit down, Mam.'

'Why? I'm learning a new recipe called beef strong enough.'

The younger woman fought a smile. 'You can't cook that until you see the whites of your diners' eyes. And it's stroganoff. If you want soured cream, put a bit of lemon in, and don't forget the nutmeg.'

Anna sniffed and sat down. 'Well? What more do you have to say for yourself, besom?'

293

'Don't fuss. I've something important to say.'

'Oh yes? Is this you telling me to leave?'

'No. Whatever happens, your home will always be with me. This is me telling you that you'll be needed more than ever.'

'Oh, I see. No rest for the wicked, then.'

'No rest for any of us, Mam.' Rosh paused. 'Now, don't go off at the deep end, because you might just drown at last. Look, I don't want to leave Phil's money sitting in a bank making bits of interest. I want to use some of it to build a family business, something for the kids to fall back on, sell, or whatever.'

Anna nodded.

'So I've bought the shop, and it comes with plans for a café at the back. There's a chap called Clive Cuttle who used to do the six till two shift in the shop, and Mrs Bailey's asking him to come back. The two till six in the evening will be covered by somebody else, because I'll be running the other side of the business.'

'On your own?'

'No. At first, everything will be literally home-made. The kitchen will be big enough to cook in, but for a while I'm going to buy pies and cakes made by housewives round here. We have to get the food to the shop, so I start driving lessons next Monday, one lesson a day for two weeks including Sundays after Mass. If I fail, I'll try again.' Rosh looked at her mother. 'What's the matter now?'

Anna was fanning her face with a hand. 'I can't speak.'

'Why? What the plucked chicken's up with you?

294

Please tell me what stopped you talking, because I'd love to know how to make you shut up at will.'

Anna dried her eyes. 'I'm proud of you. I am. Is there a refrigerator?'

'Yes, and I'm getting one for here as well. You and I will make scones and fancies fresh every day. So, very simple to start with, but all beautifully presented with good cutlery and crockery. No gingham. I was going to call it No Gingham, but I changed my mind. It's Home from Home.'

'Nice.' The older woman blew her nose. 'It's so exciting and so brave. Home from Home is just perfect. Are you excited, Rosh?'

'I am. A bit scared as well, but I feel like a kiddy on Christmas Day. Now, before you get cracking with your beef strong enough, I want you to write a list of everybody who won the best cake or pie prize at the church and the school. Roy's already on the list; his short pastry is second to none.'

'That lad loves you, Roisin.'

'I know.'

'And you don't love him?'

'No. Yes. I don't know.'

Anna raised both arms in a gesture of despair. 'You've gone all undecided, so. What's the craic? Did you get a sudden visitation from your guardian angel, or are you doing all this as a bet?'

Rosh blew a loud, wet raspberry in the direction of her mother. 'I'm trying to be truthful, trying not to open my mouth unless I'm absolutely sure. Upsetting those people earlier–'

'Has upset you. I'll give this a week. By the time you're driven daft – literally – by learning to drive, you'll be back to your usual gobby self.

Now, will I curdle the cream by adding lemon to it, or will I put the cream in with the meat before squirting the lemon?'

'Please yourself. The children won't eat it anyway.'

'Just as well,' said Anna smartly. 'There's enough just for you, me and Roy. The kids are having a bit of yellow fish with a poached egg.'

Rosh's heart skipped a beat; Roy was coming to dinner. It wasn't love. Love was a blinding moment that led its victim all the way through life until... Well whatever it was, it wasn't like this. Roy was growing on her like mistletoe on a host tree. Not true, because he gave more than he took. He was not a parasite. The kids loved him. Did she?

Anna chose to eat in the kitchen with the children. 'I'll keep an eye out here,' she yelled to Rosh and Roy from the doorway. 'Alice has decided she won't eat anything yellow. Don't ask; her mind works in mysterious ways its wonders to perform.'

'Has your mother gone Biblical?' Roy whispered.

'I don't know. Was that from the Bible?'

He shrugged; he didn't know, either.

Rosh decided to cut to the chase. 'This is her way of matchmaking,' she said. 'Next time, there'll be wine, flowers, crêpes suzette and fingerbowls. She's made up her mind, and there's nothing I can do about that.'

Roy swallowed nervously. 'And?' he achieved eventually.

'And what? She's my mother, a law unto herself.'

'Rosh?'

'What?'

Roy paused for a few seconds. 'Is there a chance for me?'

'Yes,' she snapped. 'Eat your dinner. This beef strong enough's no good cold.' There were tears in his eyes; she couldn't bear to look at the tears in case they brimmed over. 'You're a patient man. Continue patient, please, because I'm not ready.' Love was a blinding moment... The 'yes' had been automatic, almost sight-impaired. It had come from her mouth, not from her brain...

The doorbell sounded, and Rosh thanked it for its timely intervention. But her relief was short-lived, because Lipstick and Nail Polish stood on the step behind a bunch of flowers almost as big as the kitchen. 'For your mother,' she said. 'Dad's sorry.'

'So am I.' Rosh took the flowers and placed them in the hall before stepping out to the car at the kerbside. 'Mr Collingford...' He really should invest in some new glasses. 'I am so sorry,' she continued. 'I shouldn't have... I bought a shop this afternoon.' She was babbling, and she knew it.

'What sort of shop?'

Rosh blinked stupidly. 'Sweets, tobacco, newspapers...'

'On the ground floor?' he asked.

'Yes, of course.'

He nodded, causing his spectacles to perform a tap dance on the bridge of his nose. 'We need to talk, Mrs Allen. But I must leave you now. I shall see you here on Tuesday afternoon at two o'clock. Is that a suitable time?'

'Yes. Yes, of course.'

Lipstick and Nails climbed into the driver's seat, gave a little wave, then took off quickly.

Rosh closed her mouth with a snap. What an odd day this had been. She'd had the interview, said her piece, discovered that she'd cursed the wrong people, bought a business, chosen a colour scheme for the café. And she'd given a half-yes to a not-quite proposal of marriage. 'A lifetime lived in a day,' she whispered as she rescued the flowers.

Anna was rendered speechless, and that was another novelty. An apology from a Collingford? She gathered all the vases in the house and began the business of containing the multitude of blooms and spreading joy and happy comment all over the place. But her tone changed when she reached the dining room. 'What's wrong with your food?' she demanded.

'Nothing,' Roy replied. 'We got talking, then the Collingfords came to the door.'

'Talking?' A white vase was plonked in the centre of the dining table. Tall flowers prevented Rosh and Roy from seeing each other, which was just as well, as they were perilously close to hysterical laughter. The situation was surreal.

'And you were talking about what?'

'Maroon-and-white striped curtains.' Rosh kept her voice as sombre as she could manage. 'For the café.'

'That is a cartload of my eye and Betty Martin,' announced Anna.

'Who is this Betty Martin?' Roy asked innocently.

298

'She is just a saying,' Anna snapped. 'And I can tell from your faces that you weren't talking about anything maroon and white.'

Roy nodded. 'You're right, of course. It was royal blue and cream.'

Anna stormed out.

Rosh moved the vase. 'Coffee at your house, I think, sir. We can't have a conversation without Big Ears poking a lughole in. Oh, and you're on coffee and listening, and I'm on talking.'

Across the road in Roy's house, they drank his excellent coffee and listened to a concert on the Home Service. Coming here had probably been a mistake, Rosh mused. Whilst her mother was a nuisance, she was also a distraction, as were the children. What a day this had been. 'Roy?'

'Yes?'

'When you asked if you had a chance with me, what did you mean? What exactly do you want from me?'

His gaze remained steady. 'Just to be with you. You know full well how I feel, how I've always felt. I think Phil knew, too. A day when I don't see you is empty. Just be quiet for a minute and listen to this bit. Close your eyes and allow Beethoven to touch your soul.'

She obeyed until the movement ended.

'Beethoven says it all, Rosh. His father was a cruel man, or so I've heard. The torture and the passion are in all his symphonies. What I feel for you is in there, too. Because words are not enough.'

Roy had been reborn with his father's death. He had become louder, livelier and a great deal more optimistic. Because these improvements showed in all areas of his life, he now acted as the glue that held his legal offices together, the one man who knew where everyone else should be at any given moment of any day. Rosh was turning into the shy one, she reminded herself now. Always a gutsy woman, she found herself very aware of him, of the changes in him, and she was suddenly quieter. Why? What was happening? 'You're supposed to be listening,' she reminded him with mock severity.

'And you're supposed to be doing the talking.'

For once in her life, she was almost stumped. It had been her idea to escape to his house, to leave behind Mam and the children, since everybody valued Roy, and Rosh's mother in particular had taken on the role of matchmaker. 'My mother has us married off already,' she began carefully.

'I noticed,' he said.

'There's been just Phil for me, you see.'

Roy had lived in Phil's shadow for what seemed like an eternity. 'No woman has lasted more than a fortnight, Rosh. I seem to have a low boredom threshold. Oh, and we're not young any more.'

She bridled slightly. 'Speak for yourself. I'm thirty plus a bit, and that bit is negotiable. On a good day, I'm thirty-one; today, I was thirty-twelve, because I hurt some people.' She paused. 'Am I hurting you?'

'Not at the moment, no.' And he told her about his pain.

During the litany that followed, Rosh remained motionless. He hurt when she walked away from him and when she approached him. A table between them grew to the size of Everest, while his bed was the loneliest place on the planet. 'I'm obsessed,' he admitted finally.

She agreed with that. 'Yes, you're a lunatic. We definitely know each other well enough. But we need to make time for us away from here. And be aware, she'll be watching. There's no sense in trying to hide anything, because there'll be gossip no matter what we do.'

'I know. But I disagree with you; there's no need for any courtship ritual.'

Yet again, Rosh had no idea what to say.

'We already know each other completely,' he whispered.

Rosh inhaled deeply. 'Not quite completely. So we go directly to bed without collecting two hundred pounds? Like jail in Monopoly?'

He laughed. 'I didn't say that. Though it is just about the only thing we haven't done together. Perhaps you're right. We need to get away from this area and learn to be together without the past dogging our heels. And out of reach of your mother's sharp eyes and ears.'

'She doesn't need a special mention in dispatches. She's a constant, a permanent fixture. Even if we do come through, Roy, she stays.'

He chuckled. 'Poor Eric. He's got new teeth, new trousers – even a new cap. He loved his old cap, you know. And she still makes his life a total bloody misery. What?'

But Rosh had curled into a ball of agony. Strange, how laughter could make a person ache so much. After a few seconds, she managed to catch her breath. 'He came round on Thursday, and she was cleaning cupboards. So she handed everything over to him, sat down, and read his paper.'

'Cheeky mare,' grinned Roy.

'I've not finished. Neither had she. She examined his cupboards, said his work wasn't good enough, and made him do it all again.' Rosh dried her eyes. 'But she has knitted him a lovely cardigan. He told me privately that it itches something terrible on the back of his neck, but he has to wear it, and I mustn't say anything. Oh, it's a shame.'

'I know how he feels.'

'You know how he feels? When did you last scrub cupboards for me?'

'But I would if you asked me.'

'Yes, you probably would. Tragic, isn't it?'

'Not particularly. I love you, and I won't allow you to have dirty cupboards.' After this statement, he crossed the room, sat next to her and pulled her into his arms. 'Stop me at any time,' he said seriously. 'Like the ice cream man – stop me and buy one.'

She didn't stop him. Sensations long forgotten returned within seconds, and she pressed him closer to her by encircling his neck with her arms. For her, the embrace became urgent, almost desperate, yet he went carefully, almost with reverence. His hands on her clothed body simply rested on her softness, and she had her answer. This was meant. It had been organized by someone or something outside the two of them. Phil?

Breathless, they parted and reclaimed their share of oxygen.

'What were you selling?' Rosh asked. 'Stop me

and buy one?'

'Me. I was selling me.'

'You're priceless,' she told him.

He looked at the clock. 'Eight minutes.'

'What?'

'Our first kiss lasted eight minutes.'

Rosh clobbered him with a cushion. 'You timed it?'

Between blows, he pleaded innocence. He'd just happened to glance at the clock when crossing the room. No, no, he hadn't timed it, but might she stop hitting him so that they could try to beat their record?

She threw down her weapon. 'I'm off home,' she announced. 'I'm not stopping here to become a plaything for a bloke with a stopwatch. No, I'll wait for the real ice cream man, thanks.'

'Coward,' he cried.

'Shut up, you'll have the neighbours in.' She struck a pose, hand on thrust-out hip, mouth chewing non-existent gum. 'How much? How much will you pay for my time, mister? I'm good on the flat, not bad over the jumps, and I'm experienced in dressage.'

'Three-day eventing?' he asked.

'You couldn't afford me for three days, love. I doubt you could afford me for three hours – we've Norwegian ships in, you know.'

'One hour, then?' he begged.

She nodded, removed the pretend chewing gum and stuck it to his windowsill. For the first time in ages, she was playing a game that could have only one result. 'Follow me,' she commanded. 'And you'll never last an hour with Lola, sailor.'

'Who's Lola?'

Lola arrived home at nine thirty. The children were in bed, thank goodness, but Hawk-Eye remained lively; Rosh, wondering how she might escape upstairs to erase all signs of Lola, could hear Anna clattering pots in the kitchen. Oh, God. The prodigal daughter closed her eyes and leaned against the front door. Twenty questions. Any minute now, torture would begin.

It began. 'What time do you call this?'

Rosh didn't open her eyes. 'Lola,' she replied.

'What?'

'I call it Lola.'

The smaller, older woman dragged her daughter into the dining room. 'Well, I must say–'

'No, you mustn't.'

But silence was not an option in Anna's book. 'I must say you look as if you've been dragged through a hedge backwards.'

'You should see the other fellow, Mam. Battered, he is.' Again, she closed her eyes as if the lids would provide some armour against the inevitable onslaught.

A short pause served only to announce the advent of Anna's next paragraph, which allowed little room for punctuation. 'You didn't ... you haven't been and... Rosh, whatever will you say in Confession? You know it's a mortal sin outside marriage. You'll be giving the priest a heart attack, so you will. And such a good girl, you were. I have never expected this sort of behaviour from you, but. Howandever, I'll give you the chance to explain yourself.'

Rosh pleaded the fifth amendment.

'That's for Americans, Roisin.'

'Lola's probably a Yank. She's very modern.'

Anna glared sternly at the sinner. 'So you decided to try before you buy?'

Rosh opened her eyes. 'Mother? That's rather vulgar coming from such a good Catholic woman.'

Anna tapped a foot. 'Well?'

'I did. I tried before I bought, and I'm glad. I've always felt something for him, but I wasn't sure about the intimate side of things. We'll probably be marrying once I get the café on its feet.'

'Oh. Oh, Jesus.' Anna ran back to the kitchen.

Rosh lingered by the dining-room door. Mam would be weeping under a tea towel. Whenever anything of huge emotional moment occurred, it was run, find a tea towel or similar covering, sit, weep and moan. Yes, a moan emerged. 'It'll be all right, Mam,' she called.

'I know, I know. Oh, and God knows that's a fine young man.' Snivelling was duly resumed.

Rosh puffed out her cheeks and blew. This was Becher's Brook cleared with no injuries. 'And I can love again,' she whispered. 'It's allowed. Thank you, Phil. It isn't goodbye. It'll never be goodbye.' She sat at the table on whose surface two portions of beef strong enough with rice had been allowed to congeal. Had they eaten, she and Roy might have been too weighted down for what followed...

He was lovely. She wanted to go back and sleep with him, wake with him, listen to a bit more of Beethoven's Sixth. Roy was a true romantic without being soppy or silly. He took charge but didn't dominate, was kind, considerate, yet very masculine, and she loved him. Rosh was alive

305

again; she had never fully realized how important the love of a good man could be. 'Mam?'

'What?'

'Cocoa would be nice.'

A loud sniff was followed by, 'What did your last slave die of?'

'Lost the will to live and went into a decline. Last seen trudging over the mountains into Yorkshire.'

'But that's enemy territory, Rosh.'

They drank their cocoa in the front room.

Neither noticed the man across the road. As night spread its black umbrella across clouded skies, the two women chatted happily about a dress suitable for a second marriage, about brides-maids, hats and flowers, a venue good enough for the wedding breakfast.

'I'll make the girls' dresses,' Anna promised. 'But you and I are going haughty culture.'

'We'd need an allotment.'

'Eh?'

'For horticulture.'

'All right, haute couture. You know I know what I mean. I know you know I know what I mean. I know—'

'Shut up, Mother.'

Clive Cuttle remained motionless, eyes fixed on the most beautiful woman in Liverpool. He didn't like women. He hated women. The good-looking ones were the worst. He still remembered *her*, all light and happiness, long, chestnut hair, a laugh like tinkling bells, pretty face, heady perfume, perfect smile.

He woke one day and she was gone. At the age of eight, he had been abandoned to the streets of the Dingle, a drunken, abusive father his only companion in a house that had become filthy. And she never came back. Sometimes people fed him, but there were occasions when nothing was available, and he had stolen from shops, waste bins and houses.

At school, no one would play with him. He stank to high heaven, and that fact had prompted him to take clothes from washing lines and shops. Shoes had been a problem, as they were seldom displayed in pairs, and residential areas had become hunting grounds for footwear. Money for the public baths had prompted further exploration, and he had, of necessity, grown bolder and rather reckless in his mission to remain alive and acceptable.

Until he'd been caught, of course. That final beating had put him in hospital and his father in jail. Children's homes. The joy of three square meals, a bath every night, clean clothes and outings to zoos and seaside towns. The misery when he discovered he had no social skills, no way of knowing how to converse or play with his peers. An outcast. An outcast because of *her*, because of Mam.

Women were a curse. His mission was to clean up the streets, just as he'd cleaned up himself. So over there in that house sat a candidate ideal for cleansing. He had no intention of working for her. If she disappeared, old Ma Bailey would sell the business to a bloke who would leave Clive Cuttle in charge. Rosh Allen was a marked woman.

Eleven

Cleansings are never easy. I keep telling myself to hunt on foreign soil, but I take no notice of me, never have. Liverpool isn't very far away, or I could get to the Wirral, Wales, St Helens, Warrington, yet it doesn't work that way, does it? They aren't hunted, sought out and chosen by me. No. They arrive. They arrive and challenge me simply by being there. Some don't even need to talk to me; I can tell from the attitude, from facial expressions, from the way they walk. She's the one. Why? Why not the one standing next to her, or the other across the road? What's so special?

Dad, may he rot in hell, always said Mam was a whore. Seems he got word about her selling favours down in London. Good looks make women bad, he said. Dad turned evil into an art form, but only after Mam had gone.

Well, I am like my father, blast him, and these women send me to the dark side. It's like an illness. Yes, they make me sick. My hell is here and now, on earth in the year 1959. They got cocky since the war, the females of the species. They knock home a couple of rivets, build a bomb, throw an aeroplane together and whoa! They suddenly own the world. Not my bloody world, though. I didn't fight my way through North Africa to come home and be owned by a woman.

Oh, yes, there she is in a house paid for by the death of her man. Dangerous. Too close to me, to my home and my job. With each one, I've taken another step

308

nearer to arrest and trial. Roisin Allen has friends and family; this is no stray bitch wandering the Dock Road looking for customers. She has a mother, some children, a man friend just across the road. And I shouldn't be bringing trouble to Waterloo, should I? Mind, I've got away with plenty up to now, and they weren't all at a great distance.

The last one I did was from a large family. Where did I bury her? Why can't I remember all the big things I've done? When I'm at home and I get the stuff out of their boxes, when I touch their clothing and bits of jewellery, all the details come back to me so clearly. The terror in the eyes before the chloroform hits, the cutting, the strangling, that wonderful sense of peace when it's all over. They're all different, you see. Yet I can only live through it properly when I hold their belongings. Those items aren't so much trophies as aides-memoires. Cheap perfumes, waxy red lipsticks, the scent of fear, the odour of blood as it trickles, seeps, pools and clots. I keep pieces of their lives and, via those tokens, I relive my triumphs.

And here's my next. Old Bailey dying like that hasn't helped. Old Bailey. That's where they try murderers, isn't it? Worked at that shop for years, I have. Just the two of us, and we rubbed along quite nicely. Now this. Mrs Bailey's delighted about a café. It'll be all net curtains, frills and fancies. Mrs Allen. I've walked up and down Lawton Road a few times today. She's a friend of that bloke with a limp; he used to buy a paper in the morning on his way to the bus stop.

Funny. I hardly noticed Mrs Allen till Mrs Bailey told me I'm to be offered an extra ten bob a day because of what the new boss calls my unsocial hours.

I like those hours, early morning, no one about, air fresher before mankind starts to soil it with all the comings and goings, chimneys spouting smoke, buses pumping out poison. Lady bloody Bountiful offered me a bribe I didn't need. And in the hours that followed, I saw how beautiful she is, almost as lovely as Mam used to be. Mrs Allen arrived. Oh yes, she pulled into my station and I applied the brakes.

I watched her during today and this evening. And him, the limping clown who probably follows her everywhere when he's not at work, his eyes never leaving her, his body aching because he's wanting a taste of her. Straight away, I would know when they've had each other. She's already blushing and he's looking anxious, hoping she won't say no. She won't say no. I only need a glimpse to know all about them. I'm like that. I know people. Young widows are always on the lookout for the next victim. You'll never get her, Roy Baxter, not when I've finished with her, because she'll be as dead as a coffin nail.

The day my father died in Walton Jail, I cried like a baby. Not because I missed him, but because I never got to kill him. That last beating left me different, no use with a woman. The doc says it's probably psychological, but I know I'm not a man. Don't know where my mother is, whether she's alive or dead, can't get her, can't punish her. My old man's dead of natural causes, but there was nothing natural about the way he beat me for trying to stay clean. Jack the Ripper? I'm Clive the Cleaver. Never used a cleaver, but you know what I mean; it has a ring to it.

I've got all the cuttings in my flat. Some earrings, a chain with a cross dangling from it, beads, underwear covered in blood. I'm not as evil as Jack the Ripper,

310

since I don't remove body parts, but I cut them up inside to leave them as messed up as I am. Yes, I kill them. Even with the mask, you never know, one of them might recognize me and tell the cops. Perhaps I should try to keep this one alive and useless to men... No. She has to go.

If she buggers off out of it, Mrs Bailey will go back to the number she first thought of, the bloke with a chain of small shops. I'll be left in charge, my own business to all intents and purposes, and a wage big enough to afford a car– Hang on. Something's happening in the house.

Ah. Mrs Allen's mother's bedroom light's on, and she's closing the curtains. Her light's out now. Mother in bed, kids in bed, no sign of life in the limper's house. I've got my mask, the chloroform, a handkerchief. I'll just nip down the side, see if her kitchen light's on. She'll be found. I've no way of shifting her, no transport, no spade. My bike's at home with its sidecar. But for a reason I can almost fathom for once, it has to be now and it has to be her. Before the paperwork on the shop's done, I'll do her.

Anna's neglected beef strong enough was fast becoming a distant memory, so Roy had decided to go for fish and chips, since he and Rosh were both hungry after their exertions. He couldn't keep the smile off his face. If it hadn't been for his leg, he might have danced up Lawton Road and along College Road to George's Chippy. The off-licence was open, so he might buy a nice bottle of wine on his way back home. Home. She was going to marry him, and he would be part of a family at last. Lola had gone home, but Rosh would be hungry.

He glanced at Rosh's shop. Soon it would be up and running, smart little café round the side, staff continuing to run the sweets, tobacco and newsagency part of the business. He was so proud and so in love that he wanted to shout, to wake the world and enlighten mankind. But no, he was going for chips. He wiped the grin from his face and joined the queue. *Act sensible,* he warned himself inwardly. *Don't show yourself up. More to the point, don't show Rosh up.*

To redirect his thoughts further, he engaged in a conversation whose subject seemed, at first, to be of little interest to him. But no. Everyone should be paying heed, because the matter under discussion was missing girls and one corpse. There was probably a serial killer on the streets of West Lancashire, and he needed to be found before more girls disappeared. Women had been warned not to go out alone at night, to lock doors and send for police if any suspicious behaviour was noticed.

A fat woman in a red coat was airing her views loudly. 'See, they were mostly prostitutes and the like, them that's disappeared. But Susie Crawford weren't. Him next door to me's a copper, and he said they found all sorts inside her. You know. In her private bits.' The last two words were mouthed soundlessly, their sole accompaniment the sound of bubbling chip fat. 'I'd call him an animal, but there's no animal as bad as what he is.'

'Terrible,' said Roy. 'I wonder if he's finished?'

The red coat shrugged. 'Him next door to me

what's a copper says they don't finish till they get caught. Or till they die. It's as if they can't stop themselves, you see. Somebody should stick a knife through him. Not the copper; I mean the queer feller. He wants burying ten feet down under a ton of concrete.'

Roy nodded. 'So they think all the missing girls died at the hands of the same chap who killed Susie...?'

'Crawford, her name was. Nothing to do with biscuits, not rich. Student teacher, she was. Lived round the corner from me sister in West Derby, lovely girl, magic with kids.' Red Coat sniffed. 'Just stick him in a room with Susie's mam. She'll bend his bloody membership card for him. She's that mad with grief, I bet she's got the death certificate filled in except for his name. Wanders about looking for motorbikes and sidecars, she does. A young couple seen one near where Susie's body got found.'

Motorbike and sidecar? No. Plenty of people had those. But he was an odd-looking fellow, that Clive Cuttle. He seemed to look at people without seeing them. He knew his tobaccos, all right, but he wasn't really customer-friendly. A bright stripe of pure terror painted its way from the base of Roy's spine right up into his skull. He didn't know why. Something was out of context, out of place. Something was usually attached to a motorbike and sidecar. On foot. Clive Cuttle had walked up and down Lawton Road several times. Was he there now? Didn't he like the idea of working for a woman? 'Er...' He ran, leaving the door to close itself behind him.

313

Running with a limp wasn't easy. And what would Rosh say when he turned up for no good reason? She didn't know he'd gone for chips, did she? The motorbike-and-sidecar man wouldn't choose her; she was a decent woman, not a prostitute. But Susie Crawford had been a normal girl, a student. Rosh was buying the shop. Damn this leg; damn football; damn the hospital that had done just about everything wrong.

He had a key to Rosh's front door. Where was it? Right-hand trouser pocket? No, it was in the breast pocket inside his jacket, and his fingers curled tightly round the metal once he had it in his hand. He left his boots outside, because the bad leg had a tendency to stumble its noisy way through life. With only socks, he missed the lift in his footwear, but he had no option. If he was wrong, he'd look a right idiot.

'Bugger,' he whispered. He was going to walk – no, creep – with no surprise chips, no fish, no shoes, no dignity, and no mushy peas, all because Clive Cuttle was a miserable-looking man with a motorbike and a surly manner. Silently, the door swung inward, and Roy thanked the saints that he'd remembered to oil it a few days ago. If he was wrong, if she was just sitting there with or without Anna, he'd ask if he could borrow some cocoa, and say his shoes had started to hurt.

A sickly smell mingled with a different odour, one Roy didn't recognize as the metallic stench of newly spilt blood. Anna stood halfway up the stairs in a long blue nightdress. Roy put a finger to his lips and shook his head. Something was wrong. In an otherwise heavy silence, some small sounds emerged from the kitchen.

For as long as he lived, Roy would never account completely for the next two or three minutes. Blood. Rosh on the floor naked from the waist down. Man in a mask pushing, pushing things ... broken glass. Green glass. Shards being thrust into–

Carving knife. Man dragged off beloved on floor. Black mask. Bless me, Father, for I have sinned. Man on linoleum, knocked out by me. Knife through neck into floorboards, its thrust so violent that evil now impaled. How strong an angry cripple can become. I hear the red-coated woman in the chippy saying that someone should stick a knife through him. 'Stay away, Anna.' Cover Rosh. Small bottle labelled chloroform on floor. Cloth nearby. Handkerchief, I think. Tick-tock, tick-tock. 'Go upstairs, Anna. The kids mustn't see...'

He heard her climbing the treads. Remove the mask. Clive Cuttle. No breath, no heartbeat, no more. Rosh breathing and bleeding. Phone. Must get phones put in our houses. They thought I broke Dad's neck, but I broke this man's instead. Do not touch her. Do not remove anything from her. It will cut again on its way out.

He had to get out, had to get to the phone box.

Phone. Three nines. Police and ambulance. 'I killed him. He was killing her. Like the others, I suppose. Come quickly, she's bleeding to death. No sirens, please. Her children are in bed.'

A blur of frantic activity. Rosh taken to hospital, Anna with her. Pretty young policewoman to sit here in case kids wake. Body carried out eventually. I killed him. Now I know how Tom Walsh felt when he deliberately scooped the scum off the water at that wedding party. His wife looks like Rosh. But Rosh is the more beautiful of the two.

They are taking me to the police station. I don't care. As long as they save my Rosh, I don't give a tuppenny damn. Do policewomen know about children's breakfasts? Will she know about Alice? Alice throws a right wobble if she's given the wrong stuff. Phil, make sure Rosh gets through this. Talk to the Big Man upstairs, tell Him she's needed and wanted...

Thus Roisin Allen and her mother came to be at the Women's Hospital where Tess Compton lay in recovery. Remarks were passed among the staff, while Don Compton, who was very busy working on a boudoir for his wife, wondered about these almost identical twins. Well, not twins, because his Tess was a few years older than Mrs Allen, but this Roisin was a very near copy. It was like seeing double. Surely there wasn't a second bundle of trouble like the one he'd married? There sat Tess, every inch the angel, every ounce the naughty child. She was lovely.

'I've brought your knitting, pet,' he said after kissing the top of her head.

'So I've to work myself to death in here as well? No rest for the wicked, is that the case?'

'Leave it till you're more comfortable, then.' He sat. 'The woman in the side ward who had the operation a couple of nights ago – has she come round yet? Is she any better?'

'Did you bring the rest of the wool? No. I think

316

they're keeping her like that deliberately. They want her asleep while she heals a bit.' She lowered her tone. 'She's been hurt in a terrible way, Don. They were hours sticking her back together, so I've heard. That was one total madman. Kidnapping girls and women and killing them seems to have been his hobby. I'm glad he's dead.'

'Was she raped?'

She nodded. 'But not in the usual way.' Tess dropped her voice even further. 'They say he used broken glass and a vegetable knife. Police reckon he's that serial killer – I bet all those missing girls are buried except for the one where he got disturbed. Anyway, he's a goner as well. Mrs Allen's man friend killed him, and he got arrested. Who'd arrest somebody for killing a killer? But he must still be inside, because she's had no visitors except her mother and an old man called Eric. It's a terrible business altogether.'

'Kids?' he asked.

'Three. Two girls, one boy. Neighbours are helping to look after them, because their grandmother's here most of the time. These stitches are tightening up, Don. I feel as if I've been in a hot wash and my seams shrank. But I had a walk today, poked my head in to see how she was doing. No change. But I'll tell you what – she could be my sister. I'll knit you a winter woolly when I've done this cardigan.'

Don tried not to laugh. Tess still had a butterfly mind, flower to flower, one subject to another, no warning, no application for permission–

'Don?'

'What?'

317

'I asked what colour you'd like.'

'Brown.'

She sighed. 'I want to come home.'

'You can't. I'm decorating. And I'm doing your round for Johnson's. Mark's collecting the football pools on his bike. I'm terrified in case anything blows away, but Anne-Marie's got Saturday mornings off because you're in here, and she rides pillion. They both have security bags practically padlocked to the insides of their leather jackets.'

Tess's arms folded themselves, while her expression was extra sober. 'So you let her have a leather jacket?'

He nodded in mock shame. 'I did.'

Tess tutted. 'Leather jackets are like tattoos – they're for the lower echelons.'

'The what?'

'The uneducated.'

She would never change fully, but he no longer wanted her to change in every area. 'Mark's educated,' he said. 'As for tattoos – yes – I'd kill her myself. I was bad enough when she got her ears pierced.'

'I know you were.' She chuckled, then placed a hand on her healing scar. 'Don't make me laugh, it hurts. Go on home to this bordello you're making for me.'

'Boudoir.'

'Yes, that as well. I don't want anything vulgar.'

'Right, Miss. Is detention over now?'

'It is.'

He kissed her. In a way that truly mattered, she had managed, albeit by accident, one radical

318

move away from her past. There could be no more babies, no more danger of her upsetting Rome by making love for its own sake. 'I love you, Mrs Compton,' he said.

She tilted her head to one side. She knew he melted when she tilted her head to one side. 'Who was she, Don?'

He didn't hesitate. 'Just Molly.'

'Fat Molly?'

'Yes, fat Molly.'

'All right. Make sure it doesn't happen again. Go on. Get on the end of a paintbrush and make the bedroom nice for me.'

Don stepped away. He'd thought she would throw a tantrum, but she'd taken it quite well. Didn't she love him enough to mind what he did and with whom? Then he saw her expression. She was smiling at him. Perhaps the operation, the threat of death, had made her mature a little?

'They're not feeding me,' she complained. 'Bring me some custard creams, a pasty from Wetherton's, a packet of crisps and a bottle of ice-cream soda.'

'But they said—'

'And a quarter of liquorice allsorts.'

He sat down again. 'Look, love. You've half a mile of stitches down below, and that's just on the outside. Inside, every layer's stitched with stuff that melts away, so you can't go packing the food in. They explained this. You'll get wind. That's why they're cutting down on your food.'

The smile remained. 'You want me in your bed?'

'I do.'

'Then I'll settle for the pasty.'

'I'm not bringing you a pasty.'

'Half a pasty.'

'No.' She hadn't grown up. She would never grow up. The forever child from a wooden caravan in a barn was still here. Hunger was something she hated and dreaded above all else. The whole Compton family was a well-fed unit, and even the wildlife in the front and rear gardens was pleasantly plump. Tess was reliving a deprived youth because she was desperately hungry. 'I'll think of something,' he promised.

'You're a good man.'

'Glad you noticed. Glad I noticed how scared you are of having nothing to eat and too many children.' He nodded thoughtfully. 'Yes, it's time we got to know each other. We need a few meaningful talks, love.'

A group of people entered the ward, shepherded in by the sister.

'Collingfords,' Tess pronounced. 'Look at the flowers. You could fill a small graveyard with that lot. They're at war with Johnson's, but they'll never win. Johnson the Dyers and Cleaners are the cream. Which is why I work for them.'

'Of course.'

Tess folded her arms again. 'Mrs Allen's mother's a very small but very loud lady. I've talked to her – well, listened to her when I got as far as the corridor. She says her sleeping beauty's just bought a shop, and I'll bet you a pound to a penny the Collingfords are setting up a collection service. They'll be looking for a base in Waterloo, and I reckon she's been chosen.'

'You know it all, don't you, Tess?'

She nodded. 'I wasn't behind the door when they gave out brains. A meat pasty, not cheese and onion. I don't like their cheese and onion.'

The Collingfords disappeared into the side ward.

Don awarded Madam his full attention again. 'No pasties, our kid. You'll swell up, and your bowels will press on your operation. A couple of butties is my final offer, no negotiation. And you have one bite, then wrap it up again in the grease-proof.'

She stared bleakly at her bedcover. 'If we found anything, we had to hide it. If somebody suspected that you had found something, you got beaten till you told them where it was.'

'This is different, Tess.'

'But the hunger feels the same.' She looked up at him. 'I had arms like twigs, Don. With a little hammer, you could have got a tune out of my ribs. I've dug up raw potatoes and eaten them. She said I look like her.'

He scratched his head. 'Who said?'

'I wish you'd listen for once. Mrs Allen's mother said I look like Mrs Allen.'

'Right.' He would never keep up with her, would he? Her mind shot all over the place like spilled mercury, fragments breaking away to travel in many directions. She should wear a warning sign, *I am quicksilver*, so that the populace might be warned before dipping in.

'Don?'

'What?'

'Are you still working for her?'

'Eh? Oh ... not just now. I've got time off for bad behaviour.'

'Will you go back?'

'I don't know. I might man Injun Joe's phones while he goes out sleuthing. And I can help you with your jobs, stop Mark looking at you all soft while you're football pooling. I think our Anne-Marie's just an excuse so he can be near you.'

Tess sighed in the manner of a ham actor. 'I can't help being beautiful, can I?'

'No, you can't.'

The ensuing silence was shattered by a blood-curdling scream and the sound of nurses' feet pounding in the direction of the little side ward. The Collingfords emerged and were shunted into the corridor.

'Blood and Sahara,' Tess muttered. 'I thought she'd wake up a bit at a time, not like a train screeching through a tunnel. Go and see if she's all right. Go on.'

Don stayed where he was. 'What? Everybody but the pope's in that little room. It'll be worse than the Saturday crush at the Odeon. Anyway, it's none of our business, is it?'

'She looks like me.'

'And?'

'Ask the Collingfords – if they're still here.'

'I don't know the bloody Collingfords, do I?'

'But you can ask is she all right, offer them a cup of tea, seeing as that nurse who fancies you gave you the freedom of the kitchen. Yes, Lucy. I've seen her looking at you like a starved cat staring in the fish pond.'

In the end, he did as he was told and approached a very sad man in the corridor. His two women companions seemed to have deserted him. 'She wanted someone called Roy,' the sad man said. 'But Roy's in hospital, too. The police doctor said he wasn't fit to be let home, so he's had to be ... well ... certified. When Mrs Allen's mother told her he'd been certified...' His voice died.

'I'm sorry,' Don said lamely. 'The whole ward heard the scream and they're all worried. Can I get you a cup of tea? They've a few biscuits in the kitchen, too.'

'No thanks. My daughter's gone to bring the car a little nearer, and my mother's in the ladies' room. We came just to bring flowers, because we were due to meet for a business discussion, and we found out about this terrible attack.'

'And she woke?'

The man nodded, then adjusted a pair of very mobile spectacles. 'She asked for this Roy. Her mother said he was in hospital, and poor Mrs Allen screamed. I hope she hasn't damaged herself further. I think she believed that Roy had been hurt by the man who hurt her, but that's not the case.'

'So she knows he's not hurt?'

The glasses slipped again. 'The truth's bad, too. Telling her he's judged insane hasn't done any good. She's trying to get out of bed to go off and find him. Ah. Here come my ladies. Thanks for talking to me, Mr ... er?'

'Compton. Don Compton.' He stood and watched while three sad people walked away. It was a frightening world. But he had to go back and report his findings to the wife. If he didn't, he would be paying in pasties and paint for some considerable time to come.

The scenery had changed dramatically, suddenly, and more than once. There had been a kitchen, a brutalized woman – his woman – then a police station. She had followed him to the police station. A corner-of-the-eye job, Rosh lay on the floor of the interview room, only to disappear when Roy moved his head to get a fuller view of her.

He had been in this place before to answer questions about his dad. Someone mentioned that. 'Where is Rosh?' he asked. 'Is she in the other room?' But he knew she wasn't in the other room, because she kept coming and going on the floor here, didn't she? Then there was him, Clive bloody Cuttle with his cutlery – Cuttle and cutlery? What an appropriate name the monster had. He was appearing and disappearing in a corner. His item of cutlery was a sharp, vicious vegetable knife.

They told him Rosh was in the Women's Hospital in Liverpool.

'I killed him,' he said. 'But I keep seeing him.'

They knew Roy had killed him, and they said so. 'He's not here. He's on a slab somewhere.'

'What's he doing over there in that corner?' Roy asked. There was a huge carving knife through the man's neck, and it had stuck in the wall behind him. But when Roy turned to look, the apparition did a disappearing act.

They brought tea. And more tea. 'I went for

chips,' he told them.

So they brought him chips.

'I don't want them,' he said. 'I want the real Rosh, not the one who keeps coming and going. And that thing in the corner's back, too.' He was strangely calm. 'Green glass.' What came in green bottles? Was it wine?

'Yes, we know, lad.'

More of them arrived. Solid, real, clothed in navy blue. Whispering. Why were they whispering? They had news. 'Is she dead?' Roy shouted.

A young one entered; he was wiping his eyes with a handkerchief. A weeping policeman? Was he real? Yes. No light passed through him. 'She's alive,' a constable answered.

Handkerchief. 'It was on the floor,' Roy announced. 'And the stuff smelled sweet, the stuff he used to make her sleep. He had a handkerchief.'

'We know.' The man who spoke had three stripes on his sleeve and very sad eyes. 'These officers here found things in his flat, Mr Baxter. As you can see, my lads are upset about what they discovered. Shoeboxes with names on. Those names and the contents of the boxes were the property of missing women. You stopped him. You wiped out a one-man plague.'

'Is she dead?'

'No. They're mending her. She's young and healthy and they can get plenty of blood into her. Your Rosh is in the best place, son. Good nurses, brilliant doctors – it's second to none.'

Roy's eyes moved sideways, though his head remained still. 'Why is he still hanging on the wall like one of the ten green bottles? He used a green bottle, you know... And why is Rosh on the floor here?'

'Because you can't get what you saw out of your head. And you can't forget what you were forced to do.' The pavement outside the police station was three-deep in photographers. The nationals were arriving, too, since this broken man was a hero. 'It's not murder, Mr Baxter; it's rodent control.'

'I'm a Catholic.'

'So am I, but I've shed no tears when somebody I arrested went to the gallows. Cuttle would have killed her. You stopped him, and you stopped him killing somebody else after Mrs Allen.'

'So she's not dead?'

'She's not dead.'

'How do you know she's not dead?'

'Because they told me they'd every hope of getting all the glass removed and of making her whole again. They'll sedate her for a few days to keep her still and numb the pain.'

They were alone now, just Roy and the sergeant, plus transparent figures that seemed to come and go as and when the urge overcame them. 'They aren't real, you know,' Roy said. 'As long as I know they're not real, I'm all right. Right?'

'Er ... yeah, I'd say so.'

The see-through figure in the corner raised two fingers in a lewd gesture. Roy shot out of his chair and ran towards Clive Cuttle. Real or not, he needed ten shades of waste matter knocking out of him.

When the police doctor entered, Roy's knuckles

were bleeding.

'What's that wall ever done to you?' the new arrival asked. So Roy clouted him as well.

Dragged by the sergeant back to his seat, Roy fought to regain a level of steady breathing. The one-eyed medic sat next to the sergeant's empty chair. 'Keep hold of him,' the doctor recommended. 'I'll have a shiner tomorrow, and I don't want another.'

The heroic killer of Clive Cuttle was asked questions about the date, the year, the Prime Minister, Rosh and her children, their address, his address.

'What are you writing?' Roy demanded.

'About your state of mind,' was the reply.

'State of mind? State of bloody mind? I haven't got one. I've a mind, but not a state of.'

'Then why did you hit me?'

'Perhaps you've a face only a mother could love. Or I'm having a nervous breakdown – how the hell should I know? You're the doctor.'

'And you're not aggressive by nature, are you?'

Roy shrugged. 'I suppose not. But I killed him. I knifed him so hard, he was pinned to the floor. I can still see him over there in that corner.'

The doctor sat back. This was no psychotic; Roy was a man who had been driven to the edge and beyond. 'Every normal person, Mr Baxter, including you, me and the sergeant, is capable of killing under certain circumstances. Cuttle's final victim is the woman you love, I take it?'

Roy nodded. 'Even if it hadn't been her, what he was doing sickened me.'

'And you're having a bloody awful reaction. You need a rest. Peace, quiet and relaxation. Will you go to hospital voluntarily?'

'No. I want to be with Rosh.'

'You can't be with her. She's in a hospital for women only. Look, I'll be straight with you. The images you've seen in this room tonight are created by your brain. It's acting like a cinema projector, and this is, I hope, a temporary situation. But I can't let you wander off, you see. I can't allow you to pick up pieces until you've put down the burdens you're carrying now.' A suicide attempt could not be ruled out; if Rosh Allen died, this man would make sure he joined her.

'The kids need me. She's not dead, is she?'

'She's alive, Mr Baxter. Look at me. Look me in my one eye. If you go home and carry on seeing Cuttle, how many more people will you punch? For your own safety and for the sake of others, you must go to Whiston tonight. You'll be assessed, helped, then sent home to look after the people close to you.'

DIARY OF ROY BAXTER, PSYCHIATRIC UNIT WARD 6, WHISTON HOSPITAL.

Drs Fisher and Thorne, you said this would be a good idea. It is almost winter, and my section has run out long ago, but I remain voluntarily. Looking back on all that's happened, things got too much for me. Leaving aside (as if I ever could) the incident with Cuttle, life was already catching up with me. More responsibility at work, chasing round to be there for Rosh and her family, the leap from despair to hope, the supersonic dash from hope to joy – as I said, all these things were too much for me.

I can say now for the first time that excellent news can be as wearing as bad news. That looks so silly written down, yet it's true, and I am ordered to be truthful in this journal. My father's nastiness and my mother's goodness are on display now, as is the need for a family, for Phil's family. When Rosh promised herself to me, I was overwhelmed and weakened in a way that remains to this day beyond my comprehension.

My darling comes to see me regularly. Alice broke through whatever her barrier was, and she's now as normal and terrible as the next child. Philly is piano soloist with a youth orchestra, while Kieran is heavily into biology and other sciences. Anna, my wonderful soon-to-be mother-in-law declared her intention to starve the two girls so that their bridesmaid dresses will fit. Rosh has healed. The first few visits she made in a wheelchair, then she progressed to crutches, then a walking stick.

At first, she was very pale, frighteningly so. What do you want me to say here, docs? That I was terrified of losing her because she looked so fragile, that Cuttle came back and mocked me, that what wasn't there became more real than actuality? All right, I'll say it. I've said it. Yes, I remember my one night in the bounce-off-the-rubber-walls room, and he never returned after that, because I killed him all over again in my head.

I've become institutionalized. And I've made some decisions. I'll let you know my conclusions very soon, because I don't want to here. I'm not ungrateful, and I shall miss Stuart writing advanced maths problems all over the walls, Louisa and the ten-foot scarf she won't cast off the needles, Ellen with her Bible and Chris with his flying saucers and his belief that we all

arrived here in spaceships thousands of years back –
there may be something in his hypothesis. Above all, I
shall miss the two of you.

Christmas soon, then 1960. In these months, you
have turned me round and shown me that I have
much to offer and much to live for. I still admit that I
would have chosen not to live if Rosh had died. You
were right. I needed this space away from everything,
needed to grow stronger with your help. But I can also
say now that I did the right thing and I am not a
murderer. Oh, and I don't believe in ghosts any more,
not the Clive Cuttle type, anyway.

More later.

Anna's arms were folded tight across her bosom.
'Anyone would think a king was coming to dinner. Don't forget the little ermine cape, now. You look like a Christmas tree dressed by Alice. Remember? She hung so many ornaments on one side that it fainted.'

'Shut up, Mother.'

'As for when he's home to stay – well, I don't agree with your plans!'

'I'm not leaving him on his own overnight.'

'Then we'd best find out when he's coming out of the hospital, and get the wedding booked for that day.'

Rosh continued to apply mascara. If her mother didn't shut up soon, there would be another episode in this house. Roy couldn't come home and face a wedding on his first day. He had saved her life and had paid for it by falling apart. She owed him everything, and he'd already won her heart on the very night that ... just before it happened. An involuntary shiver passed through her body.

'And you might not be fit yet for ... messing about.'

Sometimes, just sometimes, Rosh felt like crowning her mother with the cast iron frying pan. 'Take the three of them to the cinema like you promised. I'll not have him mithered.' The kids had taken some comments and questions at school and in the neighbourhood. There was no way of shutting them up, not after what they'd been through, and they might just push Roy over the edge again. Especially Alice, who now talked at the speed of an express train. The press had been tethered; even now, reporters were forbidden to waylay the young Allens, but plenty of local people had kept the fires burning.

'If it wasn't for the shop, I'd move,' Rosh announced. 'It has to be just the two of us tonight, Mam. Shall I drop you off at the cinema?'

Anna shook her head. 'A walk will do us good. Go on. Go and fetch him.' She was so proud of this beautiful daughter. Like most strong Irish girls, she had healed at a miraculous pace. After the initial shock about Roy's condition, Rosh had shunted her thoughts into some kind of order and resumed her focus. Having progressed weeks later to a walking stick, she had passed her driving test in a month before turning her attention to something she called pelvic floor. Pelvic floor involved little yelps of pain, a lot of determination and a screwed-up face, but she persevered.

'As soon as Roy's home, we'll get that shop started up,' Rosh said. 'I'll employ temporary help until Roy's ready.'

'Ready for what?'

'Ready to work there.'

Anna dropped into a chair. 'He's got a good job, Roisin. Very highly thought of in legal circles, that man of yours. And you'll have him selling newspapers and tobacco?'

'I am not letting him out of my sight, Mam.'

'Don't you know that people shouldn't be to-gether twenty-four hours a day?'

Rosh awarded her mother a withering glance. 'I've managed it with you when I was a child and when we lost Phil. If I can tolerate you–'

'It's not you I'm concerned about, madam. It's him. You'll drive him mad.'

'He's visited mad already and wasn't too keen on it. Anyway, he can make up his own mind. The leg's no better, and he's as thin as a peeled rake, so I shall be looking after him as best I can.'

'Hmmph.'

'Same to you.'

'We'll be off, then.' Anna went to capture the grandchildren.

Rosh blotted her lipstick. Roy hadn't been here since the death of Clive Cuttle. 'Worse for you, my love, because I was out of it, unfeeling as a stone, and you had to take a life. And you already felt guilty because of wishing your father dead.' She was bringing him back to this house, to the scene of the ... the incident. Would he 'see' Cuttle in the kitchen? Would the breakdown recur, would he suffer?

She pulled on a coat. November shivers were something she could do without. Should she change her mind and allow a member of staff to come with him? No. She and Roy needed to talk in private.

'I can't do without him much longer. He's the only man alive I can love the way I loved Phil.'

'I know.'

Rosh turned. 'Can't even talk to myself, can I?'

'Not while I'm around, no.'

Rosh kissed her children, told them she hoped they would enjoy the film, made sure they were dressed warmly, then found her keys. The little van purchased for the shop was making its first long journey tonight. Whiston wasn't far away on a map, but it was a stretch for a woman who'd driven just locally until now.

When she reached the grim, grey place, he was seated on a chair in the central corridor. So thin, he was, and there were streaks in his hair where the colour was fading. But this served only to make him more attractive, and she ran to greet him with her arms widened to receive him. 'Handsome devil,' she whispered after kissing him.

He was quiet. Leaving this place had not been easy on the few occasions when he'd been taken out shopping for a couple of hours. But this was different. He was with his sweetheart, his princess, his backbone. Yes, he was going to a place that had been bad for a while, though its longer history was cloaked in happiness. He would be all right.

She set off back towards home. 'You'll be all right,' she said, as if reading his thoughts.

The smile was audible in his reply. 'I know. As long as I have you, as long as I'm with you, whatever happens, I shall always be all right. Don't worry about me.' Rosh had been through the real hell, yet he had managed to crack up and make a spectacle of himself. A hero? Heroes didn't come apart at the seams and allow the terror to show.

Rosh was very worried. Should they eat in her house, the place in which he'd put an end to the evil predator Clive Cuttle? Or should they go across to the house in which he'd seldom been happy since the death of his poor mother?

'And how are you?' he asked.

'Oh, I'm great. The café's done, but with just sixteen covers until I open the kitchen and expand the menu. I'm a driver, as you can see, and the children are wonderful. Alice is still different, has to carry an article from home wherever she goes, but she's top of her class with an adult reading age. Philly's on the up with her music, and Kieran's always attached to a book, mostly medical.'

'Your mother?'

'A pain in the bum, so normal, I'd say. She started a campaign about dog dirt, so some neighbour or other collected piles of cat poo and deposited the lot outside our front door. That put a stop to her. Then she joined the Labour Party. I feel ever so sorry for them. If anybody can spoil their chances locally and nationally, it's my mother.' She was prattling nervously, and she knew it.

A rusty laugh emerged from the passenger's throat.

'I've not finished.'

'I know that, sweetheart. Don't ever alter.'

She blinked. Driving in darkness with eyes filled with tears was not a good plan. 'So what did she do? She ragged all the Tory posters off shop windows and the like, painted Hitler moustaches on the candidate's stiff upper lip and, where she could, pulled Conservative leaflets out of letter-boxes and replaced them with Labour.'

'Was she admonished?'

'Oh, yes. But she says all's fair in love, war and politics. I hope you know what you're taking on, lad.'

He knew what he was taking on. He remembered a precious child having a shave with him, another playing the Moonlight Sonata until he wept, a third engaging him in a discussion about the nervous system and which parts of the brain were in charge of various functions. A family. And this delicious woman in his arms and in his heart. Well, they were all in his heart, Anna included. 'How are you physically?' he asked.

'Improving. I couldn't run a mile, but I'm a lot better.'

'So am I. I've decided to be home for Christmas.'

'Good.'

The conversation continued in slightly stilted fits and starts until they reached Lawton Road. This was a big step over a small distance, and they both knew it. But Roy climbed out of his seat, walked round the van, and opened the door for Rosh. 'Come on, Twinkletoes. Scene of the crime and all that. Let's get it over with.'

Inside, he took her coat and hung it with his on the hall stand. Without a word, he walked into the kitchen and stood open-mouthed at the view. A new, bigger table covered the place where Rosh had lain, while a large refrigerator eliminated the spot where Cuttle's life had ended. The flooring was new, as were sink, cooker, cupboards and shelves.

Rosh was behind him. 'I thought change would be a good thing. Mr Collingford from the dye works is going to use the upstairs level at the shop for his dry-cleaning. For now, it'll be a collection and delivery place, but he might bring machines in, and we'll get more rent. I bought this new kitchen with the retainer he paid. Nice man, decent family. They visited me in the Women's, you know. Brought enough flowers to open a florist shop.'

'This is lovely,' Roy said. 'And when you sell this and I sell my place, we can buy somewhere with a garden for the children and the cats.'

'All in good time. I think we need to think–'

He kissed her to stop her thinking about thinking. His right hand travelled over the nape of her neck and up into that abundance of hair. It was a hard kiss, hungry, determined; it was the embrace of a decided man. When it ended, he spoke to her. 'The future can wait. By its very nature, it must wait. After all that's happened, I need to get back into my stride – my limp – at my own pace. The same applies to you, but without the limp. We'll marry when we're ready, and I'll have the pleasure of helping Phil's children on their way through life. If you'll have me. Am I enough?'

'Oh, yes. You're enough.'

He was ravenous in more ways than one. 'As

long as it's not beef strong enough.'

'Nothing so posh, I'm afraid. It's a stew type of thing where you just throw things in and hope for a good result. But there's cobbler on top. Like dumplings, but lighter and nicer. Shall we take our chances?'

He nodded.

Although she had set the dining-room table, they sat in the kitchen, in the very room in which he had ended Clive Cuttle's reign of terror, commenting on the meal with its scone cobbler topping. He had finally overcome the trauma, had dismissed the nightmares and the visions.

They went across the road for coffee, Rosh carrying a pint of milk, since none had been delivered to Roy's house for months. Eager to keep him to herself on this first occasion, she was determined to save him from her children's joy. If Alice saw him, she would enter one of her states of rapture, yap, yap, yap, isn't everything wonderful, and when are you getting married? But he saw them from the window, watched as they entered the hall and switched on the lights. 'They've grown,' he commented.

'Yes, they do that. It's a habit they develop during babyhood, and they seem unable to break it until they reach twenty or so. The bridesmaids' clothes will have to be re-invented because...' Because he'd been away for months, yet she could hardly say that. But Mother, being Mother, had found material in a sale and had motored on with her sewing despite the fact that no date had been fixed.

He turned. 'But you do love me? You aren't

marrying me out of gratitude or pity?'

'Yes and no. Yes, I love you squillions, and no, there's no pity. Some gratitude, no pity. All right? Will I do?'

'I've loved you, Roisin Allen, since you were fourteen. Perhaps even earlier. I remember being impressed because you were only a girl, but you could pick up worms and caterpillars. And you had silky hair. That such a pretty thing would lift up a beetle and count its legs was brilliant.'

'I'm a treasure,' she said. 'There's no better word for me, is there? Shall we get you back to the asylum?'

But they didn't get the chance. Alice arrived first. 'We saw the lamps switched on in your house.' She stretched out her arms and claimed him. 'I missed you. I never had a shave.'

Philly and Kieran were on their sister's heels. They greeted him in a quieter way, but their beaming smiles said so much more.

Anna pushed her way in. 'I came out of the bathroom, down the stairs, and there they were – gone. Completely disappeared. Can't even answer the call of nature, can I? I trust you're well, Roy?'

Alice wouldn't let go.

Anna tutted. 'Looks like the poor man's become attached to something or other. Alice, put him down.'

The little girl frowned. 'I haven't picked him up. He's too heavy for me. You know he's too heavy.'

'And she's giving me the dirty looks again, Roisin.'

'She's a realist, Mother.'

338

'Is she now? Well I wish she'd take a realistic look at the benefits of broccoli. She used to eat it, didn't she? Now she has to have her dinner without trees, and—' Anna turned. 'What the blood and bone is all this?'

Rosh understood immediately. Some neighbour or other had been promised payment if he or she contacted the press. 'Let's get it over with,' she suggested to her fiancé. 'There'll be plenty of flashes, because it's dark, but better now, when you're going to escape back to Whiston for a while. Come along, nine-day wonder.'

They faced and dealt with a barrage of questions, were photographed as a group, and as a couple, then had to accept more questions. When would they marry, had she healed completely, how had he been treated during his breakdown, were the children happy about their soon-to-be stepfather, what did Anna think about the hero and about her daughter's second marriage?

When Roy was asked for details about the killing of Clive Cuttle, Rosh stepped forward. 'Wonderful,' she declared. 'You finally display your true colours, and you're about as sensitive as a box of cabbages. There's no more to be said, but any further harassment you will pay for. We are determined to protect each other's well-being, and you have already been warned about speaking to or in the presence of my children. I am tempted to say something very rude, two words about sex and travel, but my children are with me just now.'

Anna spoke up. Anna would always speak up. 'Away with you now, you no-good pack of rats.

339

See the doors open all down this road? Just a click of my fingers, and every one of your cameras will suffer accidental but fatal damage. So bog off.'

The rats dispersed.

Rosh watched as ten or more cars left the road. She imagined the headlines – *Hero Returns to the Bosom of his New Family, Killer of a Killer Allowed Home from Mental Ward.* She'd allowed the children to be photographed because it was inevitable, and she needed to control the vermin. But no more. They'd had their pound of flesh, and if they were still hungry they could feed off the bones of some other innocent souls.

'Our wedding will be soon and in secret,' Roy whispered into her ear. 'Two witnesses, the kids and your mother.' Inside, he picked one letter out of a pile created by Anna, who had been in charge of mail to the empty house. He kissed all members of his future family, led them out, and climbed into Rosh's car. Unable to tell the children that he would be their new stepdad even sooner than they thought, he simply waved at them as the vehicle pulled away. Anna, too, needed to be kept in the dark, since she had a leaky mouth when it came to gossip. But he loved her. No one who knew Anna Riley could fail to love her. 'Rosh?'

'Yes, love?'

'Remember when you were in the Women's?'

'I doubt I'll ever forget it, babe.'

'Well, there was a Tess there, Tess Compton. Your mother talked to me about her. She was in for a hysterectomy.'

'The one who looked a bit like me? Her husband was a grand chap, or so Mam said. With a limp.'

340

'I see. Only your mother told me when she visited me in Whiston that he got his at Dunkirk.'

'Right. And?'

He swallowed. 'I think there are three of you.'

'Three? Three of me? How the heck did that come about?' She parked the car and stared at him. 'What are you talking about? I am a one-off.'

'This letter's from Tom.'

Rosh let out a long sigh that was almost a whistle. 'Tess Compton's Tom?'

'No. Tess has a Gordon shortened to Don.'

'With a limp?'

'Yes, with a limp. Tom hasn't got a limp.'

'Well, thank goodness for some better news at last.' Roy's mouth twitched. 'He's got a Maureen instead.'

'Oh, I am pleased.'

Roy could contain himself no longer. He burst out laughing and doubled over with the pain of it. When had he last had a good old belly laugh? With tremendous difficulty, he composed himself. 'There are three women who look like sisters. Well, really, there are more. Only we don't know where a lot of them are. And they might not all look like you. But another older two from the previous generation–'

'Oh, give up, Roy. You lost me with the abbreviated Gordon and his abbreviated leg. Have you been taking your tablets?'

'I don't have them any more.'

'Well, get some for me. I think I'm going to need them.'

341

Twelve

'He won't know where we are.' Maureen's Tom was carrying the umpteenth cardboard box into their new house. He'd passed a few remarks about always having wanted to be a dray horse, a pack mule or a slave, but nobody took any heed. Roy had been on his mind for weeks. 'I'll have to go and see him. I wrote when he was in Whiston Hospital and got no reply, so then I sent a letter to his home address, but we've moved now and there's nobody left in any of the prefabs to–' He stopped and surveyed the state of his son, who seemed to be legs only for the time being. 'Seamus, put that dolly tub down before you do yourself or somebody else a mischief.'

Seamus, who had elected himself chief of an elite Martian force invading Earth, dumped his spaceship. He hadn't banged into anything, had he? And Mam had a new Hoover twin-tub with rubber wringers, so she didn't need the dolly and posser any more. Everything always had to be so serious. Even Reen, his married sister, was in a bad mood because of moving house. They'd waited ages for these three-in-a-row homes, and they still weren't satisfied. Taken all round, remaining a child seemed a jolly good idea, because children were the only people capable of making the best of a situation. Imagination was what the adults lacked.

Maureen, in her oldest clothes and with a headscarf transformed into a turban, faced her husband. 'Do you have plans to stay alive today? You and our Reen and her Jimmy have to help my mam as well. It's three households moving all at the same time. This is a very important day for all of us. So concentrate and stop moaning. You can think about Roy tomorrow. There's loads of stuff to carry, and some of it's heavy.'

'I know all about heavy lifting,' he answered. 'It's called moving a mountain. It was bad enough shifting your mother's furniture every time she wanted a change in the prefab, like about once a week.'

'Me dad's too old for messing about with wardrobes. We don't want him ending up with a hernia. He's aged a lot just lately.'

Paddy had that effect on people, Tom thought, though he kept the opinion to himself. Folk deteriorated quickly in Paddy's company. With Maureen in a mood, Paddy in a paddy and Seamus now head-first in a tea chest, this was hardly the time for clever quips. But Roy Baxter was in all the papers, as were Roisin Allen and her children. Roy was a hero. Even before the killing of Clive Cuttle, Roy had been Tom's hero.

'Seamus, get out of that box before I nail a lid on it,' Maureen snapped.

'He saved my life as well as hers,' Tom said, shifting a chair to one side of the fireplace. 'And you've seen her photograph in the papers. You know she has to be a Riley. She's the spitting image of–'

'Who has to be a Riley?' Seamus emerged from

343

his coffin.

'Shut up,' chorused his parents.

'Can I have a–'

'No, you can't.' Again, the response arrived in perfect unison. They hadn't even waited to see what he wanted, had they? He might have needed a plaster for a cut, an aspirin for a headache, an ambulance to save his life. But he didn't matter, because he wasn't a chair or a box of bedlinen. He stood in the front doorway. It was an all right street, he supposed. No air raid shelter for secrets, but there again, there was no war, was there? Or was there? There wasn't much peace, that was certain.

Moving house seemed to put everybody in a bad mood. Seamus alone was making the most of the experience. Reen kept moaning because she hadn't enough furniture for a two-and-a-half-bedroom house with bathroom plus downstairs lav, Jimmy was fed up because Reen was moaning, Seamus's parents were at loggerheads about photos in the papers, while Gran kept screaming at Granddad because his legs couldn't keep up with her tongue. Nothing could keep up with Gran's tongue. Even a huge jet engine would have its work cut out to catch up with her.

The lad went out to explore his new setting. As he passed his older sister's house, her voice echoed. 'I want a dining suite. That's a dining room, so it stands to sense we should have a...' Seamus ran away before she added anything else to her list. Some folk were never satisfied. Building was still ongoing at the other end of the street, and it all looked very interesting. There was a cement mixer. If he wore his best smile, they might let him have a bit of a go with that.

Inside, Maureen faced her beloved opponent, who was showing signs of flagging. She didn't want the poor soul breaking down again. 'Sweetheart, he's a good man. What Roy Baxter did for you that day when you were so ill speaks for itself. And you know why he went to bits, because killing anybody, gangsters and serial killers included, can never create happy or even ... or even acceptable memories. He followed in your footsteps, Tom. Like you, the poor beggar had no choice. He fell apart, but you'll see him soon. For now, can we get on with this move? Even though we're in November, I shan't be lighting a fire till later, because this is hard, warm work.'

'It's certainly that, all right.' Tom went next door to check on the elders and borrow a screwdriver while Maureen sorted out her new kitchen. He found Paddy sitting on the stairs in her hat, coat, gloves, scarf and fur-lined winter boots, the ubiquitous black shopping bag by her side. 'You all right?' he asked. 'You look wrapped up ready to move into an igloo with Eskimos and a fish supper.'

She nodded. 'Me old bones is froze stiff. Kevin's gone for more stuff. And you can tell Maureen and Reen that we'll have plenty of help later, because some dock workers are coming along – I've just now had word. But for a bit of a minute, I need to talk to you about something important.'

It was one of those hardly rare enough moments when Tom felt he should have signed the Official Secrets Act; she was about to give

345

him information he didn't need, didn't want, and couldn't pass on in some sort of attempt to share the burden. 'Right,' was all he managed to say. There was an almost indefinable edge to her tone, which confirmed his belief that she was about to impart knowledge he would be ordered to keep to himself. It wasn't fair. Why him? Why not some other poor bugger for a change?

'Tom, if I do something that you might call out of character, will you tell them I'm all right?'

'No, I won't do anything of the kind.'

'But Tom, you've always been the one to back me up when–'

'No. Tell your husband. I'm fed up with being your storage box. It's not as if I got democratically elected. What am I supposed to be? Some sort of chief whip put there to keep order on the back benches? And we're hardly a quorum, just the two of us.'

'I can't tell Kev.'

'Why?'

'Because he'd go into a purple fit with yellow spots. He would find a way of putting a stop to me, I know he would. You might all think I'm in charge, but once he puts his foot down, well...' The last word hung in the air, and she made no attempt to add to it.

Tom, knowing full well what was on her mind, maintained his stance. 'Then I'm with my father-in-law. If he wouldn't want you to do whatever it is you're going to do, then I wouldn't want you to do it.'

She nodded, a grim smile on her lips. 'You're picking up on the Irish way of expressing your-

346

self. And I know that you know what I'm talking about.'

'I don't.' He did. Of course he did. Every adult in the family knew, though they never spoke about it.

'Well, then. We'll leave it there, shall we? See, I know you're a grand chap. When I do what has to be done, it will be noticed. Deal with it. And don't let me down, Tom.'

He'd forgotten what he'd come for, and had to root about in the memory department. Women were truly gifted when it came to the messing up of a fellow's mind. You went to borrow something or other, only to return with a head filled with rubbish, and often without the article you'd gone for. 'Screwdriver,' he exclaimed triumphantly.

'Same to you.'

'Have you got one?'

'Mantelpiece, front room, next to the clock. Why do you need it?'

Tom jerked a thumb in the direction of next door. 'Your daughter has a screw loose.'

'I see. I think I was already aware of that, thank you.'

'On a cupboard door.'

Paddy chuckled. 'Then she has more than one screw loose.' When he turned to leave, she called after him. 'Don't say anything to her. Don't tell anyone.'

He turned in the front doorway. 'How can I tell anybody something I don't know? Do I lead her to believe that her mother's told me a secret and I don't know what it is? You'll have me as daft as the rest of you.'

Paddy shrugged. 'Please yourself. Whatever, I'm doing it, and I'm doing it alone.'

Tom fled before she could reveal any more of her plan. Months earlier, she had announced her intentions, but she'd said nothing of late. He guessed that she'd been waiting for the move from prefab to house before embarking on her mission. That there was sense in her argument could not have been denied then; nor could it be denied now. London gangsters seldom hurt or killed women. Unless some poor soul got in the line of fire, no female would be hurt. Even among the bad boys, there existed a code of sorts.

'Where've you been?' Maureen snapped. 'Three-course lunch and a pint, was it?'

Talk about frying pan and fire! He was stuck between a cauldron and the Liverpool Blitz. 'I had to look for it. Get out of my way while I fix the hinge properly. Builders? They couldn't make a sandcastle in Blackpool.'

Maureen gazed round her new home. It was all right, she supposed, though it needed a bit of colour. 'When can we paint and decorate?' she asked. 'I fancy a nice shade of mauve in the kitchen.'

'Three months.'

Maureen's jaw dropped. 'Three months? Three months living with this dirty pink stuff all the way through?'

'It'll go lighter as it dries.'

Maureen was further appalled. 'You mean we're living in a damp house? More to the point, are you telling me that my mam and dad are living in a damp house?'

Tom descended to terra firma. He slammed down the screwdriver and awarded his wife a laboured smile. 'Right. Go and get the removals men again, pack up here, tell your mother and our Reen to pack up, and we'll go back to our prefabs. All right?'

'No. I don't want to live in a tin hut either.'

'A tent?' he suggested.

'No.'

'The Park Lane in London?' He wagged a finger under his wife's nose. 'Now, think on before chucking stuff. I kept the right sized window glass down yonder for the prefab, but I've nothing for here, so don't go throwing the pans.'

She glared at him. 'When was the last time I threw things?'

'When Seamus took the school camp money to run away and find his brothers.' Tom looked round. 'He's disappeared again, hasn't he? No flaming wonder, with his mam and dad going at it hammer and tongs. Maureen, this is a fresh start in a new house. Don't quarrel with me. Don't turn into your mother, queen of all she surveys, controller, nuisance–'

'There are kids round here who wouldn't eat except for Mam lending families a few bob.' Maureen calmed herself. 'But she's up to something. I can feel it. I can almost hear it crackling in her head like a wireless not tuned in properly.'

Tom recognized his chance, but said nothing. If he started a war between mother and daughter, it could take a document far more complicated than the Treaty of Versailles to straighten things out. With three houses stuck together in the terrace, any argument would spread like plague before becoming the subject of gossip throughout the whole neighbourhood.

The rest of the day passed without incident. Dockers arrived, beds were carried upstairs effortlessly, as were wardrobes and chests of drawers. Seamus returned, muddy and frowning. When asked how his circumstances had deteriorated so terribly, he made no reply, but was heard muttering under his breath about poor drainage at this side of Bootle, and he wasn't going to be a builder when he left school.

Maureen placed him on the stairs and went to light a fire. 'Don't move,' she called while balancing coals on newspaper and firewood. 'Don't even think about moving; don't think at all. In fact, don't even breathe deeply, cos this is a new house. The water will be hot enough for a bath once this fire gets going.'

Seamus sat on the uncarpeted stairs and thought about not thinking. But thinking about not thinking was thinking, wasn't it? How could a person not think? Even asleep, he thought about things. That was called dreaming. The trouble with adults was that they had all the authority but no sense. 'Straighten your face before the wind changes.' 'Don't swallow chewing gum, because it'll wrap itself round your heart and kill you.' Where were their brains? On holiday somewhere? He was fed up.

Mam arrived with a paper poke containing chips. 'There you go, my lad. From the chippy. After your bath, I'll do you a nice fried egg butty. That's if I can work out the flame-throwing monster in the kitchen. Then you've got that great big bedroom all to yourself, a lot bigger than in the prefab. We can't decorate till the plaster's gone off properly, but when we do, it'll be red and white for Liverpool FC, eh?'

The nice thing about mams was that they kept you right. You got cooked meals, clean clothes with no creases, and your hair looked at every week for nits. They tucked you in, helped with homework and saved up for a television set. Dads were OK, too. They mended bikes, built go-carts out of pram wheels and wooden boxes, took you on the ferry or for a kick-about with a football. So life wasn't all mud and tellings-off. It was a mixed bag with a fried egg butty for supper. Oh, well. The chips were good, but his hands were filthy...

Don's head couldn't rid itself of a picture of Molly floating round in that big house all by herself. Was she still going out George Formbying? Was she eating properly, was she happy, had she found someone to talk to? She and Matt had been so close, so wrapped up in each other. After his death, poor Molly had fallen apart until Don had entered the picture. Had he not become close to her, the business might have died of neglect and– Oh, what a mess. He'd caused more trouble than enough, hadn't he?

He felt as guilty as Cain, as original sin, as Lucifer, the fallen angel who turned his back on glory before moving south to create hell. Molly had her lovable dogs, some tropical fish, her temperamental cookery and her money, but what she really needed was human company. Could he be that? Just that? Why was life so bloody complicated? Why couldn't a man and a woman remain friends when an affair ended? Humans were an odd lot.

Tess mumbled in her sleep. She often did that, and he found himself almost praying that she wasn't stuck in that apparently endless nightmare about the caravan, the hunger, the bed-wetters. For how long had he cursed her selfishness? Why hadn't he remembered her beginnings? More to the point, why hadn't she trusted him enough to explain to him about her fear of more pregnancies? He couldn't have got life any more wrong if he'd tried. Was he some sort of Jonah?

Because Tess was no cold fish. Recovered at last from the surgery, she often instigated lovemaking, and he quickly realized that she had been denying herself as well as him, and that she, too, had suffered. Had he been a Catholic, he might have understood, but he'd promised only that any children would be reared as Catholics, no more than that. Perhaps he understood at last the Roman disapproval of mixed marriage.

He loved her. She wore him out with her butterfly mind, her sudden enthusiasms and her squirrels, but he wouldn't swap her for all the tea in China. Squizzles, she called her pets these days. The Lennon boy had donated the word free of charge. The pretty little rodents now ate out of Tess's hands. She wore gloves, because the buggers had teeth like razors.

Molly. There had been no phone calls, no meetings, no work. She had ordered him to stay away until Tess was well, and Tess was well. She

352

was so well that Don was sometimes exhausted by her; his marriage had travelled at the speed of sound from famine to feast. He was happy to be tired, yet miserable about poor Molly. Today, he would visit her. The business was up for sale, but it needed to be in good order, and he should make sure that it was, that the books were clean and that no custom had been lost. She must not miss out; this could well be his last chance to be of service to her.

Tess reached for him. 'Bad dream,' she said. 'Just hold me.'

'With pleasure.' He was at his most contented when his face was in her hair, when her head tucked itself into his neck. This was the wife he had almost lost, and he had no intention of misplacing her again. But Molly mattered. Molly had been good to him in many ways, and this was a debt of honour that demanded to be paid. He had to tell her that his concern for her remained, that she was by no means forgotten.

When Anne-Marie and Sean had left for work, Don advised Tess of his intentions. She was melting fat for her bird lollipops. 'I'll come with you,' she said, her tone nonchalant. 'I'd quite like a little outing.'

Don shuddered and sat down rather suddenly at the kitchen table. 'You can't do that, love. I have to talk business with her, look at the books and so forth. It wouldn't be right in a business meeting.' Molly was a sensible woman, but Tess remained capable of creating a stir if her feathers got ruffled.

'I'll be very quiet,' she promised. 'Like a little

mouse, but without all the squeaking. You will scarcely know I'm there.'

'You will be quiet, because you won't be there.'

She turned from the cooker and looked at him. Little strands of hair framed a face any artist would be pleased to commit to canvas. 'I'm not letting you out of my sight, Don Compton. I've been lonely for too long. She'll want you back, I know she will.' After a pause, she continued, 'You're handsome and good and kind. She'll be missing you.'

Two lonely women, both of them his own fault. 'I'm not going to the house, Tess. I can't go to the house, because I'd have trouble tearing myself away from the dogs. Anyway, she'll be at work.'

'Then so will I.' She turned off the burner and mixed hot fat with birdseed and bits of bacon.

'You don't trust me,' he accused her.

'I don't trust her, either. She shouldn't have messed about with somebody else's husband. She's a ... a lowlife.'

Don hung his head. Molly was nothing of the kind. She was isolated, and he knew how that felt. 'You took it so well when I told you.'

'I was too busy worrying about stitches and thanking God that I'd come out of the slaughterhouse alive. Now. As soon as I've got this lot in their moulds, we're going. If you leave before I've finished, I'll follow in my van. So stick that in your pipe and blow bubbles out of it. My mind is made up.'

Don decided in that moment that honesty wasn't always the best policy. He would have done better with a lie, a tale about meeting Injun

Joe in connection with a job, or a story concerning the planning of darts matches. When truth hurt, it was best left to one side like a bit of jetsam that might float away on the tide of life. 'All right,' he said after a lengthy pause. 'But no trouble.'

'Fair enough.' She went upstairs to make herself beautiful while Don sat and tried to read his newspaper. This promised to be an interesting morning. He would be unable to talk privately with Molly, and that was a grave disappointment, since he wanted to make sure she was all right. Doing the books under Tess's gaze might prove difficult, and he wished he'd kept his stupid mouth shut. But the damage was done, and her highness was upstairs making herself inappropriately smart. This time, she would be applying war paint. He allowed himself a tight smile. Tess would look wonderful in a potato sack, and she knew it.

Madam returned gowned and crowned, a very straight spine adding further to her regal appearance. The crown was a hat with a tiny veil that covered none of her face and precious little of the golden blonde hair. A matching suit fitted so well that it looked tailor-made to show off wonderful calves and ankles, while the ensemble was completed with good shoes, good bag and kid leather gloves. As was the way with many women, she planned to make her non-spoken statement via the outdoing of the perceived opponent by leaving her behind in the area of fashion and general appearance.

'You look wonderful,' he said.

'I know.'

She knew. And she wasn't shy about her beauty, wasn't prone to dismissing her looks as unimportant as most females did. An undersized child had blossomed into a stunningly attractive woman. 'You may have gone a bit over the top for a builders' merchant's yard, love.'

'Yes, perhaps. But that'll be because we're going on somewhere when your business at the yard is over.'

'Like Windsor Castle?'

'No. Like a posh restaurant in town.'

He couldn't tell Tess how much she owed to Molly. If she were to learn how he had come by this house, God alone knew how she might react. 'She's a good person, Tess.'

'Good women don't mess about with someone else's husband.'

Don sighed. 'You and I weren't happy, love. I didn't know you were ill and that messed-up hormones were making you worse and giving you panic attacks. Molly was company more than anything else. She was alone, and I was alone.'

'But you weren't going to stay with me, were you, Don?'

After a quick shuffling of his thoughts, he came up with a reply. 'She didn't know that. She thought we were moving as a family, because she knew I loved you. I didn't realize it then, but she did. In fact, she was always on your side, always asking after you and telling me to get back home. She's good, Tess. Even good people sometimes do wrong.'

Tess sniffed and tapped a toe two or three times. 'All right, Romeo. I'll give you twenty minutes' travelling time – that's ten each way – and half an hour to say goodbye and check her books. So it's fifty minutes. Out of the goodness of my heart, I'll stretch it to an hour. One hour. When you get back, I want you booted and suited, then you can take me somewhere plush for lunch. I'm still in here, you know.' She placed a hand on her chest. 'Inside, there's still a hungry infant who turned into a silly, selfish woman. And I want four courses.'

'Yes, ma'am.'

'Including sorbet.'

'Who?'

'It's a palate cleanser.'

Don nodded. 'Can't you just take your toothbrush?'

For answer, she clouted him with the best handbag. 'Get gone. And don't let me down, or your privileges will be curtailed.'

'Oh. Do I get a general anaesthetic?'

'No. You'll feel the pain and enjoy it.'

He folded his paper and rose to his feet. 'Ah. Now we enter the sado-masochistic phase, eh? Can I tie you to the bed and talk to you in Greek?' He kissed her very fiercely.

When she regained the ability to absorb oxygen, she hit him once more with her bag. 'You've ruined my make-up,' she accused him.

'That's all right, then. You've won an hour to put it right.' He left.

Tess smiled to herself. He wouldn't walk out on her. Mind, there was a clause in the marriage ceremony, a piece that contained the words 'till death us do part'. Nobody got out of here alive.

357

The smile faded. He couldn't die before she did. She had to go first. Oh well, she needed to sort out her face. People with smudged lipstick couldn't enter a place that served sorbet.

Meanwhile, Don followed a familiar route to the place where he had worked for over ten years. Although Molly understood that their close relationship was over, she surely deserved a visit, an update and another thank you. Oh. An Under Offer notice had been pasted over the For Sale sign. He got out of the car and saw that the gates were padlocked. What now?

He looked at his watch. She Who Needed To Be In Charge had imposed a limit, but he had to get to Molly's house. There was no anger in him; being annoyed by Tess was no longer allowed. Few people in life escaped undamaged, but some were more damaged than others. Inside Tess's core dwelt an unloved child who would never be satisfied.

Molly wasn't at the house, and there was no barking. A Sold sign stretched diagonally across the estate agent's board informed Don that he was probably trespassing. Pressing his nose against the living-room window, he discovered that the tropical fish had been removed. She would never have left without letting him know, surely?

The answer? He knew exactly where it lay. Instead of using his key to the front door, he walked down the side of the house to the huge back garden. And there it was, in a flower bed well away from the house. A gardening glove that seemed to have been dropped accidentally lay on frozen soil. With difficulty, he eased his already cold fingers into the icy item before using it as protection while reaching into a holly bush. And there he found the black box inside which he and Molly had occasionally left messages for each other whenever plans went awry.

Firstly, there was a folded note for him – no name, no address, just a small piece of lined paper with a few words scribbled on it. *Lots of luck to you, D. Every good wish for the future. Be happy. The other letter can be read by anyone, even T. Bye, my love. M xxx*

Don carried the sealed envelope back to the car. His name was written on the front. As he sat staring at it, a dart of sadness pierced his heart. It was possible to love two women simultaneously. Molly had been his anchor, his best friend. He could still hear her laughter, remember the smell of a disastrous moussaka, fumes from which might have been used against an enemy in the event of war. Somewhere far away, tucked in the back of his head, he heard the strumming of a ukulele and her 'turned out nice again' voice delivering a rendition of 'My Little Stick of Blackpool Rock'.

Would he never see her again? Never was a long time to be without a best friend. But there was Tess, his re-enlivened wife, and he absolutely adored her. The extra layer in Molly's make-up was probably connected to her age, because she had babied him. Where was she? Where the bloody hell had she gone with the wonderful dogs and the satanic angel fish?

He checked his watch. Unless he wanted to run into extra time, he'd better get this read, since the referee was waiting for him. Waiting for him. When they'd lived above the launderette, she'd taken little interest in his whereabouts. He could have been in Timbuktu for all she'd cared. He'd been steak pudding and peas, no more than that. Now, like most other wives, she wanted to know the location of her man.

But no. He didn't need to open the envelope here in the car, because the extra little scrap of paper, now discarded in the dustbin, had re-assured him. Even Tess could read this letter without taking umbrage. They might read it together, then. But as he drove away from the past, from an area of his life that had contained love, kindness and consideration, he felt a great hole widening in his chest. No Molly, no daft dogs, no hum from the filter in the fish tank. He remembered the trout. *They're staring at me. Do I cut their heads off?* That had been followed by another trip to the chip shop. Molly. A mistake a minute, a laugh a minute. But no man could have two mistresses, and he had to be satisfied with his lot. Nothing on the planet would ever persuade him to abandon his Tess.

When he reached home, Tess had changed her clothes and was kneeling on the kitchen floor, her head in the gas oven.

'No need for that,' Don said. 'There's a whole river down the road if you want to commit suicide. A kitchen's no place for a corpse, even one as pretty as yours would be.'

She emerged with a smudge of dark grease on the end of her nose. 'Listen, bird-brain of Britain. You did the Sunday dinner, right?'

He fought laughter. No one with a smudge like that one could expect to be taken seriously. 'I did.'

'It was lamb, right?'

'It was.'

'Lamb spits,' she pronounced.

He considered that for a moment. 'Actually, it was dead at the time. If it had been prone to temper tantrums, the inclination would have died with the rest of it. And anyway, it was just the one leg.'

Tess scrambled to her feet. 'You should have wiped down before the oven went cold.'

'Sorry.'

'Then after wiping down, put the cloth in the sink with bleach diluted in hot water.'

'Yes, ma'am.'

She awarded him one of the more sudden of her army of smiles. 'You're back early.'

'I am. And you've had a change of clothes.'

'Change of mind,' she answered quickly. 'I rang a few restaurants, and nobody serves sorbet. That was definitely a sorbet suit. I was far too well dressed to live the sorbet-less life. We'll have to go to London.'

'No problem. But will they sell steak pudding and peas?'

'How was she?'

'She's gone, love.'

'And no.'

'No what?' He scratched his head in the manner of Stan Laurel.

'They won't serve steak pudding.' She caught sight of herself in a mirror above the kitchen table. 'Why didn't you tell me?' she asked crossly.

'Because you look cute, and because I thought I might sell you on to Billy Smart's circus next time it hits town. They could do with a glamorous clown.'

She rubbed away the offending mark. 'What do you mean, "She's gone", anyway?'

'She's gone. As in not there, no sign, no sound, business under offer and house sold.'

Tess sat down. 'Without letting you know?'

Don nodded. Seated opposite her, he placed the unopened letter in the centre of the tablecloth. 'I found this.'

'Oh. What is it?'

After repeating his Stan Laurel imitation, he offered his opinion in the matter. 'From where I'm sitting, I'd say it's an envelope.'

'Don't get clever with me, Don Compton. It doesn't suit you.'

'OK.'

Two pairs of eyes were glued to the white oblong next to the cruet set. 'Open it, then,' Tess ordered. 'It's addressed to you, not me.'

He tore back the flap and withdrew the contents. 'Cheque for a grand there,' he said. 'Severance, I expect.'

She shook her head. 'Payment for services rendered, if you want my opinion.'

'I'm no gigolo,' he said.

Tess swallowed nervously before turning pink. 'Well, I think you're good at it.'

'At what?'

She paused for several seconds. 'Managing a business, of course.'

But he knew what she meant and was disproportionately pleased. He unfolded the letter and read it aloud.

Dear Don,

I owe you so much, and nothing could compensate for the way you saved the business after I lost my beloved Matt. However, I trust that the enclosed will help replace your car and buy something for the house. I also hope Tess is better, because she had a tough time with that terrible illness.

A lot has happened since I last saw you. I was doing a wedding for an older couple, childhood sweethearts who met up again after both were widowed. It was so romantic. They love George Formby songs, so I was at it for over an hour, until I got hoarse.

At the same event, I met a man called Henry, which he doesn't like, so he goes by Hal. He plays the piano. We started talking during a break, and we got on really well. He's not after my money, because he has plenty of his own and, like me, he plays and sings mostly for the fun of it.

Anyway, to cut a short story even shorter, we started spending time together. He lives in a huge flat over his music shop in town – he sells instruments, records, sheet music and so forth. By the way, he thinks John Lennon and his group could go far.

It turned out that he was selling up, like me. He wants to retire to Cornwall, and we've been looking at bungalows down there. We've both sold more or less everything and we're moving to Cornwall and renting until we find a nice place to buy there or in Devon. I know you'd like him, Don. He even does all the cooking which cuts out the danger of food poisoning so we dovetail very well, because he can't iron to save his life!

I gave my tropical watery friends to a young man who loves them, so the angel-devils and the others will be cared for. Saying goodbye to Matt's house wasn't easy, but we must all look to the future however long or short it's going to be. The good thing is that both Hal and I feel as if we've known each other all our lives.

The business has been bought by a Chester firm called Williamson and Co. Ltd. I have recommended you to them in case you feel like carrying on once Tess is back to normal. I managed the books – hang the bunting out immediately – and Mr Williamson was quite impressed by the turnover. They want to reopen as soon as the paperwork's done, so they may contact you in the near future.

Tell Tess and your children I wish them the best of everything.

Yours sincerely, Molly.

'So she's definitely gone?' Tess asked. 'That isn't some sort of code saying meet me outside Lewis's and we'll book a room nearby?'

Don shook his head.

'I bet there'll be somewhere in Chester.'

'What?'

'Somewhere in Chester with sorbet.'

She was at it again. Her mind leapt about with all the senseless agility of a newborn lamb. Ah, yes. Lamb. 'What about the oven?' he asked.

'You're doing it.'

'With my knee, that would be difficult.'

'That means I'll have to do it. Put the kettle on and make a cuppa. Then you can take the money to the bank; it'll do for our Anne-Marie's wedding. Have you seen the price of wedding gowns lately? Some are twenty quid. Twenty pounds for something that gets worn once. And you can't get even a decent finger buffet under twelve shillings a head. There'll be no sorbet for that, I shouldn't wonder.'

Don closed his mouth with a snap. 'She's not seventeen yet, Tess.'

'I know that. And I was married at that age.' Her head disappeared into the oven again.

She was right, as usual. Anne-Marie was growing out of her parents' arms and into the embrace of Mark, her wealthy yet down-to-earth boyfriend. Even John Lennon had been dismissed as ordinary, and her outings to Allerton for a glimpse of Paul McCartney had stopped. The couple went to stock car racing and speedway in Manchester, enjoyed films and concerts, and were members of a local jazz club where they listened to both modern and traditional bands. 'Are they engaged?' Don asked.

Tess emerged from the cavern, banging her head on the way out. 'Now look what you've made me do. What did you say?'

'Are they engaged?'

She stood up. The old blouse was ruined, as was the wire wool with which she'd been scrubbing at grease and grit before wiping the oven down with a tea towel. 'I wonder if we should spend that money getting your knee sorted? Then you can do this job sometimes.' Even her hair was filthy. 'I don't think they are,' she added.

This time, Don had managed to keep up with his wife. Their daughter was not engaged. Yet.

'You're in a state worse than Woolworth's on Christmas Eve. Come on, let's get you bathed.'

'What about your knee?'

'I'm not wasting money cleaning up after Hitler. I'd rather rub my wife down with a damp cloth.'

She nodded. 'Yes, and you kneel to do it.'

'Do I?'

'And there's no cloth. You never use a cloth or a sponge.'

He nodded sagely. 'My hands do just as good a job.'

'And then I get dragged off to the black and red bordello you made for me.'

'Boudoir. I must finish it, must put that mirror on the ceiling. Don't blush. You're dripping grease all over the place.'

Tess folded her arms. She was definitely not having a mirror on the ceiling. Did he realize what people might think if they walked in? 'We could have a party, and they might leave their coats on the bed. It's already colourful.'

He sniffed meaningfully. 'It works for me.'

Tess closed her eyes, tutted and shook her head. 'No mirror. You go within a hundred yards of a mirror, and I'll make sure you have seven years' bad luck even if you don't break it.'

'Get up the stairs.'

'No.'

'Are you taking advantage of a Dunkirk hero?' The electricity was still there. It was the same as it had been twenty years ago, before Sean, well before Anne-Marie. He was the luckiest man in the world. How many marriages resurrected themselves after so long a drought? It was as if little sparks of blue fire flashed in her eyes as she challenged him. 'Choose your weapon,' he suggested.

She picked up a sad, superannuated dish towel, the very one with which she had wiped down the oven after the scrubbing. 'This'll do for me,' she said, her chin tilting in defiance. 'Choose yours.'

He grinned. 'You're already familiar with my weapon of choice.'

'Vulgar man.' She stalked past him and clomped noisily upstairs.

Don sat for a while with Molly's letter and the cheque. Perhaps he should see a specialist about his knee. Molly had wanted that. It was unlikely that anyone could make him walk without the limp, but the pain was tiring, especially at this time of year.

The bath was filling. A slow smile spread its width across Don's face. In a bottom drawer of the chest in the hall, Sean's water pistol rested. The lad still used it in summer, usually in an effort to drown his dratted little sister. 'I'll use warm water,' Don whispered. 'Cold would be cruel.' He fetched the item and filled it at the kitchen sink. 'Second weapon of choice, you come with me. Let's prove to her that the bathroom ain't big enough for the both of us.'

Christmas threatened. Shop windows were all lit up, dressed trees glittered in almost every parlour, while the faces of many women wore a slightly worried expression. Was a turkey twenty-five minutes a pound, or was it twenty? Some gave up altogether and went for a couple of chickens. They understood chickens; twenty minutes a pound, then twenty minutes extra at the end. Problem solved. Right, so how many were coming for dinner, and who hated sprouts? Would the royal icing on the cake be the death of Auntie Ivy's dentures, and would Granddad repeat last year's performance and swallow a sixpence from the pudding? Oh well, at least all the presents were wrapped and ready.

When the women stopped worrying, the men took over. Christmas Eve found every shop crammed with white-faced males who tried to buy perfume they'd never heard of, underwear without looking at it, or scarves. Scarves were for those who had failed the first two fences. They were safe, as were slippers, books, and manicure sets.

Roy didn't take a safe route. Having sold his story to the most notorious of Sunday newspapers, he no longer felt persecuted, since he had made the decision to be exposed, but with a degree of control. Yes, people stopped him in the streets and yes, he put them off politely. But the quiet, invisible wedding was not going to happen, because Rosh's daughters wanted the dressing up, bells ringing, a party afterwards. When it came to her honeymoon attire, he dealt with it head-on. Armed with a list of his beloved's measurements, he entered the dragons' den and bought whatever took his fancy. And quite a number of flimsy items managed to take his fancy. How he had changed!

On another expedition and with all his girls in tow, he bought rich cream silk taffeta for the bride,

368

the same material in sky blue for her daughters, a good suit for Kieran, and a mid-blue jersey silk for Anna. It would be a grand wedding.

Kieran was not interested in shopping, so he had stayed at home reading about the nervous system.

'I hope the suit fits him,' said Anna when all five sat down for lunch in a café. 'And I'm cutting out no frocks till the first banns are read. Two good dresses, these two grew out of while Roy was away. I shall sell them. Alice, eat your soup. It's all right, you can start when you're ready. Say grace in your head – God won't mind.'

'I know,' Alice replied. She was starting to put her foot down, especially where Gran was concerned. But now she awarded attention to her partner-in-shaving and future stepfather. 'You've seen Mam's material,' she pronounced with gravitas. 'Isn't that unlucky?'

'Only when it's a frock,' he replied, the sober tone matching hers.

'I've seen the pattern,' the child continued. 'But it won't be quite like that, because at the top, where the–'

'Quiet, love,' Rosh begged.

Alice grinned. 'I was going to tell him lies,' she giggled. 'I was thinking of purple sequins and red bows.'

'You're a terrible child, and thank goodness for that. Asparagus, my behind. See? See? Would you ever take a look at the expression on her face? She never liked me, and it shows.'

'Aspergers, not asparagus, Mother.'

'I know.'

Roy continued to sit on his secrets; not literally, as he would have broken them. He had bought everyone a watch. The notoriously naughty newspaper had 'purchased' the wedding, and he was using the money for his lovely females. Photographers and journalists would be there, and Roy imagined the headlines. *Serial Killer's Surviving Victim Marries Her Hero*, and *A Happy Ending to a Tragic Tale*. He and Rosh had decided not to care. The two older children knew what had happened to their mam; even Alice understood enough. And they all loved Roy, though he never pretended to be their dad, and he'd made sure that they always remembered Phil.

He bit into a sausage roll. It seemed to have no personality whatsoever, no sausage, and a bit of flaky that was more air than pastry. He returned it to the counter and demanded a replacement. A year ago, he couldn't have done that, but his fiancée had given him backbone, pride and strength.

The manager was summoned. 'What's up?' he asked.

Roy lifted up the delicacy in question, put it to his eye and said, 'I can still see you. This roll may have enjoyed a passing relationship with sausage meat, but they never married.'

The boss folded his arms. 'How do I know you haven't took the meat out and ate it?'

'Because I say so.'

'Right.' There followed a lengthy pause. 'You're him, aren't you?'

Roy shuffled a bit in order to redistribute his weight.

370

'You're him what closed the book on that murdering bastard. They found all the bodies cos of you, too.'

Nobody moved, and silence reigned. Roy didn't need to look over his shoulder, because he got reactions like this at least twice a week.

The manager carried on. 'Fancy him writing on them boxes. All the details about when and where, the soft olly. It said he seen people setting fire to that car with three men in it, too, but that led to a dead end.' He grinned, pleased by his own untutored genius. 'Do you get it? Dead end, like?' He was now displaying teeth like a picket fence that wanted a coat of paint. 'Proud of you, lad.' He placed six sausage rolls in a bag. 'Any time, son. Don't pass by. You come in for a free dinner whenever you like.'

The subsequent applause resulted in the swift departure of Roy and his family. Except for Alice, who ran back inside to deliver a curtsey.

Anna grabbed her attention-seeking granddaughter. She was taking the two girls to a matinee at the Odeon. 'Stop showing us up, you little besom. Come on, or the best seats will be filled by the time we get there.' She marched off, one hand gripping Alice's. Philly shrugged, waved goodbye and followed the others.

Roy and Rosh looked forward to a couple of hours of privacy. They sat in her van where she changed her shoes before starting the engine.

'Rosh?'

'What?'

He cleared his throat. 'Remember that time I said there were three of you?'

371

'Yes. And?'

'I've been writing to Tom. Haven't seen him, because they've not long moved house and he's pushed for time with running the Co-op as well, but he's convinced that his mother-in-law is your mother's sister-in-law.'

'Eh?'

'Tom's mother-in-law was a Riley till she married an O'Neil.'

'Right.'

'And your dad was a Riley.'

'Common enough surname.'

'And Tom's mother-in-law, Paddy, has a name like yours, but with a Conchita instead of a Carlita. Spanish names – a string of them. Then, when you were in hospital after the ... trouble, and while I was in the loony bin, there was that hysterectomy that looked just like you.'

'I look nothing like a hysterectomy, Roy.'

'I'm just repeating your mother's words. Anyway, your mam was too worried about you to bother about who was whose second cousin twice removed, or whatever, but another patient told her this Tess woman lives on Menlove Avenue. I don't know what she was before she became a Compton, but she's supposed to be the spit of you, only older.'

Rosh pondered the subject. 'So my dead dad was this Paddy's brother?' Her fingers tapped on the steering wheel. 'Liverpool was full of us. The granda sent everybody to Liverpool and told them to find each other and stick together. My mam told me that. But saving up for tickets was a long job, Dad used to say. So they came in fits and starts, moved to where there was work, and that was the end of the clan. Mam says she thinks some emigrated abroad, so–' She shrugged. 'Can we leave this till after the wedding? That'll be enough emotion for me without bringing the long lost into it.'

Roy, completely alone in the world for much of his life, could not understand his fiancée's reluctance to make contact with her extended family. He remarked on it now, and waited for her reply.

'Dad used to call them the wild bunch. No education, no manners, no idea of how to behave. My mam says she heard some had gone completely to the bad, but she's not really sure. As for me – well, I've managed this far without them, and I'd rather not rock the boat.' She awarded him a smile. 'Let's go and look at Home from Home.' The shop was up and running thanks to a man who knew his tobaccos, and his daughter, who did the half-shift. Loyal customers were back, and many newspapers were delivered daily to houses in the area.

Roy knew better than to pursue the subject. Once Rosh made up her mind, it would be easier to shift Gibraltar with a washing line than to get her to revise her position. Their love life had been interesting for some time, because he'd been terrified about her insides. So she'd battered him with a pillow; it had taken two days to get rid of the feathers. She was back to normal in the female department. No, that wasn't true; she was back to glorious.

They stopped on College Road and walked up the side to her domain. It was beautiful, classy without being showy – just like its owner. The kitchen had been fitted, and cooking would commence one week into the new year. 1960. How time flew for a happy man.

'When's the wedding?' he asked.

'March.'

'I can't. I have a limp.'

In the absence of pillows, Rosh clouted him with a tea towel. Sometimes, this man could be hilariously annoying.

Thirteen

On a bright, icy January morning in 1960, Seamus, recovering from a severe head cold, was off school, and he was mooching and rooting. These two verbal participles had been introduced by his grandmother; mooching meant wandering about aimlessly, while rooting referred to his tendency to put his hands, eyes and ears where they didn't belong. Well, he was bored, and boredom wasn't right for a lad with a good rate of recovery from illness and an inquisitive mind. There was no conversation to be overheard, so he had to indulge in rooting. Anyway, what did they expect? Did they think he'd sit quietly in a corner with a poetry book? Perhaps he could take up knitting or crochet?

He was alone. Dad was out at work, busy being the manager of a big Co-op, while Mam's day was split between Scouse Alley and Paddy's Market. She helped her mother until after lunch, then gave the rest of the day to her father on his good quality second-hand clothing stall. Reen and Jimmy were both at work, and Seamus was fed up. There was nothing of interest in his own house, nothing exciting in Reen's, so he ended up in Gran's place. Downstairs was all holy statues under domes of glass, last year's straw cross saved from Palm Sunday, rosary beads hanging next to the fireplace and, most treasured of all, a framed Papal Blessing centre-stage on the chimney breast. Upstairs was a bit more entertaining; upstairs sometimes housed secrets.

He wasn't supposed to go upstairs unless he was sleeping here, but he was drawn like a piece of base metal to the magnetic powers of Gran's boxes. There were four of them, originally made to contain new shoes, now utilized to guard letters, photographs, birth, marriage and death certificates, curls of baby hair, insurance policies and the like. There was knowledge to be gleaned; if the adults wouldn't talk, papers might.

Oh, yes. Gran's house, positioned between the homes of her daughter and granddaughter, was tremendously interesting on the upper floor. He could look at the photographs, some sepia, some in faded black and white, with the most peculiar-looking people frozen for ever on paper. One of the photos had been focused on the doorway of a Liverpool cellar dwelling, and its subject was a woman standing on flags at the top of steps, a swollen belly advertising pregnancy. Another, taken from further away, showed a water pump in the middle of the same yard. The woman in the doorway was probably Gran, and the pump provided water for thirty or forty families, many of whose members lived in windowless, under-ground rooms. It had been a difficult life, and Gran seldom referred to it these days.

But Liverpool had cleaned itself up since then. In a sense, even Germany had done it a favour, because the living conditions of many had improved no end after the war. Mind, Seamus did miss the prefab, because it had owned a garden.

The paved yard here was rubbish. Dad had promised to clear it, get topsoil and plant grass, but it would always be small.

Seamus replaced the box, opened a drawer, and found photos of his older brothers, Michael and Finbar. They were hiding in Rainford, a village a few miles up the East Lancashire Road. This was all because of some trouble in London, the details of which were unclear to Seamus, although his eavesdropping skills were second to none. Nobody spoke about it, so there was nothing to hear. But, at last, he had found something to see. There was a letter from a man in London. He seemed to be chairman of an Irish club, and he was volunteering to take Gran, who was referred to as Mrs O'Neil, to the Kray house.

What was a Kray house? Was it like a public house, a terraced house, a mansion? It was probably a mansion, because London people were rich, and they walked about with their noses in the air. 'I bet that's where the saying comes from,' Seamus said quietly. 'If you walk about with your nose up, pride does come before a fall.'

The girl who'd played Mary in the school nativity play last month had been too proud of herself. With her head held high, she had taken a tumble over the hem of her frock. Her nose was bloodied and her dignity lay truly shattered, yet worse was to come. She landed on Jesus, partially hidden and, as yet, unborn, and the Messiah had been decapitated.

Seamus giggled. Even now, he could hear her bawling in the wings. 'The doll's head came off, Mam. I shown meself up. No. I'm not going

377

back. I'm not. They'll all be laughing at me.' Oh yes. There were worse things than having to wear a silly suit at Reen's wedding. Especially now, when at least four other lads had been forced to wear the resurrected bits and pieces. So. The nativity play had been abandoned, and a happy carol concert had filled the gap.

He sighed heavily. Now, when the path of life seemed smoother, Gran was going to London. Yes. Here was a coach ticket and a letter. The vehicle would leave Liverpool at midnight and, after several comfort stops, would arrive at Victoria Coach Station early the following morning. The date on the ticket was for next week, and nobody had said a word.

Mam would turn loony. Gran had been the first to go down with the cold, and it had left her with a cough that seemed reluctant to say goodbye. Bronchial, she called it. She should not be setting off to London with bronchial. He would have to tell Mam, but when?

'Oh, God.' He sank onto the bed. If he ran to Mam too early, there would be an absolute nightmare of a week, because neither would give in to the other. 'I have to be clever,' he whispered. 'I have to wake Mam in the night and say I saw Gran leaving with a big bag, then Mam can follow her. Let's hope there are some tickets left.'

It might all go horribly wrong, yet he could think of no alternative. If he talked to Dad, there'd be trouble, and Dad might open up to Mam. When it came to keeping secrets, his sister Reen was like a colander – full of holes. But Gran had been so ill, and she shouldn't even think about London; it was hundreds of miles away, like some foreign country. They didn't even speak English. He'd seen films with Londoners in them, and they talked in something called Cockney, which was rubbish.

But there was no other way. If there had to be trouble, it should happen on neutral territory and well away from home. The idea of Mam and Gran going at it hammer and tongs even for a day wasn't pleasant. A whole week? 'What if they get the same bus, cause a riot and the coach crashes?' he asked the room. 'What if they never come back? It'll be my fault for not doing anything about it. I can't win, can I?'

Whatever a Kray house was, it didn't matter. Gran's secret journey, one she wouldn't normally choose to make, had nothing to do with sightseeing. She couldn't care less about Buckingham Palace and Big Ben and mansions. No. All she worried about was family, because too many had gone into the bowels of London, never to be seen again. Who was still in London? Nobody. But two brothers were in hiding – probably as a result of having been in London. This proposed expedition was likely to be their fault. Oh, what could he do, what should he do?

With his brain spinning at a high rate of knots, Seamus replaced Gran's property, making sure that everything was as he had found it, with the ticket underneath the letter. It was time to go next door, since either Mam or Dad would call in to feed him and build up the fire. He wasn't allowed near the fire, which wasn't his fault. So he'd set light to some toast weeks ago – didn't everyone make a mistake sometimes?

Still, at least it was warm in his own house. Finding out Gran's secret had been an exhausting experience. Seamus curled into a fireside chair and fell asleep.

'I hope you know what you're doing, Baxter. I don't want you blaming me when you get out of step with legal procedure. And there'll be homework on top of everything else, because they can't do without you, but how can you be a legal secretary after tea with Alice chattering, Philly doing her piano practice, and Kieran mithering about the human reproductive process? I wish he'd hurry up and get on to neurology or whatever. You'll have all that going on around you.'

'I shall be fine.'

'Oh. Shall you, indeed? So you'll be in a hot kitchen all day, then stuck to a typewriter every evening? Are you some kind of superman?'

They sat together on his sofa in his house. He was selling the place furnished all the way from beds and wardrobes to cutlery and cruet; it was going lock, stock and carpets to a young couple who were absolutely delighted. Due to be married in March, Roy would move into Rosh's house while the other newly-weds would move into his place.

It was all dovetailing beautifully as long as Anna stayed out of it. Roisin's mother, who was showing signs of buckling under pressure, was not exactly glowing with the joys of spring. Rosh had taken her dress material out of the house for two reasons. First, she didn't want Roy to get a glimpse of

380

work in progress. Second, her poor mother had enough on her hands with bridesmaids' dresses and her own outfit. 'Mam's cracking up again. To use her own famous words, she's mortallious troublesome. Philly says if she gets pricked once more with a pin, she's running away to London, taking up the oboe properly and busking in underground stations. Alice says she'll go with her sister and play drums and tambourine.'

'And Kieran?'

Rosh shrugged. 'Well, he's not being fitted for a frock, is he? And he's not what you might call musical. I'm a bit worried, though, because since he took up human reproduction there's every danger that we – you and I – might come under the heading of practical demonstrations. We could well have a spy in our midst.'

'Bugger.'

She laughed. 'No, just ordinary sex.'

There had been nothing ordinary about it, Roy mused. He'd been terrified of hurting her after all she'd been through, though she'd certainly tried to hammer home the fact that she was Irish, tough, a quick healer, ready, willing and able. It had taken a while, but he had finally coped. Which was just as well, as she had threatened not to marry him, since she was fast becoming a recycled virgin. There was no one in the world like her. Even now, in the wake of the Clive Cuttle business, she remained unafraid. He had dreaded going with her to the shop, yet she hadn't turned a hair.

'What are you thinking about?' she asked.

'You.'

She placed her head on his shoulder. 'Tell you

381

what, kid. They loved your cottage pie today. One bloke did an Oliver Twist, brought his plate back and asked for more.'

Roy chuckled. 'Did you make him pay?'

'Course I did. We're not a charity.'

'But whatever, we look after your mother, because that's not charity.'

'Of course we look after her. She thinks it's the other way round, of course, and that she looks after us.'

'Take the girls and their dresses to your dressmaker. Anna's showing the strain, love.'

'What?' Rosh sat bolt upright. 'I know she's not young, but she'll go mental if I do that. She'll take it as criticism, you know she will. There'll be weeping and gnashing of teeth, moaning about nursing homes, scrap heaps and lack of appreciation.'

But he had an answer to that. The wedding cake was made and ready for decoration. 'Let her do it. I've got it in three tins, and I keep prodding it with a knitting needle and pouring in brandy, but I've no idea when it comes to icing and marzipan. She can do a lot of that sitting down, Rosh. Anyway, mothers don't last for ever. Let her be in a bad mood. At least she's still with us.'

Rosh knew how dreadfully Roy had missed his mother. She'd done her best to talk him out of the guilt he felt. According to her fiancé, his father had been as bad as Cuttle, though his body count was lower. Baxter Senior had sent his wife to an early grave, and Baxter Junior, who had seen and heard much suffering, had done nothing about it.

'It wasn't your fault,' Rosh said yet again.

'I should have poisoned his tea.'

'And put yourself at his level? At Cuttle's level?'

Roy shook his head. 'Poisoning would have been much kinder than Cuttle, and a hundred times less nasty than the way my old man treated my mother. She was a wonderful woman, and so is Anna, but in a different way.'

It was Rosh's turn to laugh. There could be no two women as unalike as Roy's mother and hers. Roy's mother had received bruises both mental and physical, while Anna had inflicted damage, mostly with words and attitude. 'My father was the saint in our house,' she said. 'Mam was sort of corrosive. Is that the right word? Or is it erosive? She wore everybody down till she got her own way. It's taken years, but she's got the Collingfords on her side at last.'

'I thought you were handling the dry-cleaning stuff.'

'Well yes, and he's paying rent to me. But Mam will come down on a Thursday and check that the tickets match the tabs. It makes her feel as if she won, because they gave her a job in the end. They'll be paying her a wage, you see. So that's a victory for her.'

'Marvellous. Give us a kiss.'

'Hello?' Anna's voice crashed through the letterbox.

'Beer and pork scratchings,' Roy exclaimed. 'We all know she reads minds, but there are a couple of gardens, two pavements and a road between her and us.'

'Never underestimate my mother.' Rosh went to open the front door.

Anna joined them in the front room. 'Now don't start,' was her opening salvo. 'I've been to the doctor's and got a diagonal nose is. All right, diagnosis. Arthritis in me hands. That's why I keep impaling your daughters on pins. So will you please ask your dressmaker to deal with the girls' dresses and my suit? Oh, and I've found somebody to decorate the cake. Is that all right?'

'For goodness' sake, Mam. You should have said something about the pain. Did you get some pills?'

'I did, but I don't like the looks of them. Purple, they are. A very lurid shade of purple. They're in a drawer, Morecambed.'

Roy scratched his head.

Rosh translated for him. 'The pills are a last resort. She nominated Morecambe as the same. So anything Morecambed in our house is there only in case nothing else works.'

'What's wrong with Morecambe?' Roy asked.

Rosh sighed. 'Torrential rain the day she visited. She's got it into her head that Morecambe will be washed into the bay any day now. Last resort she'll consider visiting, because it's going to be flooded. In my opinion, my mother's decision to stay away is good news for Morecambe.' She was trying to make light of the situation, but she knew that her mother must have been in great discomfort if she'd visited the doctor. Doctors were for cowards and layabouts. Yes, they were yet another Morecambe. She turned to Anna. 'You know we love you. Whatever, you'll be looked after.'

Anna tutted. It had taken time for her to pluck up the courage to confess her failing. 'It's not sympathy I'm after, Roisin. And I'll not be giving up using my hands, since they're the only pair I happen to have just now. It was all the cutting out and tacking that did for me.'

Rosh disagreed. 'You've been a workhorse all your life, Mam. Phil had so much respect for you – remember? He always called you Mother. What you have to know now is that you can rest sometimes. Slowing down isn't a sin. Roy and I can cope with meals, and I'll go part-time when I've found a couple of dependable girls for the café. Start thinking about yourself.'

Anna folded her arms. 'Well, I have been thinking. I've a great big cleaning-up job to do, and it can't be left.'

'And what's that?' Roy asked. 'Can we help you?'

'It's the rubbish in the kitchen. I'm going to shift it, and not before time.'

It was Rosh's turn to look puzzled. There was no rubbish in the kitchen. It sometimes looked like a war zone after all six of them had eaten, but that was easily sorted out. 'My kitchen's not messy,' she insisted. 'I've always kept a clean house – with your help, of course.'

'It's not your mess, not the kids', not Roy's. It's mine. I shall take it away the day you get married. I'll bring it back from time to time, and I'll try to stop it standing there, twisting its cap in its hands.'

'Mam?'

Anna took a very deep breath. 'My name is Mrs Holt. Well, somebody has to look after him, so. We didn't want to steal any of your thunder, so we did it quietly. Yes, for once, I was quiet. We'll

385

be living at his house after your wedding, but if I stay out all night before then, I'll be just at the bottom of the road with my husband. Ah, he's a lovely man, but. So don't be worrying about me, because Eric can do all the fretting from now on.'

Rosh burst into tears.

Anna wriggled herself into the space next to her daughter on the sofa. 'See? You've the both of us here now, me and Roy like bookends propping you up. So why are you keening? Are you not happy for me?'

Rosh nodded. Of course she was happy. All she wanted was for Mam to be content and safe. But the happiness was mixed with a selfish sadness, a childish emotion that bubbled up and spilled out down her face. This was her mam, and her mam was meant to stay. Why did she want to go getting married at this stage in her life?

Once again, Anna read her daughter's mind. 'Marriage isn't there just for young folk, you know. We're put on this earth by the good Lord to look after each other. Eric needs me, and I need him, somebody of my own generation. He's a good man. There's not a bad ounce in him. Though he has come out of his shell, and he tries to tame me.' She sniffed. 'He won't win.'

Rosh raised her head. 'The children will miss you. Alice doesn't like too much change—'

'Neither do you, madam. I'm doing nothing wrong, am I? Sweetheart, I need no permissions. The last time I looked, you were my daughter, and God knows I love the bones of you, but I'm not dead, Roisin. So we know where we stand. Until the day I die, I'll be here for you. All of you.

I'm worried, but.'

Rosh dabbed at her damp cheeks. 'Why?'

'Kieran. Have you seen his reading matter just now? Naked people and private parts. Last time I saw him, he had his nose in some woman's perjacker.'

'Per-what-er?' Roy's eyebrows had travelled north and were almost hidden by his hair.

Rosh sniffed. 'Her word for female parts. Goodness knows where she found it.' She turned to face her mother. 'They're only drawings, Mam. It's not as if they're photographs of real folk. He's studying.'

Anna stood up. 'Studying, is it? And what if a priest happens to call? Or a pair of nuns? Can you imagine that, now? We'd be needing smelling salts. There's Alice at an impressionable age, Philly trying to concentrate on her piano, and he leaves the darned book open at a page showing a man's wotsit in a state of doo-dah.'

Roy fled the scene as quickly as botched surgery would allow. In the kitchen, he wept into a tea towel; he couldn't let the laughter out of his mouth, so it took a route via tear ducts down his cheeks. Yes, he was getting a wonderful, vibrant wife, but the rest of the bunch might be termed interesting, at least. Wasn't eccentric nearer the mark? Life would never be dull.

'You should make him study upstairs,' Anna was saying now.

'And make a big fuss of it? I'm glad he's such an open book.'

Roy swallowed another chuckle. Open books were the basis of Anna's argument. There wasn't going to be a minute of normality, was there? He'd moved from the dry, dusty atmosphere of the law into a kitchen where he did what he loved best – cooking. He'd be leaving the peace and deadly silence of this house to move into relative chaos across the road; he would share a life and a bed with the woman he adored, while Anna's house was going to be very near. Eric would be henpecked, of course.

'Come out of that kitchen immediately, if not sooner,' Anna ordered.

He thought about that. It was his house, his bloody kitchen, yet she still ordered him about. *He* was being henpecked, never mind poor old Eric. Like a naughty schoolboy, he returned to the front room. 'You rang, ma'am?'

'Don't you get cocky with me, Roy Baxter. I knew you when you were snotty-nosed and covered in mud. You make sure you look after my girls and my boy. And if he carries on looking at those books, put your foot down. The good foot, not the other. Tell him to study that kind of thing in private.'

Roy nodded soberly. 'Privates in private, then.'

Anna looked at her daughter. 'Do you ever feel like hitting Roy?'

Rosh nodded. 'But only in private, and never in the pri–'

'That'll do.' Anna marched out of the house, slamming the door in her wake.

The two remaining adults howled like children. It was the sort of laughter that gives rise to pain and tears. 'Where did you find her?' Roy managed. 'Under a witch's broomstick?'

Anna shrugged and dried her eyes yet again. 'She's elemental. She's like earth, wind, fire *and* water. My mother just *is*. She's probably the result of a mating between a Titan and a Valkyrie. And I'll bet you any money the Titan suffered more during the encounter.'

'Rosh.' He pulled her close. 'Let's give them a surprise party in the café.'

'Why?'

'Celebrate their wedding.'

She frowned. 'Are you sure they said you were all right in your head when you left Whiston?'

'Listen, you,' he answered. 'I have a certificate to say I'm sane. Have you?'

'No. But I can tell you this much: my mother doesn't like surprises. You already know that.'

'Pretend Mr Collingford wants to see her at the shop. Then she'll get all dressed up like a Christmas tree. We'll let Eric in on the secret. Though if he owns a suit, I've never seen it.'

'Course he has a suit. Must have. Can you see my mother marrying somebody in a flat cap and overalls covered in paint and sawdust? But listen to me properly, Roy. We'll just have champagne, lemonade for the kids, and a wedding cake. If she'd wanted a shindig, she would have had one, believe me.'

They went upstairs. Conversation seemed easier when they lay down together. Anna would not come back; the closing of curtains informed her that shenanigans were ongoing.

But on this occasion, there were no immediate shenanigans. Like a long-married couple they lay, spoons in a drawer, his mouth in her hair near the left ear. 'Irish stew,' he said. 'With beetroot and red cabbage. Apple crumble and custard. A few finger things like vols-au-vent, some crudités, a bowl of punch. Dips and–'

'Shut up. I'm sick unto death of menus. My whole life is menus, both work and home. I know you do the cooking in the café, but we all bake at night, and I decide what's what and who's which and why.'

'She's your mother. We should do something.'

'Eric would spill beetroot-coloured vinegar down his shirt.' She wriggled backwards, could not have been closer without sharing his skin.

Roy smiled as sleep claimed her. Sometimes, his happiness became almost too big to be contained, and this was one such occasion. He couldn't laugh, couldn't cry or speak, because his precious girl was asleep in his arms. So he thought about her, remembered her.

The bullies. She and Phil had dealt with them. Phil left bruises; she gathered handfuls of hair, torn clothing, books. Blood under her nails, screams, threats and curses pouring from her throat, no pause for breath, no thought for self. Goal shooter in the first netball team, top scorer at archery, top scorer in the secret, hormone-fuelled dreams of every boy in Upper School. His Amazon, quieter now, yet more powerful than ever.

'Touch him again and your head will be so far up your arse, you'll be dining on your own shit.' That line from Phil, of course. Even in a fight, even bloody and breathless, Rosh had managed to retain a degree of dignity. Roy had loved her then, and he loved her now so much that it hurt, as if it wouldn't fit in the space he had inside.

Best man day. Their wedding, his purgatory. Long white dress, she wore. Simple, almost unadorned, just a whisper of lace at the throat. Phil, strong and handsome, no stupid leg, no ill-tempered father mocking him, dragging him down. Roy would look after her now; daily, he reminded Phil of that, hoped that his huge spirit approved of the new liaison.

She turned in his arms. 'Love me,' she commanded.

'It will be my pleasure, ma'am.'

'And mine. You'd best make sure of that.'

Roy leaned over his captive audience. 'Would you like to see the wine list? Or a selection of my crudités?'

'No, just the pudding trolley, thanks.' Then she kissed him very fiercely.

'See?' he said when he managed to escape. 'I knew you were hungry.'

Tess Compton sat in front of her dressing-table mirror. 'I've got lines,' she complained. 'I'm getting old. Crows' feet? I look as if I've been attacked by a full-grown eagle.'

Don managed to contain a bubble of laughter. With hands clasped behind his head, he sat propped up by pillows while watching his almost brand new beloved as she patted cream into the offending areas. 'I hope you're not going all greasy during the day as well. When I grabbed you last night, you nearly shot out of my arms all the way up to the ceiling.'

She turned. 'Don't exaggerate. Anyway, this is day cream. It's very thin, and it gets completely absorbed.'

He was completely absorbed. He felt he might be quite happy to watch her for the rest of the day. 'There's an oil slick on your pillow case,' he stated boldly. His mind wandered into the past, where he could never have made fun of her, where she had been a sour, bitter, old-before-her-time woman, an automaton. Underneath all those confused hormones, Tess had been there all along. 'You're lovely,' he told her. 'I wouldn't swap you for a quarter of Horniman's. Maybe I might for half a pound of my favourite tea, but–'

'Oh, shut up. I've got lines.'

'*You've* got lines? You should try living with you. My lines have got lines. I'm like a map of the London underground railway. If you want the Bakerloo line, it runs all the way up to my hair.' In ham actor fashion, he exhaled sadly. 'My wife doesn't understand me.' God, she was beautiful. 'You're getting ready for Mark,' he pretended to accuse her. 'Flaunting yourself in front of your only daughter's only boyfriend. It's the same every Saturday.'

'And you're off to see Injun Joe, so don't forget your headdress and peace pipe.'

He smiled to himself as she got dressed. Until relatively recently, he'd never seen her unclothed or even in underwear. There was something undeniably moving about watching an attractive woman while she donned clothing. It was a form of ritual, filled with little moves and habits she had probably developed since she was a teenager.

During the early years of wedlock, she'd been shy about her body; then the dreaded hormone imbalance had kicked in, and they had both begun to exist in nightmares. 'Tess?'

'What now?'

He allowed a few beats of time to pass. 'Did you marry me for my dad's bit of money?'

She grinned. 'It was taken into consideration, and you know why.'

'Oh, yes. I do now.'

'But, in so far as I was capable of loving at that time, I loved and valued you, Don. Whatever was wrong inside me must have started to affect me when Anne-Marie was a little girl. I was never the cold, calculating bitch I seemed to be. Sometimes, I heard myself and was shocked. Then, that day in the launderette, the first panic attack. Fortunately, I had only two that floored me completely.'

'After which, we got the literally bloody day.'

She pulled on a stocking and rolled it up a shapely leg. 'The day that saved us. I thank God for fibroids, cysts and all the other alien growths I carried for years. I thank Him often for giving me back to me, because those invaders owned Tess Compton for a very long time.'

Don chuckled. 'Now I own you.'

'In your dreams, lad. This is 1960. In case you haven't noticed, women took over in 1939 and got a bit feisty. We've been in charge ever since, but we allow men to believe they still have power. Just watch this space, Tarzan. Twenty years from now, we Janes will be running the country from the front instead of leading from behind.'

'Oo-er. I'm terrified.'

'So you should be. Because when a woman tells you to jump, there'll be hurdles of varying heights. I'll fetch you a cup of tea before Mark gets here.' She blew him a kiss before leaving the room.

He shook his head and wriggled down under the covers. His Tess was strong now, as was the other one. The other one, in her single room at the top end of Tess's ward, was also strong. Her ordeal had hit headlines both local and national but, according to the press, she'd gone on to open a shop and a café up in Waterloo. And there were more of them – Tess was well aware of that. A long-dead Irishman had saved to send them to England, and they had come across the Irish Sea a few at a time. Don's wife, filled to the brim with terrible memories, had walked away from her siblings as soon as possible. For that, she should not be blamed.

He rolled to the other side of the bed and breathed her in. To his knowledge, she had made no attempt to reconnect with her family. They'd be different now, older, separated from each other by marriage and workplaces. The bigger, healthier ones who had deprived a small thin child of food, who had beaten her and screamed at her, no longer existed. That animal-like behaviour would have ceased by now, surely? Their life had been so wild that the survival of the fittest had been unwritten and unspoken law.

Anyway, he must shift himself. Injun Joe had become fed up with a series of temporary assistants, and today he would probably offer Don the job of office manager, which was just a posh term for someone who answered phones and lined up appointments. Joe was a great local character, a man who wanted all European invaders removed from America, because it belonged to the natives. After the clearance, buffalo would be reintroduced, and the indigenous population could go back to the way they used to be, tribe fighting tribe, hunting parties arguing about which was whose buffalo, and a jolly time could be had by all who managed to hang on to their scalps.

'Daft,' Don said as he dressed. 'Still, it takes all sorts, I suppose.'

A cup of tea, followed by his wife, entered the room. 'Make sure you eat before going to see soft lad. If you ask me, Joe's as mad as a flea in a tin.'

'Well, he's good at his job.'

'Job? Taking photos of cheating husbands?'

'And wives,' he reminded her. 'Takes two to join a St Bernard's waltz and change partners after a certain number of steps.'

Tess blushed. 'I wouldn't swap you.'

'Not for a ton of Horniman's?'

She hesitated. 'Make it Typhoo, and you're on.'

And she was gone. Since losing some of her innards, she had moved on from a moderate, ladylike pace to greased lightning. Grease. Night cream, day cream, all-over-after-a-bath cream, foot cream to ward off the horrors of hard skin, eye cream, hand cream – everything but ice cream.

Oh well. Time to get down Smithdown Road to Joe's place. Because Joe was about to become master *and* servant all in the one body. Joe Dodds, Injun Joe, the man of many disguises, was going

395

to round up the Riley clan and drive them out of hiding. With a whip, if necessary. It was time.

Seamus had heard the term 'in two minds', but he was in several. He adored Gran. She was his hero for most of the time, but she was naughty. He couldn't tell her not to go to London, because she was his senior, and anyway, he'd be forced to admit to mooching and going in drawers upstairs in her house while he was supposed to be ill. He might have to confess his sins to somebody, but it wouldn't be Gran.

Mam would erupt if he talked to her. World War Two and the Blitzkrieg in Bootle might pale into insignificance compared to the wrath of Mrs Maureen Walsh. She had been known to start, choreograph and play an active part in battles on the green in the centre of Stanley Square where they had lived in their prefab, so Mam had to be left out of all calculations.

Reen, his sister, was simply daft. All she went on about these days was wanting a baby and dining-room furniture, not necessarily in that order. She'd be no good with babies, because she kept losing things, putting them down somewhere or other, then running round her house shouting, 'Where did I leave the whatever?' The whatever varied in size from a key to a basket filled with washing, so Seamus didn't fancy a baby's chances unless it cried all the time. Which it would. Anybody with Reen for a mother would cry all the time.

This left Seamus's grandfather, a grand chap who was slowing down noticeably these days. He wasn't ill; he was just hesitant. And he was worried about Gran, because his noisy, beloved wife had a terrible cough that was proving difficult to shift.

Oh, bugger. Seamus wasn't supposed to even think that word, but this was a terrible situation, and a boy lost control when life tied itself in knots with very little warning. But the conclusion had to be reached even if he walked towards it with leaden legs. It had to be Dad. Something had happened to Dad a couple of years back, and Dad had suffered from nerves; would that happen again? Oh, this was too much responsibility for Seamus. He wasn't even a grown-up. He couldn't carry the weight of the world on his shoulders. Could an adult bear the load?

There were priests, of course, but they knew nothing about complications. They could reel off the rules, but hadn't the ability to understand that sometimes those commandments and laws had to be bent a bit. It was a lack of creativity again. Most of the adults Seamus knew didn't own the sense required to work out difficult answers to complicated questions, so how was a mere child expected to manage? Teachers were the worst; unless it was long division, gifts of the Holy Ghost, or the Battle of Hastings, their knowledge wouldn't fill the back of a stamp.

This was Saturday. The Co-op shut at half past twelve, but Dad often stayed behind to fill in order sheets and clear his desk of paperwork. Yes, this was Saturday and, on Thursday, Gran would be on the midnight coach to London. The Krays were gangsters. Seamus had found that out by asking at the local branch library. And this knowledge had pushed the lad right to the edge.

He had to talk to someone, and the someone needed to be Dad.

Mam and Gran were out preparing lights for a coming-of-age party. They had to transform Scouse Alley into a nightclub with a licence for drink, so at least they were out of the way. It was noon. Time to start walking towards the Co-op. Oh, God. Could he? Should he? Of course he should. If Gran ended up dead, killed by gangsters, it would be his fault for saying nothing. He was going to get into trouble whatever happened or didn't happen, so he might as well be in trouble with a live gran rather than a dead one.

In spite of dawdling, Seamus reached the Co-op before the last customers had completed their shopping. He sat on the wall and waited until his dad appeared at the door and ushered out the stragglers. 'Dad?'

'Hello, son. Here.' Tom threw half a crown which Seamus caught deftly. He needed no instructions. He was to go to the Fat Ladies' Chippy and buy fish, chips and peas, which he and his dad would share. The favourite times in his life thus far had been Dad days. He loved going out with Granddad, loved all his family, but sharing a meal with Dad was Seamus's idea of bliss. Well, it would be bliss if he didn't have to spoil it all with... By the time he got back, Dad's staff had all gone home, so there were just the two of them.

They sat at Tom's desk in the office and ate from the paper with their fingers.

'What's the matter?' Tom asked.

Seamus shrugged. He didn't know where to start.

'I can tell there's something bothering you. I've eaten more than my fair share of these chips already.'

Seamus opened his mouth. 'It's a funny name for a chip shop. They're fat, and they don't care, do they?'

'It's called marketing, Seamus. They turn a negative into a positive and sell more chips.'

'Right.'

Tom studied his son. The lad couldn't sit still at the best of times, but he was a bag of nerves today. 'I haven't much to do here this afternoon, so I'm ready when you are.' He paused, waited for a reply, got none. 'You'd best get on with it, because your mam and your gran are going to need help down yonder.'

Seamus swallowed audibly. 'It's bad. If I tell you, there'll be trouble. And if I don't tell you ... well... I have to tell you.' He took a deep breath. 'Thursday midnight, Gran's getting on a coach in town and travelling to London. She's got a ticket hidden with pictures of our Michael and our Finbar in that big chest of drawers in her bedroom. If you tell Mam, there'll be murder. They'll be like two cats in a dustbin.' His shoulders dropped slightly as the tension left his body. Dad was in charge now.

Tom stopped eating. 'How the blood and sand did you find out?'

'Mooching and rooting when I was off school. I didn't know what to do or who to tell. Gran – well – she'd hit the roof. Mam would start on Gran, then they'd both hit the roof. Granddad's a bit old, Reen's daft–'

'So that leaves me.'

'Yes.'

'Hell's bells.'

'I know,' Seamus said. 'But with me having an imagination, I've got an idea. Will you listen to it, Dad?'

'Course I will. All contributions received with gratitude, son.'

So the plan poured from Seamus's troubled mind and into a room in which the aroma of cured bacon flitches mingled with the heavenly scent of ground coffee.

Silence ruled for several seconds. 'You're quite a clever boy, aren't you?' Tom asked.

Seamus nodded. 'See, if you tell Mam before Thursday, you'll be stymied. She'll go for Gran's throat, and that'll mean war. So you have to get Friday and Saturday off work, and pack some of Mam's stuff and yours without her noticing. That won't be easy. I'll help if I can.'

Tom's fingers drummed on the desk behind which he sat. 'So, suitcase in the boot, take your mam out to the pictures, then for a meal–'

'Yes, and make sure it's gone eleven before you leave the restaurant.'

'Which gives me just about an hour to tell your mother and calm her down. Then we follow the coach.'

'Yes. Because if you bought tickets and rode on the same bus, there'd be murder on a moving vehicle.'

Tom blew out his cheeks and exhaled. 'Like the Orient Express. Then we get to Victoria Coach Station and wait for a man to pick her up. And we follow him–'

'To the Kray house, yes.'

Tom couldn't eat any more. Three shots from a tiny gun, three bodies, three machine guns, three helpers when it came to disposal, three months in his own silent, crazy world. Roy helping him. Roy with the girlfriend who looked like Maureen, the girlfriend who'd almost died at the hands of a serial rapist and murderer. He hadn't visited Roy for ages, because life was packed to the brim with work and with helping his mother-in-law at Scouse Alley. Scouse Alley, scene of his crime.

'Dad?'

Tom pulled himself together. 'You'll have to stay with your granddad or our Reen.'

'I'm not stopping with her. Jimmy got her some second-hand furniture, but all she goes on about is wanting new. It's either that or babies. She's like a record with the needle stuck. Anyway, Granddad will need me. Because you can't tell him, either. He's going to be upset when you all go – if you do it my way. So he will definitely need me.'

It occurred to Tom in that moment that he had an extraordinary son. The poor boy must have lived with his ill-gotten knowledge for several days, and he'd taken it upon himself to find a feasible solution. 'I'll have to do what you've done, Seamus. I'll have to think. But it seems as if you've worked out the only sensible solution. Let's just hope I can keep that coach in sight for two hundred miles.'

Seamus nodded. 'It stops a few times at all-night cafés. If you have to leave the car, be careful in case Gran notices you. Take food. If you need

401

the lav, be extra careful, or you could come face to face with her. It won't be easy, Dad.'

'I know. And another thing I know is that I'm proud of you. No, you shouldn't be rooting in Gran's bedroom, but on this occasion, I'm glad you did. And thanks for working it out, son.' He wrapped the cooled food and took it to an outside bin. It was a bitterly cold day. By Thursday, life might well become hotter than hell.

On the same Saturday, Don Compton walked into Injun Joe's tepee. In reality, it was an office, but it was made smaller today by a rack from which hung many of Joe's disguises. Three overalls covered in paint, mud and oil were separated from the rest at one end of the rail. Cleaner items, including suits, shirts and ties, were arranged at the opposite end of the metal rod.

A table against one wall was covered in wigs and hats. 'Heck, Joe. What's this? A fancy-dress hire shop?'

Joe raised a hand. 'How,' he said gravely.

Don removed his hat and sat down. The walls were covered in feathered headdresses, photographs of people termed Red Indians, lengths of cloth hand-woven by the same people, wise sayings translated into English, hundreds of peace pipes and some paintings produced by Navajos. 'How,' he replied eventually. 'Is that what I say when I answer the phone? How?'

'No. We work as white men.'

'And speak with forked tongue?'

Joe laughed. 'You taking the urine?'

'No. Why are all these clothes here?'

'Your missus will collect them Monday for cleaning. The rest are still in the walk-in wardrobe. I often disguise myself when following people for clients. Sometimes I'm a window cleaner, sometimes a painter – whatever, I try to blend. So, are you ready to start?'

'I am. But you know what you said about training me up for field work?'

'Yes?'

Don studied the man across the desk. He had what might be best described as a lived-in face with a big nose, big ears, skin like tanned leather and thinning hair scraped back in a ponytail. He spent a month of every summer with natives, moving round American settlements in a hired car. No wonder he looked weather-beaten.

'Yes?' Joe repeated.

'I've got a limp from Dunkirk. I'd get noticed if I followed somebody.'

Joe shook his head. 'No. People would never suspect a man with a limp. It's called a double bluff. If they think they're being followed, and if they catch sight of you, no way will they believe anybody in their right mind would send somebody with a limp. So not only are they being watched, they're being watched by a man they'll dismiss immediately from their thoughts. After a few minutes, they won't even see you. Then, when you come back and tell me where and when, I take over.'

'Right.' It was all as clear as mud, but Don had to go along with it. 'I want to hire you,' he said.

Joe's eyebrows travelled up his lined forehead. 'Divorce?'

'No. Quite the opposite, if I'm honest.'

'So you're looking for somebody else's wife or husband? Because I know you're still with Tess.'

'I'm looking for a lot of wives. And brothers, uncles, nieces, second cousins, first cousins, cousins twice removed–'

Joe held up a hand and stopped the flood. 'Right, that's it. This calls for a stiff drink. Will you join me in a single malt?'

'Would we both fit in the glass?'

Joe stood up. 'If I leave out the ice, we might just manage.' He poured two hefty measures and passed one to his new recruit. 'Cheers. Start again, please.'

Don passed an envelope across the desk. 'It's all in there. Rileys. Started coming over early this century – many will be second or third generation by now. Somewhere in County Mayo originally. And don't tell Tess. I don't want her to know what I'm up to. She had an unhappy childhood, and she's never let it go. There's one in Waterloo, I think. She survived Clive Cuttle's final attack.'

Joe stood up and paced about in the narrow space between desk and window. 'I remember that. Glad he got killed. But if Tess doesn't want to see her family, why–'

'Because they'll be different now. To get rid of her past, to stop the nightmares, she needs to see them as they are now. It's all written down in the envelope. Some slept in gypsy caravans. There was an orchard, there were horses. The old man made poteen and sold it all over the place. Some will remember that, and younger members of the family will have been told the stories.'

'Are they all in the Liverpool area?'

'No idea. Some may have emigrated to America, Canada, Australia–'

'Hang on. Are you suggesting I go abroad?'

Don reassured him. 'Just find as many local ones as you can.'

So it was all agreed. Don would take a cut in pay, and Joe would find Tess's missing links. Not all of them. But, with luck, enough to put an end to many years' disturbed sleep. She deserved some peace, didn't she? Between them, they polished off half the bottle. And it was a twelve-year-old single malt Scotch...

Fourteen

'Where the blooming heck have you been till this time? It's gone seven o'clock. Ten hours? Who works a ten-hour day? I've been worried sick.' Tess could see the pain etched into her husband's face. He was pale, too. Don wasn't one who allowed his hurts to show, because whatever he went through nothing could ever be as bad as Dunkirk, where he'd been among the luckier men. One of the many good things about Tess's husband was his refusal to sulk. This was pain, real pain, and it was upsetting her.

'I'm all right,' he muttered. 'Don't fuss.' She worried about him. He mattered to her. Even in a state of exhaustion, he managed to experience a dart of elation. Tess was a beautiful woman with a frightened heart. For better, for worse, and for all points between, she was his. 'I'm just tired out, love.'

'Have you been walking on that leg?' she asked. He looked terrible, and she hated seeing him in such a state. Injun Joe should have more sense than to run her Don into the ground like this. Already disabled by war, he needed more damage as much as he needed smallpox.

Don achieved a tight smile. What did she expect him to do with that leg? 'Legs are for walking on, Tess, and I've only the one pair. And I can't leave the bad one at home. My other leg

406

might be quite lonely without its twin. How would I screw it back on again, anyway? I've a feeling it got cross-threaded way back in 1940 when I hit the ground so hard that I dented the beach and nearly caused an earthquake–'

'Stop the clever talk, Gordon Compton. Your dinner was nearly in the squizzles, because the greedy little beggars will eat just about anything. And our Sean's wearing that hungry look he collects at work every day. I had to tell him no when he asked if he could eat yours, so he's upstairs with two salmon sandwiches and a plate of jam tarts. I sometimes wonder whether that lad has a tapeworm. Sit.' She pointed to Don's usual place. 'And don't moan at me if it's gone a bit claggy in the oven. Wait till I see Injun Joe – I'll crown him with one of his totems, and I shan't tell you where I'll stick his peace pipe, because I'm a lady.'

He sat. It occurred to him that the lady no longer existed in the bedroom, and he was very pleased about that. He glanced down at claggy gravy. Claggy was a word she'd picked up from her mother way back. Did she remember her mother and dad? Would she know any of her brothers and sisters if she passed them in the street? Would she even want to know them? Tess was such a complicated soul. She'd always been difficult, but he understood her at last. He should have tried harder and earlier, because she was a woman worth knowing.

A 'ta-ra' was followed by the slamming of the front door. Sean must have eaten his fill at last.

'And your eyes look funny,' Tess said as she left the kitchen.

407

Alone, he stared bleakly at a couple of chops that looked as if they'd seen better days about a hundred years ago. He didn't know whether to eat them, or to have a go at soling his shoes with them. God, he was tired. His eyes looked funny? So would hers if she'd been forced to endure what he'd been through. Anne-Marie followed her brother. Thank goodness for that; there'd be no rock and roll pouring down the stairs this evening. A diet of Elvis Presley and Bill Haley was probably worse than these blinking chops. If he didn't shape, Don would fall unconscious right here in the kitchen, his face resting on two pieces of dead sheep. In fact, if Tess pegged him out on a clothes line, he might sleep a full eight hours.

Injun Joe was ... enthusiastic and in disgustingly rude health. Within a matter of days, he had located every male Riley from Liverpool, the Wirral, Chester and Warrington. There were dozens of them. Each real candidate unearthed and visited today knew another whose surname changed when she married a man called... What had been his name now? Endless phone calls, ages spent poring over electoral registers and baptismal records – it was hard work.

Those located were checked thoroughly regarding a white house with a black door, exploding sheds, an open-fronted barn with four gypsy caravans parked side by side, orchards, potato fields, valuable horses and a granddad who was said to have died with a ticket for Liverpool in a pocket. It had been a bloody long hell of a day, but thank God for Tess's memory and her ability to describe her childhood home.

House calls. Always children in the mix, sometimes a gran who remembered vividly being in Mayo, often a parent whose dead progenitor had spoken about the wild days. So many tales, so much vivid description. From time to time, they weren't the right Rileys, and those occasions were easier, because there was no calling over the shoulder, 'Mary, come and tell about the day when the granda caught on fire and you all beat him half to death with rugs and blankets.' Endless cups of tea, pieces of cake, slices of buttered soda bread, the odd tot of Irish whiskey. In the end, Don had become an automaton, nodding and shaking his head as appropriate, grateful for the journeys in Joe's car from one Riley address to the next. If he'd heard that name one more time, he might have ended up in a mental hospital with rubber walls.

He pushed away his plate. He felt as if he would never eat another meal in his life. This Irish lot seemed to be of the feast-or-starve school of thought, as most Rileys had gone from nothing to plenty, and they shared their plenty with visitors, all but nailing them to their chairs until they'd consumed a variety of offerings. Eating was compulsory; the refusal of food and drink constituted an insult against the cook of each establishment. Insult the provider of sustenance, and you annoyed a whole family, so going with the flow had been their only option. That was another thing about Injun Joe – he clearly had a bottomless appetite.

Tess returned. 'I'm sorry, love. Are you ill?'

Don shook his weary head. 'Just weary-worn. I've been learning my new trade in case he wants me out on field work.'

She tutted. 'You're not fit for field work. Did he not give you a tractor?'

Knowing that his wife was being deliberately daft, he shook his head sadly. 'They're not used to agricultural doings down the Dingle and in Sefton Park. We were looking for somebody who's gone missing. I mean, most of the time, I'll be in the office taking details and booking appointments, but Joe says I need to know what the business is about. He's quite right, I suppose.'

Tess sat opposite what was left of her poor husband. 'Who's gone missing?' she asked.

And he wanted to tell her that she was the missing person, that he and Joe had been searching for her huge clan. At this rate, they'd need to book St George's Hall for the reunion. 'Erm ... a bloke with three kiddies and a young wife. He went to the shop for bread and milk last week, never came back.'

'I wonder why he did that?' she pondered aloud.

'His wife's a mitherer. He was probably escaping from prison.'

Tess pursed her lips. 'Are you saying I'm a mitherer, Don Compton?'

'I wouldn't dare. You'd only batter me with the nearest weapon, and there are too many knives and rolling pins in this kitchen for my liking.'

She jumped to her feet. 'Right, let me have five minutes. I'll run you a nice, hot bath, then I'll give you a massage.'

Alone again, Don closed his eyes. So many of

410

them. Siobans, Oonaghs, scores of Marys, several Theresas, Maureens, Kathleens, Eileens. There were half a dozen Josephs, a few Johns, some Jacks, one Malachi, a Finn, a shedload of Michaels – was it time to stop? Padraigs, then the English version, Patrick, and some fellows who knew other folk who'd married Rileys and moved on to America. A Jean and a Joan were twins in Canada, while a Stella had gone to Australia on the ten-pound ticket and now owned thousands of sheep. Though according to the tale-teller, she was having a bit of trouble with rabbits and a giant kangaroo... Oh, how he needed sleep.

He kept telling his mind to stop, but it wouldn't be quiet. Had he opened a can of worms, or had he found a way of bringing peace to Tess's haunted nights? Joe had kept all the details; Don didn't want any written evidence in his house. No more was expected of him. The boss would do the rest alone; there were people in West Derby, Bootle and Waterloo, but Don had done his bit. The Waterloo people included Tess's double, the one who had survived that terrible Cuttle fellow.

He was sore. The walking had hurt, as had the reading of fading parish registers. 'I'd better get my eyes tested.' He glanced down at his dinner. Little bits of lamb fat were creating white globules in the gravy. Don felt sick. Would this day ever end? He ached all over his body – even his hair felt sore. That was daft. Nobody had sore hair, because it died as soon as it struggled through the skin. With his body aching from top to toe, he slumped in the chair and closed his eyes.

'Don?'

This time, his smile was real. The nasty, selfish wife had disappeared, had been replaced by a piece of magic by which he was fast becoming totally bewitched. She often bathed him. Some instinct born of ancestors who had been forced to self-medicate had come through in her engineering, and she owned miracle hands. His leg, a limb that had suffered the cruel ministrations of qualified doctors, had never been hurt by the new Tess. She knew how to handle it; in fact, she knew how to manage the rest of him, too. 'Coming,' he called. Oh yes, he would place himself in her hands any day of the week, because she owned a great gift. For her and only for her, he would climb the Everest that the staircase had suddenly become.

He lay in the roll-top bath while Tess massaged his head. She wasn't gentle, wasn't harsh, since she seemed to know exactly how much pressure to apply in order to lower his level of tension. Gradually, he relaxed until he courted the edge of sleep while she began on his neck and shoulders. Even the pain in his beleaguered leg lessened as he gave himself up to the power of her fingers.

The leg would remain untouched until the rest of him was dried, powdered, and on the bed. The leg didn't get powdered, since she used oil on it. She was wonderful. Tess could do this job professionally, perhaps even as therapy within the health service, but she was happy with her dry-cleaning round, her football pools, the family and her famous birds and squizzles. She'd settled. Yet he had been sure for so many years that she would never be satisfied with her lot.

In the beautiful bedroom, she worked on his leg. Although shrapnel had blown his knee to smithereens, Tess was aware of referred pain. It took several paths, and she traced each one, smoothing out knots in tissues, finally arriving at the injured joint. 'Don?'

'What, love?'

'You know they've moved?'

'Who's moved?'

'The bits of metal and stuff.'

'Shrapnel.'

'Yes. They're trying to get out. It's as if your knee finally recognizes them as foreign bodies. We've money saved. Rodney Street or Harley Street – let's pay someone to have a look. Let's beat the queues and go to the front for a change. It's time somebody examined it to see can they get the pieces out.'

Ah, there was her bit of Irish. Just occasionally, her words arrived rearranged by habits collected in childhood, during the hungry time when her siblings had stolen her food, when she had been cold in bed.

'Don?'

'What?'

'Shall we go private?'

'On one condition.'

'Oh?'

'Lock the door and lie down with me.'

'But you're tired.'

'That'll be why I'm on the bed, then.' For some beautiful things, a man was never too tired.

Seamus was like a flea trying to choose between

two dogs. He couldn't seem to keep still. Fortunately, his mother was out quite often, though when she did clap eyes on her son, she voiced the opinion that there was something up with him. 'What *is* the matter?' she asked after tea on Wednesday. 'Come on. You know I'll get it out of you before bedtime.'

'Nothing's the matter,' he lied, nose pointing downwards to his shoes.

'Look at me.'

He didn't want to look at her. He didn't want to look at her because he and Dad shared a secret of gigantic proportions. 'What?' he asked sullenly.

'What? What?' Her hands were on her hips. 'You're bright red. Have you got a temperature?'

'No.'

'Are you sure?'

'Yes, I'm sure.'

'Then you're hiding something from me. Like when you were going off to find your big brothers and we thought you'd be camping with school. I can always tell. That's one thing in life you can be sure of, Seamus: I always know when you're hiding something.' It was true. The lad was completely transparent, and Maureen thanked God for that. Had her two older sons been as easy to read, she might have managed to keep them away from the corrupting element of London's East End and its boxing clubs.

He shuffled about a bit. Mam was the one person who made him shuffle more than Gran did. And she had a temper. Gran had been heard to declare that their Maureen's temper could rip the skin off a rice pudding from a distance of forty paces. Then an idea lit up his mind. Pauline Critchley. Yes, he would tell her about Pauline. 'Mam?'

'What?' Her arms were folded.

'Pauline Critchley says she loves me.' Well, at least it was a truth. 'She kissed me.'

'Where?'

'Behind the air raid shelter on the playing field.'

'That's a terrible place to be kissed.'

He nodded. 'Makes me nervous. I never know when she's going to jump on me. I'm not safe. I'm going to need eyes in the back of my head. She says we're getting married and having two children, one of each kind.'

Maureen straightened her face as best she could. 'Did she kiss you on your cheek or on your lips? That was my question.'

'Cheek,' he answered. 'And I got into trouble because I hit her. See, the way I look at it, if a person kisses you when you're not expecting it, that is doing an assault. So I clouted her.'

'Where? And don't say behind the air raid shelter.'

'In her stomach. And she goes running off to old Vera screaming and shouting and–'

'Old who?'

'Sister Veronica. The tall one with a face like a very wrinkled prune. I got a hundred lines. So that'll be why I've gone all red, cos I am in a very bad mood.'

'Right. Are you sure that's all?'

'Is it not enough?' he asked. What did Mam want? Jam and whipped cream on top? 'Mam, I don't want to be kissed by Pauline Critchley.

She's got warts. When she grows up, she'll get a black cat and a broomstick and hairs growing out of them. Her warts, I mean.' Seamlessly, he carried on. 'Is it all right if I go to Mark Tattersall's house? He got a new train set for his birthday and he said—'

'Off you go, then.'

'Thanks, Mam.' He left at speed, slamming the front door in his wake.

Maureen sank into a chair. Everybody was a bit odd. No, not quite everybody. Mam was vague and in slow motion, but she'd been quite ill with bronchitis. She kept staring through the windows at Scouse Alley, as if expecting ghosts to walk towards her. Three ghosts? Was Mam waiting to be haunted by the men dispatched by her son-in-law?

Dad wasn't quite up to scratch, but he was probably reacting to his wife's altered behaviour. He'd had a few bad nights, too, what with looking after Mam and being kept awake by her hacking cough. Reen and Jimmy were OK to the point of boring, as there had been no changes in their department. God love her, but there was no real evidence of life in their Reen. She had a new dining suite ordered, but there was no sign of pregnancy. At least she only had one subject to complain about now.

Then there was Tom. Like Seamus, he was a bit jumpy, though he didn't hop from foot to foot. Tom's unease displayed itself in words, or in the lack of them. She couldn't allow him to slide back into depression, so she'd agreed to go out with him tomorrow night. And she'd picked up a lovely dress and full-length coat from Dad's stall, completely unworn and with all the shop tags still attached. It was a deep pink. She had to think about accessories. Yes, that would keep her occupied for half an hour.

Seamus was not at Mark Tattersall's house; no, he was freezing to death in the old prefab. He'd hung on to a key, and he came back from time to time just to remember stuff. Voices from the past seemed to echo like his footfalls in the empty space. All that remained here were shapes where pictures had hung. When he played his torch over the walls, he could pick out where the calendar had been, where photographs of himself, Reen, Finbar and Michael had occupied space for many years. They were like echoes, too, but he saw rather than heard them.

Sister Olivia had told Seamus that he had a clever way with words, and that he might be a writer when he grew up. Or perhaps he could become a journalist. No. He wanted to drive trains or buses. Or he could join the RAF and learn to fly planes. But first he had to survive some very difficult days that would include a small irritation named Pauline Critchley.

He lit a fire, and the smoke blew back at him. Mam would go mad if she saw him now, playing with fire in a house where he had no place. But he could think here, because no one was watching. He remembered Reen and her dolls, recalled being punished for drawing a Hitler moustache on a thing she'd named Emily. Fifteen years old at the time, yet Reen had hung on to those nasty, staring things with pot faces, posh clothes and real hair. Emily stood up on her own unless one of Seamus's cars knocked her over. Yes. He nodded; his cars had knocked the doll off its feet repeatedly. More punishment. It was his fault, because Reen's dolls were kept on shelves, and he used to lift them down and use them as targets. His family had endured its troubles, and he had contributed to their pain.

Now this. Gran was going off to foreign parts tomorrow night, and his parents were intending to follow her. Well, Dad was, but Mam didn't know yet. Gran had looked troubled when informed that she and Granddad would be looking after Seamus, but she hadn't been able to say anything. Because once poor Granddad nodded off, she would be away to catch the London coach in Liverpool. All hell would be let loose. A missing mam would take the place of Reen's complaint about dining-room furniture, while poor Granddad was going to be confused and hurt.

He crept nearer to the fire and closed his eyes. In his head, he heard them all. Mam, after a night containing too many Guinnesses, screaming when her head was dunked in a sink filled with cold water, Gran berating her drunken daughter, Dad grumbling as he stood over his toolbox in preparation for dealing with breakages, Reen weeping because Mam had shown her up, neighbours grouping outside for a glimpse of the fun. Saturday Night Theatre, the locals had labelled Mam's falls from grace.

Dad making kites. He had made one for his son, then one for each child in Stanley Square.

He was like that, Dad. He helped anybody and everybody as long as he could manage financially and time-wise. Kids came to him with broken bikes or broken hearts, and Tom Walsh dealt as best he could with every problem presented to him. Poor Dad. A two-hundred-mile drive with a shrieking wife in the passenger seat wasn't going to be pleasant.

In this very room, Seamus had listened while the Cooperative Society had been explained to him. In a way, the customers owned the shops and they shared in dividends at the year's end. 'That's why, as manager, I get no perks, because we all share. It makes sense, especially for poor people.' Dad was a good man, a brilliant man. And he had to go to London to stop Gran getting hurt while she did something about getting Michael and Finbar back.

Seamus had found out all he could about the Kray twins. They were good at boxing, and they had an older brother named Charlie, and a nice mam called Violet. Reggie was in prison, Ronnie was at home. Did Gran know that? In spite of all their misdeeds, the two men were capable of acts of great kindness, while their mother was honoured by them at all times. Would Mrs Kray like Gran? Would Mr Ronald Kray like her? After all, Gran could be a bit sharp at times.

The thing about Irish women was that they came in two sorts. Perhaps he was guilty of over-simplification, but he was only a kid. There were the loud ones like Gran, and they showed you up all over the place. Then there were the quiet ones. They went to Mass every day and kept a bowl of holy water just inside their front doors. Every time they went in or out, they blessed themselves against the evil world they were about to enter, or to sanctify the home to which they had just returned. They wore mantillas, dark clothes and flat shoes, and always carried big prayer books with holy pictures used as bookmarks.

Nuns were the same. If they were loud, they tended not to use canes or straps, because they could shout you down; the quiet ones were more dangerous, as they said little and let their weapons do the talking. Given a choice, Seamus would opt for the loud ones every time.

Gran was a loud one. He hoped with all his young heart that she wouldn't shout at Mrs Kray. According to Seamus's small amount of research, nobody shouted at Mrs Kray, because her lads wouldn't allow it. But sometimes Gran couldn't help herself. She climbed on her high horse and stayed there until she fell off exhausted, or until she became bored.

However, the Kray household seemed to be on the side of Finbar and Michael. Months ago, Seamus had eavesdropped on a whispered conversation from which he had gleaned this fact. The Krays had helped Finbar and Michael escape from London. All he could do now was hope for the best. By tomorrow night, he'd be in Gran's back bedroom, Gran would be on her way to London, and so would Mam and Dad. 'I'll be looking after Granddad when it should be the other way round,' he told the space around him. Oh well. There was nothing he could do, so he had best go home.

This was home, yet it wasn't. 'I miss you,' he told the little house.

He doused the fire, switched off his torch and walked into the kitchen, inserting the key into the back door. No light was needed to enable him to perform that small action, as he knew this place even in darkness. And he suddenly realized that this might well be the last time he would come here. The awareness of life's transience, a concept that had taunted every poet down the ages, suddenly hit him. There were no certainties. Nothing stood still. Soon, there would be no prefabs.

In the end, Rosh decided to have the celebration at home. She couldn't just sit back and fail to celebrate the wedding of Mam and her new husband. So she recruited the residents of Lawton Road and cobbled together a plot that might just work with some luck and a good following wind.

When Anna and Eric were dressed and ready, they were sent to the café for a meeting with the Collingfords about dry-cleaning and the possibility of opening a functioning unit with all necessary machinery in the rooms above café and shop. As soon as they had left, a mad flurry ensued; neighbours arrived with food and decorations while Roy, Rosh and the children ran upstairs to don their best clothes.

By the time all five were ready, the ground floor of the house had been transformed. There were fairy lights on the walls, and plates of food with a wedding cake at the centre on the table. A huge sign wishing the couple well was hanging over the piano where Philly had sorted out music ready to play. Alice, pretty in yellow, wore a crown she'd saved from Christmas, while Kieran stood in the hallway ready to warn everyone as soon as he saw Gran and Eric returning. Rosh looked at him for a few moments. He was almost adult, and she ached as she realized that he was all but ready to move on in the world. Her son would be a great doctor, she knew it. Wherever Phil was, he would be proud of their boy.

The kitchen was a drinker's paradise, with three or four types of beer and several wines, white, red and rosé. It was going to be a great night apart from one small fly in the ointment. Anna didn't like surprises.

Neighbours rushed about applying finishing touches, while Roy simply stood and stared at his fiancée. God, she was beautiful. The dress, dove grey and deceptively simple, showed off every line, every curve of her body. She had no idea, had she? Or had she? There was a little devil at the core of Roy's intended; she possibly knew that the eyes of all the men were on her.

'They're coming.' This stage-whisper came from Kieran. With the rest of the neighbours jostling for space, he squeezed his way into the kitchen. 'Quiet,' he ordered before switching off the lights. Rosh and Roy waited in the doorway.

When Anna arrived, she failed to notice that her daughter had changed into her finery. 'They've given us over a hundred pounds' worth of china. For a wedding present. Who told them we were married?'

Rosh offered no reply. Roy coughed in an

422

attempt to cover up a giggle from the darkened kitchen.

Anna rolled on. 'Bone china. Can you see this fellow here with his little finger sticking out while he drinks tea? And if he put a bigger finger through the cup handle, he'd need goose grease to get it out. Or surgery.' She peered at her beloved Roisin. 'You're up to something.'

'She's always up to something,' Roy replied. 'In fact, the whole road's been up to something. I tried, Anna, but there was no holding them back.'

Light suddenly flooded the house while Philly played a wedding march. The Collingfords arrived with a dozen bottles of champagne. Mother Collingford wedged herself into a corner chair with her own bottle of bubbly and a glass, and there she remained for the duration. Alice, who had a fondness for her elders, kept the old lady fed and entertained. Had Alice not taken it upon herself to supervise and feed her, the poor woman would probably have suffered alcohol poisoning.

Wedding presents were opened and exclaimed upon. Anna looked at a pretty figurine before turning to her husband. 'Don't hang your cap on this,' she warned, 'or I'll hang you on my line.'

For the first time ever in public, Eric swiped back. 'Listen, you. That's my house, and what's mine is yours, but as I said before, that doesn't make you the boss.'

Neighbours within earshot froze for a few seconds. They knew Anna Riley of old, and she wasn't one to allow anyone else the last word. But it seemed that she had finally met her match, because she simply laughed and blew Eric a kiss.

The party revived, and Philly began to play a medley of wartime ballads.

Under the cover of the inevitable sing-song, Roy and Rosh slipped into the hall where they found an extremely odd-looking man. Rosh picked up the wedding gift she had wrapped so carefully for Mam and Eric, but she kept her eyes fixed on the intruder. 'Yes? Can we help you?'

'Well, I seem to have come to the right place at the wrong time.'

'We're in the middle of a party,' Rosh said. What a strange way for a grown man to dress. He wore a Stetson, a fringed jacket and denim jeans. He dressed very adventurously for a person so clearly on the brink of middle age.

'But it's the right place, because you are the spitting image of Tess Compton.'

Rosh dropped her package and thanked goodness that she'd bought bedlinens instead of glass or porcelain. 'The hysterectomy,' she replied almost without thinking. 'I was in a single room because of ... because of what happened.'

He held out his hand. 'Joe Dodds. Private detective looking for Rileys and anyone related to Rileys. You are one hundred per cent Riley.'

She shook the proffered hand. 'Fifty per cent only. My mother was an O'Connor, then a Riley, now a Holt. I was a Riley, then an Allen, soon to be a Baxter. Mam and I are working our way through the alphabet. This is Roy Baxter, my current intended.'

Joe's mouth twitched. Of one thing he was certain: they were all characters. 'So your dad's dead, I take it?'

'He is. And this is my mother's wedding reception. Let's go across the road, because she doesn't do surprises. The party's enough – she couldn't be doing with much more excitement.'

As soon as they had settled in his front room, Roy spoke. 'There's a Tom,' he said. 'His wife's Maureen, and she's an older version of my Rosh. Tom has a job at the Co-op. His ma-in-law feeds dock workers during the week and runs an Irish club some evenings.'

Joe burst out laughing. 'Oh yes. That'll be Paddy. She's a star turn. Took over an old building that used to be owned by Lights – they made lampshades and the like. Paddy added a section on, turned it into an L-shaped building, but she keeps the newer bit partitioned off while she feeds dockers. So Lights is its evening name, and they call it Scouse Alley during the weekdays. Maureen is Paddy's daughter, and she married Tom. Yes, I've met them.'

Rosh was taking it all in. 'Then Paddy must be my mother's sister-in-law.'

Again, Joe laughed. 'I couldn't possibly make a family tree. I think you'll all have to work on that after the reunion. We've decided to hold it at Lights some time in late spring or early summer. Are you game for that?'

'As long as it doesn't interfere with our wedding. Don't do anything before the middle of April. We're having a honeymoon down south, probably Cornwall.'

'Right you are.' With a flourish, he handed her something. 'My card.'

Rosh looked at it. 'Injun Joe?'

'That's me, ma'am. I'm an honorary member of two tribes, and blood brother to several native Americans.'

'How exciting,' she exclaimed. 'So you go and live with them sometimes?'

'I intend to retire there. It's a life worth living and, of course, my wife's there. Daughter of a chief, no less. We have two children and wonderful neighbours. Most of my income goes to my family. Anyway, I must let you get back to your party.'

Roy and Rosh waved him off.

Across the road, Anna was waiting at the door. 'Who on God's good earth was that? Looked like he'd stepped out of a silent movie.'

'It's Hiawatha, I think,' Rosh mused aloud. 'Or was Hiawatha a woman?'

Roy wasn't sure, and he said so.

But Anna was too excited to listen. 'We're going on a train and a boat,' she announced proudly. 'Isle of Wight, where the old queen died. Mr Collingford has a house there, so he's lending it to me and Eric for our honeymoon. They've got servants.'

Rosh tried to imagine Mam with servants, though the exercise was a complete failure. For Anna Holt, the kitchen was her natural habitat. Servants? They might well be sent packing with little spotty red handkerchiefs on sticks over their shoulders, plus instructions about never darkening certain doors again. The Collingfords could lose their staff. 'That's lovely, Mam,' she said. 'I believe the Isle of Wight's a pretty place.' God help the Isle of Wight. Was it big enough for her mother's personality?

'And thank you, Roisin,' Anna continued. 'We've really enjoyed ourselves. I'm that proud of our Philly – she's been playing something called rack man enough. It was very fiddly, but her fingers flew like butterflies over the keys. A gentle touch, she has. Of course, she'll have got that from me, so.'

'It was Rachmaninoff,' said a voice from behind her. The words came from Eric, of course. 'As for the gentle touch...' The invisible man sighed heavily.

'Isn't that what I was after saying? Rack man enough?' She stood back to allow Roy and Rosh to enter the house. 'And Alice all settled – she never had asparagus syndrome, did she?'

Rosh shook her head in despair. Mam still refused to employ the real word. And the reason? It was the Irish choice, this marked tendency to make light of frightening situations, the decision to laugh in order to stem the tears. It was a strange form of bravery, yet it was courageous in its way. While Anna feared for her younger grand-daughter's welfare, she refused to show it. 'She probably hasn't got asparagus, Mam.'

Wicked eyes fixed on Rosh. 'Are you taking the wotsit out of me, Roisin Allen?'

'Wouldn't dream of it. And I'm glad you enjoyed your party.'

The expression on the older woman's face softened. 'You're a good girl, and you've a good man alongside of you.'

'I know. So have you, Mam.'

'Ah, he's manageable.'

Eric winked at his new daughter. 'That's what she thinks. She knows the rules, Rosh. Stay off my allotment, let me read the paper in peace and leave me to have a lie-in on a Saturday. I love her, but she'll not walk over me.'

Anna bit her lip and looked at the ceiling.

Rosh kept her face straight. Something had happened to Mam, and this man seemed to be the one who had interfered with her determination to retain the throne. 'Be happy,' ordered Roy.

Anna and Eric walked away.

Rosh took her good man's hands in hers. She wasn't forgetting Phil. She could never forget that wonderful husband. There were things about him that she'd always remember – like the way he tilted his head when pretending to tell her off, his beautiful smile and his terrible toast. It was always either anaemic or black as hell. 'I'll never be sorry I married him, and I'll never be pleased that he died,' she said before pausing for thought. 'But I'm glad I have you. Do you understand? Do you know you're very special to me?'

'Yes.'

'Don't get too cocky, though.'

'I won't.'

'Or I'll deal with you.'

'Right.'

She stared at him. 'Are you laughing at me, Baxter?'

'I wouldn't bloody dare.'

He was laughing at her. He was laughing at her inside, where it didn't show. Because of the party, she couldn't do anything. Yet. 'Just you wait,' she mumbled before leaving him where he was.

Roy chuckled. Would it be a wet dishcloth across the head? Or might certain privileges be withdrawn? Worse still, would she set her mother on him? A black cat wove itself round his ankles. This dark character already felt sorry for him. 'Oh, Lucy-Furry,' he whispered. 'You know, don't you?' It was going to be the dishcloth again.

Seamus was now a cat on bricks so hot that they must have been manufactured in hell. She was going. She was going tonight, but he felt sure in his bones that she would be leaving a note for Granddad. According to Mam, her parents' marriage was the best ever, so there had to be a note.

A stair creaked. Her suitcase was under the stairs, brown with scarred corners, an old belt strapped round its middle in case the jumpy bits snapped open again. Blackpool. Out of the house by nine in the morning, cruet threepence a week, baths to be booked a day in advance, and don't come back into the house before half past five, because the evening meal began at a quarter to six. A big woman in flowered aprons and navy carpet-slippers, overfed on her own importance, face twitching when the smallest suitcase burst open and Gran's unmentionables deposited themselves in the lobby. The key was lost, so a belt of Granddad's was promoted to a new position as guardian of Gran's bloomers.

Another creak. Seamus wrapped a pillow round his head, willing his grandfather to stay asleep. New houses shouldn't creak, should they? Dad had explained about timbers expanding and contracting in response to temperature fluctuations, but somebody should have found a cure by now. They – whoever they were – had dealt with diphtheria and were on their way with smallpox, so surely a creak could be eliminated? It wasn't much to ask.

He replaced his pillow. Even the silence seemed loud. There was probably no such thing as complete silence, anyway, what with cats and dogs fooling about, and drunks on their way home from a night on the ale. Granddad was snoring. Sometimes, he woke himself with a very loud snore, but he'd better not do that tonight.

Seamus wasn't sure about God. Being unsure about God was probably a sin, but only if there was a God. So just in case there was a God, he apologized for being uncertain and begged for Granddad to stay asleep. The longer he slept, the further away Gran would be, and what she was doing probably needed doing. Finbar and Michael would want to come for a visit and bring their children, even if one was only a girl.

It was possible to leave the house without slamming the front door. All you needed was to keep the key in the Yale, hold it turned to the open position, then allow the lock to slide home with barely a click. She'd gone. She must have gone, because the London coach was due to leave in half an hour, and it was quite a walk to town.

Then there was Mam and Dad to think about. They'd been to a play or a concert, then on to a restaurant. Oh, God. If there was a God. Mam and Dad would be closing in on Gran now. She knew their car; she knew them. And how would

430

Mam take the news that she was about to follow the London coach all the way to – where was it? Victoria, that was it. It wasn't a train station; it was a bus depot. He needed sleep, because tomorrow was a school day, so he stretched out and counted rabbits because sheep were boring. And it was already tomorrow. And Granddad would hit the roof.

Fifteen

Tom couldn't say anything in the restaurant until the meal was over and he'd taken a discreet indigestion tablet. Eating hadn't been easy, though he'd managed a bit of soup and an omelette, while Maureen had consumed enough to keep the average carthorse going for a fortnight. He had steered his lovely wife away from Guinness, but she'd managed two glasses of red wine with her steak, and a healthy flush was beginning to stain her cheeks. It wasn't just the black stuff, then. She was probably capable of getting inebriated on just about anything – with the possible exception of dandelion and burdock or household bleach.

'Drink your coffee, love,' he suggested. 'We need to be off soon.' He was off already, he told himself inwardly. He was right off his head for even considering this London business. It could even turn out to be dangerous, and he wasn't armed this time; neither was his wife. Daniel entering the lion's den must have felt almost as scared.

Sometimes, Tom imagined that he had never truly regained his sanity, and this was one of those occasions. Only the mad would jump into choppy waters without a lifebelt. One of his eyelids suddenly developed a twitch, and he hoped it wouldn't be noticed. She never missed stuff like that, never missed much when he came to think.

432

Like her mother, his wife was becoming Eyes and Ears of the World, though compared to Paddy this one here was a mere apprentice, still wet behind the lovely little ears.

Maureen was taking her time, savouring every moment, every last drop of the cream that had accompanied her lemon meringue pie, every mouthful of coffee. But she clearly remembered where she was, since she refrained from licking the pudding dish. He had to smile in spite of the situation. This wife of his certainly liked to taste life, preferably in large chunks.

'Don't worry,' she said. 'A few minutes won't make much difference. Seamus is next door with Mam and Dad, so he's safe enough. Let's hope they are, because he's been like a cat on hot bricks this past week.' She looked round the restaurant. It was definitely the poshest place she'd ever eaten in; in fact, it was probably the most expensive restaurant in the whole of Liverpool. Her new suit looked wonderful, so she was as well dressed as any other woman, and probably prettier than most.

Sighing happily, she sat back. Oh, she could get used to this, all right. She might work in Scouse Alley and on Paddy's Market, but she could hold her own in any company. That was one of the benefits granted to beautiful people. 'Why do you keep looking at your watch, Tom?' He was beginning to remind her of their youngest son, all fidgeting and anxious glances. 'What's going on?' she asked. 'What with you and our Seamus, it's been like a circus in our house. I nearly sent for a safety net last night in case I hit the roof, because you were both getting on my nerves. Come on, you. Out with it. And your eyelid's twitching a bit.'

Could he tell her in here, or should he wait till they were in the car? In the car, she might clatter him with her bag, and they could well be too late to follow the London coach if she required restraining. This upmarket place was almost empty, but they might be thrown out and banned for life if she kicked off in here. And if police were summoned... Yet he was desperate, so he waded in because there was no time to test the water. 'We're not going home tonight,' he said quietly. 'And I'm warning you just once – any loud noise out of you, Maureen, and I'm going through that door on my own. Do you understand?'

She didn't understand, but she nodded.

'We're driving to London in about twenty minutes, so get used to the idea.'

Her jaw dropped for a split second. 'In the dark?'

'In the dark. The coach just off Lime Street leaves at midnight, and we have to be on its tail. Don't start. One false move out of you, and I will definitely go on my own. I'm taking no nonsense this time. Whatever you want to do, I'm off to London.'

'On the coach?'

'In the car.'

'But why do you–'

'No buts, girl. For once in your life, just do as you're told. I've no time for questions and mithering. It's like when you had to...' He looked round and decided that the other late-night diners were far enough away. 'Like when you had to give me the gun at the wedding. It was an executive decision I felt forced to make. Now, I've paid the bill and left a tip, so let's be having you.'

She blinked stupidly. 'What's the coach station got to do with it?'

'Your mother.'

'Eh?' Maureen's voice raised itself.

'Don't shout,' he said sternly. 'Your mother's going to London overnight. A man from some Irish club's meeting the bus in the morning and taking her to see Mrs Kray somewhere in the East End.'

Seconds ticked by. 'Why?' she asked eventually.

'To get our two sons out of whatever difficulty caused our Reen's wedding to turn into a bloodbath. The Krays are on our side. Your mam's trying to get some help so our lads can come out of hiding. They can't spend the rest of their lives keeping a low profile, and your mam knows that.'

She folded her arms. 'She's been ill. Look, you can drive round to Lime Street and drag her off the coach. Her chest isn't right, and she shouldn't be taking all this on herself, should she? I mean, she could end up with double pneumonia, and that'll do nobody any good, will it? She could end up in hospital for weeks, and we don't want that.'

'No,' he answered. 'We don't want that. She may need looking after tomorrow when she gets where she's going. That's why you'll be paying a visit to the Kray house with her. I've a feeling it'll be something like a mothers' meeting, so I'll stay in the car. Come on. I've put a few things in the boot in case you and your mam decide to sleep over.'

435

Maureen rose to her feet. Surely this was some kind of dream? She needed to wake up and push herself back to normal. 'Why don't I just travel on the coach with her?'

'You think she'd allow that? Look, she'd go mad, you know she would. Paddy will put herself in danger, but she wouldn't want you doing the same. She would get off the bus and bugger off home. Then she'd go through it all again, and we might not manage to stop her or keep up with her. But when we get to London tomorrow, it'll be too late for her to kick off.'

'Oh, my God. I can't believe all this has gone on behind my back and—'

'Go to the ladies' room,' he ordered. 'It may be a while before we get another chance. I'm off to the men's. We've a long night in front of us. That coach makes more stops than the bus to South-port.'

When they met up again, Maureen was toe-tapping in the open porch. The weather wasn't good, and her breath hung on the air each time she exhaled. What if it snowed? Worse still, what if they hit frozen fog? He'd packed her bag with-out telling her. How long had he known about Mam and London? Who'd told him? Why hadn't he told her? It was her mother, after all.

As he approached the double doors that led to the exterior, Tom noticed the foot. The foot was not a good sign; toe-tapping had been known to act as harbinger for handbag-swinging, words that should never see the light of day even on a dark night, and broken windows. If she broke this lot of glass, it might cost hundreds to replace.

But she didn't have a cast-iron frying pan, so the chances of smashed panes were minimal. He, however, might get a thick ear, and he didn't fancy driving through the night in pain. She needed dealing with immediately, before she got completely out of hand.

'What's going on?' she asked before Tom could frame a single word.

'I'll tell you in the car once we get behind the coach. Until then, button it, Maureen. I mean it. You start lashing out with words or handbag, and I'll dump you in a ditch. You've had all your own way for long enough. Anyway, I'm giving up being a battered husband. This is for Finbar and Michael, so if you don't care about your sons, bugger off home now and I'll go by myself.' His heart was beating like a drum in a marching band.

'Who do you think you're talking to, Tom Walsh?'

He gazed up and down the street. 'Well, seeing as you're the only one here, I must be talking to you. Unless the invisible man's joined us. If he has, tell him to come back later, because I can't see him at the moment.'

'Don't try to be clever,' she snapped.

Right, that was it. 'I don't have to try.' The words were forced through Tom's gritted teeth. 'I work for a nationwide company, and I'm about to join the board as Manager Representative. I can forecast trends, order correctly to the last ounce, predict what'll be the next individual big seller, and take the rug out from under any salesman who tries to pull the wool over Co-op eyes. So trying isn't necessary. Trying is what you are, because you'd try the patience of angels, saints, and the bar staff at the Eagle and Child, who are noted for their tolerant attitude.'

Maureen's jaw dropped again, so she snapped it shut. She was beginning to realize that the gentle soul she'd married was fast approaching the end of his tether.

'Come on,' he ordered before walking away.

She staggered behind him on heels that weren't easy. If she'd known about London, she'd have brought something more sensible to change into, but nobody ever told her anything, did they? And he wouldn't have brought her make-up. Very few men understood the value of war paint when it came to unusual situations.

Tom was mulling over a different unusual situation. Roy from Waterloo, who had helped Tom climb out of a pit named despair, had turned out to be almost a relative. Injun Joe and a chap named Don were trying to round up the Rileys. There was one here right behind Tom, a part-Riley of the female persuasion, and Riley women weren't easy. He wondered whether Injun Joe might have bitten off more than he could either chew or smoke in his peace pipe, because Maureen, whom Tom loved dearly, was a difficult little besom who spoke with forked tongue. If the others were anything like Maureen and Paddy, Injun Joe was going to need all his warriors and a bit of curare to dip his arrows in.

'Tom?'

He stopped and turned. 'What?'

'Help me. These shoes are awkward.'

She was a beautiful besom. Paddy, who was a

tall, well-built woman, had been a stunner in her time, and her daughter, slighter of frame, was another pretty one. 'Come on, love,' he urged. 'Take your shoes off and I'll carry you to the car.' He would carry her for the rest of his life if necessary. Nothing was ever perfect, but Maureen was still the woman of his dreams.

Another nightmare that might register on the Richter scale. Tess was fighting her way out of the involuntary paralysis that is a companion to real sleep. Her voice was returning to her. 'It's mine,' she muttered. 'Give it back, give it back.'

Don reached up for the cord and switched on an overhead light. She started beating him with curled fists, and her eyes were slightly open. 'Come on, my beautiful girl,' he whispered. 'Get past this. What about your squirrels and your birds? Who'll look after them if you're too tired in the morning?' He gripped her flailing arms before planting a demanding kiss on her parted lips. It worked. She knew he was here; she knew she was not alone.

Eyelids fluttered before raising themselves fully. When her arms were freed, she wrapped them round him. 'I'm sorry, I'm sorry,' she muttered. 'Dear God, I'm getting worse. I shouldn't be hitting you. It's not your fault.'

She was getting worse. 'Tess, it seems the safer we are, with us all working now and a nice house to live in, the more you have to lose. And because you're asleep, you can't reason with yourself, and I should understand better than most. Many's the night I've been on that beach with dead mates in bits spread all round me.'

'I know.'

He planted a chaste, matrimonial kiss on her forehead. 'Baby, we have to pull you out of it. Bugger my knee, because this is more important.'

'Oh yes? Are you sure?'

He nodded. 'I'll nip down and do us both a mug of cocoa, eh? No falling asleep before I get back.' He peeled back the covers and stood up. 'Read your magazine. There's an article about Skaters' Trails carpet being the worst thing invented since original sin. It'll remind you about your good taste.'

'Oh, shut up, Gordon.'

'Don't you "Gordon" me, or I'll tan that pretty little bum.'

She plumped her pillows and leaned against them. 'Promises,' she snapped.

In the kitchen, Don made the half-milk half-water cocoa. While it was heating, he noticed the mousetrap on the floor. It wasn't the old one, the one that killed small rodents; this was a cage with a lump of cheese inside. It was designed so that the animal would be trapped, but not hurt. Smiling to himself, he shook his head slowly. She was a character, all right. The woman who had been a nightmare was now a dream, but her dreams were nightmares. Twin tears travelled down his face. The bad was rooted deeply within her, so a long shovel would be required to dig it out.

The doctor, while unwilling to discuss too thoroughly the ills of another patient, had spoken in general terms about childhood trauma and the effect it might have in later years. Hunger and

440

physical abuse could leave a soul bruised for a lifetime, but treatment was available. Should a patient require private care, he would gladly write a letter of introduction to a Rodney Street therapist.

So, if it was to be a straight choice between a difficult knee and the mending of Tess – well, there was no contest. Physical pain was a nuisance, but he could go on a waiting list and take his turn. No, he was not prepared to jump a queue for himself while Tess was in such dire need. There were people who would listen to her, strangers schooled in the art of counselling. She needed a friendly ear attached to someone dispassionate, a professional who knew how to extract the terrors and deal with them.

He carried the cocoa upstairs on a little tray. She was sitting bolt upright, hands clasped round raised knees. 'Don?'

'What? Here's your cocoa.'

'Thanks.' She took her mug. 'You know what?'

'Me? I don't know anything, love. Thick as a brick, me.'

'I'm serious. You know how selfish children are? Remember our Sean pinching Anne-Marie's banana when he already had his own?'

'I suppose so. She was as bad, though. They both grabbed what they could and when they could.'

'Exactly.' She paused. 'They were hungry, too.'

'Listen, sweetheart. Our kids were well fed and well enough upholstered to be a couple of arm-chairs.'

She shook her head. 'Not them. I mean my

441

brothers and sisters back in Ireland all those years ago. See, a kiddy is centred inside itself. Boy or girl, it knows pain and hunger and running about for no reason at all. Like squizzles. Just little animals. Truth is, I wouldn't know or care what the others had to eat. I concentrated on me.'

Don sipped his cocoa. 'Survival instinct.' She was analysing herself; at the same time, she was taking under consideration the needs of other family members. Was this the beginning of the end? Could she talk herself out of a dilemma that had lasted for so many years?

'I was the easiest target.' For minutes, she sat and said nothing. Then, finally, she wondered aloud where they all were. How carefully she had avoided mentioning them until now. 'They won't have crossed oceans,' she said quietly. 'We were all sick coming across from Ireland. None of us had sea legs. I had no legs at all, so I lay on deck trying to muster the strength to jump overboard and have done with it.'

'Might they go on aeroplanes?' Don suggested.

Tess shrugged. 'Where we lived, I think we'd only just caught up with the invention of the wheel. I can't see our lot putting their lives in the care of a big metal tube in the sky. They'll be around. Somewhere.' She sighed. 'I bet they'd go mad if somebody stole from their kids. I bet they've forgotten what they did to me.'

'Then your parents should have guarded you, baby.'

She laughed, though the sound arrived hollow. 'He was always drunk, and she was worn out by his other hobby, which was sex. They're long dead

442

now, both of them. He drank his way to the grave. For Mammy, his death was probably a blessed release because of her nerves. He used her as a punch bag later on in life, because booze had probably deprived him of the ability to perform in bed, so he found other outlets for his aggression. She suffered. By God, she suffered until he got pushed through the gates of hell. By which time, she was a shadow. I expect she never recovered.'

Don decided to remain silent. She seemed to be getting somewhere without any help.

'I ran when I was fifteen. Last day at school, I just packed my few bits and pieces and fled. Sent a letter to my mother, which someone would have needed to read to her. I put no address, and I got a job in a shoe shop, shared a bedsit with a girl called Paula. We slept top to toe in a single bed, but I'd never felt so free. When you met me, I was under-manager in that shop, and I had my own rooms, if you remember.'

Don drained his mug. She'd scarcely touched hers.

'Our kids were grown when I really fell in love with you, Don. Then when I lost my insides, I knew I didn't have to be like my mother, with loads of kids and no food. I could enjoy ... things. I probably did have strong feelings for you, but I couldn't show them. And the business of being a Catholic ... well, you know how irritating that can be.'

He waited.

'I saw Mammy's death notice in the paper. Forgiving myself for not going to the funeral is something I've never managed. I suppose she had a few peaceful years without him, but I bet she remained a frightened woman. I never even visited her. How would we feel if our kids left home and never came to see us?'

'With or without Elvis?' he asked.

'Oh, Don.'

'I know and I'm sorry. Forget Elvis. I love our children and would hate to lose them.' He paused. 'Would you like to find your family, Tess? Do you feel ready for that?'

'I'm not sure.'

Should he tell her? Could he tell her that Operation Riley was already under way, and that some of those discovered were her siblings? No. It would be better to present her with a fait accompli down at Scouse Alley. The decent people he had met bore no resemblance to the hungry children who had denied the existence of their little sister. 'It might cure you,' he suggested.

'Let me work my way up to it, love. Come on, lights out. Let's try to get some sleep.'

Another person suffering severe sleep deprivation was Seamus Walsh. After a doze that lasted minutes, he suffered a rude awakening. Granddad had surfaced. It was probably Gran's medicine time, and the habit seemed to be proving hard to break. He must have found the note, because he was up and down the stairs like a yo-yo with a long string. The coach would be leaving soon, surely? And why was Granddad grunting and groaning? Something unusual was happening, and the something unusual was climbing the stairs yet again. Seamus felt as if his heart might stop at any minute.

Kevin O'Neil stood in the doorway. 'Get dressed,' he snapped. 'I'm not waking our Reen, so you'll be coming with me. We have to follow the London coach. It's nearly time for it to set off, so don't be dawdling and messing about.'

'No, we don't need to do that.' The child squinted when light flooded the room. Electricity seemed a lot brighter than it used to be.

'What do you mean? Come on, don't sit there blinking as if you're innocent. I thought you'd been a bit weird lately. What do you know? What haven't you told me?'

The boy bit his lower lip. 'Mam and Dad are following the coach.' He groaned under his breath. When was he going to learn what not to say?

Kevin folded his arms. 'You what? You knew your gran was going to London, and you said nowt? And with her chest the way it's been? Well, we've no time to be picking bones, but you'll be a bloody skeleton when we come home. Get in that van. I've put a mattress and bedding in the back, so crawl in and stay there with your head down. I'm posting a note through our Reen's door.' He left the scene.

Seamus kept his pyjamas on, piling on top the clothes he had been wearing earlier. With his outdoor coat over an arm, he went out to meet his Armageddon, which had suddenly taken on the shape of his grandfather. But Granddad was already scraping a bit of ice off his windscreen. 'Get in,' he hissed. 'And shut the door properly. I don't want you to shoot out somewhere outside Birmingham, because I need a word when we get back. You're in trouble, lad. Very big trouble.'

When was he not in trouble? He could remember very few days on which he'd scraped through without being accused of something or other. So what was the difference? It would have been more remarkable had he not been in some kind of grief, then somebody might tell him for once that they were impressed by how good he'd been.

To give them their due, the remarks on his much improved school report had given rise to kisses – which he could have done without – book tokens, three quid in change and a kit for a Spitfire off their Reen. He was clever. He knew he was clever because even old Vera with the prune face had said so, while Sister Beetroot – really Beatrice – had declared that his compositions were good enough to enter in national competitions. He had a good imagination. Yes, he had a good imagination, and he was shut in the back of an old van with two blankets, an eiderdown, an old army greatcoat and some skirts and blouses intended for the Paddy's Market stall. Oh, yes. As Gran might have said, it was a hard life as long as you didn't weaken.

He couldn't see anything. There were two little windows in the van's rear doors, and they afforded a brief glimpse of the lit-up Liver Birds, though nothing else of interest was visible. Then the van stopped.

Kevin called over his shoulder. 'I can see your mam and dad's car skulking up the alley. And your gran's on the coach.' He tapped the steering wheel. 'I don't know whether to go and drag her off. Lie down. Did I tell you you could sit up?'

'No, Granddad.'
'Then lie down.'
'Yes, Granddad.'
'You taking the wee-wee, Seamus?'
'No, Granddad.'

Kevin almost exploded. 'Now look what you've made me do. The coach is pulling out. I could have got her if you hadn't taken my mind off things.'

Seamus closed his eyes. No matter what, no matter when, no matter where or which, the ills of this world would always be placed at his feet. If somebody dropped another atom bomb on the Far East or started an avalanche in the Swiss Alps, it would be down to Seamus Walsh of Prescott Street, Bootle, Liverpool, Lancashire. Should an earthquake swallow up Buckingham Palace, he'd be the one in the Tower.

'Your dad's following the coach, and I'm following your dad.'

So who was daft? Seamus pondered this for a few minutes. Sensible people would sort this out. Oh well, he might as well hang for a sheep. 'Granddad?'

'Go to sleep.'

'I was just thinking.'

'God help us.' Kevin changed gear.

Seamus continued. 'When the coach does one of its stops, Mam and Dad should lock their car and come with us. You'd have two drivers and you could take turns. That saves petrol. Mam could have a sleep with me, then you could swap with her and have a rest while Dad drives. They can lock their car, and pick it up on the way back.

It makes sense.'

For an idiot, Seamus did make a lot of sense. Kevin grinned to himself. Seamus had taken after his dad for brains, though his mam wasn't exactly backward at coming forward, was she? 'We'll see, lad. Now get your head down and try for forty winks. This is going to be a long night.'

Rosh turned over. She wasn't ready to wake up, because she'd been having a lovely dream about being on the English Riviera in springtime with Roy. There were palm trees, some exotic-looking flowers starting to bud, and clotted cream teas stolen by this county from Devonshire, its next-door neighbour. She and Roy had a bridal suite with four-poster bed, a full bathroom including shower and bidet, and a bedroom balcony that overlooked a bay populated by fishing boats. Tomorrow, they would hire a boat and crew to take them out for–

But she couldn't get back to sleep. She couldn't get back to sleep because some fool was hammering hell out of the front door. Bleary-eyed, she blinked till the luminous dial on the alarm clock made sense. It was ten past midnight.

She got up and peered through the curtains, but she couldn't see anything, since the intruder was shielded by the open porch. Though she did notice that Roy's lights were being switched on. He watched over her and the children constantly. Right from the beginning of their courtship, he had taken on the job of caretaker, a sort of lieutenant to the absent Phil. He was lovely. Rosh pulled on a dressing gown and opened a sash window. She bent down and placed her mouth at the two-inch gap she'd created.

'Who is it? If you wake my children, you'll be a bit dead, and don't expect a decent funeral, because you'll go in the Mersey, burial at sea.'

Her mother stepped back onto the path. 'It's me,' she said unnecessarily.

'I can see it's you because of the street lamp. Stop hammering. Even poor Roy's awake – look across the way. You've probably woken everybody at this end.'

Anna, muttering under her breath, stepped into the porch once more.

Rosh went down and opened the door. She was not in the best of moods. 'Where's your key? I hope you haven't lost it.'

'I thought it was in me pocket, so I did. But this is the key to his house.'

Rosh blinked stupidly. 'You mean your house. It's your home as well as his, isn't it?'

Anna sniffed and stalked into her daughter's hall. She was carrying two lidded baskets. 'It will be, because I'll make sure of it. May God forgive me, but I'm in a fight and with no intention of losing. He's taken a step too far.'

'God has?'

'Eric has.'

'I see.'

'No, you don't. I'm banned from the allotment, and no one knows more than I do about arable farming on any scale whatsoever. He interferes with my cooking and cleaning, won't let me help with decorating, says I've to leave the garden alone. As for the Isle of Wight – well...'

'Well what?'

'He kept going into a huddle with the gardener, something to do with raspberry canes, a south-facing aspect, and growing orchids in a greenhouse. But there was more to it than that. A lot more. I was absolutely disgusted. Honeymoon? He spent more time with his new best friend.'

'There was more to what, Mam?'

'Him and the gardener.'

Rosh staggered back. 'You're not telling me Eric's bilateral?'

'You what?'

'Is he queer?'

It was Anna's turn to lean for support on a wall. 'Oh, give it up, Roisin. He's no more homo sapiens than your Roy.'

'You mean homosex–'

'I know what I mean. Don't be telling me what I mean, because you're as bad as I am, asking is he bifocal. Oh no, this is another matter altogether, one that means war. So I need troops. That's why I'm here just now, because he's already starting to fix battens to the wall.'

Roy fell in at the front door. 'What's happening? Is Eric all right?'

Anna nodded. 'Just now, he is. Whether he'll continue so is very much a matter of opinion.'

Rosh shrugged and stared at her intended. He bore a marked resemblance to an unmade bed that had recently housed several small children and a couple of dogs. In his current condition, no way would he look right in a bridal suite complete with four-poster, its own bathroom containing shower and bidet, plus an off-the-bedroom balcony overlooking a Cornish fishing village. 'Who got *you* ready?' she asked. 'Is it a fancy dress do?'

Roy knew when to ignore his beloved. 'What's happening?' he asked again. 'Come on, say something rational, Anna.'

'He's happening.' Anna jerked a thumb over her shoulder. 'Holt. The creature I married, otherwise known as my biggest mistake so far.'

Roy sighed. His mouth felt like the bottom of a bird cage, and he desperately needed a cup of tea. 'Fight among yourselves,' he said. 'I'm putting the kettle on.'

Anna watched as he walked away. 'He might look better with a kettle on,' she declared. 'It would cover his hair up, I suppose. I'll sleep on the sofa.' She walked into the front room.

Rosh followed her mother. 'Why are you here?' she asked.

'Oh, so now I'm not welcome in me own daughter's house.'

'Don't be silly, Mam.'

'Silly? Silly, is it? I'll tell you what silly is. Silly is two grown men dressed like God knows what poking about in beehives while the creatures were asleep for the winter. There was no need to go dressing up, because you never see a bee till summer.'

She sat down. 'In fact, Eric got very excited about everyone but the queen being dead and the females working themselves to the grave for just six weeks every year. So he comes back from the Isle of Wight wanting to keep bees on his allotment for cross-pollination purposes or some such thing. The allotment bosses said no, and there's

451

no room outside the back of the house, so he's building a pigeon loft against my kitchen wall instead. Pigeons. Rats with wings. He can't have bees, so he wants pigeons. Good job we came home after three days, or we might have ended up with a zoo.'

Rosh tutted. 'Those rats with wings got medals after the war, Mam. If it wasn't for domesticated pigeons, we would have lost even more men.'

Anna grunted. 'And where would a bird pin a medal? Anyway, that's as may be, but I don't want pigeon droppings on my washing. They don't care where they do it, you know. So I'm not having it. I won't have it. I will not put up with it.'

Roy came in with mugs of tea. 'What's the score?' he asked.

'Several direct hits from varying heights,' was Rosh's response. 'Eric wants to keep pigeons, and Mam's making him choose between her and his feathered friends.'

Anna took a sip of tea. 'Oh no,' she said. 'He can choose between life or death for his precious birds, because I'm here for my cats. If he wants his pigeons to live, he'd be better leaving them exactly where they are, un-purchased.'

Roy rubbed the sleep from his eyes. 'You can't take the cats, Anna.'

'And who are you to be telling me what I can and can't take?'

'Alice's nearly-stepfather,' he replied. 'That child was a worry for Rosh and Phil, and the cats have been part of her improvement. Function-ally, she's up to scratch on the social level, though

452

she's still a bit quiet occasionally. But her work's brilliant, and she's a fantastic artist. Are you going to take Winston away when you know Alice tells him all her problems? And Lucy-Furr, who curls up every night with your youngest grandchild – will you take that bit of comfort, too?'

Anna blinked. She hadn't thought this through properly. 'We could share them.'

'They'd be straight back here as soon as your back was turned,' Rosh pronounced. 'Cats belong to a place; these two have chosen my children, too. I know Lucy's a pest, but we love her. You mustn't do it, Mam. Anyway, they could get run over dashing from house to house.'

Anna sighed. 'All right, then. I need new cats. You see, that nice little man who came a-courting thinks he can best me.'

'But he loves you, Mam.'

'I know he loves me. And he also fights me in his quiet way. It's like a continuous joke that isn't even funny.' She swallowed. 'Well, I hate to say this, Roisin, but he's cleverer than I am.'

Roy placed a hand on Anna's shoulder. 'You took the mickey out of him good and proper for ages before the wedding, love. He's just keeping one step ahead, that's all. I've noticed he holds you back in company when you try to show him up. Anna, why can't you see he's playing you at your own game?'

'I don't mind the game, Roy. But I can't bear the losing. Do you mind back to the times he just stood there twisting his cap because I made him nervous?'

'I do,' Roy answered, his face in serious mode.

'So he marries me, then takes that as permission to do as he pleases.'

'Does he hit you?' Rosh asked.

'Is there a knife in his back? No, it's not that. It's the way he pretended to be such a nice man.'

'He is a nice man,' Rosh insisted. 'He's just not the docile fool you thought you were getting.'

'I'm the fool,' Anna cried. 'I let him make me the fool. All that tippytoeing round me so I'd marry him, all that pretending to be helpless.'

'Mam, he would have sold his soul to marry you.'

'Then why doesn't he treat me better?'

A glance passed between Rosh and Roy; both knew that Rosh would have to say the next line. 'You mean why doesn't he lie down and let you walk all over him? Perhaps you go too far, Mam. Phil had your measure. He respected you as a strong, determined woman, but he saw through all your games. Roy does, too. Roy takes the edge of your tongue often enough and doesn't rise to the bait, but one day he might.' She glanced at him, and was pleased to see that he continued to wear a grave expression.

It was plain that Anna failed to see where she'd gone wrong. Her first husband had seemed content enough even though she'd managed to produce just one living child. He'd been a bit untidy, and she'd told him off once or twice about that... No, she had to be truthful to herself. She'd nagged a bit. She'd raised her voice on several occasions.

'Mam?'

'Be quiet, I'm thinking.' She was thinking it was

454

too late for her to change. Even her humour had a sharp edge, but she was Irish, wasn't she? The Irish were quick to laugh, quick to cry, quick to lose temper. It was just that Eric had seemed so docile... 'I never tried to fool him, did I?'

'No,' said Rosh. 'You had him scrubbing cupboards, sweeping paths, painting ceilings. And he's put his foot down not on the rung of a ladder, but where you'll trip over it. Yet he's not a bad man. He loves you, but he wants a partnership, not a mistress and slave arrangement.'

At this point, Eric Holt entered the theatre of war. Unlike Roy, he had made a bit of an effort and was reasonably tidy. 'Hello, Rosh. Hello, Roy.' He looked at his bride. 'Hello, love.'

Anna angled herself differently so that she was facing the fireplace. She didn't want to look at him.

Eric looked at the other occupants of the room. 'I haven't got her permission to be here, you see. It was her bloody-mindedness that attracted me, but it's hard to live with.'

Anna glanced over her shoulder. 'That's right. Talk about me as if I'm not here.' Having made her views known, she turned her back on the trio once more.

The slow, plodding Eric seemed to have disappeared. 'You turned away from us, so you're *not* here,' he said before continuing to speak to her daughter. 'I can't take an interest in anything before sitting through the statutory conference. She's rearranged all the kitchen cupboards, moved all the furniture in the living room, and tidied me wardrobe. Tidied? I can't find anything when I need it. She's thrown out half of me gardening clothes.'

Rosh winked at her stepfather before employing her next weapon. 'Well, that's the way she is. You knew what you were taking on, so don't moan. That's my mother, and she's a good woman who doesn't want pigeon doings all over her tablecloths.' She sighed dramatically. 'Oh, I can't see this working, can you, Roy?'

Roy agreed. 'No, she'll have to come home. Leave her with us, Eric. We're used to her.'

Eric played the game. 'Fair enough. I suppose you know best. She even shortened the honeymoon because she didn't like the servants. I got on OK with the gardener, but we shared interests, you see. Anna kept looking for dust and saying the cook couldn't cook. So we came back.'

'And was that when you started wondering?' Rosh asked innocently. 'Whether you'd done the right thing?'

'That's right.'

Rosh winked again. 'Speaking for myself, I don't think you're man enough for her. Even if she wants to come back to you, we'll stop her. But it's your fault. She hasn't changed at all, yet you have. No, you'll never manage her, and you should have realized that from the start. You shouldn't marry someone and then decide to change them.'

Eric coughed. 'You're right,' he said mournfully.

Anna jumped up. 'Hey, that's my husband you're criticizing. Leave him alone, but.'

Eric hung his head. 'They're right, Anna.'

'But we always...' She blushed. 'We make up

456

afterwards, don't we?'

Roy squatted down and studied a mark on the wallpaper. 'Lucy's been at it again.' His voice trembled slightly with subdued laughter. Anna was like a child in many ways. When something was removed, she wanted it back, though that didn't mean she would treat it with anything approaching respect.

'What about your pigeons, then?' Rosh asked.

'It's a trellis I'm building for honeysuckle,' he answered. 'I told her it was for pigeons to pay her back for getting rid of my grey cardigan.'

'Cardigan?' Anna shrieked. 'It was a cardi gone, cos there were more holes than wool. You were a walking moth factory. I considered hanging a bell round your neck to warn folk to avoid you.'

Eric chuckled.

'See?' Anna stood and waved a hand in his direction. 'Mockery.'

'Mam, he's not–'

'And don't interfere in private matters again, Roisin.' She used the raised hand to push her husband into the hall. 'We need no advice,' she threw over her shoulder before slamming the front door.

Roy was doubled over in pain on the floor. Rosh dropped into an armchair. 'What happened then?' she asked. 'Did she or did she not come knocking on my door?'

The only response managed by the heap on the rug was a howl of laughter.

'Some flaming use you are, Roy. The slightest thing, and you crack up like a raw egg. She brought cat baskets. She called him for everything.

457

She wanted Lucy and Winston to kill his pigeons.'

'Which he isn't getting,' Roy managed.

'They're like a flaming pantomime.'

'Ugly sisters?'

'Something like that. Go home. You look like something that fell off a flitting.'

'What?'

'An expression of my mother's. A flitting's done at midnight because the rent's not been paid. A horse and cart arrives, and everything's thrown on the back, family included. They have to be quick, so stuff and people fall off.'

'Right.' He sighed. 'So glad I asked.' He looked at his reflection in the mirror. 'You're right, of course. I look as if I fell off a moving vehicle.'

'Naturally,' she said.

'Just like your mother.' He donated a perfunctory kiss and went home. Some people didn't appreciate other people...

Sixteen

'Have you written the full number plate down? It won't be the only coach bound for London Victoria, you know. When we get to a comfort stop, we'll need to be sure which bus is ours. We'd be in a right mess if we ended up following the wrong one. You can't be too careful with these things.'

Maureen sighed heavily and stuck her tongue out sideways. He didn't notice, anyway. If she'd stripped off and walked in front of his car with a red flag, she would have been no more than an obstacle in his path. 'You sounded very much like a Co-op manager just then, Tom. Or some old schoolteacher. For the forty-seventh time, yes, I have written the number plate down. It's here in my purse as safe as houses, your honour.'

'Are you sure you did it right?'

'Are you sure you don't want a clout with this handbag?'

'Are you sure you don't want to spend the night in a ditch?'

Maureen gritted her teeth. Tom was hunched over the steering wheel like a hungry, toothless old man hovering hopefully above a plate of food that threatened to defeat his dentures. He'd maintained that attitude throughout Lancashire and Cheshire, and was continuing through Stafford-shire with his nose perilously near to the windscreen. She found herself hoping there would be no sudden stops, because he'd get thrown through the window and die under the wheels of his own car. Even without ice, braking might be treacherous, and she fingered the rosary in her pocket while praying for black ice and freezing fog to keep their distance. Getting to London alive would be preferable to the alternative, she told her Maker.

At last, the vehicle between Tom's and the coach turned left. 'Ah, that's better,' he said. 'I can see what's what now. I thought that chap was going to be with us for ever.'

Maureen tutted. 'The coach driver will notice you're following him all the way. He might phone the police. Say there's somebody rich on the coach, he might think we were planning a kidnap and looking for a chance to hold somebody to ransom for thousands. If we get arrested, who'll help Mam then, eh?'

'Bloody hell, Maureen.'

'What?'

Tom snorted. 'Don't talk so daft. Rich people don't go on the overnight bus to London; they don't need to. First class train compartment for them, or even a hired plane.'

Mam was on the rear seat of the coach. If she turned round, she might see them, so Tom had to keep some distance, and Maureen understood that. Although the roads were quiet, it was dark, frosty and unsafe, and the coach didn't move quickly enough to be a great worry. 'Will they stop soon?' she asked. 'I need a wee.'

'There's a bucket in the boot,' was his terse reply.

'There's a which in the what?' Incredulity lifted the tone of her voice.

'You heard me. When we get to Stoke, your mother might go into the café and rest rooms, so it's a bucket in the car if you can manage it, or squat behind a wall or a bush where you can't be seen. Other than that, cross your legs till we reach London, because that's the only option you'll have left. Don't wet my car.'

Maureen was flabbergasted. 'And if I get a bit peckish, what happens then?'

Tom groaned. She'd not long ago eaten half the contents of a restaurant's fridge, so why should she suffer hunger? Like their youngest son, she was a gannet. 'There's a flask of soup, a flask of tea, some sandwiches and half an apple pie in the boot. Oh, and some butterscotch toffees bought specially for you.'

Maureen shook her head in disbelief. 'I hope they're not in the bucket.'

'They are in the bucket,' he replied calmly. 'Because it's brand new, and nobody's peed in it yet. Before anybody pees in it, I shall remove the food and the flasks.' In certain situations, a Riley woman could drive a man so far round the bend he'd think he'd been flushed down the drains of Bootle. 'You are annoying me, love. I have to concentrate, and I can't do that if you mither.'

What did he think a wife was for? Even a decorative female had certain functions to perform, and holding a husband in check was one of them. Except for her, the prefab would have been full of bike and car bits, as might their new house become if she didn't watch him. She fed him well,

461

brought money home, kept his clothing washed and pressed. And she tried to keep him happy-ish, because she dreaded the return of the black time when he'd disappeared inside himself. The trouble was, she loved him too well. 'Tom?'

'What now?'

'I'm sorry for moaning.'

'It's all right. I'm used to it.'

'But Tom?'

'Yes?'

'Remember those old films they sometimes showed as specials? Keystone Kops?'

'Oh yes, I like them.'

'All chasing one another and messing about and falling over folk with the music quickening up all the while?'

'Right. Where's all this leading?'

'To us, Tom. This is like Keystone Kops, except there's no music. I think me dad's behind us. He's following us following me mam. Don't do anything daft, because it's too icy, but I'm sure it's him. I wonder what he's done with our Seamus?'

Fortunately, the coach turned at this point, leading them into a large parking area containing many lorries and several coaches. A sizeable cafeteria was advertised as *Open 24 hours a day, seven days a week*. It was clearly there to serve those who kept the economy moving quickly by driving goods and people in all directions. 'You try and have a word with your dad while I watch the coach,' Tom said. 'Keep yourself as well hidden as you can.'

They stopped. Tom kept his eyes riveted to the single-decker on which his mother-in-law was travelling. He saw her getting off, watched as she approached the transport café. Paddy was a tall, strong woman, yet she suddenly seemed small as she ambled along like an aged person. She wasn't well. This excursion wasn't doing anyone a lot of good, but his mother-in-law was likely to be suffering the most. She'd probably booked her ticket before becoming ill, and she'd stuck to her plans in an attempt not to overcomplicate matters, but she should have waited. God help her, she had to be all right. Paddy could be a difficult woman, but he loved her to bits. At times like this, which had been mercifully few, he realized how much he cared for his in-laws.

Maureen shot out of the car and cursed the high-heeled shoes again. The ground was frozen and rough, so she struggled until she reached her father's van. He opened the door. 'Quiet,' he said. 'Our Seamus is asleep behind me.'

'I'm not,' piped a voice from the rear.

'If I say you're asleep, you're asleep.' Kevin gave his attention to Maureen. 'I didn't want to wake our Reen. She can't look after him properly anyway. I found a note from your mam, got the truth out of this young beggar of yours, and here I am. Seamus and your husband cooked this plot up: theatre, posh meal, then follow that coach.'

'No,' yelled the supposedly sleeping one. 'It was all my idea, cos I knew Mam would go mad, and you'd go mad, too, so neither of you could be told till the very last minute. Me dad's the only person I can trust because he doesn't drink Guinness, doesn't smash windows, doesn't tell me off for every little thing—'

'Shut up,' chorused the two adults.

'He's had another idea,' Kevin said. 'Lock your car and get in here. You could have a lie down with Seamus on the mattress in the back, and Tom and I could take turns with the driving. I suppose it makes sense. I mean, we're on your tail, you're stuck to a bus, and I'm stuck with him.' He jerked a thumb in Seamus's direction.

The boy peered over the parapet created by his grandfather's shoulder. 'I have a lot of ideas if people would only listen. Old Vera and Beetroot both say I have a future in some kind of–'

'If you want any future at all, you'll sit quiet,' Kevin said. 'Maureen, go and ask Tom how he feels about leaving his car here. We can pick it up on the way back. I'm sure we won't stay long down yonder.' He hoped they wouldn't; he didn't want Seamus to see the posh end of town. If soft lad caught sight of Buckingham Palace and Westminster, he might well get ideas above his station, and bloody London had swallowed more than enough of the family already.

'Me feet's killing me in these shoes, Dad. You go.'

Seamus shot up again. 'Let me go,' he suggested. 'I'm smaller, so I can hide better. Dad listens to me. I don't drink Guinness and break windows.'

'No, you just tell lies,' Maureen snapped.

'I don't tell lies.'

'That's a lie for a start,' his mother accused him. 'All right, you go. But be quick. Your gran's gone inside for a cuppa, so make sure she doesn't see you. Remember, she has eyes in the back of her head.'

Seamus needed to be a shadow. That was it – he'd be The Shadow and write adventure books. He opened the rear door as narrowly as possible and slipped out onto cold, uneven ground. Members of the Mafia to the left of him, the New York City police to the right, four precincts plus two important fellows covered in braid and medals and whatnots. He avoided crossfire by bending low next to Granddad's van. Light blazed from the speakeasy, but it was a hundred yards away. The FBI would be here in minutes. It was time to consult his assistants.

'Hunter One,' he whispered into his hand. 'Hunter One, maintain position. I repeat, position to be maintained. I'm going in at once. Alone. God bless America. Over and out.'

'Have you seen this daft boy of yours?' Kevin managed to contain his laughter.

Maureen, in the van's passenger seat, had grown used to her son and she said so. 'He's on a secret mission for Sunray Major. Sunray Major is deeper than M15, M16 and M17 point three. No one's ever seen him.'

'I'm not surprised. Who's Seamus talking to?'

'Oh, that'll be Hunter One.'

'Who the blood and liver pills is that?'

'He'll be Captain Overlord's assistant.'

Kevin left some space before asking, 'And who the hell's Captain Overlord when he's eaten his porridge?'

'Our Seamus. We listen to this every night, me and Tom. It's better than the Light Programme. A few nights ago, he saved the whole country from a plague sent over from Germany in a box

465

of liquorice allsorts. Mind, he didn't do it on his own; he had Hunter One and Sunray Major on his torch. He uses the torch because it has a built-in walkie-talkie.'

'But it hasn't–' A smile broadened Kevin's face. 'Bless him,' he said softly.

'He's clever, Dad. Underneath, I'm so proud of him I could sing, and that would empty this car park in ten seconds. But he's still a lying little toad. Though lovable with it...'

Seamus continued along his perilous route. All around him, vehicles were peppered with bullet holes. Scar-Face and his boys were determined to reach the speakeasy, and the cops were equally determined to wipe out the Mafia. A semi-automatic machine gun ack-acked in the background, and Captain Overlord crouched lower, since he had to stay alive until he could hand over control to federal agents.

'What are you doing here?'

Still absorbed in the game, Seamus froze.

'Seamus?'

Ah, it was Dad. 'I'm coming for you, cos Mam's shoes are killing her. I was bending down so that Gran wouldn't see me. Granddad woke up, you see. He was in a very bad mood, and he shoved a mattress and stuff in the back and made me come with him, because he'd found Gran's note about London. So I said it was all right, cos you and Mam were following the coach, but he just went mad because we hadn't told him.' He folded his arms. 'The trouble with this family is you daren't tell the truth. Lock your car, Dad. We can pick it up on the way back. You can share driving the van.'

'Seamus, you're always one step ahead.'

'I know. I wish you lot would grow up and listen to me.'

Tom shook his head in disbelief. Life seemed to get weirder by the minute. 'All right. I suppose that makes some sort of sense, two drivers and one car.' He opened the boot.

'Course it will make sense. It was my idea. Dad?'

'What?'

'Why have you brought that bucket?'

Tom managed not to snarl. 'Never you mind.' He'd heard enough about buckets to last him a lifetime. He paused suddenly. 'What if the van breaks down? See, if one of us breaks down, we'll have a spare vehicle. Come on, let's get your mam. We need the van and the car as well, son.'

Once again, Tom found himself carrying Maureen back to the car. She was at war with her shoes, with the slippery earth, with her dad for being daft enough to follow them, with her husband for not having the sense to pack some flat shoes, with Mam for kick-starting all this bother, with– She was dumped with minimal ceremony in the passenger seat of her husband's car.

He walked round the vehicle and slid in behind the wheel. 'Stop whingeing, or I'll swap you for Seamus. I'm sorry I forgot the flat shoes, sorry you may have to pee in a bucket, sorry I couldn't arrange better weather. And it would have been nicer if we could all have travelled together, but if your dad breaks down, he'll have us to turn to, and vice versa.'

Maureen mumbled under her breath. The girls at Scouse Alley wouldn't know how to cope without any supervision, and there was no way of letting anyone know that she and Mam would both be missing. And they'd just branched out into Lancashire hotpot, shepherd's pie, meat and potato under a lid of shortcrust pastry, or pasties and chips occasionally. And here she was, with her young son, mother, dad and husband, all of them going into the dens of London's East End gangs, which wasn't much to look forward to. Seamus would miss another day of school, and he'd already had time off with his cold. But she might see Finbar and Michael again, plus her grandchildren. She was young for grandmother-hood, but she'd manage.

'Stop wittering,' Tom said. He usually didn't mind the wittering; like the radio, it was an accompaniment to everyday life. But on a journey like this one, he needed a bloody rest. At home, he could walk into another room, but here? God, he wished he'd left her at home, high heels, pink suit and all.

There was another stop outside Birmingham. England's second city was just a cluster of lights down the road, and Maureen was not impressed. 'They talk funny,' she said. 'And it doesn't look up to much, does it?'

'Bigger than Liverpool,' was Tom's reply.

'They still talk funny.'

Tom raised his eyebrows, but said nothing. In the opinion of many, the Scouse accent was not exactly music to the ears.

She opened the door.

'Where are you off to?' Tom asked.

Maureen reached into the back of the car and pulled out a tartan rug. 'I'm going to the ladies' room, then I'm getting me mam. She'll travel to London in the back of this car – or in the van – wrapped up and warm. We'll carry on following the coach, and she'll meet her Irishman as planned. This time, I'm making an executive decision. Being a bloke doesn't mean you're the only executive in the car. She's my blinking mother, and this is about my blinking sons. So you button it, baby. It's your turn to do as you're told, just for a change.'

What was the flaming point? For a few seconds, Tom watched his wife stumbling about in heels high enough to present a danger to low-flying air-craft. She could end up with a sprained or broken ankle at this rate. He followed her yet again, carried her yet again. When they reached the coach, he propped her up next to a nearby wall. 'Stay,' he snapped.

'Don't use that tone of...' She was too late; he was approaching the coach driver.

Fortunately, the driver was one hundred per cent Scouse with an agreeable attitude and an accent thicker than Tate and Lyle's treacle. 'No problem,' the young man was saying. 'I remember it, cos it has a belt holding it shut, like. Follow me and give us an 'and, mate. Yeah, you'd best take her if she's ill.'

So Mate followed Brian, who issued a condensed version of his life on his way to the back of the coach. He was twenty-seven, worked nights to keep away from the wife who got on his nerves, his mam was in hospital with all the worry and a stomach ulcer, and his dad, a waste of space and oxygen, was dead through drink.

While luggage was deposited on the tarmac, Brian gave birth to twins – little sods – a whippet, and some koi carp in his back garden. He never voted Tory, liked a flutter on the 'orses and the 'ounds, thought the Queen Mother was great, and couldn't be in a house where cabbage had been cooked.

By the time Paddy's case had been recovered and the rest replaced in the boot, Tom knew everything there was to know about bypassing lecky meters to make the bill smaller, feeding a family of four for two weeks with a sack of spuds, four dozen eggs, some beans and a few loaves, and where to get a decent imitation of a road fund licence. The one thing Tom didn't know was whether he was coming or going. The remark he'd made about Jesus feeding the five thousand fell on stony ground, as did a few suitcases, though Brian remained unperturbed.

He shook Mate's hand. 'Thanks for the interestin' conversation,' he said. 'Lonely life, drivin'. I hope your mam's soon better.'

Tom, slightly dazed, returned to his propped-up wife. Without words or ceremony, he replaced her in his car before marching off to find Paddy. This was going to be one of those moments, like had he been good enough to marry their Maureen and was he a real Catholic boy? Paddy was not only the eyes and ears of her world; she was also the voice.

Then he saw her. He'd seen her earlier today –

well, it was yesterday now – and she'd seemed all right. But a suddenly old female walked towards him, her face grey and drawn, her eyes ringed with darkness, her forehead lined and worried. She was alone, contained inside a head that wouldn't stop thinking, and he remembered that, by God, he did. This poor woman was in a place he had visited, and he must help her out.

As soon as she noticed him, she stood stock still. 'Tom?' Relief flooded her body, making her so weak that she lurched towards him, her legs unable to bear her weight. 'Tom! Oh, Tom. Thank God it's you.' Only then did she realize how frightened she was. Big, brave Paddy who ran Scouse Alley, who threw grown men out of Lights, was reduced to a helpless fool.

He grabbed her and placed the car rug across her shoulders. 'We're all here, love. Me, Maureen, Seamus and Dad. We couldn't let you do this on your own. Don't cry. Don't let them see how tired and worried you are. Remember, Finbar and Michael are our sons, so we should be involved in getting them back.'

She sniffed back wetness created by cold air and emotion. 'I'm just so tired, so completely worn out.' She couldn't be bothered to ask how they'd discovered her plan and why they were here. Nothing mattered now. With her family around her, she could cope with just about anything. Tom led her across the car park to Kevin's van. Kevin, having taken one look at his wife, came at her with medicine bottle and spoon. 'Here, love. You forgot it.'

Seamus joined Tom while Gran was helped into

471

the back of the van. Even the child was quiet because he could see that she wasn't quite herself. He walked with his dad back to the car, where he climbed into the rear seat. This was one time when he decided to keep his mouth nearly shut, because the less Mam knew, the better.

'She's with your dad,' Tom said.

'I know, I've been watching. Is she all right?'

'Just tired,' Seamus said helpfully. 'She can rest stretched out in the van.'

Paddy, prone on the mattress in the rear of her husband's vehicle, fell asleep almost immediately. In her dream, she saw her brothers and her sons, all four lost to the London gangster and boxing communities. But her grandsons were alive and well, as were her great-grandchildren. The trouble with having strong and combative boys was that they started with boxing clubs, went to London, and...

Groaning, she rolled over and pulled the covers up to her chin. She reached out for Finbar and Michael, for their wives and children, but they were dragged away by an invisible hand. Her arms weren't long enough to grab them from the jaws of criminality. It couldn't happen again, mustn't be allowed to...

The woman smiled and poured tea into delicate china cups on a tray. 'Call me Violet, dear. Now, I know all about troublesome boys, because I've three of my own. Turn your back for a minute, and they're either knocking somebody about in a boxing ring or, worse still, bare-knuckle fighting. And they don't look after themselves properly, do they? What rubbish would they eat if we weren't here to feed them?'

Paddy tried to answer, but the woman rattled on. She had a lovely smile and was possessed of a kindness that was real. She was also strong and overflowing with love for her twins. 'Charlie's a lovely chap,' she said. 'He's my eldest. But my twins is special. You just know, don't you, dear? That moment when you hold them for the first time, you just know these things. Instinct, you see.'

Paddy took the line of least resistance and continued to listen. 'Men?' The lady of the house chuckled mirthlessly. 'Best left out of it altogether, my love. Oh yes, we have to remember them ladies that threw themselves under horses and tied themselves to railings and got force-fed in clink. Only when this country's run by women will we get any sense.'

The sleeping Paddy moaned. Didn't Violet understand that her children were now grown and members of the gender she dismissed as stupid and dangerous? Had she no true perception of the crimes that were being perpetrated out there on the streets of the East End? Or had she simply turned her back on reality; was this woman living in a parallel universe?

Ronnie Kray came in. The smile he donated didn't reach his eyes. There was something cold in his stare, as cold as the unidentifiable and unquantifiable Epping Forest graves. Yet when he looked at Violet, his whole demeanour softened. It was clear to Paddy that whatever else Ronald was guilty of, he adored his mother.

'My Ronnie misses his twin, don't you, dear?

473

They hate being separated. Reggie's away for a while, isn't he?'

Ron nodded. 'A little holiday,' he said. Paddy knew they meant prison. He turned his attention to the visitor. 'It'll be all right, missus. I'll sort it. Tell the boys not to worry about a thing, but they're better out of London.'

Sort it? Would sorting it mean further death and destruction? The man wasn't dressed for killing. His suit was very posh, probably bespoke, with bright red silk lining the jacket. There was money here, so perhaps he would use some of it to ensure her grandsons' safety. No. She wasn't like the adorable Violet Kray. Paddy O'Neil was sure that the payment for the freedom of her grandchildren was likely to involve a few corpses. She shivered.

He beamed at her when she thanked him. But he still had flat, empty eyes. Fear continued to shudder its silent way through every fibre of her being. Tom, her much-loved son-in-law, had killed, and he'd been hollow-eyed for months, but this was different. Some inner instinct told Paddy that Violet's Ronnie had always been ... well ... odd and possibly dangerous. Yet there was something endearing about him. He was gentlemanlike in the presence of older women, so there was a level of respect rooted deeply beneath all the negative stuff.

Ah yes, the present. She rooted round in her bag for Violet's gift. It was a framed print of Liverpool's waterfront. Violet's smile was a hundred per cent genuine. 'I bet it looked nothing like this after the Germans had rearranged it. But it's lovely now, eh?'

Paddy tried to tell her that the Liver Building and most of its stalwart companions had survived with very little damage, but her throat seemed paralysed when it came to delivering a speech of any length. In return, she was given a photograph of Violet's boys. All beautifully dressed, Charlie in the middle, Ronnie with what looked like a huge boa constrictor draped across his shoulders. The snake looked settled; its eyes were reminiscent of those of its owner.

He was saying something about liking snakes, about a person knowing where he was with a python. 'If he doesn't like you, you're dead,' he said. 'If he doesn't like you, you're dead. If he doesn't like you–'

'Paddy!'

She woke with a start. 'What?'

'You're dreaming and shouting.'

'Am I? It's a wonder I can sleep at all in this boneshaker.' She was still tired, but she wasn't afraid any more. And Mrs Kray's blue-and-white front-room wallpaper was beautiful.

At last, the journey ended. Paddy's Irishman, who had expected just one woman, was typically unfazed by the increased head count. Like most Irish folk, he liked plenty of company, and he took them for a good breakfast in a café not far away. After booking them into a small hotel, he left and promised to return that afternoon. 'Then I'll take you to see Mrs Kray,' he told Paddy.

'And we'll follow you,' Tom said. 'Maureen can go in the house with her.'

Atypically, Paddy said nothing. She knew exactly what was going to happen, because God had sent her the dream. How did she know? She didn't know how she knew, but she knew.

'Mam?'

Paddy looked at her daughter in the crumpled pink suit. 'Thank you for coming,' she said, her voice unusually quiet. 'I felt so ill and tired last night, but look at me now. Sometimes, I forget to remember how much I need all of you. The best moment in my whole life was when I saw our lovely Tom walking towards me. Now, we should all rest and get changed later.' She paused. 'This is a big day for all of us, especially for Finbar and Michael.'

Seamus stood at the window of the room he was sharing with Mam and Dad. So this was London? It was just like Liverpool: buses, houses, shops and people. 'Where's the soldiers in daft hats?' he asked. 'And the soldiers stood in boxes? They can't talk to you, and if you pull faces they're not allowed to laugh.'

Paddy opened the door. She was on her way to the next room, where Kevin was already asleep. 'Seamus, this is a big, bad city with a lot of good people and beautiful places in it. I tell you this now for your own good. It killed two of your great-uncles and two of your uncles. It's put your brothers in a difficult situation. Let the soldiers in daft hats stay where they are, horses and all. The royals are a long, long way from here.' She left the room.

Kevin opened one eye. 'You all right, queen?'

'I am,' she replied. Queen? Hadn't she just told

476

Seamus that royalty was miles away? Oh well, never mind – at least she was smiling. Her chest and mind were both clearer, and she felt better than she had in weeks. Taken all round, it was going to be a great day.

'Why wouldn't she let me go in with her?' Maureen, reasonably well kitted out in her navy suit, felt like a bridesmaid who hadn't been allowed to accompany the bride up the aisle. Not that the house looked up to much. It was yellow, for a start. Why the heck would anybody build rows of terraces that looked as if they had liver disease?

Tom worked hard at remaining patient; after many hours in a confined space with his wife for company, he needed the forbearance of Jesus Himself. 'This is the bit she has to do on her own, love. She needs us here, within reach, but she doesn't want to upset the family. Mrs Kray expected one visitor, so she's got one visitor. Now, give it a rest, will you? I'm going on no more long journeys with you, Maureen. Can you not sit still?' Tom glanced over his shoulder at Kevin and Seamus, who was clearly bored. He wanted to see soldiers and Buckingham Palace, but he was stuck somewhere with a daft name, Bethnal Green. There was nothing green about it.

'There's another fidget here in the back,' Kevin said. 'Like a cat on hot bricks. If he doesn't slow down, we'll need to get him checked for St Vitus's dance. Or he may just have ants in his pants. Again.'

Seamus puffed out his cheeks and blew hard. He wanted to see Hyde Park, Piccadilly Circus,

Westminster Cathedral, the palace. There were big shops, bigger than anything in Liverpool, but here he sat outside a boring yellow house in a boring yellow street—

'Seamus!' Maureen snapped.

'What?'

'Stop breathing.'

'I can't. If I stop breathing, I'll die. Beetroot says oxygen is a requirement if we're going to sustain life.'

'Sister Beatrice, you mean. I'm not talking about ordinary breathing, but the huffing and puffing is getting on my nerves.'

Well, she was getting on Dad's nerves, but at least Seamus was fast learning the benefits of near-silence.

They all stared at the door through which Paddy had disappeared some forty minutes earlier. A huge black car sat outside the house. Inside, Paddy would be thanking the Krays for helping Finbar and Michael to get out of London. 'What will it cost?' Maureen mused aloud. She kept the rest of her thoughts to herself. Would Mam find out the names of the three dead? Would the men killed on Reen's wedding day become real people with widows and children?

'It won't cost anything,' Kevin replied.

'I wasn't meaning money.' Maureen found her rosary. At times like this, the only help available came from a different dimension.

Tom watched his wife while she closed her eyes and began to move her lips through a Pater, ten Aves and a Gloria. His own prayer was, as usual, less conventional; he simply begged the Lord to bring home his boys and make his family whole again.

The door opened. Paddy emerged with a man and a woman in her wake. The Krays waved at the people in the car; Seamus waved back. Violet crossed the road, and Tom opened his window. She told them it had been lovely to meet Paddy, and invited them all to come in next time.

Then it was Ronnie's turn. 'Any time you want a holiday in London, let us know and we'll fix it for you.'

As they drove away, Paddy began to cry. Wedged in the back seat between Seamus and Kevin, she didn't really have enough space when it came to sobbing. After a couple of minutes, when the Kray street was behind them, Tom parked again. 'What happened?' he asked.

Paddy shook her head. 'Back to the hotel,' she achieved finally. 'Book another night and we'll travel home Sunday, after Mass. There's a Catholic church nearby. If ever God wanted a visit from us, this is the occasion.'

Seamus kept quiet. Now was not the time to start going on about soldiers who appeared to live in standing-up coffins outside the palace.

When they reached their hotel, they all piled into the room occupied by Maureen, Tom and Seamus. The extra bed meant extra seating. A maid brought up tea and sandwiches, and everyone waited for Paddy to speak. Still clearly distraught, she described the dream she'd had in the van. 'Everything was right except for the wallpaper and the photograph of Violet's sons. But even so, Ronnie was talking about getting a snake. And until three weeks ago, the wallpaper had been blue and white, so–'

'Great,' cried Seamus. 'Can I have a snake?'

'No, you can't,' came the answer from four adult throats.

Seamus sighed. The Shadow might have had a python to play with between chapters. He could imagine himself sitting at a typewriter with a cold-blooded friend keeping watch.

'But after breakfast in the morning, Seamus, you'll get your precious tour of London. I'll book a car to take you and your dad to see the sights. It will have to be quick, because daylight hours are short and we need to get back to Liverpool the next day after Mass.'

The lad wanted to kiss Gran, but he restrained himself. There was no point in complaining about kisses if he started to dole them out. 'Thank you,' he said. He would see London after all.

'What upset you, love?' Kevin asked his wife.

Paddy scarcely knew where to find the words. 'Seeing a good, kind man with something wrong in his eyes,' she answered eventually. 'Reggie wasn't there. They said he was away, and I think they meant prison. Ronnie's generous, kind and helpful. I know in my bones he would never hurt a woman, a child or an elderly man. He'd be the first one there if I needed to cross a busy road. He'd never see a child without food or something to play with, and he worships Violet.'

'So what's the but?' Maureen asked.

'Gangs,' came the reply. 'Rivalry. There's a great, gaping maw that swallowed my brothers and my sons. But Finbar and Michael will soon

480

be safe, because Violet ordered it.'

'And your dream?' Kevin asked.

'Very near to truth. I gave her the Liverpool waterfront, and she gave me this.' From a brown paper bag she lifted a piece of framed embroidery. It was beautifully done with a border of flowers. Stitched onto the cloth were nine words. *The hand that rocks the cradle rules the world.*

'That's beautiful,' Maureen said. 'Did she do it?'

Paddy shook her head. 'It's antique. Ronnie paid a sum for it. The money goes to the local children's home. See what I mean? He looks after the poor and afflicted, then he turns and...' She snapped her fingers. 'Violet's a fierce feminist, yet she's blind where her boys are concerned. I like her. It's a while since I met a more likeable woman. I invited her to Liverpool, and you'd have thought I'd offered her the crown jewels. She won't come, because she won't leave her boys, but she was pleased all the same.'

Tom was careful in the presence of his youngest son. 'The three men in the car?' he asked casually.

'No idea, Tom. I didn't ask. It was a happy conversation for the most part, and I wasn't about to spoil it.'

'Were you afraid at all?'

Paddy smiled at her son-in-law. 'Not as frightened as he is.'

Tom thought for a moment. 'What's Ronnie Kray afraid of?'

'Of himself. Of the demon behind the eyes. And I sensed that he can't function properly without his brother. After all, they are two halves of one whole. Identical twins are from the one cluster of cells. He looked lost.' She slapped her knees with both hands. 'Let's forget all this and eat. Tomorrow we rest, and Sunday we're home.'

Seamus heard little. He was going to see the sights of London, and nothing else mattered.

'Don't tell anybody we went to the Krays' house.' This litany had been drummed so deeply into Seamus's brain that he actually took notice of it. But he wrote four pages of foolscap and took them in to school. He handed them to Vera with a letter from Mam that pleaded urgent and unexpected family business in London as the reason for Seamus's Friday off. Having donated his masterpiece to the form teacher, Seamus put his head down on the desk and fell asleep.

Sister Veronica set the rest of the class some work before sitting down to read what Seamus Walsh had written. At the top sat the legend, *It is gone midnight and I am writing this by torchlight. I have to write it now before I forget bits.* It was difficult to keep a straight face while reading this boy's work. He had a way with words, and a dry humour that seemed very mature for a lad of his age, but she was determined to persevere.

BUCKINGHAM PALACE

It's all right. I mean, there's nothing wrong with it, and some of the railings are fancy, but it's just a very big house. It wasn't what you'd call clean, either, cos some of the stones were darker than others. She was in, because there was a flag up, and Dad says a flag up means she's in residence. If you rang the doorbell, which you can't, it might take her ages to get to the front door. Not that she'd answer it, anyway. Dad says a lackey would do it. Not sure what a lackey is, but I'll find out in the dictionary. I bet they need maps to find their way round that palace. She's got corgis. Corgis are snappy little dogs, Dad says. But Queen Elizabeth rules them with a rod of iron. Is the rod of iron that thing she keeps with the ball that has a cross on top? I hope she doesn't hit them with the rod of iron, cos that would be cruel.

The men in daft hats are there, and Dad told me to leave well alone, but I tried to make one laugh. He didn't laugh, and I thought he was a statue, so I asked was he a statue, and his mouth twitched. So they are actually alive. Boring though. I'd hate to have to stand there doing nothing. What if they got an itchy nose or something? Would it be off with their heads?

Anyway, I saw the queen's house, and I suppose it's OK, but I wouldn't like to light all the fires every day.

ST PAUL'S

St Paul's has a big dome. It's not Catholic, so we didn't go in. During the war, Mr Churchill said St Paul's was so important that it had to be saved at all costs. So it was saved at all costs, as Mr Churchill was boss of the war. Oh, it has a lot of steps up to the front door, so that's the other reason why we didn't go in, because the car was waiting. So that's all it was, just steps and a dome with a bit of a point on top.

I think it was a round building. A circle. I don't know what all the fuss was about. They'd have been better saving people at all costs than saving that thing

483

at all costs. It might not have been round. I might be mixing it up with something called the Albert Hall. That had a lot of steps, too, so it wasn't worth the bother.

When playtime arrived, the nun ushered the class out to the yard. She put a finger to her lips. 'Let him sleep,' she whispered. 'He's been on a long journey.' She referred not to London, but to the advances Seamus had made over the past eighteen months. The boy had matured, and he owned a special eye for detail. Also, his spelling had taken something of a turn for the better.

She sat at her desk once more.

THE EMBANKMENT

It's just a river, but it's wide with bridges everywhere. Tower Bridge is smart, but the others are ordinary. All kinds of boats on the water, lots of people talking and shouting. They talk funny, but I knew what they were saying cos I've seen films with London people in them. There are beautiful buildings with really posh door-ways and poles – Dad says they're called columns. It was lively down there, but not as busy as our Liverpool docks.

Course, we're not posh, so we don't have an embankment. We have Liverpool, Birkenhead, Wallasey, the Pier Head, but no embankment. Trust them to need a fancy name for it.

Sister Veronica grinned. He was perceptive, and very decided for a mere child. And he'd been up half the night straining his eyes to write this in poor light.

And there he sat now, dead to the world, tousled head resting on an open maths book. His family should be proud, because a cheeky little urchin was fast becoming a personable young man. Still cheeky, though.

PALACE OF WESTMINSTER AND OTHER PLACES

Now they're talking. This is really, really nice to look at, much prettier than the queen's house. There's Big Ben for a start. Dad said the name Big Ben is just one huge bell inside the workings, but everybody calls the whole clock Big Ben. There's bits of gold up at the top. I wonder how many people died building it? A lot have died falling off Liverpool Proddy Cathedral, and it's still not quite finished.

Dad said this was the people's palace and I asked him what he meant. The House of Commons is in there, full of idiots, he told me. The daftest thing about it is that people like my dad voted for the idiots, so voters must be stupid too. Mr Macmillan is the boss in the Commons. But I never saw such a wonderful place, right next to the river, all towers and fancy windows. It's ours. It's the people's palace. The queen isn't allowed in the House of Commons because she isn't one of us.

I wanted to go in, but there were no tours and our car was waiting again. Then we went to Downing Street and my dad took a photo of me with a cop on the steps of Number Ten. It's not a mansion, it's just a house stuck to other houses, but I bet it's posh inside.

We had something to eat in a café on Piccadilly Circus. Hundreds of people rushed about outside, all busy, and not looking at each other. The chips in

London are not as good as the chips in Liverpool and the vinegar tasted funny. Dad said it was probably watered down, cos London folk will do anything for a quick quid. I think he doesn't like London much.

I will go back one day, but just to visit. There's a lot of trouble with gangs and fighting and people getting hurt and I don't want that kind of thing. But there's a street called Fleet Street where newspapers are made, and I might go there, I don't know yet. Then there's another place called Threadneedle Street and the Bank of England is there. Stupid name for a street.

And one of the places we went to had yellow houses. I never saw yellow houses before. They looked strange.

Regent Street and Oxford Street have loads of shops, some of them very big and they're not yellow. But while I watched all these people running about, I thought they looked lonely and they'd be better off up here where we talk to each other. Thousands of them dashing round, nobody stopping for a chat or anything. Dad said you could probably drop down dead in the West End and nobody would notice for a week.

Oh, I nearly forgot. Westminster Abbey's very nice. Me and Dad stood outside and heard angels singing. Only they weren't angels, they were boys. Our driver told us that. The singing made me tingle all down my back and I don't know why. Dad had to use a hanky to dry his eyes, and said it was the cold air stinging them. But it wasn't. It was the choir. The song made you want to cry. I don't understand how that happens.

It's nice to be able to say that I've been. But coming back home was great. Too many people in London for my liking. They travel under the ground, too, all packed like animals, squashed together beneath the pavements. It's no way to live. That's what Dad says, anyway.

The sister known as Vera placed Seamus Walsh's work in a large cardboard envelope. He could keep all his pieces in there. Soon, he would go to the grammar school, but she intended to give him a head start. With one or two others, he would be offered advanced lessons in English Language. If he didn't become a writer of some sort, she would eat her habit, wimple included.

Seventeen

Molly was married. Don chuckled to himself when he read the notice in the paper. She needed happiness, closeness and a good marriage, and he hoped she would be blissful, since she deserved nothing but the best. With her dogs, her ukulele and her tropical fish, she was one of the most wonderfully eccentric people he'd met. Singing in pubs, performing at birthday parties, weddings and the occasional bar mitzvah, she was perpetually on the go. Her energy had been contagious, and she'd shown him how to be truly alive at a time when Tess had appeared not to want to know him.

He would never forget Molly, partly because his love for her had been real, mostly because of all she had done for him and his family. This lovely house, his wonderful born-again wife, the treatment Tess was undergoing – all these things had been made possible by a generous, big-hearted woman. He owed her everything, yet he knew she would never accept repayment even if he ever found the ability to repay.

Tess, armed with a bright yellow duster, entered the front room. He could tell that she wanted to talk, and that she was trying to hide behind the duster. What was she up to this time? The next few minutes would tell, he supposed. Now that he'd learned how to almost manage her, life was good. Oh well, let her get on with it. Like an electric kettle, she took a little while to reach boiling point, though she didn't overspill as frequently as she once had.

Never mind. The job with Injun Joe was going well, Sean and his best friend were trying to establish their own garage business on the Dock Road, while Anne-Marie, now a fully qualified hairdresser who had almost recovered from Quarry Men fever, seemed to be edging towards marriage with Mark. So taken all round, life was good. Except for ... yes, she was going to speak.

'I don't want to go. I'm not ready for it. It's all too soon and too complicated.' Ah, so Tess was in a darker mood today. She was trying to put her foot down, and she knew as well as he did that she was in the wrong. Yet in a way, he found her more endearing when she was acting all Contrary Mary. Without her unpredictability, her odd little ways with wild animals, those sudden smiles that lit up a whole room, life would have been considerably duller.

'I'm not doing it,' she said sternly. 'They can reunify themselves without any help from me.'

Don tutted. 'But it's what you've been working towards. Look, we can go, sit at one side, then come home. If you don't want to get too involved–'

'And what would be the point of that? It's supposed to be a Riley reunion, and if I don't want to join in I shouldn't go. Nobody can make me go.'

He could. He could and he would. 'You must go. Dr Banks said you ought to go. In the weeks you've been seeing him, you've come on in leaps and bounds. And that young woman's going to be there, the one who had a single room while you were both in the Women's. She looks like your sister, but she isn't. Joe found out she's not one of your caravan crew. Tess, knowledge is power. Take hold of it, shake it, see what falls out.'

Tess carried on dusting furiously while Don kept an eye on her. All she seemed to achieve was the stirring up of particles which settled elsewhere. Real dusting involved a slightly damp cloth and concentration, so it was plain that she was simply working out her fears on the furniture. 'Tess, I love you to bits.'

'I know that.' She flicked an angry cloth at a chiming mantel clock that had been a birthday present from Don.

'So would I set you wrong? Would I ask you to do something that might hurt you and send you hurtling back into nightmares?'

Tess sighed and sat down. 'No, you wouldn't do anything to hurt me, and vice versa. I'd have been much happier to spend the cash on your knee, as you well know.' She paused, nervous fingers plucking at her yellow duster. 'It's you. You're the reason I'm better, because you're always there in the night. That's as important as a mad doc droning on about my mother, my heightened sense of guilt, and the brothers and sisters. Then, of course, we have the buckets.'

Don managed not to smile. 'Buckets? What the blood and sand have buckets to do with anything?'

'Exactly.'

'Mind, you'd miss having a bucket if you needed to mop a floor, Tess.'

She threw the duster at him. It missed and draped itself unbeautifully over a Wedgwood dish. 'We all have a bucket,' she told him sternly.

'Some have more than one,' Don replied. 'The rich might have several to match different rooms.'

'These are buckets you can't see, Gordon. Oh, I wish you'd behave and listen. Did you read in the paper that Molly got married?'

Here she went again, off at a delightful tangent. It was up to him to guide her back to the path. 'I did. She used to sell buckets, now I come to think. Builders' buckets. Great big buckets for great big builders, they were.'

Tess stared through the window. A squizzle was pinching bird food again. Sometimes, the creatures you loved could be very annoying. There wasn't much bird food left, as she stopped feeding everything in spring, yet squizzles still knocked at the door, didn't they? Birds adapted. But squizzles and Tess weren't good at change. Hungry little rodents, squirrels were, so she understood them very well. Even when they weren't hungry, they wanted food to save for later. How well she remembered that. 'Little thieves,' she said quietly. 'Poor birds hardly get a look-in.'

'Buckets?' he reminded her.

'Some are bigger than others,' she said.

He bit back a quip about a child's seaside bucket and spade.

'They fill up,' she continued. 'A big bucket fills more slowly than a little bucket even if the stuff that fills it pours at the same rate.'

Don was with her so far.

'People with little buckets have to empty them more often to make room. When a bucket overflows, a person can go to pieces. I have to keep emptying my bucket by forgiving myself. So we're paying fifteen quid an hour for him to ask me how full my invisible bucket is. Daft. It's my opinion that he should see a psychiatrist.'

'Put your coat on.'

She stared at him aghast. 'The children will be home soon. I've chops to grill and the vegetables want peeling and–'

'They aren't children, love. Sean wears more oil than a tanker carries, and Anne-Marie can cook. They've both got legs, so they can walk to the chippy. Now, they're a couple of bucketfuls you can empty immediately. They aren't babies any more. With luck and good management, they'll be making you some more babies in a few years. You'll be a lovely granny.'

'Shut up. I'm a young woman.'

'A beautiful young woman,' he said.

What was he after, she wondered while ordering him to write a note for the offspring. It wasn't sex, because he didn't lead up to that with fuss and compliments. That was their own little world, their private kingdom. Once in the boudoir he had created for her, they became different people.

No, he was planning something, and she guessed that he had already begun the spadework. She would arrive at the Riley reunion hog-tied and in a wheelbarrow if necessary. And she trusted him to know what was good for her; despite her own doubts, she knew he was probably right. He was

492

usually right, often annoyingly so.

Obedient in coat and gloves, she stood in the front-room doorway. 'Where are we going?' she demanded.

'Out.'

'Gordon!' She stamped a size five foot. 'Where to?'

He shrugged. 'I'll let the car decide. Let's have a mystery tour, eh?'

The car chose Southport. The sedate, Victorian resort was so in control of itself that even holidaymakers were quiet in the summer.

But this was not summer, and the days were still short. Don parked on the coastal road while the sun put himself to bed. 'You see?' He took her hand. 'The sun's gone. And look what he's left behind just to remind us that he was here today. Colours. And with him goes today, and the colours fade until this day becomes yesterday. He'll be back tomorrow, and we'll call that today. All new. Every day is new.'

'Could be cloudy.'

'But the sun will still be there, love, supervising everything. We have to carry on into tomorrow; it's what we do – we follow the sun's sense of order. And soon, very soon, you can take hold of one special day, an important occasion. You can walk up to them and ask why they took your bloody dinner, and how dare they remain alive when they starved you halfway to death. Empty your bucket on their heads. Do unto others what they have done unto you. Steal their sausage rolls and ask how they like it. Better still, throw their food on the floor and jump on it.' He grinned impishly.

'I couldn't do that.'

He shrugged. 'Then I'll do it for you.'

'No!'

'So your bucketful of crap is never going to land on their heads?'

'Language, Don.'

She often used a few choice words in the throes of passion, but he decided not to mention that fact. A man had to take his pleasure where he could. 'You were starved by your brothers and sisters. Don't tell me off for swearing, but this is your chance to kick seven shades of shit out of them.'

A short silence followed. 'But they were children, too. They were probably as hungry as I was.'

'Then it's your chance to forgive them. In my opinion, forgiveness would leave your bucket bone dry. It's facing them at all that's your problem, because you walked out and left them to it. They had to look after your mother. So a lot of it's guilt mixed up with the anger. You do know I met some of them the day I went out with Joe?'

Tess nodded.

'Decent people, ordinary people.'

'Yes.'

'We didn't let anyone know who I was or where you were, because I told Joe just as much as he needed to know. Tess?'

'What?'

'The knife sharpener – remember him? That's one of your brothers. Luckily, he didn't recognize me.'

'So Jack the Knife's my brother?'

'He is. There's at least one builder, a postman,

494

a greengrocer, two hairdressers–'

'And a partridge in a pear tree?'

'We never found one of those. But you've at least two nephews at university.' He waited for a response, but none came.

'Tess, there were times, you see, when I felt I'd never have made it without our Ian. I know I don't see him often with the hours he works and him living in Chester, but knowing my brother's somewhere is enough. You need to make them real, sweetheart. They're there, they exist, they're people. Whether or not you see them, they're part of you. Whether or not you like them, the fact is–'

'Shut up, Gordon. The fact is that if you carry on carrying on, I'll walk home.'

'Good luck with that – it's well over fifteen miles, so it would take you till next Tuesday. Behave yourself. I'm treating you to a meal.'

'I'm not dressed.'

Don laughed. 'If you weren't dressed, we could fulfil a dream of mine. Sex in the sand dunes.'

'Too cold,' was her quick response. 'You'd shrivel like a roll-mop herring.' Tess, when tottering on the brink of coarseness, was a delight. 'And sand is hard,' she added.

'How do you know that?'

She turned to face him. 'Picnics. And it gets in your sandwiches. Three bites of a ham sarnie, and you feel as if you've been to a sadistic dentist.' She nodded. 'It gets everywhere. Everywhere.'

He mused aloud about restaurants, wondered if anyone served roll-mop herrings, until she dug him in the ribs. 'Take me home. We'll call at the chip shop and you can keep your herrings.'

'One condition, Tess.'

'I'll go, I'll go. Just stop mithering on at me. Take me home, and I promise I'll go.'

His face was a picture of manufactured innocence. 'Go? Go where?'

'The Riley reunion. I'll be good, and I'll go, and I won't kill anybody.'

'Oh, right. Fair enough, I suppose, though what I really meant was ... oh, never mind.'

'What's the matter with you now, Don?'

'That wasn't my condition. I'll take you home if you'll follow me to the kasbah.'

'You what?'

'The sand dunes.'

She pulled his ear. Hard. Well, it was no more than he deserved.

The letter, spread out and almost untouched, sat on the kitchen table between Mr and Mrs Roy Baxter. Rosh stared at it as if in possession of manufacturing specifications for the Holy Grail, terrified of touching it, fearful for its integrity, doubting its very existence. How on earth had her mother managed this?

'So it all happened while we were on our honeymoon.' This statement from Roy was surplus to requirements.

'I don't know how to feel,' Rosh said. 'This is my baby, and she's too young. But I'm so proud of her I could burst, but I...'

'You can't hold her back.'

'Yes, I know. It means...' She rose and walked to the window. Out there, her children had played, had learned to tolerate each other, to interact with

496

visiting playmates, and to bear the inevitable tumbles that accompanied early years. 'It means she knows how good she is. It means I lose her too soon and too suddenly. It means my mother took her to London for the interview without telling me. Where the hell is Marylebone Road, anyway?'

Roy glanced at the letter. 'Northwest London.'

'Oh, well, that makes everything so much clearer, doesn't it? Then there's the vicar. I can understand her turning down the idea of a place with one of the tutors, and I know she wouldn't want the room offered by those nuns, but a vicar? She'll be living with a Protestant, a Cromwellian, one of Henry the Eighth's lot. No better than heathens.'

Roy puffed out his cheeks and blew. 'Catholics have to start making room. The same applies to Protestants. It's as if everybody goes through life reading just the one book from cover to cover. A second book with a different opinion does no harm. Look, Rosh, I don't want to argue, but you don't own Philly, and she doesn't own her gift, because it has to be shared. If Shakespeare had buried his pen, if Turner had decided to paint his bedroom instead, if Beethoven had decided to be a sailor or a butcher – what then?'

'I don't know. I don't care. I wasn't their mother, was I?'

'A child like Philly needs input while she's young enough. She absorbs things so quickly – remember the viola?'

Rosh sank into an old rocking chair that used to be Anna's. She missed her mother, but not enough to want her back. One newly-wed couple

497

in a house was quite enough, thank you very much. 'I'm frightened, Roy.'

'I know you are, love. I'm not exactly on the edge of my seat with joy. But she won't be the only youngster at the Royal Academy. There are other prodigies. And she'll still go to ordinary lessons as well.'

Rosh felt as if some giant had ripped out her heart and used a hammer to batter it. Kieran would go relatively soon; he had worked out that Edinburgh was the best seat of learning for doctors, though because he was English and without doctors in the family he was mildly worried about his perceived suitability. Alice? Who knew? She was an all-rounder who kept her distance even now, preferring the company of older people to that of her peers. But a series of assessments had ruled out any form of autism, so she was within the bounds of normality, whatever they were.

Roy sought a change of subject. 'This reunion? Are we going?'

'Of course we're going; they're my father's family. And when the time comes, we're on puddings. I got a letter from that Injun Joe person. He said all culinary offerings of the sweet variety would be welcome, but the Scouse Alley people are doing the savoury side of the buffet. So apple tarts, custard tarts, fancies, maids of honour – the usual mixed bag. It'll be a riot. Some daft young beggar's booked a rock band, then there's a ceilidh, some Irish dancers–'

'And Philly.'

Rosh shrugged. 'She'll play if the piano's good enough. That's if they have a piano. No, let her be a child, let her meet other people her own age. Maybe she'll see a future up here and decide to stay. I mean, what if she's not up to scratch for the Royal flaming Academy? She might not make it as a concert pianist. How will she feel if she isn't better than the best? And how do we know this vicar won't try to convert her once he's got her in that church of his?'

Roy wasn't about to repeat himself. If Philly could make a living via music, the thing she loved most, that would be enough, surely? She didn't need to be a concert performer; her main aim for now was to progress to a church organ with several manuals, dozens of stops, many pedals and a life of its own till reined in by a maestro. The vicar's church had a great organ, but Rosh didn't want her daughter learning anything at all in a Church of England establishment. 'Rosh, there are evil priests and nasty nuns. There are also some bloody good vicars and some marvellous atheists. It's about music, not about a view of God. She can go to war with a real monster in that church. The organ's no piano, no walk in the park. But she wants to get to grips with it.'

'She is too young for London. They'll keep the place till she's eighteen, surely? If she wants to mess about with a church organ, she can find one in Liverpool.' Rosh left the room.

Roy sat with his head in his hands. Because he had the advantage of a slight distance between himself and Rosh's children, he was able to view them not quite dispassionately, but sensibly. He had never been an outsider, even when Phil had been alive, yet the qualities of these young people

499

were not clouded in his mind. Alice was going to terrify everybody, because her brain, scarcely apparent while everyone treated her as the baby, would burst forth like a dandelion clock in the wind once the other children had left home. She would make an excellent teacher, he decided.

Kieran, now, was a different bag of tricks. Apparently totally focused on a future in the medical profession, he remained open to suggestion and receptive to all learning. Through Roy, he had explored law, particularly the criminal aspect. Fiercely opposed to capital punishment and aware of several innocents who had hanged, he rather fancied the idea of defence work. He liked having Roy around, because he had been buried beneath the weight of females since the death of his father, and Roy seemed to understand him.

This left Philomena. Strange that Rosh and Phil should have chosen to name a girl Philly after her father. Philly resembled neither of the other two. She was quiet, naturally refined, and completely engrossed in music. In other subjects she performed adequately, but music was her soul. With a borrowed viola, she had progressed in weeks from delivering sounds reminiscent of a cat in agony to playing her own compositions. She performed well on clarinet and oboe, but keyboards were her main passion. And something in the girl's eyes informed the world that yes, she would go all the way to the top. Thus far, she lacked the arrogance of the self-absorbed diva, yet she would probably gain it later in life. The love demanded by genius came not from a partner, but from a crowd that kept its distance.

In fact, broken relationships often formed a trail of debris behind those owned by an audience, the public, the world.

Roy raised his head. Did she have that special quality, the rogue element that separated the few from the many? And why was he, a mere step-father, so engrossed in his wife's children? Couldn't he sit back like most incomers did, let their mother do the work and the worrying? No, he couldn't, because Phil and Rosh had been his best friends since school, and he loved her. Her troubles were his troubles, yet hers would always be the final decision.

He followed in her footsteps to their bedroom. She was crying. 'I can't let go yet, Roy. The fault's in me.'

He stood behind her, hands on her shoulders, his eyes fixed on her face in the dressing-table mirror. 'We have to go and meet the vicar. And we need to see this Royal Academy place. She's old enough in her head, Rosh.'

'But I'm not.'

'No mother's ever ready to let go. If she'd turned thirty and was about to walk to the altar, you wouldn't judge any man fit to deserve her. It's never a good time.'

'You want her to go?'

'No, but that doesn't mean she shouldn't. She'll be with others of her own age, other musically gifted kids. Rosh?'

'What?'

'Are you going to take a dangerous chance here? If she doesn't forgive you, can you ever forgive yourself?'

The tears dried. She hadn't looked at it from that viewpoint. Because of her nature, Philly hadn't leapt for joy when the offer had arrived. For a girl in her teens, she was very much in charge of her emotions. 'I think she cried herself dry when Phil died, Roy. Then she turned to my mother, because I was in a state...'

'And after that, she minded Alice,' Roy said quietly. 'I am not criticizing you, babe. You were bloody devastated. She grew up very fast, because she's like you, sense of duty and all that. And Kieran changed, Alice changed – we all changed. But if you put a stop to her now, she might finally react. Or, if you want to look at it a different way, we can sell the shop, the café and this house. We can all go to London. Your mother and Mr Collingford can sort out his upstairs dry-cleaning business.'

Her jaw dropped for a split second. Uproot the other two as well? 'Kieran's at a critical age, and as for Alice–'

'Kieran has brains enough for Harrow,' Roy said. 'He'll survive no matter what. Alice is young and would settle eventually, don't let her fool you. Houses are expensive, so we'd probably need to get a flat, but–'

'And uprooting everyone is the answer? Oh, no.'

'It's an interesting city, Rosh.'

'The Lake District's interesting, but we're not going to live there, either.' She knew the ball was in her court. When it came to decisions like this one, the ultimate responsibility would always be hers. What would Phil have said? How would he

502

have reacted? Rosh closed her eyes and concentrated. 'First, we talk to her,' she said at last. 'It's her life.'

'That's right.'

'Then, if she's determined to go, we make an appointment with the Academy, then with the vicar. She'll need permission from the bishop to attend a non-Catholic college and to live in a vicarage.'

'Where does that come in the list that gave Moses a hernia?'

'It's a law of our Church.'

He nodded. 'Oh, yes. Do you know why? They want our money in their collection plates. "Contribute to the support of our pastors"? That means don't encourage other Christian faiths, don't try to see a different viewpoint, go through life with sand in your eyes, no ecumenical movement, no space for thought, no thought for education. Well. As far as I'm concerned, it's a definite case of no permission required.'

'Is your sermon finished?' she asked. 'Send the plate round, because I think I've a bent halfpenny somewhere and a couple of shirt buttons.'

He laughed at her.

'It's all right,' she said. 'I know what you mean. You'll be a lovely dad.'

He grinned. 'Alice loves me.'

'They all do.' It was too soon to tell him that she thought she had a little foreigner on board, one that might arrive with *Made in Cornwall* stamped on its rear end. Roy deserved to have a child of his own, but she knew it wouldn't be easy for her. The delivery of Alice had been difficult and, since Cuttle's attack, internal scarring might interfere with the birthing process. Caesarean section?

'What are you thinking about now?' he asked.

'Not much,' she replied. Which was true enough. An invisible bundle of cells wasn't much. Was it?

The weeks flew by like a wind off the Irish Sea, and the big occasion was upon them. Maureen rolled up her sleeves and marched through the living room. 'I'll kill him,' she pronounced. 'I'll wring his flaming neck.'

Tom lowered his newspaper. 'You said that yesterday, but he's still walking about somewhere. What's he done this time?'

'What's he done? What's he done?'

'That was the question, love. Do I get an answer?'

She continued to the front door and threw it open. 'Seamus?' she yelled. The first syllable emerged on a note towards the middle of the scale, but the 'mus' was thrown high into the air like a pigeon being released from confinement. Each child knew the call of his or her mother. Seamus, probably on the run, failed to put in an appearance.

'Maureen?'

'Five. He's buggered off with five Cornish pasties. I'm up to my eyes in sausage rolls and vols-au-vent, and he's nicking stuff faster than I can cook it. We might as well have a prayer meeting instead of a reunion, because there'll be nothing to eat. It'll be known as the day of the starving Rileys.'

This was Tom's afternoon off. The Co-op closed at lunch time on Saturdays, and he came home for rest and relaxation. Some chance of that in the current climate. Should cooking while moaning become an international sport, his Maureen would be on the winners' podium with the best. Some of the baking was going on at Scouse Alley, but Maureen and her mother were working from home. It was all right for Kevin. He'd escaped to Paddy's Market, and good luck to him.

'He can't eat five himself,' she said now.

'How much are you prepared to bet on that?' Tom asked. 'Anyway, you've got him all wrong this time, missus.'

'Have I?'

'Oh, yes. I gave him and four friends a pasty each, and they're decorating. You know he's good at that, because he does the room up every Christmas for the pensioners. So in future, before you kill him, ask me first.'

Maureen blinked. 'Why didn't you tell me?'

'Because you weren't here. You were next door having a row with your mother. These houses may be well built, but I reckon they could hear the two of you in Glasgow and London. I got every word through the party wall.' He raised the newspaper and continued reading while his dearly beloved flounced off back to her baking.

At the kitchen table, Maureen lit a rare cigarette. The argument with Mam had been about Reen. Maureen's only daughter, who had never been the sharpest knife in the drawer, was failing in the pregnancy stakes. All her friends had babies, and Maureen had discovered a stash of

505

baby clothes and equipment in Reen's spare bedroom. If the girl wasn't held back, there'd soon be a cot, pram and high chair with no baby to occupy them. Poor Reen. She was truly broody, and her sadness showed in the way she moved, the way she failed to hold up her head, the way she talked to the floor. It was almost as if she couldn't face people because she was infertile, abnormal, less than a woman.

Maureen dashed away a tear almost angrily. Special classes for reading, extra arithmetic homework, Finbar and Michael having to protect their sister from the taunts of her peers – little Reen had never been lucky. She now had a good job in a factory canteen, where she had risen from the ranks to hold the post of deputy manager. Her skills had been picked up from her mother and grandmother, sometimes at home, often in Scouse Alley. She was capable of calculating the amount and cost of food required, yet she couldn't have managed long division even had her life depended on it.

Maureen's idea of tackling the problem was to go via the medical route, but Paddy disagreed. 'If the good Lord wanted her to have babies, she'd have them. She can scarcely take care of herself and the house, Maureen. She loses interest. I wouldn't trust her not to forget the child, leave it at the shops, and come home wondering what she'd mislaid.'

From there, it had all gone downhill. Both women had stuck to their guns, and both were frazzled from cooking for endless hours. Maureen insisted that her daughter had every right to children, and that an investigation into the couple's breeding equipment would do no harm.

Paddy, however, was not convinced. In her loudly expressed opinion, this was God's way of telling the family that the girl should not be a mother, since she would not be an adequate one. 'What if her slowness of mind gets passed on?' Paddy had screamed. 'And the eejit she married isn't up to much, is he? All he's bothered about is Liverpool Football Club and beer. Leave things alone, Maureen.'

It was stalemate. Fortunately, Reen and Jimmy had gone out for the day, so they had heard none of this.

Tom stood in the doorway. 'Come on, love. We've got this big do tomorrow, and your mother's talking rubbish. We'll do all we can for Reen and Jimmy. They may not be a pair of clever clogs, but you saw how they were in Rainford with Finbar's Beth and Michael's Patrick.'

Maureen's face brightened. Her two older sons had decided to stay in Rainford, where they had a huge window-cleaning round and a pair of ancient stone cottages side by side with pretty rear gardens and beautiful interiors. In a way, they were like dolls' houses, especially when her tall sons entered by ducking under door lintels. The properties, already over two hundred years old, had been built for the Earl of Derby's farm workers, all of whom must have been no taller than five and a half feet.

'Maureen?'

'I heard you, love. I was just thinking about our boys and their families. It's nice where they are, isn't it? Thank goodness for Mrs Kray, eh?'

'And for your mother. Don't forget her part in it. She's different from us, and a lot older. Her faith begins and ends with the Catholic Church and that makes her difficult. Look at it another way, though. By setting off on her own to London in poor health, she proved she cares. But in this case, I'm with you. I think our Reen would find her feet as a mother. It would be the making of her.' He paused for a few heartbeats. 'Go and make friends with your mam. Go on. We've a big day tomorrow.'

The phone rang. Unused to the new intruder, both jumped. 'Bloody hell,' Maureen breathed, one hand pressed to her chest.

Tom went to deal with the offending instrument. 'Hello?'

He was quiet for several seconds. 'You what? Can you say that again, please?'

Maureen waited impatiently while whoever it was repeated whatever they'd already said.

He covered the mouthpiece. 'It's Maggie from Scouse Alley. She says the place is full of nuns.'

'What does she mean?'

'What do you mean, Mags?' He listened before covering the mouthpiece once more. 'She says there's two of them, but it feels like a crowd.'

'It would do,' Maureen replied. 'Ask what they're doing.'

'What are they up to?... Right ... right, I see.'

'Well?' Maureen's hands were on her hips.

Tom shrugged. 'Mags says they're putting signs up.'

'What signs?' She started with the foot-tapping

508

business. Nuns had no right to put signs up in Scouse Alley. 'If it's the Sermon on the Mount, they can take it down again.'

Tom smiled. 'Oh, hello, Seamus. You what? OK. Well done, lad. Yes, yes, I'll tell your mother.' He replaced the receiver.

'What's going on now?' Maureen demanded.

'He says nuns can do curly writing. So they've made two signs, one for the door and one for inside. The door one says *Riley Reunion,* and the inside one says *Bless This Family.* Seamus asked them to do the signs in curly writing.' He walked towards her. 'All's well, you see.'

With the wind fast abandoning her sails, Maureen sank. Fortunately she landed in a chair. 'Well,' she said thoughtfully, 'it just goes to show there's more to that little monkey than meets the eye.'

'There must be, love. He's got what he refers to as a pair of penguins decorating the room. Maggie was frightened to death. For her, seeing a nun's like walking under a ladder – bad luck. Let's hope her roast beef survives the shock.'

Maureen began to laugh.

'What's funny?' her husband asked. His flies were fastened, he wasn't wearing bits of lavatory paper after a disastrous shave, and he wasn't making funny faces.

She pulled herself together. 'Bless this family? I'd better go and see my mother. You can't have a family with no mam.'

Rosh cuddled up to her man. Asleep, he was lovely, because he had disgracefully long eyelashes that almost rested on his cheeks. In fact, if she took the curl out of them, they probably would...

'Oi,' he shouted after his rude awakening. 'What are you doing now, madam? Trying to poke my eyes out?'

'Just messing about,' she answered. 'Are you properly awake?'

'I am. Blind, but awake. You want me to make tea, don't you? You want a poor old crippled man, blind in one eye, to struggle down the stairs without waking the Three Musketeers, make tea, let it brew, pour it into cups, and—'

'Yes.'

'You're cruel.'

'I am.'

He went. On Sundays, he always did morning tea. This was a special Sunday, because Rosh was about to mix with members of her extended family, as were the children and Anna. He was looking forward to meeting Tom again, and Rosh could scarcely wait to see Maureen.

Roy chuckled to himself. Never in his existence had he experienced such contentment. The house he had sold was happy at last, too, because it contained newly-weds who were expecting their first child. Taken all round, life was good. With his tea tray, he went back upstairs.

Rosh was brushing her hair at the dressing table. 'Now, Baxter,' she said. 'About ... things. I'm mended enough for the making of babies, but not enough for squeezing them out.' She swivelled round. 'You're going to be Daddy to a Caesarean section.'

Items on the tray wobbled a bit, so he placed it on the bed. 'Erm...' Had he heard right?

'Sit down, Bax,' she ordered.

He perched on the edge of the bed. 'I brought your tea.'

'Yes.'

'And your hair's like a halo.' What a stupid thing to say.

Rosh grinned impishly. 'You've gone white. Don't go showing me up by fainting in front of my relatives.'

Roy swallowed. 'A baby?'

'That's what humans usually have.'

'My baby.'

'No, it's the milkman's. Well, I think it's the milkman's.'

He had always been sure that he would never have a child of his own. But here he was, married to the most beautiful woman he'd ever known, and she was– 'They have to cut you open?'

She nodded.

'Because of Cuttle?'

'Scar tissue or something. Yes. Forget about him. All that matters is this baby.' She stared hard at him. 'I'll be all right. Oh, for God's sake, you can stop dripping tears. I'm not turning up with you all red-eyed, either. Red eyes, white face – all we need is a bit of blue and we can call you Reunion Jack.' She sat next to him and drew him close. 'Don't make me start crying, or we'll be going nowhere.'

'Isn't three enough?' he managed.

'I'm being given a fourth. Don't worry. Some poor women go through this half a dozen times and right into their forties. Four's a nice even number. I'll miss Philly, but I reckon Alice will step up to the plate.' She paused. 'We've done the right thing, haven't we? The vicar's lovely, and he has a nice family.'

'And a big organ.' Roy groaned when she dug him in the ribs.

'The Academy people talked posh, but they were all right too,' she added.

'They were keen to get her, as well.' Roy rubbed the elbowed rib. 'A baby,' he sighed. 'I'm going to be a dad. I thought I'd never be a dad.'

'Wear your best suit today,' she ordered. 'And a tie. You can take it off if others do. Just the tie, I mean. And,' she wagged a finger, 'no stupid, Cheshire cat grin...'

He kissed her. It was by far the best way to stop her nagging. Oh, but he was one lucky man. Another long-abandoned dream was going to come true.

Don stood at the top of the stairs. 'Anne-Marie?'

'What, Dad?'

'Help. I need help. Come and deal with her, because I've given up.' Tess had tried on so many outfits that the bed and all other surfaces in the room were draped as if ready for decent burial. Naturally, she had gone back to the number she'd first thought of, a beautiful blue suit that matched her eyes perfectly, but there was no telling which way she'd jump next.

'Don't leave me, Don,' Tess shouted. 'I need your input.'

His input? His bloody input? Twenty-five

guineas he'd spent on the blue suit, not to mention shoes, gloves and bag. She'd been after a hat as well till he'd put his foot down hard. They were going down towards the Dock Road, not to Royal Ascot or Buckingham Palace. The way she was carrying on, the reunion would be over before they got there.

'What shall I do?' Anne-Marie asked.

'Panic,' he replied. 'That's what I'm doing.'

'I refuse to panic,' was Anne-Marie's haughty response.

Tess appeared. She shut the bedroom door and looked her husband up and down. 'What's all the noise for?' she asked innocently. 'I hope everybody's ready. We don't want to be late, do we?' Without another word, she led her family downstairs. Pulling on her gloves, she wondered again what all the to-do had been about. After all, it was just a fuss about nothing.

Nevertheless, when they reached Scouse Alley and Don helped her out of the car, she hung on to his hand. From the other side of an open door, rock music poured. 'Don't leave me,' she whispered.

'I won't.'

Anne-Marie was already halfway across the parking area. 'It's the Quarry Men!' She dragged Mark inside.

'Remember your breathing, Tess,' Don whispered. He was glad Sean hadn't come. Sean was under a 1939 MG with no intention of shifting till he'd got the beggar moving. Sean was more sensitive than he appeared, and he hated to see his mother in a state. 'Don't hold your breath, or

513

you'll end up hyperventilating and in a panic. They're just people. You even know one of the guys in the band. When they stop playing, you must go and talk to him.'

'I can't go in.'

'You can go in. I'll bloody carry you in if I have to.'

'All right, all right, I'm coming.'

It was chaos. The only bit of organization was the work of Injun Joe, who was standing at a table marked *Photographs etc.,* and there was a lot of et cetera. People were adding snaps, wedding pictures, portraits of men in uniform, scraps of paper marked with addresses and phone numbers, and other bits of memorabilia. From the extension pounded the music of John Lennon and his pals, and all the young had been drawn round the corner like iron filings responding to the positive side of a magnet.

Don could feel his wife trembling on his arm. Then, apparently out of nowhere, two more Tesses strode towards them. One was older than his own Tess, while the other was several years younger. The latter was Cuttle's victim, the poor soul who'd been in hospital with Tess. And they simply drew her away from him. One minute she'd been a shaking wreck; the next, she was engaged in animated conversation with two women who had introduced themselves to him very briefly. One was Roisin Baxter, while the other was Maureen Walsh. Don picked up a sausage roll and wandered towards the music.

Lennon was singing, and he wasn't bad. Perhaps he'd do all right without serving an apprenticeship for a trade. Mark and Anne-Marie danced energetically, as did the offspring of other Rileys. The Quarry Men finished their set and began packing up their gear. Anne-Marie sidled up to her dad. 'You thought he should go and be a plumber? John Lennon a plumber? Just you wait and see, Daddy-oh.' She returned to her boy-friend, who was being scrutinized by several other teenage girls.

Don shook his head. Daddy-oh? Not again – he was sick of that title.

Then it kicked off, and the young were not responsible. A row broke out near the centre of the longer arm of Scouse Alley. 'She didn't,' a man yelled. 'She went over to Derry and married a Protestant.'

'She did not!' shouted another. 'Finished up in Dublin, married English, but he was Catholic, and they farmed in Suffolk when they came over. I should know, she was my sister. They had a Suffolk Punch stud, and–'

Another man chimed in. 'Your sister? She was anybody's for a drop of gin.' He was the recipient of the first blow.

'There's your Suffolk Punch,' cried the pugilist.

Maureen's older sons dragged the men apart. Finbar and Michael were big men, both trained boxers, and they soon put a stop to the fracas.

Paddy grabbed the microphone. 'I'm ashamed of yous,' she announced. 'Brawling in front of children. I am Paddy O'Neil, and you are inside my property. It will take me two minutes, no more, to turn this place dry. Then we'll see do you fight without grape or grain in you. Maureen

515

– easy on the Guinness.'

People shuffled uncomfortably. They had come to meet their kin, and a few of their kin were scarcely civilized.

Paddy continued. 'Those who know people who arrived here drunk, get them out. Now.' She waited while the sober offloaded the inebriates. There were several scuffles in the doorway, so Finbar and Michael stood guard. Paddy waded on. 'I am Irish myself, as you can no doubt tell. My mother married a Riley. We have, here in Liverpool, some grand Irish folk. But we also have those soaked in alcohol and nostalgia, always keening for home, their true address somewhere at the bottom of the Irish Sea, because they know and love home, depend on England and curse England. Well, let me tell you now that my family was a poor one, and most of us are glad we crossed the water. This is home. Liverpool is home.'

Don felt his jaw drop. Tess was borrowing the microphone! 'I was a Riley,' she said clearly. 'Slept in a caravan with seven others, plus my mother and father. We sometimes ate in the ganga's white house. I am Theresa Marianne. My oldest sister was Concepta Maria Conchita – can't remember the rest of it. If my brothers and sisters are here, hello to you.' She handed back the mike.

Don lowered his head and blinked away some wetness. So frightened, so slow to move when getting dressed, so shaky out there in the car park. Unpredictable? Even a word as big as that was not sufficient to cover the glorious, beautiful woman he had married. Her two clones clapped when Tess was picked up and carried away by a brother she might never have recognized had he not sharpened knives on his wheel just outside the Smithdown Road launderette. Jack the Knife took her to meet the rest of her family.

But for the most part, the three 'sisters' spent time in each other's company. Some invisible yet irresistible hand steered the three husbands into a corner. Tom and Roy had already met, though neither mentioned the original occasion. It would go to the grave with them, since both were honourable men.

Roisin's Roy was the first to speak up. 'I never know which way she'll jump,' he said happily. 'Every day's a new chapter, and it doesn't necessarily join up with any previous text.'

Don nodded. 'Tess tried on so many dresses this morning, you'd have thought she had shares in Lewis's. She collects squirrels. Not like stamps, she doesn't have them in the house, but she feeds them and talks to them. There's one called Alex who knocks on the bloody kitchen door. If I open it, he scarpers, but he begs from her. She can't resist them. Or birds. It's like a flaming wildlife sanctuary.'

Tom chuckled. 'Small fry, your two,' he said. 'Mine's the best girl in the world, but she has a gob on her like the Mersey Tunnel. And she breaks things. Temper? Give me a leaky boat on a stormy sea any day. Safer.' He nodded. 'But I wouldn't swap her for all the gold in Fort Knox.'

A proud Roy pointed out his stepchildren. Alice held an old lady captive and captivated in a corner. 'That'll be our teacher, I reckon. Kieran's probably for medicine, possibly for law. But

Philly, the beautiful blonde, has won a place at the Royal Academy. She's a great pianist.' But he didn't mention the unborn, because that would be Rosh's job when the time came.

'I've just my daughter here,' Don said. 'She's over there with her boyfriend. My lad's mending a car. What about you, Tom?'

Tom pointed to Seamus, who was half hidden under a table. 'There's my youngest,' he said, 'up to his eyes in jelly and custard. The big fellows on the door are mine, too. And my daughter's over near that long table studying her shoes.' Poor Reen. There were babies and children everywhere, living reminders of her own failure to produce. Her husband was drinking himself towards coma, while she lacked the confidence to mix with strangers.

Anna and Paddy found one another, of course. They were sisters-in-law, since Anna had been married to one of Paddy's brothers, one who had never gone to London to involve himself with gangsters. The two got on like a house on fire, as did their husbands. The rest milled about, men clapping men on shoulders, women weeping when they discovered the long lost, people lining up for the ceilidh.

The ceilidh was insane. Most seemed to own left feet only, and no two people knew the same dance steps, so corns and bunions were shown little respect. At the end, there was just a pile on the floor, the whole lot screaming with laughter.

Don, still in the company of his fellow sufferers, saw the blue suit among all the carnage. If twenty-five guineas had gone to pieces, that sight made his spending sensible. She was dancing with Jack the Knife, her lookalikes, and several others to whom she was probably sister, aunt or cousin.

This had been a good day.

Home From Home

The Irish Sea was frisky, to say the least. But on this occasion Tess felt no sickness, no urge to jump into the water to end it all. Paddy and Don both looked rather green, yet Tess maintained her dignity, even managing the occasional smile when she noticed the condition of her stalwart companions. They had taken her home; now, they were bringing her home.

She closed her eyes. In the middle of nowhere, a hotel had sprung up. Its name was the Middle of Nowhere, a title expressed in English and in its Gaelic equivalent on exterior signs. The Middle of Nowhere was crammed with people, Irish, English and American. Words and drink flowed, singing broke out, an accordion played while a young woman performed a less than steady version of a jig. Midsummer in the back of beyond was certainly lively.

The place was packed; its last two rooms had gone to Paddy and to Don and Tess. They breakfasted next morning on porridge topped with thick cream and a touch of orange liqueur. Then they walked the slow walk, travelled on a pilgrimage back in time to a white house with a front door that had been black.

The roof had caved in, and the weather-battered door had lost most of its paint. Through a broken, filthy window, they caught sight of the ganga's chair, which rested in its old place, though rain had done its damage over the decades. Here and there, bits of the poteen sheds hung on, while the orchard, running wild, was dense with untended foliage.

'Are you all right, Tess?' Don asked.

She opened her eyes. He'd asked the same question when they'd reached the open-fronted barn.

'Yes, thank you,' she said both times.

There were no caravans. Stables had rotted, arable fields lay fallow, cattle from various surrounding farms wandered and grazed where they chose. But the most remarkable thing about the place was its pure beauty. The abandoned white house said something about Ireland's regeneration, as did the hotel down the road. At last, people had begun to value the middle of nowhere, because the middle of nowhere mattered in this madly busy world.

But above all, there was the greenness. Yellow-greens, blue-greens, moss greens, emeralds, St Augustine's school-uniform bottle greens, shiny greens and dull ones, light fern greens. Green upon green upon green. Endless. 'So unashamedly lovely,' Tess said. 'It celebrates itself. My squizzles would love the orchard.'

And she didn't want to leave.

Paddy, drying her eyes after the sight of her old home, said she didn't know about the state of things and how to get proof, but this was Riley land, and she would see what could be done to mend things, make a holiday home where the family could come and stay in turns.

And Tess still didn't want to leave. She found the field from which she'd dug potatoes and turnips to eat raw, stared at the spot where her caravan had stood, remembered the older ones stealing her food. But none of that mattered any more, because this was her place ... well, one of her places. Calm, so calm. She even went to find the grave of the little stillborn, and it was there, marked by a cross on the trunk of a tree whose canopy shaded one who had never breathed. 'Sleep well,' she told her brother or sister.

'Tess?'

She opened her eyes. 'Yes, Paddy?'

'Don's being sick over the side somewhere.'

Tess smiled. 'Then he'll know how we felt coming over the first time. I wanted to die.'

'You're talking in your sleep, but.'

'I'm not sleeping, I'm thinking. Look after Don.' Tess closed her eyes again, and was immediately back in Mayo.

They walked back to the hotel and rested on their beds for several hours. Well, they were supposed to rest, though Don was kept awake by his wife's ceaseless chatter. But Tess knew that her man was happy because she'd finally faced her demons.

After lunch, they had another little walk, but not in the direction of the white house. It was then that Tess realized that there was something going on. Paddy and Don kept looking at each other, then at their watches. 'What are you two cooking?' she asked.

'Soda bread,' came the terse reply from Paddy.

A small man rode towards them on a donkey.

522

He stopped. 'A Riley,' he said, pointing at Tess. 'Sure, they threw up these pretty little fillies for generations.' He grinned, baring a total absence of teeth apart from a lone ranger at the front. 'Would ye have a drop of petrol on ye?'

It was the party of three's turn to grin.

'Because I've tried everything else on this lazy article.' The animal resumed walking. 'Did I tell you to go?' the man yelled. 'I never even put you into first gear...' His voice faded as the animal picked up a bit of speed.

'Old Ireland alongside the new.' Don pointed towards their hotel. 'You know, girls, I have a sneaking hope that the old won't die out altogether.'

'Ah, it won't,' Paddy promised.

They rested on their beds before dinner, and during wakeful moments Tess thought about the changes in their lives since that first gathering. Everyone met once a month at Lights. A family tree of sorts had been constructed, and she was reconciled with her siblings. The Three Musketeers, Don, Tom and Roy, enjoyed nights out together, as did their musketeeresses. There were family dinners, outings, birthday parties, weddings. She belonged. She belonged with Don and the children; she belonged with the Rileys, too.

No more nightmares. No longer were the bottoms of wardrobes filled with tinned food. She almost missed the fear of poverty and hunger, which was silly. It appeared that even the worst parts of life were woven into a person's background, and that was stupid. She turned to the bright side. Reen was pregnant at last. For Paddy's sake, and for Reen, Tess was glad, though the father-to-be didn't look up to much.

They woke, made themselves ready for supper, then went downstairs for a drink before their meal. They were accosted by their hostess, a bustling, busy little woman with the broadest smile on earth, which this evening was just one expression of many mixed emotions. 'You see. I said to Vinnie – didn't I, Vin–' She turned, but her husband had done a disappearing act. 'Would you ever look at that, now? There he is – gone. Don't you find, ladies, that whenever they're needed, they're never in the place where they should be?'

'Oh, yes,' Paddy said gravely. 'It's the disappearing act of the lesser-spotted human male.'

The landlady shook her head. 'Well, yours back in Liverpool might be lesser spotted, but mine's covered in freckles even in places the sun should never have visited. It's the O'Malleys, you see.'

Paddy didn't see, and she said so.

'Well, here's the thing. There I go, rattling on, and you with no idea of any of it. The O'Malley clan booked tables in the dining room, special occasion, and Vinnie, God mind his soul, forgot to mention it, so I'll kill him later. Don't want blood on good Irish linen, so. You're in the annexe. I think it's called an orangery, though I don't know why, for I never managed to grow as much as a hyacinth in there.'

They followed her through to the annexe, a huge glass room with blinds at all the windows. The sun had gone on its westward journey, so the blinds were not closed, and the beauty of the countryside was all around them. A long table

524

groaned under the weight of food, and a poster hung from the ceiling. *Eat your fill, Tess. From your brothers and sisters.*

'There,' smiled the landlady. 'All paid for by your family over to Liverpool. God bless, and I hope you enjoy.' She surveyed the table. 'I expect you'll never shift it all, but.'

Tess laughed. She laughed then, in that glorious country, and she laughed now, on her way home.

'Tess?' Paddy touched her shoulder. 'Your man's stopped heaving for the while, but I want you to come and look. Come away with you now.'

The ferry busied itself over the bar where sea became river. 'Look at that now,' Paddy commanded. 'Sure, it's a different beauty, but it remains a lovely, welcoming sight, does it not?'

Tess agreed. That famous waterfront hove into view, its huge buildings made smaller by distance. They were home. The ferry chugged its way towards dock, bringing them nearer to their goal with every passing minute.

'And here we have it,' Paddy said. 'The lights of Liverpool. We're home.'

The publishers hope that this book has given you enjoyable reading. Large Print Books are especially designed to be as easy to see and hold as possible. If you wish a complete list of our books please ask at your local library or write directly to:

Magna Large Print Books
Magna House, Long Preston,
Skipton, North Yorkshire.
BD23 4ND

This Large Print Book for the partially sighted, who cannot read normal print, is published under the auspices of

THE ULVERSCROFT FOUNDATION